Rock Chick Revenge

Published by Kristen Ashley
Discover other titles by Kristen Ashley at:
www.kristenashley.net

ISBN: 0-6157-8214-0
ISBN-13: 9780615782140

Rock Chick Revenge

Kristen Ashley

Dedication

This book is dedicated to Gib Moutaw,
who's cooler than Lee, Eddie, Hank, Vance, Luke, Mace and Hector all put together.
Keep whistlin' in the dark, my brother.

Chapter 1

Bad Ava, Good Ava

I sat in my hunter green Range Rover, hands resting on my steering wheel, forehead resting on my hands, wondering what in the hell I was doing. Not only that I was parked on 15th Street outside the Nightingale Investigations offices, where Luke worked, but any of it, all of it, the whole shebang.

Do it, do it, you know you want to do it. Teeny-tiny Bad Ava, wearing a lacy red teddy, red stockings, spike-heeled, patent-leather red pumps and devil's ears, sat on my right shoulder and whispered in my ear.

Don't do it, go home, do yoga, light candles, meditate. Teeny-tiny Good Ava, wearing a white satin teddy edged in soft, fluffy feathers, gold high-heeled sandals with straps that crisscrossed up her calves and sporting a glittery gold halo, sat on my left shoulder and whispered in my ear.

"I'm going nuts," me, the real Ava, said out loud.

You aren't nuts. You want to see him. You've wanted to see him for four years. Girl, you are shit-hot now. Let him get a load of you! Bad Ava reminded me.

This was true. Not the shit-hot part, the other parts.

Go home, call Sissy and tell her you can't do it. Then call Luke and ask him over for dinner like a normal person. Don't do this. Don't! Good Ava cried.

Argh!

Do it, go in there, suck him in, chew him up, spit him out. Men stink! Bad Ava encouraged.

Luke doesn't stink. We like Luke, Good Ava protested, leaning around my neck to glare at Bad Ava.

Bad Ava gave Good Ava the finger. Good Ava poked her tongue out at Bad Ava.

I ignored them.

Men did stink. This was true. Men were scum. All of them. Luke too.

Probably.

I had known Luke Stark since he moved in across the street when I was eight years old and he was twelve. He was the most gorgeous boy I had ever seen in my little girl life, and when I saw him at his Dad's funeral five years ago, I realized he had turned into the most gorgeous man.

Men stunk, on the whole, but Luke had always been ultra-nice to me. But then, as a kid, I was fat, four-eyed and had mousy brown hair. And when I saw him at the funeral, I was still fat (more so), four-eyed and had mousy brown hair. So I figured all that time he probably felt sorry for me.

Now I was seventy-five pounds lighter, wearing contacts and had my hair streaked blonde. A partial streak, just the top and sides. The bottom back I left alone, and for some bizarre reason, against the blonde, it had turned a burnished chestnut color that was the same color as both my glamorous sisters' hair. The hair I had always wanted all my life, even prayed for but never had, until now.

Last time I saw Luke he was wearing all black: black suit, black shirt, black tie. It *was* a funeral but Luke had always been partial to black, and I was glad because he looked good in it.

Even when he was a teenager he usually wore tight, black t-shirts, black motorcycle boots and jeans. I noted this like I noted everything about Luke.

He had black hair, and on first glance black eyes, though his eyes were really a dark, dark indigo and totally yum.

At the funeral, I noticed he had grown a beard. Not full and thick, but short and trimmed and it looked great on him.

I nearly melted into a puddle when his eyes moved through the graveside crowd and stopped on me. They got soft, and one side of his mouth went up in one of his half-grins that made him look so yumalicious you wanted to pounce on him. Instead of shoving the mourners aside and pouncing (which would have been highly inappropriate), I just gave him what I hoped was a jaunty wink and a stupid half-wave. The grin went full-fledged (guess the jaunty wink worked, but then again my stupid, dorky behavior always seemed to amuse Luke) and he turned away.

That was the very day I decided to turn my life around and that was the day I turned my life on its fucking head.

I rued that day.

I never thought I would rue anything, but I rued that day for certain.

However, now I needed Luke.

I knew from my Mom talking to his Mom (they were still friends even though Luke's Mom had moved into a condo in Governor's Park and my Mom had moved to Phoenix), not to mention from Ally and Indy, my Rock Chick friends, that Luke was some kind of kickass mercenary, bounty hunter, private investigator-type guy who worked for Ally's brother and Indy's fiancé, Lee Nightingale.

Luke had always been a badass.

Two days after he moved in across the street I caught him in the alley smoking cigarettes. He was twelve and smoking in the alley, and at eight I thought that was way cool.

When he grew up, he drove muscle cars (loud and fast) and motorcycles (again, loud and fast) and sat in his Dad's garage with the door rolled up, lifting weights. I watched this out of my bedroom window, and it was better than anything on television, believe you me.

He always had a different girlfriend and you could tell they were all easy, but a nun would turn easy at one look at Luke.

And he was also always getting into trouble. I heard his Mom telling my Mom about it a lot. He'd been picked up by the cops more than once while out carousing.

He was a tough guy in high school, and he roared off the day of his graduation after one of his many rip-roarin' fights with his Dad and became a tougher guy (I heard his Mom… well, you get the drift).

And right now, I needed a tough guy.

"Shit," I said out loud.

You go get him, girl, Bad Ava said.

Be nice, Good Ava said.

Before I could chicken out, I got out of the Range Rover and went into the building.

I had serious second thoughts about my choice of clothing the minute I opened the door to the offices of Nightingale Investigations. I thought tough guy, mercenary, bounty hunting private eyes would have shithole offices. Couches with the stuffing sticking out, filing cabinets with wire baskets on top overflowing with papers, dirty coffee cups, debris floating around—stuff like that.

Nightingale Investigations' reception area was all smooth gleaming wood paneled walls, expensive leather couches (with no stuffing coming out at all), a huge cowboy print in a heavy, carved-wood frame, a bronze statue of a bucking bronco in the corner and a mammoth reception desk with a state-of-the-art computer on it.

The desk was the only thing in the room not neat and tidy. It was a mess, and there was a pretty older black woman sitting behind it. She had the biggest afro I had ever seen in my life and she appeared to be both eating a calzone and painting her fingernails a frosty, raspberry sherbet-type color.

I was wearing seriously faded Levi's I'd found in a vintage clothing store (and they were *the best*), my black Green Day t-shirt over a white thermal, black flip-flops and my silver. I was a silver freak, and that day, as with every day, I was dripping with it: four silver necklaces, five silver bracelets on my right wrist, three on my left, long, silver hoops at my ears and nearly all my fingers had heavy silver rings or bands on them. I'd slopped my hair in a messy knot on top of my head with a ponytail holder and I'd gone makeup free.

I was pretending I had nothing to prove and no one to impress.

I should have worn a dress and heels *and* makeup. Not to mention done something with my goddamned hair.

Hell and damnation.

"Can I help you?" the lady behind the reception desk asked, breaking me out of my idiot thoughts.

I looked at her.

I hesitated, for a moment, wanting to run, then I took a deep breath and said, "I'm looking for Lucas Stark."

"You got an appointment with Luke?" the lady asked, looking through the total mess on her desk, not that she would ever find anything.

"No, I'm an…" I hesitated again, wondering if I wasn't perhaps the stupidest woman in the world, I licked my lips and went for it, "Old friend."

"He ain't here, girl. You want, I can call him," the lady offered, looking at me closely.

"No," I replied quickly, relieved beyond belief that Luke was somewhere else.

There it was, the gods telling me that this was not meant to be. I was going to go with that. Big time.

"I'll just…" I stopped and looked around, deciding to get the fuck out of Dodge. "Forget it. Could you please just tell him Ava Barlow was here? I'll try to catch him later."

I was rethinking telling this woman my name (too late now) when she smiled huge like she had just thought of some hilarious joke but wasn't going to let me in on it.

"No problem to give him a bell," she pushed. "I got his number on speed dial."

Oh crap.

"No!" I cried, suddenly sounding desperate, because suddenly I *was* desperate. I shouldn't have come there. I could get the goods on Sissy's stupid-ass cheating jerk of a husband myself. It couldn't be that hard. I didn't need Luke. I didn't need anyone. "Really, thanks, but I'll just go, I've got to be somewhere anyway."

I started edging away, deciding on escape.

"Just hang on one tick," the lady said, ever helpful, getting up and waving her hands to dry her nails. "I'll just talk to the boys in the back. Maybe they know where he is."

Eek!

Boys in the back?

A door opened and a man (most definitely *not* a boy) walked in and at one glance at him I stared.

At first I was worried it was going to be Luke, but it wasn't. This guy was tall, dark-haired with jade-green eyes, a lean, muscled body to die for and he was unbelievably gorgeous. Not your average, everyday gorgeous but otherworldly gorgeous. His green eyes were on me and he looked like he, too, thought something was hilarious.

I thought distractedly, considering everyone looked about ready to laugh, that this must be a fun place to work.

"Luke just called in," he said to the black lady but his eyes never left me and all thoughts of a fun place to work flew from my head because all thoughts flew from my head. "He'll be here in five."

I had a silent freak out and wondered why, now that I needed advice, Good Ava and Bad Ava disappeared. I noticed too late that Hot Green Eyed Guy was standing between the exit and me.

Crap.

"Hi, um…?" I looked at him.

"Mace," he said and I blinked.

Yikes.

What kind of name was Mace? He certainly looked like he had some non-Caucasian ethnicity to him, maybe Polynesian, and who was I to say what Polynesians named their kids, but *Mace?*

"Well, Mace, I need to go," I told him.

He shook his head.

I stared at him, thinking maybe he didn't hear me right.

"I need to go," I repeated.

"Luke'll be here in five," was all he said.

He stood with his arms crossed on his chest and I got the (correct) impression that for some reason he wasn't going to allow me to leave. I found this somewhat alarming. I gave up on him because he was big guy and he didn't look like he was easily swayed and turned back to the receptionist.

"Um, really, I've got to go. I just remembered a dentist appointment. They get kind of touchy when you miss your appointments."

This made her laugh.

"No, really. Sometimes they charge you," I went on.

"Girl, so I can watch whatever's gonna happen next, *I'll* pay if they charge you," the lady said.

Okay, it was safe to say I'd left the real, sane world and entered a loony bin.

"What's going on?" I asked.

"First, I'm Shirleen," she told me.

"Um... hi?" I asked, still not following, and wondering why it was clear I couldn't leave and everyone in the room (but me) was okay with that.

"Hey there," Shirleen said. "Second, to understand what's going on you gotta know all that's gone on before you. Since Luke'll be here in five—"

"Three," Mace interrupted from behind me. I glanced over my shoulder at him, beginning to feel out-and-out panic, and then turned back to Shirleen.

"In three," Shirleen continued. "There ain't enough time. Just trust me, girl, go with the flow."

She was making no sense at all.

"What flow?" I asked, then shook my head because I didn't have time for information about the flow. I had to *go.* I turned and started toward Mace. They couldn't actually keep me there. I was pretty certain that was against the law.

"I'm leaving," I said to him.

His hard body went alert. I not only saw it, I felt it.

"Luke wants you here," he told me.

I took two steps toward him, which meant I was a foot away from him and about ten away from the door. I tipped my head back and looked at him, surprised at what he said.

"He doesn't know I'm here," I stated.

"He knows," he replied.

"He doesn't," I pushed.

"We told him," he shared.

"How'd you know?" I asked.

He pointed and I followed his arm to see a camera in the corner of the room. The light on it was green.

Goddamn.

The boys in the back had been watching.

My eyes went back to him.

"You can't keep me here," I said.

He shook his head to tell me I was wrong.

This made me angry.

I had kind of a temper (okay, so maybe one could say I had a helluva temper) and right then I needed to go before Luke got there, and I calculated I had about a minute to make my getaway. Not being able to go got the better of me, and frankly, when I had a moment to look back, I was kind of shocked it took that long.

"Get out of my way," I snapped.

I charged ahead and tried to dodge him at the last minute. He caught me and swung me around. I struggled, and laughably quick he subdued me, my back pressed tight to his front, my arms crossed in front of me, his hands at my wrists.

We were both slightly bent at the waist and I was still struggling, flipping out that suddenly I was stand up wrestling with a guy named Mace at the same time trying to pull free, when the door opened.

Mace and I stayed locked together, but we both froze and our heads jerked toward the door.

Luke stood there.

Fuckity, fuck, fuck, *fuck*.

I noticed instantly he looked even better than ever. Tall, at least four inches taller than me (and I was five foot eight), lean and built, wearing a skintight black t-shirt, black cargo pants and black boots. His thick hair was clipped short to his head. Not a buzz cut, but short. The beard was gone and in its place was the baddest-ass mustache I'd ever seen, thick and black across his lip and trimmed neat down the sides of his mouth.

Holy cramoly! I wanted to know at that very moment what it felt like to have that mouth, with that 'tache, on me, *any* part of me. I didn't care which part and I wouldn't have been choosy.

His eyes came to me, slid to Mace then back to me.

Then one side of his mouth went up in a half-grin. At the sight I melted into Mace, and even though he had to feel the fight had gone out of me, he didn't let me go.

"Too late again," Luke muttered, sounding amused, his eyes on me, but I got the feeling he wasn't talking to me.

"Not quite," Shirleen told him and she sounded like she was trying hard not to laugh.

This exchange confused me, but I had no time to ask or say anything at all. Luke's eyes moved away from me and scanned the room. Obviously looking for something then not finding it, his gaze sliced back to Shirleen.

"Where's Ava?" he asked. His eyes narrowed, the arms around me tightened and both my captor and I straightened.

"What do you mean, where's Ava? Boy, you looked right at her," Shirleen answered.

I heard a door open, but since it was behind my back and there was a big, solid guy there, I couldn't look. Not that I would have. Luke's eyes had cut to me and pinned me to the spot.

I went still and he stared at me.

"Hey Luke," I said, feeling and sounding stupid.

His brows came together. "Ava?" he asked.

"In the flesh." I tried for a jaunty smile, even though Mace still hadn't let me go and I felt like a big dork.

Luke did a body scan then his eyes came back to mine. "What the fuck happened to you?"

There was definitely a sort of pissed-off accusation in his tone. Not the reaction I had dreamed of (quite a lot) when Luke saw the new me.

"I got contacts," I told him.

He glared at me.

"And I dyed my hair."

The glare turned scary.

"And I lost seventy-five pounds."

For some reason, at this Shirleen burst out laughing and I could hear other laughter in the room as we'd been joined by more people that I couldn't see. I just kept my eyes on Luke who looked, for some insane reason, about to blow.

His jaw clenched and his gaze moved to the man behind me.

"You wanna let her go?" he asked, but it wasn't really a question and the tone of his voice was downright frightening.

The arms around me loosened and I took a step away.

Luke stayed where he was.

"What're you doin' here?" he asked, still weirdly pissed-off and still angrily glaring at me.

I decided instantly I didn't need a tough guy. I was going to go it alone so I lied, "Thought you might want to get a beer."

"I called you," he said, changing the subject suddenly, seemingly oblivious to our audience.

Crap, I was worried about this.

He *had* called me, half a dozen times after his father's funeral. Two I missed because I was out. Four I had listened to, sitting there while he was leaving the messages and I didn't answer. None of them I returned.

"I know," I said softly.

"After my father died, I called you," he stated, and the laughter swept out of the room just as quickly as it came in.

"I know," I repeated.

"You didn't call back and now you wanna have a beer?"

His tone was even more frightening than before. I wouldn't have thought it was possible, but there it was.

"Um… maybe not," I muttered, deciding that perhaps I should go home, go to bed, get up again and try the day differently, next time making smart decisions about my actions (read: not going to Nightingale Investigations).

"What're you doin' here?" Luke asked again.

"I told you," I answered.

"You lied," he stated.

My mouth dropped open. I had lied of course, but how could he know that? And anyway, he was accusing me of lying in front of other people.

I felt my temper flare.

"I did not," I snapped (and lied again).

"Bullshit."

"Don't you say 'bullshit' to me, Lucas Stark."

"Don't lie to me, Ava. What're you doin' here?" He wasn't going to let it go.

"I *was* going to ask you out for a beer. Then I remembered I have a dentist appointment and now I'm late so I'm just going to..." I was preparing for escape. I took two steps toward the door, mid-rant, and Luke moved.

One second he was several feet away from me. The next second, he was right there, bent over, and I kid you not, his shoulder slammed straight into my belly. He lifted up and started moving, taking me with him. I let out a small, surprised scream and I heard a couple of gasps as his shoulder twitched and he bumped me into a more solid position on it, his arm wrapped around the backs of my thighs. He walked from the room, opening a door and carrying me with him as he went through.

At this turn of events I was too stunned to move, much less struggle. But I did lift my head to see Shirleen and Mace, as well as another black lady, another seriously hot guy and a movie star gorgeous woman with black hair and violet eyes, all watching us go.

We were in a hall and I saw the door close behind us right before I came to myself and yelled, "Let me down!"

Luke didn't answer.

He turned and we went through another door. He stepped free of the door, turned again and I saw we were in a kitchenette slash locker room. I heard the door close before Luke turned one more time, bent forward and set me on my feet.

I would have done something (though I didn't know what that something was) to get away, but he moved into me. I had no choice but to move back and I slammed against the door.

Luke came up close, the heat from his body hitting me, his face in mine and I stilled. He was so tall and broad I couldn't see anything but him. He was so pissed-off and full of attitude I was captivated by him and wouldn't have been able to look or move away if I tried.

"What're you doin' here?" he repeated, dark blue eyes shining dangerously.

I ignored the danger, mainly because at this point I was seriously angry.

"Did you just carry me in here?" I snapped.

"Ava, I'm only gonna ask one more time," Luke warned.

I put my hands in the spare space between us, right on his rock-solid chest and gave a mighty shove. Then my eyes widened and dropped to my hands.

I was pretty certain I had given a good old shove, but he didn't move, not an inch.

Holy shit.

Okay then, new tactic.

"First, your friend physically detains me and now you're carting me around against my will!" I yelled. "I'm calling the police."

"You're gonna tell me what's going on. Are you in trouble?"

"Step back, Luke."

"Are you in trouble?"

"Step back!" I shouted.

He didn't step back. Instead, he got closer. So much closer, his body touched mine and one of his hands went to the door beside my head, the other by my hip. I was totally trapped.

I sucked in breath.

Yippee! Bad Ava shouted in my ear.

Oh my, Good Ava breathed.

It was safe to say I pretty much would have sold my soul to the devil a thousand times in my life to have Luke this close.

"Talk to me, Ava," Luke ordered. His voice had dipped low. He didn't sound pissed-off now. He sounded patient and a lot like Luke had always sounded whenever he talked to me. Gentle. Affectionate.

I should have responded to his tone, but he was so close. My head tilted back to look at him and my eyes caught on his mouth. That 'tache was hot but it surrounded the most superior set of lips I had ever seen in my whole goddamned life. I had, of course, noticed he had a nice mouth, but I never had the opportunity to stare at it in that kind of proximity.

The top lip was nicely formed, the bottom one full. The balance was perfect and there were these sexy ridges that made you want to explore. I found myself wondering if that mouth was soft or hard when he used it to kiss you. Then I found myself wondering what it tasted like. Then I found myself thinking I wanted to run my tongue along it.

"Ava," I watched it move as it said my name and my eyes drifted dreamily up to Luke's.

I was in kind of a fog, so when my eyes hit his I was no longer thinking clearly, totally lost in the moment, so lost I licked my lips.

"Jesus," he muttered, his voice soft, and now he was staring at *my* mouth.

I watched, fascinated as his face stayed hard but his eyes went warm. Ultra-warm. Warm in a way I had never seen before. He always looked at me with warmth in his eyes and I knew he didn't look at everyone that way, but as he always looked at me that way. But I knew this was different, *way* different. His eyes were warm in a way that made *me* feel warm, all over.

He wasn't that far away but he started to come even closer.

Ho-ly *shit*.

I blinked, and self-preservation in mind I shoved at him again, pulling my head back with a jerk and cracking it against the door.

The moment was broken.

"Step back!" I shouted.

Luke's eyes narrowed. "What are you playin' at?"

"I'm not playing at anything!" I yelled. "I was in the neighborhood, I thought I had time on my hands. Mom told me you worked here so what the fuck? Stop by and see an old friend. Then you all act like Neanderthal crazies. Jeez. Forget it. I have to go to the dentist. He's gonna be pissed."

I shoved again, but Luke still didn't move.

"You're lying," he said.

"I am not!"

His face came closer. The closer I thought it would have come a moment ago when, for one heart-stopping, insane moment, it seemed like he was going to kiss me. This time, it came in threateningly.

"You waltz in here after five years, not lookin' like you, not actin' like you, jittery and bitchy, somethin' I never would have expected from you. You lie through your teeth then stare at my mouth like you want to stick your tongue down my throat, and when I'm ready to give you that opportunity, you go back to bitchy and lying."

I was staring at him. I couldn't help it. I'd never heard anyone be that brutally honest before in my life.

And he told me he was going to give me the opportunity to kiss him.

Um... *wow.*

"I'm not playin' this game, Ava," he warned, snapping me out of my thoughts. Gentle, affectionate Luke totally gone, we were back to dangerously pissed-off Luke. "You got trouble, you tell me right now so I can help you. I find out another way, you'll pay."

My head jerked. "What?"

"You heard me."

I had heard him and I couldn't believe what I had heard.

"Did you just threaten me?" I asked.

"It wasn't a threat."

Read: It was a promise.

Yikes.

I didn't know what "paying" would entail and I sure as hell wasn't going to find out.

"I'm not in trouble," I told him. And I wasn't, not really. Okay, maybe a little bit. But I was worried I was about to be in a lot in trouble.

"I find out you are—"

"You won't find out I am. In fact, I can promise you won't see me again," I bit out, glaring at him.

"I'll see you again," he said in a way that I felt a thrill go up my back.

Seriously, it was high time to escape.

"Step back," I demanded.

He stared at me.

"Step back!" I shouted.

He stepped back.

I whirled, threw open the door and stomped down the hall.

Then I was twirled around, a hand at my elbow and I jerked my arm out of Luke's grasp. He was, for some reason, now grinning, face relaxed, one corner of his lips tipped up.

"Wrong way," he said, and he looked about ready to laugh.

Great.

I was a total dork, making my grand exit and going the wrong way.

I threw him a look that should have made him spontaneously combust (of course, it did not) and stomped the other way, Luke beside me the whole time. His vibe had morphed from pissed-off to amused and I didn't like it one bit.

He opened the door to the reception area for me and I hightailed it across the room, focused on the outer door, escape, and not looking at anyone.

"Later," I said to the room at large because I didn't want to appear rude.

For some reason, this was met with Shirleen saying, "I'll put money down that she's livin' with him in four days."

My confused gaze swung to Shirleen but she was looking at the movie star glamour girl who was looking at me.

"Three days," glamour girl said, smiling at me, and I thought, in other circumstances, I would have liked to meet her.

"A week. She's got spirit," the other black lady said. She was smiling at me, too. Not like I was the butt of some joke, but in a kind way.

I shook my head. I needed to focus, leave these nutsos behind and go, go, go.

I opened the outer door.

Before it closed behind me, I heard Luke say strangely, "Tonight."

Then everyone laughed.

Chapter 2
A Little Bit of Trouble

I was standing in my dinky little kitchen, taking my post-Luke episode attitude out on an innocent cucumber.

That didn't go very well, Good Ava said on a sigh, resting the side of her head in her hand and her elbow on her thigh.

I thought it went great! Bad Ava yelled enthusiastically, jumping up and down.

I tried to ignore them both and pounded the big cleaver into the cucumber, chopping it in a cucumber-decimating frenzy, trying to get the confrontation with Luke and everyone in his office out of my head.

I lived in a row house in the Highlands area of Denver. I called it The Best Little Row House in Denver.

See? I'm a dork.

It had a living room with two big arched windows at the front, separated by double doors that rolled into the walls and led to dining room, also with two big windows, these facing the back. There was a small kitchen off the dining room and a screened-in porch out the backdoor of the kitchen.

All hardwood floors, except in the minuscule kitchen, which I'd tiled in slate, with the countertops tiled in shiny black. I put in white cupboards, all the hanging ones glass-fronted and displaying my huge collection of Fiestaware.

There were two bedrooms and a massive bathroom with a claw-footed tub upstairs.

I had a big, old basement, its door leading off the kitchen. The basement had two rooms and an old coal room. It was more of a pit than a basement. Unrenovated and long-since unused, wallpaper peeling and exposed light bulbs. I only went down there to do my laundry because it creeped me out.

My row house was historically registered and had three fireplaces (dining room, living room and bedroom) and a sweet, little shady backyard with big trees kitty-corner at the ends.

It wasn't in the best neighborhood, but who cared? It had character, grace, history, a low mortgage, a garage out back where my Range Rover could be safe and I dug it.

I'd lived in Denver my whole life and was never going to move away. Denver was home. It had everything you needed: the big city choice of culture, food, shopping and entertainment all with a small town feel.

My family felt differently.

⚯

After my Dad left us when I was fourteen (rat-bastard number one in my life) and all us girls graduated high school, Mom took off to Phoenix like a shot. She hated the cold and the snow and all the familiar reminders of my father. She also liked to be tan, but felt claustrophobic in sunbeds.

I had two older sisters. My oldest one, Marilyn, moved to St. Louis after high school and got married to a car salesman, then divorced him and almost immediately got married to a lawyer, with whom she was currently involved in a bitter divorce (at the same time dating a doctor, thus moving up in her chosen career as trophy wife). So far Marilyn had managed to work approximately four months of her life and spent the rest of it in spas, malls, and on her back with sweaty slimeballs pumping away at her. I knew this because she talked about her active sex life a good deal. A kind of *gross* good deal.

Read: ick.

My other sister, Sofia, moved to San Diego and became a cheerleader for the San Diego Chargers. Sofia worked her way through the offensive line and then the defensive line (something, I might add, she also did as a cheerleader in high school). Now, retired from her career as an active cheerleader and football player groupie, she was running a cheerleading camp and engaged to a sports agent who was more of a slimeball than both of Marilyn's husbands put together. And that was quite a feat, considering Marilyn's husbands were seriously the scum of the earth.

By the way, my Mom had named us all, with high hopes, after Hollywood bombshells.

My sisters had both been bombshells from puberty, all thick, dark, shining hair, big boobs, tight asses, flat stomachs, long legs and sultry eyes.

I had to work hard at bombshell status, and even then didn't quite make it because I was a big dork.

It was safe to say my sisters and I weren't close.

Sissy Whitchurch was another story.

—※—

Sissy and I had been best friends since second grade and we *were* close. She was the bestest best friend in the world. Good at keeping secrets, happy to rip my silly and sometimes mean sisters to shreds with me, loyal to the core and always up for an adventure.

One problem with Sissy: she had shit taste in men.

Though, considering good men were non-existent, all women didn't have much choice.

However, Sissy's husband, Dominic, was beyond the pale in the shit-men stakes. Dom was a world class asshole.

Dominic Vincetti was very good-looking (and knew it), made his money dubiously (and didn't hide it) and treated Sissy like shit (and never apologized). He didn't hit her, but he cheated on her openly, walked all over her and talked down to her in a way that made my teeth go on edge.

Before Dom, Sissy was funny and sweet and there was no one in the world who was better to go to a rock concert with. She loved music like I did and she went wild at concerts, dancing, screaming. She always knew all the words to the songs and sang them loud.

After five years of marriage, Dom had forced all that good stuff out of Sissy, making her quiet, shy, uncertain and a homebody, and Sissy didn't even notice it was happening.

I noticed and it pissed me off.

Sissy loved him, though, and put up with it, and it wasn't my place to say anything. If she wanted him then I was there. My only other choice was to stop spending time with her, and a life without Sissy... well, I couldn't imagine it.

But when I changed, lost weight, dyed my hair, Dom noticed.

In fact, a lot of people noticed.

17

In fact, even though I'd dated when I was heavy, I started to get some serious male attention as the weight dropped off then more, then more. Since Luke's Dad's funeral, I'd had my first three longish-term boyfriends.

I had to admit, in the dream world I had in the back of my head, they were all practice for Luke. Of course, I never told them that, and I could have fallen in love with any one of them if they hadn't all turned out to be jerks.

There was Rick, who cheated on me (um, no).

Then there was Dave, who had a collection of pornography so big he could have opened his own store. And he called phone sex lines, like, a lot. Neither of these were bad things, as such. Except phone bills over five hundred dollars month after month were a bit much. Not to mention he wanted to have sex, like, twelve times a day, walked around naked at all times and tried to get me to go to swinger parties (um, no again).

Then there was Noah, who took my Auntie Ella's jewelry and pawned it. This, I didn't find out until he also took my ATM card, found out my PIN number and cleaned out my checking and savings accounts before he disappeared. Luckily, I had the inheritance money my Aunt Ella gave me in a different account. She gave me her jewelry and a shitload of money, but only gave Marilyn and Sofia a token, which pissed them off big time. But they'd always been mean to her and I hadn't, so fuck them.

See? All men were scum.

I wasn't a bitter, twisted spinster. I'd put myself out there and I had reasons to think that, what with my choices, Sissy's choices and my sisters' choices, not to mention my fucking Dad, who'd left and never came back, that all men were scum.

⇥⟊⟆

After Noah took off, Dom started to flirt with me right in front of Sissy. I couldn't believe it and did my absolute best not to rip his face off with my fingernails. However, there were a lot of times I wanted to rip Dom's face off with my fingernails. Not just when he was flirting with me, but when he'd ask Sissy if she *really* should be eating that second slice of pizza, giving her a shitty look when he didn't quite like the outfit she put on, causing her to go and change it, getting pissy when he was served leftovers and the like.

Sissy ignored the flirting. So did I, passing it off as a joke.

Dom took this as a challenge. Dom was the kind of guy girls responded to, mainly because he was really handsome, which sucked. I figured he could use a scar or two, put there by my fingernails, of course.

When I didn't respond, he flirted more. He started touching, and just two weeks ago he backed me into the corner of their kitchen and kissed me, open-mouthed.

I bit his tongue.

"What the fuck!" he hissed, hand swiping at his mouth and glaring at me.

He was hot—all macho, Italian bad boy, dark, wavy hair, dark eyes, slim hips, broad shoulders.

When we'd first seen him, Sissy and I had both fallen in lust. Sissy had been over the moon when he asked her out. Sissy had never been heavy. She had blue eyes and strawberry blonde hair and was pretty, petite and dainty, like a gown up human-sized fairy, without the pointy ears.

"Get away from me," I had snapped at Dom.

His face had changed from angry, to calculating. "You want it, Ava, you know you do. I've seen the way you look at me."

Like I said, he was hot, so he probably wasn't wrong. But he was also my best friend's husband.

"Get over yourself," I told him.

"I'd rather get on top of you."

I wanted to laugh in his face. That was a really bad line. Dom, I knew, because I'd seen it, could do a lot better.

Instead, I said, "Fuck off, Dom. Sissy's in the other room."

"I get what I want," he replied, and something about the way he said it kind of freaked me out. He said it like he meant it and he was looking at me in a way that made my scalp tingle, and not in a good way. I didn't know what he did for a living, but I didn't think it was good, and Sissy never talked about it, which was concerning, Sissy and I talked about everything. He struck me as a bad guy, not only because he was a cheat and a jerk, but also for other reasons.

"Dom, fuck… off," I snapped, but he kissed me again, arms going around me, tongue sliding in my mouth. I struggled and pushed. Dom pinned me against the wall, his hand going up my shirt.

We both heard a noise. Dom let me go and stepped back, and we saw Sissy standing in the door.

"Sis, girl…" Dom said, his voice conciliatory, and I wanted to kick him. I mean, what did he expect to happen?

I didn't kick him though, mainly because I was horrified and scared through to my fucking soul that I might have just lost my best friend.

But Sissy looked at me and asked, "Ava, would you help me pack?"

Then she walked out of the room.

Halle-fucking-lujah.

I shoved Dom's shoulder as I walked by him and glared, but he just repeated, staring at me with an intensity that I did… not… like, "Ava, I get what I want."

I rolled my eyes and left the room. I helped Sissy pack and she moved in with me for a few days. She cried a lot and I listened a lot, and I quietly seethed a lot more. Then she went to her Mom's place in Wyoming. But not until after we'd hatched our plan.

Sissy was going to move away and I was going to get the goods on Dom so Sissy could divorce him and take him to the cleaners.

That was the plan.

I wasn't sure *how* to get the goods on Dom. That was where tough guy, mercenary, bounty hunter, private eye Luke Stark was supposed to come into the scenario.

⊰⊱

Sissy knew Luke, had met him several times and had stood beside me at my bedroom window checking him out on numerous occasions while he lifted weights in his Dad's garage.

She also knew how I felt about him (read: big, huge, twenty-one-year old crush).

Dragging Luke into the deal was her idea.

Sissy also knew about the funeral and what happened there. In fact, she knew everything about Luke.

She knew that when I was nine and was walking home from school, three boys I detested had caught up with me, calling me Fatty Fatty Four Eyes (not original, but it hurt, anyway). She knew how Luke, thirteen and already a tough customer, came out of nowhere and punched one of them in the nose, bloodying it and making all three run away. She also knew after that was over that I made some smart comment making Luke laugh, because being teased all the time for being fat and ugly, one only had two choices: go silent and shy, or become a smartass. I chose the latter. After I made him laugh, he'd walked me home.

She also knew, after that, no kids ever teased me. Not ever again.

Further, she knew about when Luke was fourteen and I was ten. He'd had one of many humdinger fights with his Dad that I heard all the way across the street. He'd torn out of the house and I'd gone after him. I found him in a park, ass to the ground, back against a tree, his head bent, wrists resting on his cocked knees. I'd sat beside him and started telling jokes until he came out of his mood and started laughing.

She also knew about when I was twelve and Luke was sixteen, and Luke, his Dad and Mom had come over for dinner. My mother, an aging beauty queen who still had two shelves full of trophies and ribbons from "the good old days", got tipsy and announced to the table, "I'm so lucky. I have two beautiful daughters and one smart one." Marilyn and Sofia grinned at each other. My father got red in the face and looked like he was going to hit the roof. Luke's Dad chuckled uncomfortably in a way that sounded strangled, but his Mom stared at me with concern.

I squirmed.

Luke leaned back in his chair, looked at Sofia and said, "Congratulations, you must have made the honor roll." Sofia's mouth dropped open in horror (I wasn't the only Barlow girl with a crush on Luke; all three of us had the hots for him). I immediately stopped squirming and laughed so hard at Sofia's horrified expression, I snorted.

Sissy also knew about the time, only five days before he graduated from high school, when I was fourteen and Luke was eighteen, and it had become clear my Dad had left and wasn't coming back. I was sitting on our front stoop.

You could hear my mother crying and carrying on inside while my sisters argued with each other over a curling iron or something idiotic.

I saw Luke come out of his house on his way to his motorcycle. He saw me, changed directions, crossed the street and sat down beside me. He didn't say a word and neither did I. I just stared at his boots and wished he was my boyfriend, not for the first or the last time. It would have been a lot easier to cope with losing Dad if I'd had Luke as a boyfriend. Or anyone for that matter, but especially Luke.

I was close with my Dad. I thought we had a bond. I always thought it was the two of us against the other silly bitches in the house. I knew he found it trying to his patience; my mother, flighty, naggy, demanding, wanting a better life, house, car, curtains, whatever and always going on about it and going on about all the men she *didn't* chose so she could be with Dad, rubbing his nose in it constantly. I knew, too, that he lamented where he went wrong with snotty, bitchy, catty Marilyn and Sofia, though he didn't have to look too far. My Mom was a good teacher.

Dad had come into my bedroom late at night the day before he left and said, "Sorry, Ava, darlin', but I just can't take it anymore." He'd woken me up and I didn't know what he was talking about. He didn't explain and he didn't say anything more.

The next day he was gone.

"I thought..." I said to Luke, and then stopped because I didn't know what I thought.

Luke slid his arm around my waist and pulled me to his side. I put my head on his shoulder and we sat there a long time before Luke bumped his foot against mine. I got the hint and pulled back. He got up, leaned down, touched my nose then he was gone.

A few days later, like my Dad, he was really gone.

Luke came back every once in a while, though, visiting his Mom, fighting with his Dad and popping by to say hi to me.

Then he disappeared for eight years. I didn't know where he went and his mother wasn't talking or I would have found out because, normally, she told my mother everything.

Lastly, Sissy knew about Luke's father's funeral. I was twenty-four, Luke was twenty-eight. After the funeral, still at graveside, the Barlow Girl Brigade walked up to Luke and his Mom. Hugs and cheek kisses were passed around, both Marilyn and Sofia going for the gusto with Luke, but his body went stiff when they pressed against him, which was embarrassing for me, having to watch it and knowing they were my sisters. As gorgeous as they were, Luke was totally aloof from the Bombshell Barlow Girls.

That was, until his eyes moved to me and I leaned in to kiss his cheek. His arms came around me and he pulled me into a close hug, pressing his bearded jaw against my temple.

"Good to see you, Ava," he murmured, and it sounded like he meant it.

"You too, Luke," I said, pulling back a bit and looking at him. "Hanging in there?" I asked softly.

His eyes were warm, his face was hard, and he was so fucking handsome it took my breath away.

He kept his arms around me and looked down at me. "Yeah," he answered.

"Wanna get drunk?" I asked, mostly teasing.

"Yeah," he answered, definitely not teasing.

"I can probably arrange that," I told him, still trying to keep the tone light, but wanting to help ease his pain all the same. He and his Dad never got along, I knew that. Still, his Dad had been youngish and it was a shock. Massive heart attack. Not good, even if they didn't get along.

"I'll take you up on that," Luke said. Then his eyes moved to his mother. He let me go and touched my nose. "I'll call you."

I nodded. "It's a deal," I promised.

We moved away and more mourners moved into our space to offer their condolences. I walked away slowly, wanting to be in his presence for as long as I could drag it out.

It was later I overheard my sisters talking in our living room.

"God, it was sick, seeing her pressed up to him like that. All her fat, like, bulging," Marilyn said.

"I know, I think I threw up a little looking at them. He could barely get his arms around her," Sofia replied.

"I came all this way just to see him and he barely looked at me. But he hugged Ava. How fucking weird is that?" Marilyn went on.

"Maybe he's gay," Sofia suggested.

Then they'd laughed, thinking they were hilarious.

Okay, it was safe to say that not only weren't my sisters and I close, I kind of didn't like them, as in *really* didn't like them.

But for me, hearing what they said, that was it. The final straw.

That was when I made my decision, my vow, that the next time I saw Lucas Stark, and if he hugged me or touched me, no one who was looking at us would think it was sick, gross or throw up a little at the sight of us.

That was why I didn't take his calls and go out and get drunk with him like I promised I would.

Instead, I went and found a personal trainer and had a mortifying fitness test. I was put on a program, dumped all the shit food out of my house and started reading *Self* and *Shape* magazines religiously. I lost twenty pounds in the first month (water weight). The next fifty-five were a lot harder. My trainer changed my program every six weeks and drilled me like a Nazi. His name was Riley. He was always tan, and not sunbed tan. He was outside a lot, even in the winter. He had blond hair, brown eyes and a great body, and he told me I was going to be his Mona Lisa. I wasn't going for Mona Lisa. I was going for Jennifer Aniston, but I decided not to share that with Riley.

Riley was a good guy, though likely a total jerk to his girlfriends. How was I to know? Regardless, I didn't want to let him or myself down. I was dedicated and motivated and living, cycling, treadmilling, stair climbing, ab curling and weight training for the day when Luke saw me again.

Though it didn't turn out like I'd planned. Mainly because, even with partial bombshell status, I became an asshole-magnet and realized it wasn't just Sissy, Marilyn, Sofia and Mom's bad taste it men. It was just that men weren't worth the effort.

So by the time I was ready for Luke, mentally and physically prepared to seek him out, I'd gone off men. I made a new vow that I was dedicated to just as much as fitness.

I was never going to get tangled up with a man again, no matter who, no matter what.

After Noah cleaned me out, Sissy and I went to Pandora's Box on Broadway. I stocked up and got myself a rabbit vibrator *and* a smooth, sleek silver one (so I could have variety) and enough batteries to last a year. Once I got them home, out of their boxes and loaded up with batteries, I vowed everlasting fidelity to my vibrators.

That was that.

Seriously.

The end.

So there I was, now a dedicated, bitter spinster with revenge on my mind. Not revenge for myself, but for Sissy and every other woman who'd been fucked over by a shithead guy.

I stopped cleaving at the cucumber, tossed it into a bowl with the arugula I'd already nearly annihilated, and had started on the onion when the phone rang.

I threw down the cleaver and picked up the phone.

"Yo," I said.

"Yo, yourself," Sissy said to me. "How'd it go with Luke?"

I could hear the anticipation in her voice. She thought he'd fall in love with me on sight and put a ring on my finger within the hour. She loved me and thought I was funny and cool. What could I say? It sucked to disappoint her.

"Not good. I didn't ask him. I'm going it alone," I tried to make it short and sweet.

Silence for a beat and then, "What do you mean, not good?"

"I mean not good." I decided maybe I shouldn't tell her right now about how it actually went. She had enough on her plate and anyway, I wasn't ready to relive it. "I think he's kinda pissed that I didn't return his calls after his father's funeral."

"You should have called him," Sissy told me, and she'd told me this before, like, five dozen times.

"Too late now. Anyway, we go ahead with the plan as it was, just without Luke. I'll go to your house tonight."

Sissy hesitated. "I'd be a lot more comfortable if you had Luke with you."

"That isn't gonna happen."

"Okay, then maybe you can call Riley. I think he has a bit of a crush on you, now that you're hot. Maybe he'll go with you."

The idea of Riley, who'd done a body fat test on me seventy-five pounds ago (and one just three weeks ago and about seventeen in between) having a crush on me made me burst out laughing.

"Riley does not have a crush on me," I said when I quit laughing.

"Riley thinks you're fine," Sissy returned.

"Riley has a girlfriend with bleached teeth and a perma-tan," I told her.

"He broke up with her *ages* ago. Anyway, you make Riley laugh, even when he's holding your feet and you're doing ab curls."

"There's nothing to laugh about when you're doing ab curls."

This was true. I hated ab curls. I hated exercise and I wasn't that hot on cucumber, arugula, onion and bulgur wheat tabouleh. I'd rather have a huge

25

burrito with spiced meat, cheese, sour cream and guacamole and a humungous chocolate chip cookie, but I hadn't worked my ass off (literally) to go back now.

"Tell me about Luke," Sissy changed the subject, knowing, after twenty-two years of being my best friend, that I was holding out on her.

"Later."

"Now."

"Later, Sissy. It…" I stopped, then started again, "wasn't good."

"Was it bad?"

"No, it was just… weird." Weird really wasn't the word for it, but I was going to go with that for now.

"Well," she began, giving in, and her voice had gone soft. "Then don't worry about Dom. I'll come home in a few days, we'll do it together."

"No!" I said, kind of loud. I didn't want her to come back. I didn't want Dom to talk her into taking him back. I wanted her clear of him. I wanted Sissy to come back to herself and for Dom to be out of her life forever. "I'll take care of it," I finished.

"I don't…"

"Sissy, I'll take care of it."

"I don't like it. Dom's not really a guy you mess with."

"I won't get caught."

"Crap," Sissy muttered, her second thoughts clear in her voice.

"I'll be all right. I'll go tonight, search the house. It's his poker night, right?"

"Yeah." I could tell she still didn't like it. "Call me when you get home."

"Okay."

"Later, honey."

"Later."

I hung up and tossed the draining bulgur wheat in with the other junk. I chopped the onions, cried a little bit, threw them in, too. I mixed it up with a dash of olive oil, lemon juice and salt and pepper.

I got out a fork, took a huge bite and said, mouth full, "Blech."

It wasn't bad, but it wasn't a burrito and a chocolate chip cookie, either.

You know, you really should listen to Sissy, Good Ava said to me.

I think some breaking and entering will be fun! Bad Ava put in.

Shit.

I was about to head out for my evening's festivities when the phone rang.

I'd put on dark jeans, a black stretchy, fitted, long-sleeved t-shirt, black flip-flops and, of course, my silver.

I should probably have left my silver out of the equation since it was glittery and would catch the light, but I didn't go anywhere without my silver.

And anyway, I'd been to Dom and Sissy's a gazillion times. All their neighbors knew me and wouldn't blink an eye that I was there. Furthermore, I had a key (well, not really, but I knew where they hid the spare).

I didn't answer the phone. Night had fallen, it was getting late and Sissy told me that Dom's return from the poker game was up in the air. If he was doing well, he stayed out late. If he was losing, he cut it short, came home and likely took his bad luck out on Sissy by saying shit to her that made her feel like dirt.

The answering machine kicked in as I grabbed my keys and bag.

"Hey, Ava? It's Ally. Long time no see or hear, chickie. You've been, like, Ms. Invisible and loads of shit has gone down." Pause, then, "I heard you were at my brother's offices this afternoon and had a situation with Luke. Sister, what was *that* all about? I didn't even know you knew Luke. Call me, pronto. I want the dirt. Indy wants the dirt. We *all* want the dirt. We'll do drinks. Hornet, tomorrow night, seven o'clock. See you there."

Disconnect.

Shit.

Indy Savage and Ally Nightingale were Rock Chicks like Sissy and me. Those two were hilarious, crazier by far than Sissy and me, or at least Sissy recently, for sure.

We'd met at a concert years ago and went to dozens of them together. Sissy and I usually never missed one of Indy's kickass parties, she had a lot of them and she always had bowls of cashews, and everyone knew bowls of cashews meant kickass party.

Sissy and I also used to hang out at the used bookstore on Broadway that Indy owned, called Fortnum's. I hadn't been in ages, at least eight months, maybe longer. Since before Indy hooked up with Lee Nightingale.

Indy had had a crush on Lee since practically birth. Indy and Lee's parents were best friends and she and Lee and Ally and Lee's brother, Hank, had grown up together. It was super-fucking-fly that they were finally together. It made you think the world wasn't shit.

It wasn't that I didn't want to go to Fortnum's or see Indy and Ally (Ally worked there on occasion). It was just that Noah had cleaned out my bank accounts. I'd felt the need to score a couple more accounts for my at-home graphic design business to make up for the money he stole so, unusually, I was busy.

See, with Aunt Ella's money and a barely there mortgage, I didn't have to work that hard. I'd bought the house dirt cheap, mainly because it was a nightmare when I bought it, but I'd fixed it up, mostly myself. Not the electricity or the plumbing, just refinished the floors, re-skimmed the walls, did the tile work, painted, shit like that. I had a couple of business clients that kept me relatively busy, out of trouble and in plentiful amounts of my sliver. However, when your rat-bastard ex-boyfriend steals over five thousand dollars from you, it pushes you to put your nose to the grindstone.

I decided to call Ally tomorrow, after I searched Dom's house and figured out what I'd tell her about Luke.

I went to my Range Rover, backed it out, hit the button for the garage door to close and headed to Sissy and Dom's. They had a very nice popped-top bungalow in Washington Park. Sissy loved it and I liked it, too. I hoped she got it in the divorce settlement.

I did a drive-by, checking for lights and to see if Dom's BMW was parked in their back drive off the alley. It wasn't, so I parked around the corner, hoofed it up to the house, went around the side to the back and found Sissy's fake rock by their outdoor Jacuzzi which held the key. I opened it with the combination she gave me, put the rock back where I found it, went to the door and let myself in.

I didn't bother with gloves. My prints were likely all over the house anyway.

I also didn't turn on the lights. I knew the house like the back of my hand. I'd partied in it, had Christmas dinner in it, had crashed there on many occasions (normally drunk) and even helped Sissy clean it a number of times.

I didn't know what I was looking for. Shirts with lipstick on the collar? Love letters?

I had the bad feeling that I was going to have to follow Dom with a camera and take pictures of him while he was doing the nasty with some bimbo. I didn't relish that idea so I hoped Dom was a love letter keeping type of guy.

I went to the kitchen drawer where I knew Sissy kept her small Maglite and decided to start in the bedroom.

I'd seen enough movies and television to do a decent search. I started at his nightstand and found an industrial-sized box of condoms he had to have bought at some warehouse retail store. I didn't even know they made boxes of condoms that big.

I made note of this, knowing that Sissy was on the pill, therefore Dom didn't need condoms.

Sissy and I had both gone on the pill together, me for friendship's sake at the time since I'd been a virgin. I lost my virginity at twenty-three to a sweet, goofy, geeky guy named George (it wasn't awful, but it also wasn't great, by the way), but I'd been on the pill for two years before that for no reason at all.

I shrugged off thoughts of my contraception history, checked the bottom and insides of the drawer, the back and bottom of the nightstand, but nothing going.

I was moving to the closet, intent on my task, when suddenly a steel-band-like arm wrapped around my waist, a hand went over my mouth and I was lifted clean off my feet.

Freaked out, legs pumping and screaming under the hand, I was carried out of the bedroom and into the living room like I weighed as much as a ragdoll.

I planted a well-aimed, savage elbow to the side of who I suspected was Dom, someone who I not only didn't want to catch me snooping, I also didn't want to be alone with him, at all. Ever.

I heard a grunt when my elbow connected and I was dropped. Heart pumping, mind flying from thought to thought, I caught only one and that one thought was *go*.

I started to run but was caught by the back of my shirt. It went way tight against my chest and I was yanked back, again off my feet. My shoulders slammed against something hard right before I was whirled around. The arm went around me tight, pulling me against a solid torso just as the hand went back over my mouth.

"Quiet," Luke Stark clipped.

Ho-ly *crap*.

I went still and stared, though I couldn't see much of anything. I'd dropped the Maglite somewhere in the bedroom.

What in *the hell* was he doing there?

"You gonna stay quiet?" Luke asked.

I nodded. His hand went away.

29

"What the fuck are you doing here?" I whispered, not knowing what to think, or feel. Just shocked out of my mind.

Was he following me? And, if so, why?

"Could ask you the same thing," he said to me, cutting into my thoughts.

"I'm visiting a friend," I lied quickly.

His body tensed and I felt something fill the room, something crackling and dangerous. I couldn't see it in the dark, but I could feel it. I could feel it because his arm got tight and it hauled me even deeper into his body so we were pressed close, chest to crotch.

Fuckity, fuck, fuck, *fuck*.

"Stop lying to me Ava." I could tell by his tone that he was not happy. So not happy that I had to admit I was a little scared of him.

"I'm not lying," I lied.

"You're tellin' me that Dom Vincetti is a friend of yours?"

"No, Sissy Vincetti is."

He knew Sissy. He'd met her way back in the day. This was likely why his arm relaxed enough for me to pull away and put a foot of space between us, which was a far more comfortable position, believe you me.

"Sissy isn't here," Luke said to me.

"Well, I know that now," I said, like I'd expected her to be there. In other words, I lied, again.

"You often go to your friends' houses when they're not home and search them in the dark?"

Eek!

Before I could think up another lie—because it wasn't any of his business what I was doing there—I mean, it would have been his business, if he hadn't carried me through his offices like a caveman that afternoon, but it wasn't his business anymore—he reached forward and grabbed my hand, tugging me back into the bedroom.

"Luke, stop. What are you doing?"

He bent down, nabbed the still-lit Maglite from the floor and snapped it off.

"We're gettin' out of here," he said, pulling me out of the bedroom and back into the living room.

I planted my feet when he started to yank me across the room. He stopped and looked back at me.

"No. *You're* getting out of here," I flashed at him. "I'm, um... looking for the earring I left here the other night."

That sounded like a good lie.

Luke obviously didn't think it was a good lie. He gave my hand a sharp tug. I fell forward, and without a word he started walking, dragging me behind him.

I yanked my hand out of his, stopped again and cried, "Luke!"

That was when the room exploded.

One second, we were standing there, me glaring at him in the dark, him holding his body tense like he was just stopping himself from shaking some sense into me. The next minute there was so much noise and flying debris, every thought flew out of my head.

Luke moved quickly. He threw himself at me in a body tackle and we went down to the floor. He landed on top of me, body slamming into mine, and immediately pulled himself up. He wrapped his arms around my head and leaned his shoulder into the floor, my face pressed into his throat, his head tucked in, temple against the top of my forehead.

Glass, dust, plaster and bits of Sissy's adored pottery collection flew everywhere as machine gunfire blasted through the huge living room window.

I lay under Luke, pretty certain I was going to die and wishing I'd made a will. Now my sisters and mother were going to get all Aunt Ella's money. I should have left it to Sissy and a cat shelter.

The noise finally stopped, and even though it felt like it had gone on forever, it was probably less than a minute. Luke didn't move, just kept me tucked tight underneath him, and it hit me that our position meant he was using himself as a shield to keep me safe.

Whoa.

Whoa, whoa, whoa.

Stop right there.

That was too much. It was all too much. Time for me to bury all this somewhere deep and have a nervous breakdown later, when Sissy and I were on a beach enjoying Dom's money.

"Luke," I whispered and his head came up.

I was quiet because I could tell he was listening, and not to me. Then his head tilted down and I could feel his eyes on me.

I lifted my hand up between our faces, index finger and thumb held an inch apart and I said, "Maybe I'm in *a little bit* of trouble."

It was then he made a noise and it sounded an awful lot like a growl.

Chapter 3
That's Who I'm Keeping Safe

"Luke?"

"Quiet."

He knifed off me, yanked me to my feet and wasted no time pulling me through the room, through the kitchen and out the backdoor.

I didn't resist.

I didn't want to be anywhere near a room that exploded with gunfire. I was more than happy to be moving away from it, swiftly, hand in hand with a tough guy, mercenary, bounty hunter, private eye type person who clearly knew what the hell he was doing.

Luke jogged through the backyard then broke into a sprint down the alley, his hand in mine, dragging me behind him and let me tell you, it wasn't easy sprinting in flip-flops. I was going to have to rethink my footwear on my next nail-Dom-to-the-wall assignment.

I saw lights go on in houses and heard police sirens, but Luke just kept going.

It took me a moment, considering the fact that I was freaking out and perhaps fleeing for my life (on flip-flops no less), to realize that he was moving in the wrong direction.

I pulled at his hand.

"My car's the other way," I whispered loudly to his back.

He kept going, dragging me with him.

"Luke!" I hissed, tugging hard.

He didn't stop, just kept dragging me.

We shot out of the alley, stopped next to a shiny black Porsche and he bleeped the locks. He opened the passenger side door. I had to admit, even in my current state, I was impressed that he drove a Porsche.

"Get in," he ordered, snapping me out of my thoughts about his Porsche.

"What?" I asked, confused, freaked, winded from the flip-flop getaway, and wanting maybe to take a second and do a cartwheel of joy that I was still alive and not full of holes.

"Get in the fucking car," Luke clipped.

I guessed Luke wasn't into cartwheels of joy.

"My car is..." I started to tell him, but I stopped talking when his hand went to the top of my head and he pressed me into the car. He did this so forcefully my body had no choice but to comply. My legs just buckled and my ass, of its own accord, aimed for the seat. He slammed the door the minute my feet cleared the frame.

He was in the driver's side before I finished blinking away my surprise.

I turned on him.

"I want you to take me to my car," I told him. My purse was in my car and I needed my purse. My cell was in my purse, and just like anyone, I felt naked without my cell phone.

He started the Porsche (incidentally, it purred like a kitten).

Maybe not thinking clearly, I turned to the door, my hand on the handle, deciding I would run to my own car.

What happened next shocked the breath right out of me.

Luke grabbed my wrist He pulled me away from the door, leaned forward and yanked a set of handcuffs out of the glove compartment, not letting me go the whole time. He snapped a bracelet on my left wrist and the other on his right. As I was staring at our wrists bound together, he put the Porsche in gear, my arm moving with his, and we rocketed from the curb.

It took a few seconds, but then I stammered, "You just... you just... handcuffed me to you!"

"That's right," he told, me as he, or more to the point *we,* kept shifting.

"You just handcuffed me to you," I repeated inanely.

He didn't answer.

"Why did you handcuff me to you?" I asked.

He remained silent.

"Luke!"

"Quiet, Ava."

It was then I lost it. I had an excuse. I *had* just had a near-death experience.

"You're nuts! You're crazy! You're following me. You handcuffed me. We just got shot at. I can't believe this shit. Take me to my goddamned car!"

He pulled over. The Porsche moved sleekly under his command, but this was still sudden enough for me to snap my mouth shut. When he had the car idling he turned to me. His left hand shot out, wrapping around my neck and pulling me toward him.

Our faces an inch apart, he ordered, "Quiet, Ava."

"*I will not be quiet!*" I screamed in his face. "I'm freaked right the hell out. We were just shot at! I think we just ran away from a crime scene. And, I repeat, you just handcuffed me to you!"

"You got the choice to be quiet or I'll shut you up."

"Yeah? How are you gonna do that? Gag me?" I yelled.

"I had somethin' else in mind."

"Fuck quiet!" I shouted, ignoring his words, totally in Freak Out La-la Land. "I need tequila. I need my car. I need to call Sissy," I was rambling and I knew it, but I had been in a room that *exploded*.

"Quiet," he repeated, his voice holding a low warning.

I also ignored the warning. "Seriously, take me to my goddamned car."

"Why am I always repeating myself with you?" he asked, sounding slightly impatient.

"Maybe because I don't snap to when you tell me to do something like all the other women in your life likely do," I retorted, sounding bitchy as all hell.

It was at that, he jerked me forward with his hand at my neck his head slanted, and I kid you *not*, he kissed me.

For your information, those lips were hard when they kissed you.

Ho-ly crap!

I was stunned still as his mouth moved over mine. Then he let me go as quickly as he kissed me, turned back to the wheel and we moved into traffic.

I decided my best course of action at that moment was to stay silent.

It was a good thing to do. It gave me the time to bury Luke's hard, angry kiss right down deep next to him shielding me from gunfire with his body and us getting shot at.

I'd wanted Luke to kiss me, like, for ages, but not like that. I didn't even know you could kiss someone like that.

My silence and our drive also gave me time mentally to rehearse my conversation with Sissy about this incident: *Um, Sissy, you know that "Day of the Dead" pottery collection by Stephen Kilborn, you've been painstakingly collecting for years...?*

We were in lower downtown when Luke's right hand moved to flip down his sun visor, taking my left one with it, pulling me out of my unhappy thoughts.

The car slowed and he hit a button affixed to his visor then he flipped it back up, his (and my) hand moving to the stick as he downshifted.

"Where are we going?" I broke the silence.

He turned into an underground parking area and headed to an open spot, of which, I noted, there were many.

"You're staying at my place while I find out what the fuck is goin' on."

He parked, pulled up the brake and turned off the car while I processed this information, coming to the conclusion I did not want to be at Luke's place while he found out what was going on. I didn't want to be at Luke's place at all.

Before I could protest (not that it would matter), he got out his side, which meant, considering I was attached to him, I had to scramble over the seat and follow him.

"Luke, I need to get my car, my purse is in my car," I said while he closed the door behind me and bleeped the locks. I used a calmer, more rational voice, hoping to impress him with my cool attitude and get him to do what I wanted.

"One of the boys will bring it here," he said, hitting the button to an elevator.

"What boys?"

"Lee's boys."

Oh. Well then. That was my car taken care of.

I carried on to the next important subject. "I should go home. I'm supposed to call Sissy."

He turned to me, eyes assessing.

"You know where Sissy is?" he asked.

Oops. I'd just outed myself on the "just visiting Sissy at her house" lie.

Argh!

"Um… " I muttered, wondering how to backtrack on what I had given away.

"Jesus Christ. You two are in on this together," he said, yanking me into the elevator and pressing a button. We were still cuffed together, but he was holding my hand.

"There's nothing to be in on together." Oh man, there it was, lying again. I was going straight to hell.

"You two were always in on something together," Luke returned.

"We were not," I lied (again!).

Luke looked at me and I found it hard to return his angry stare.

"What about the time you two lit off bottle rockets in the middle of the night in Old Man Humphries's backyard? He nearly had a stroke."

I made a sound like "humph". "He deserved it. He shot Sissy's dog... for trespassing! How can a dog trespass?"

Luke didn't answer me. He went on, "And the time you sold a bag of oregano to Mitch and Josh Burk, telling them it was pot?"

"We needed money. There was a Kiss tribute show coming up. They never figured it out, said it was the best weed they'd ever had."

"And the time you filled Megan Carmichael's car with popcorn?"

"She was a bitch. She stole Sissy's boyfriend."

He shook his head as if *I* was the crazy person in this scenario, not him, Mr. Handcuff Man. The doors opened and we walked into a semi-dark space. It wasn't that dark since the lights of LoDo were shining in from quite a number of huge floor to almost-ceiling arched windows.

I knew it was a loft, a kickass loft, but this was confirmed when Luke flipped a switch. Soft lamps lit the space and he dragged me into it.

I didn't fight. I stared.

His loft was super-fly.

One huge room with four huge windows down one side, two windows down both the narrow sides. All the walls were exposed brick, the ceiling had duct work, painted black, and the floor was shining wood planks cut only with rugs under the bed and living room areas.

Smack center, between the four windows opposite the elevator, there was a kitchen area with a counter against the wall, a semi-circular bar facing the room, stools around the bar with stainless steel bases and black leather seats. There were shiny, black appliances including an enormous fridge.

To the side, stationed between the two windows, there was a black couch, a huge black recliner to one side, a black-lacquered coffee table and a gigantic flat screen TV was fixed to the wall.

Across from the kitchen was a big bed with a black slatted head and footboard and deep-gray sheets and comforter.

The other side of the room had a set of weights, a weight bench, a fancy weight machine and an elliptical machine. In the corner next to the weights, there was a small room made of glass block that I assumed was the bathroom.

It was obviously occupied by a man. There were clothes all over the place, magazines and opened mail in disarray on every surface and dishes in the sink. The bed had been slept in and hadn't been made.

Still, even with the mess, the tough guy, mercenary, bounty hunting, private eye business must pay well for Luke to have a Porsche and a LoDo loft like this.

I was now definitely impressed.

This lasted for two seconds, mainly because Luke had dragged me to the side of the bed and he was now unlocking the bracelet on his wrist.

"What're you doing?" I asked, watching him.

"Cuffing you to the bed."

My body went solid.

Then I screeched, "*What?*"

Too late. I should have run, struggled, something. Instead I went still, like the big dork I was, and he pushed me back with a hand to my chest. I fell to the bed. He leaned into me, and before I knew it, or even began to struggle, he had cuffed me to one of the slats.

I stared at my hand, cuffed to the slat, then I stared at him, completely at a loss for words.

He was looking down at me and he seemed deep in thought.

"I don't like this," he informed me.

He didn't like it?

I found some words. *Loud* ones.

"I don't like it either!" I shouted at the top of my lungs. "Uncuff me!"

He put a knee to the bed, grabbed my other wrist then came forward and pinned me with his heavy body. This time I struggled, twisting under him, but it was like I didn't even move. He worked at the cuffs, pulled up my other arm and slapped the bracelet on that one so I had no free hand. He did this all with minimal effort, but I was breathing like I had just run a marathon.

He got off me, stood and stared down at me.

"That's better," he murmured.

"Please tell me you're joking," I said softly and I was hoping he was. I was hoping this was all a big joke. He would give me one of his half-grins and say, "Psych."

"Be good while I'm away," he answered instead as he turned.

"Get back here! Uncuff me!" I shouted. "Luke, I'll scream my head off!"

"Do it," he invited, hitting the button to the elevator and turning to me, looking totally calm, and I wished I could throw something at him. "The loft upstairs is vacant, for sale. The people downstairs are still in Florida for the winter. Each loft is the whole floor. No one's around to hear you."

The elevators opened, he flipped the lights off and disappeared.

I screamed, "I'm going to kill you!"

The elevator doors closed and he was gone.

Well, this is a fine mess you've gotten us into, Good Ava said into my ear.

Oo, we're in Luke's bed, Bad Ava cooed into my other one.

Shit.

☙❧

When you were fuelled with adrenalin, shot at and were lying handcuffed to a bed owned by a man you had a screaming crush on for most of your life, it was impossible to sleep. Not to mention, both arms over your head was *not* a comfortable position.

So I laid awake thinking of all the ways I wanted to kill Luke.

Then I realized, when I couldn't find a way I liked, I didn't want to kill Luke because I wasn't a killing type of person.

Instead, I focused on all the reasons why I hated men.

They cheated on you. They lied to you. They stole your stuff. They made you feel like shit. And they cuffed you to beds.

I was mentally arranging and rearranging all the men I hated in order of the ones I hated the most (Luke being on the top of that list in each arrangement, for obvious reasons) when the elevator doors slid open.

He had been gone a long time. It felt like hours, though it probably wasn't.

He walked silently into the room. I saw him moving because the room was dimly lit with the city lights, but he barely made a sound. He put something on the kitchen counter and I watched, quiet and secretly fascinated, as his upper body twisted when he pulled off his tee. I held my breath as I saw skin in the moonlight, and even the definition of muscle, and what I saw was nice.

He turned to the bed, walked to it and sat on the side then bent forward and tugged off a boot.

"Please take me home," I said quietly. I had decided quiet was the way to go. All my other attempts to get my way (yelling, screaming, shouting and struggling) didn't work so I was trying out other options.

"No," he said just as quietly, foiling my new tactic and dropping his boot to the floor.

"I need to take out my contacts," I told him and this was true.

He stopped taking off his second boot then bent down, picked up the first one and tugged it back on.

"What are you doing?" I asked as he got up.

He walked to the tee he threw on the floor, pulled it on and went to the elevator.

"I'll be back," he said, standing at the elevators.

"Wait!" I called, but too late. The doors opened, he disappeared and the light from the elevator was extinguished as the doors closed.

This time he wasn't gone long and came back less silent because he was carrying a rustling bag.

"Where did you go?" I asked as he went back to the counter, threw the bag on it and then again pulled off his tee and dropped it to the floor.

"Contact solution and a case," he said, coming to the bed. He sat on the edge again and tugged off his boot.

"You can just take me home, I have, like, a million cases there and contact solution." This was obvious, but I pointed it out anyway.

"I'm not taking you home, Ava." He dropped boot one.

"I don't understand. Why? Whoever they were, they weren't shooting at me. No one even knew I was there."

He dropped boot two. "I know. They were shooting at Vincetti." He pulled off a sock.

I sucked in breath. This was news.

"They were shooting at Dom?" I whispered, unable to wrap my mind around this fact.

"He isn't a well-liked guy," he pulled off the other sock.

This didn't surprise me. As I explained, Dom was a jerk. But shooting out his living room with an Uzi? That seemed a bit much, and this was coming from a woman who was searching his house to try to find evidence to nail him in an upcoming divorce battle.

"Why would they shoot out his living room with an Uzi when he wasn't there?"

"It wasn't an Uzi. It was an AK-47. And they were sending a message."

He had turned toward me and was leaned into me, working at the cuffs.

I sucked in breath again, mainly because Luke's naked chest was close to my face and it was freaking me out and playing havoc with my vow to stay faithful to my vibrators.

I felt my hands freed and I pulled my arms down, sat up and shook them out. Pins and needles shot up them and I took a deep breath to tamp down my temper. It wouldn't serve any purpose. I was learning quickly Luke didn't like my temper and he was a lot stronger than me.

He seemed in a mellow mood and I wasn't going to piss him off. Pissing him off wouldn't get me home and I needed to get home and soon. I figured him going out and buying me contact lens solution meant he thought, for some reason, I was spending the night. My purse was in my Range Rover and I was pretty certain Sissy had called my cell, probably dozens of times, checking in. She was likely panicked. I needed to phone her and quick.

Still, I couldn't stop myself from saying softly as I rubbed at both of my arms, "That hurt."

Luke threw the cuffs on the nightstand, twisted at the waist, grabbed my left wrist and started to massage my arm.

Oh my goodness, Luke's massaging your arm! Isn't that sweet? Good Ava trilled in my ear.

Jump him! Rip his pants off! Bad Ava shouted in my other ear.

I ignored my advisors and sat, completely still, registering how nice, warm and strong Luke's hands were. They felt good. No, they felt great.

Shit.

"I needed to make sure you were safe," he told me, thankfully pulling me away from thoughts of his hands feeling great.

"They didn't shoot out *my* windows," I pointed out.

"Then I needed to make sure you didn't do something stupid."

Hmm.

One, two, three, four, five... okay, temper under control.

41

"Now that you know I'm safe and I can promise you I won't do anything stupid," *Tonight,* I thought, but did not say, "Can I please go home?"

"No."

"Luke!"

His hands went to my armpits. He got up, taking me with him, and set my feet on the floor.

I had kicked off my flip-flops and they were lying somewhere in the bed. There was something very weird about me, barefoot, standing in Luke's dark loft *with* Luke also standing barefoot and shirtless with me. There was something intimate about it, something sweet and nice and wonderful.

Hell and damnation.

He took my hand, led me across the room to a dresser, opened a drawer and took something out. He led me to the bar and grabbed the bag. Then he led me to the bathroom, flipped a switch and gave me a gentle push inside. He tossed the stuff in the sink and looked at me.

"Take out your contacts, get changed, we're going to bed."

I stood, blinking in the lit room, mouth dropped open and watching the door close through my blinking.

We're going to bed. WE are going to bed, he said. Yippee! Bad Ava yelled happily in my ear, punching the air and doing a touchdown dance.

He's so thoughtful, going out to get your contact stuff. I think he's adorable, Good Ava shared.

Oh for goodness sake. Good Ava needed a reality check. Luke? Adorable? Please.

I sighed. No reason to fight it because I obviously wasn't going to win. Tomorrow, he would take me home and I would forget all of this ever happened. This was not likely, but I was going with it for the moment.

I pulled the stuff out of the bag, noting he also bought me a toothbrush. I took out my contacts and used the bathroom because I needed it, badly. I found this mortifying for some bizarre reason. Everyone had to use the bathroom.

Still, it wasn't like I was removed in any way from Luke. There was only one other room in the place, he could probably hear. I was pretty certain I had gone through my whole life, even when he came over with his parents, or we were over it his house, without Luke ever knowing I had any need of the facilities.

Oh well, what the hell.

I washed my hands, took off my clothes, shoved my silver in my jeans pockets and pulled on the tee he had given me. It was seriously cool. Old, faded, soft and black with a Triumph motorcycle in silver on the front of it. It was huge on me, coming down over my hips to my upper thighs. It felt good on, nice and snug and I tried (hard) not to think of wearing Luke's t-shirt, at the same time trying to figure out how to steal it.

I folded my clothes neatly, as if my life depended on it. Without anything else to do to delay, I opened the bathroom door, switched off the light and walked into the loft.

The loft was still lit only by the lights outside.

Luke, I saw, my heart beginning to beat a little faster in my chest, was lying in bed, sheets to his waist, hands behind his head, staring at the ceiling seeming peaceful and Zen, as if he spent a lot of time in that position. This was all I really saw, mainly because without my contacts, my vision was blurry. Which I had to admit, still struggling with fidelity to my vibrators, was kind of a bummer.

I walked slowly to the bar, semi-feeling my way with my feet, and put my clothes on a stool. Then I turned to him.

"Can I use your phone?" I asked.

Instead of answering, he took his hands from behind his head, twisted to the nightstand and pulled the phone out of its cradle.

I walked to him and took it from his outstretched hand.

"It's long distance," I told him.

"Where's Sissy?" he asked.

I rolled my eyes, mainly because I was also noticing that you didn't get much by Luke, and that was kind of annoying.

"Wyoming."

"As long as it isn't England."

I nearly smiled at him, but stopped myself just in time.

I looked at the phone. Then I realized I had a slight problem. Although I had memorized Sissy's Mom's number, I couldn't see the keypad without my contacts. It was a new phone to me, who knew where the buttons were?

Shit.

I was wrong, the going to the bathroom thing was embarrassing. *This* was mortifying.

43

I stood there, uncertain. Then I realized I had no choice. Sissy was probably packing the car as I hesitated, ready to come down to find out what happened to me and face my house, empty, or her house, probably cordoned off with police tape. Then she would lose it, thinking Dom had killed me, or more likely, I had killed Dom.

Crap.

"Luke?"

"Yeah?"

I couldn't tell for sure, but I thought he was looking at me.

"I need you to dial the number. I can't see the phone."

I didn't know what I expected him to do. Still, I was surprised that, without hesitation, he sat up and took the phone out of my hand.

"What's the number?" he asked.

I told him. He punched it in with his thumb and handed it to me.

"Thanks," I whispered, listening to it ring.

"Good to have you back, babe," he said, his voice soft, gentle, affectionate, and I felt my body jerk in reaction to his tone *and* his words just before Sissy answered the phone.

"Please let this be Ava," she said.

"Yo," I replied, turning away from Luke, wishing I could run away from Luke, and again wondering what in *the hell* I was doing.

"I've called a gazillion times!" Sissy shouted in my ear.

"I know. I'm sorry. I… something happened and I got separated from my purse." I made it to the window by the kitchen, leaned against the brick sill and stared out at LoDo.

It was blurry, but I could still tell that Luke had a kickass view.

"Are you okay?" Sissy asked.

"Yeah, fine."

"My phone says this number is blocked. Are you home?"

Shit.

I had to make a split-second decision. Lie to her or tell her the truth, when the truth would both freak her out (her living room getting shot out and Dom, still her husband, being delivered a very scary message) and make her jump for joy (that I was standing in Luke's t-shirt in his loft in LoDo).

I decided to hedge. "Listen, I'm really tired, I'll call you tomorrow. Tell you all about it."

"Did you find anything?"

I had to give her something and that something had to be something Luke, who I was certain was listening, couldn't get anything out of.

"Just an industrial-sized box of condoms in his nightstand."

Silence.

"Sissy?"

"Guess he isn't pining for me, hunh?"

"Sissy," I said softly, feeling her pain as only best friends do and wishing she were closer so I could give her a hug.

"Get to sleep, it's late. Tell me about it tomorrow," she said.

"Okay."

"I want to hear about the Luke thing tomorrow too. Ally called my cell, said something happened between you guys. She said he carried you through the reception area!"

Oh crap.

"Ally," Sissy laughed. "She's so full of shit."

Oh *crap!*

"I'll talk to you tomorrow," I told her.

"Ava?"

"Yeah?"

"Thanks. You're the bestest best friend a girl could have."

I smiled into the phone. *That* was worth getting shot at for.

"Later," I said.

"Later," and I heard her disconnect.

I looked at the phone and realized I didn't know how to turn it off.

I didn't have to wonder long. It was pulled out of my hand because Luke, again, silent as a cat, was right beside me. He beeped it off as I stared at him and saw he was wearing nothing but a pair of dark (probably black) shorts that rode low on his hips, but were long on his thighs.

I swallowed as he walked away and put the phone on the kitchen counter. Then he turned and started back to me.

Now what?

I looked from his shorts to his face.

"Do you have a blanket?" I asked.

"Why?" he asked back, stopping close.

"So I can sleep on your couch."

"You aren't sleeping on the couch."

I looked around, confused then asked, "Why not?"

"You're sleeping in the bed."

"So you're sleeping on the couch?"

"No."

"Are you sleeping on the floor?" I asked, surprised, but figured it was maybe some Zen macho guy thing, roughing it on a plank wood floor.

"No."

Uh-oh.

"Where are you sleeping?" I continued my sleeping arrangement interrogation.

His hand shot out, and too late, I saw the blurry glint of steel and heard the clanking right before the bracelet was slapped on my wrist.

I pulled back. "Oh no," I said, my heart thumping in my chest and my blood pumping through my veins.

He slapped the other bracelet on his own wrist.

"No!" I shouted, yanking back, viciously this time, but it was like he didn't feel the pull. He just leaned in, shoulder to my belly. He picked me up, his free arm around my thighs, his other wrist bound to mine and he started to the bed.

"What the hell are you doing?" I shouted, feet kicking, pushing at his waist with my free hand.

This was too much. Too *fucking* much.

"Going to bed," Luke said calmly.

"Handcuffed to me?"

"Damn straight."

"You're nuts."

"I'm not taking any chances," he replied, tossing me on the bed and coming down with me.

I tried to scramble away. He pulled me back with a jerk on the cuff.

I stopped scrambling and stared at his fuzzy face in the dark. "Not taking any chances with what?"

"You taking off in the middle of the night, getting shot at again, kidnapped, car bombed, any of it."

I was right, he *was* nuts. "What are you talking about?"

"I'll tell you in the morning, after you tell me about your *little bit* of trouble."

Eek!

I decided to ignore the second part of that. "Tell me now."

"Go to sleep, Ava."

"Uncuff me!"

"Settle down and go to sleep," he ordered, settling himself on his back.

"Un... cuff... me!" I pulled hard at the cuff.

He jerked it again, harder, and I toppled into him, breasts to chest. His other arm went tight around my waist.

"Settle," he said low.

I glared in the general direction of his face, knowing I would never win, but not about to give in gracefully.

"I hate you," I declared.

"You don't."

"I do."

"Okay, maybe whoever this new Ava is does, but she's a bitch and I don't give a fuck if she hates me. The old Ava doesn't hate me and she's in there somewhere, I saw her five minutes ago, and that's who I'm keeping safe."

That knocked the breath out of me and cut me deep.

So deep, to hide how much it hurt, I did as he told me to do and settled into his side, my body mostly on him because my right wrist was cuffed to his left and his arm was thrown out wide to keep me there. Without anywhere else to put it, I rested my head on his shoulder. Still, I held myself tense because I was totally freaked out.

Woo hoo! We're in bed with Luke! Bad Ava crowed.

Oh, this feels nice. His chest is so hard and his body is so warm, Good Ava breathed.

If Good Ava and Bad Ava could get close, I was certain they would high five.

Jeez.

I lay there, trying to relax. I couldn't relax.

So I started talking.

"I won't get shot at again," I muttered into his shoulder.

"I'm not taking any chances."

"I certainly won't get kidnapped. The idea is ridiculous."

He was silent.

"And a car bomb, what on earth?" I mumbled.

"Babe."

"What?"

"Please be quiet and go to sleep."

"Fine," I snapped.

His arm around my waist tightened and his other hand came close to rest on his chest, forcing my hand to rest on his chest, too. I slid off his body, but he held me close to his side.

I figured I'd never in a million years, snuggled up next to Luke Stark, man of my dreams, wearing his t-shirt, lying in his big bed, in his huge loft and handcuffed to him for God's sake, get to sleep.

It took, like, five minutes and I was dead to the world.

Chapter 4

Payment

I woke up in the middle of the night when my body moved, not of its own volition.

I opened my eyes. It was still dark. Luke had turned into me, his arm holding me close, pulling me over the top of his body.

"What's going on?" I whispered, my voice sleepy.

"Shh." He shushed me and rolled, taking me with him, settling me on my other side.

Our cuffed arms were cocked and up between our bodies, and he had me close so his and my forearms were pressed beneath my breasts. His free hand slid down my hip to my thigh, pulling it up, gliding down the back of my thigh to my knee, and hooking my leg over his hip.

If I hadn't been mostly asleep, I would have probably flipped out at the intimacy of this position, struggled and maybe thrown a hissy fit.

Instead, I was warm, tired and the position was ultra-comfortable.

I snuggled into his warm body. His arm moved to rest at my waist and I fell back to sleep.

I woke up and blinked at all the sunlight coming into the room. Denver was a sunny place but this was crazy.

I stared at the wall of hard-muscled chest that was right in front of my eyes, and for a second felt confusion.

Then it all came back to me and I tensed. Inventorying my situation I realized I was pressed against Luke's side. He was on his back, our cuffed arms on the bed under our bodies, my thigh thrown across both of his, my head on his shoulder, my free arm resting across his abs.

Ho-ly shit!

I rolled away onto my back.

"You're awake," Luke said.

Fuckity, fuck, fuck, *fuck!*

"Yeah," I said to the ceiling.

He rolled toward me, hand going to my hip, his fingers putting pressure there so I turned into him and we were face-to-face. Since we were close and it was light, I could see him pretty well. He looked very awake, very alert and very gorgeous.

Holy cramoly.

"Time to talk," he said.

Eek!

I was a morning person. I usually only had to brush my teeth and have a couple sips of Diet Coke to clear out the sleep cobwebs and then I was all morning energy. Still, I wasn't ready to talk, certainly not lying face-to-face in Luke's bed.

"I need to brush my teeth," I told him.

"After we talk."

"No, seriously, I can't face the day without brushing my teeth." As I mentioned before, this was the truth.

Luke stared at me, probably trying to decide if I was lying or not. I didn't blame him. I had lied to him a lot in the last less-than-twenty-four hours.

He must have made his decision because he rolled into me, over me and reached to the nightstand. He opened a drawer and pulled out his keys. He rolled back, lifted our wrists and unlocked my bracelet. I was silent through this as I'd had another close-up view of his chest and I was fighting the urge to press my mouth to it, and I won't even mention what I wanted to do with my tongue.

The minute I was free I didn't hesitate. I jumped off the bed, hightailing it to the bathroom, totally intent on escape. It was after I used the facilities, splashed water on my face to wash away the sleep, brushed my teeth and put in my contacts that I realized my mistake.

I should have brought my clothes in with me.

Hell and damnation.

I pulled my hair back away from my face with both hands and stared into my light brown eyes the mirror. Both my sisters had sultry, dark brown eyes, which sucked and wasn't fair. I couldn't dye my eyes and I thought colored contacts looked fake.

Since I couldn't at that moment do anything about the fact that I was barely dressed, I focused on what to do with my hair.

Last time I saw Luke, my hair had been shoulder length. I'd only gone for trims since then, allowing my hair to grow long, down my back to my bra strap with thick, chunky layers cut in. It had always had an unruly wave, and length and weight had done nothing to tame it. In fact, it went all the more wild. I needed a ponytail holder. It was now a mess of waves and tangles, and currently in an untamable state without a shampoo and a shitload of product to force it under my control.

Oh well, what the hell. I had to go with it. No way was I taking a shower in Luke's bathroom, for this would mean being naked and there was no way in hell I was going to be naked at Luke's place, not even in the shower.

I dropped my hands, walked out of the bathroom and stopped dead.

A man was walking out of the elevator carrying my purse. He was blond, trim, fit and ultra-cute. His eyes cut to me and took me in, top to toe, standing there frozen and wearing nothing but Luke's Triumph tee.

Then he grinned.

Crap.

His eyes moved to Luke. So did mine.

Luke was standing by the semi-circle kitchen counter, wearing only shorts (yes, black) that were made of that breathable material with the tiny little dents in it like basketball players wore. They hung loose and super low on his hips, running long but not as long as the basketball ones, partially down his thighs. They showed not only the definition of his hip bones in sexy relief, but most of a pair of knockout muscular thighs and calves.

I would be remiss not to mention a full blown, sunny loft, contacts in view of his well-defined chest with not-too-much, not-too-little, but *just the perfect amount* of chest hair, jutting collarbone and stubbled jaw.

There was also a long, brutal looking scar tracing across his six pack.

Ho-ly crap.

My knees wobbled at the sight.

"Shit, Luke, I had two days in the pool. Christ, you tied Lee's record," the blond guy said.

Luke did a half-grin.

"What?" I asked.

The blond guy looked at me, still grinning.

"Nothin'," he said. "I'm Matt."

I pulled out of my mini-hot guy trance and walked toward him. "I'm Ava."

"I know." He was still grinning, his blue eyes dancing. I figured I wasn't in on the joke but let it slide, considering I had to focus on getting dressed and getting out of there without having Luke's talk.

"I brought your bag." He handed it to me and I took it.

"Thanks," I said, feeling like a dork, but happy to have my purse.

"Your Rover's in the garage," Matt carried on.

I looked at him and smiled, more than happy to have my car. "Thanks again."

"Your keys," he handed them to me and I took them. "Your purse is beeping."

I dipped my chin, feeling kind of weird because he was really cute and kept grinning at me.

"Thanks again, again," I said to him.

His grin faded a bit but didn't go away, and he was now watching me closely. "You okay after last night?"

Wow, what a sweet guy, Good Ava said in my ear.

Flirt! Bad Ava yelled.

As usual, I ignored them.

"Sure," I said. "It gives me something juicy to put in my memoirs."

He threw back his head and laughed. His laughter was deep and nice so I laughed with him.

"You got that right," he told me when he was done laughing.

I got over feeling weird and gave him a big smile.

"Matt."

Both our heads swung to Luke, who hadn't moved, but now his arms were crossed on his chest. His legs were planted and his brows were knit. He looked kind of pissed-off, which was confusing.

Maybe he wasn't a morning person.

Matt looked at his feet and chuckled. I threw Luke a look, walked to the counter and plopped my purse and keys on it, digging for my cell.

"I need to go out," I announced, still digging in my purse. "Get a diet pop."

This was met with silence. I located my cell and yanked it out, flipping it open and glancing at Luke. Matt had come closer and both of them were staring at me.

"Diet pop?" Luke asked.

"Do you have any?" I returned.

"No," Luke stated.

"Then I need to get some."

"It's seven o'clock in the morning," Luke told me.

"I know."

"You drink diet pop at seven in the morning?" Luke asked.

"Well… yeah. I need to wash the toothpaste taste out of my mouth."

Luke and Matt kept staring at me.

I looked at my cell. Six missed calls.

Crap.

I pressed buttons on my cell, my eyes on it, and said, "I'll just get dressed and pop out."

I really did need diet pop to wash the taste of toothpaste out of my mouth. However, this had the double duty of being my excuse to get the hell out of there, so my Diet Pop Destination was my very own fridge.

"Do you mind?" I heard Luke ask and my head came up. "Ava and me need to talk."

Matt was grinning at me again.

"You need anything else?" he asked me, amusement in his voice. "Breakfast?"

I looked at Matt then at Luke. "No, really, I'll go."

"You're not going," Luke declared.

I narrowed my eyes at Luke. "I'm going."

"Matt's goin'." Luke returned.

I opened my mouth to say something, but Matt moved.

"No problem. Diet pop," Matt said.

"Get a case," Luke told him.

My eyes bugged out. A case of diet would last me a month.

Matt burst out laughing and hit the button on the elevator.

"I don't need a case. I just need one," I told Matt.

"A case," Luke said decisively.

The elevator doors opened and Matt walked in.

"I'll get a case," he told Luke, and the doors closed.

"Really, that's unnecessary," I said to Luke.

He didn't reply.

I sighed, heavy and annoyed. He wanted a case of diet? Fine. Who cared?

53

I gave up and scrolled through my missed calls. Five from Sissy, one from Riley.

Hmm. Riley. Interesting.

"Ava."

My head came up and I looked at Luke.

Shit. It was time for the talk.

"Do you have any food?" I asked in an effort to delay. I didn't like to eat before I'd had my Diet Coke, but desperate times called for desperate measures.

"Yeah," he answered.

"Do you mind?"

His body relaxed and his lips moved. They kind of twitched, like he knew my thoughts and found me amusing, but was trying not to smile.

I squelched the desire to throw my phone at him as he offered, "Help yourself."

I dropped my phone in my purse, walked around the counter the opposite side to Luke and went to his fridge.

I was stunned to see it was packed with healthy eating options: low-fat yogurt, high-quality, multi-grain bread, tons of fruit and veggies. I spied a half a cantaloupe wrapped in cling film and pulled it out.

"Can I have some cantaloupe?" I asked, turning to Luke.

He tilted his chin up in a nonverbal "yes".

There was a cutting board in his sink. I put down the cantaloupe and went to work cleaning the cutting board.

"You're well-stocked." Again, I was delaying "the talk".

"Sandra went shopping."

"Sandra?"

"A woman I'm seein'."

At his words it took every bit of energy I had not to freeze, gasp or maybe vomit.

Of course he would be seeing someone. Luke was hot. Luke was a guy. Luke had a testosterone-fuelled job. He had to be getting it from someone. He didn't strike me as the kind of guy who would be faithful to his hand like I was faithful to my vibrators.

"Will she mind if I eat her cantaloupe?" I asked, drying the board and not looking at him.

"It's my cantaloupe. Sandra got it, but I paid for it and it's in my fridge," Luke answered.

I nodded. I set down the board, unwrapped the cantaloupe, grabbed a knife out of a big butcher block and started cutting. I tried not to think about the messy bed Luke threw me into last night and hoped he hadn't thrown me into a bed that got messy through his activities with another woman.

I failed at not thinking about it.

"Will she mind that I spent the night?"

Why did you ask that? Silly girl, Good Ava reprimanded me.

I'm so sure! He handcuffed you to him and slept with you when he's seeing someone else. What a jerk, Bad Ava huffed.

"We're not exclusive, so it's none of her business," Luke answered.

See! He's a jerk, Bad Ava ranted.

Good Ava kept her silence, likely pouting.

Luke had come to stand by me at the counter. I could see the side of his hip leaning against it out of the corner of my eye. I ignored the hip and kept cutting.

"Do you want cantaloupe?" I asked, keeping my eyes on my task.

"No, I want to stop talking about cantaloupe and start talking about your troubles."

Shit.

"Okay," I said, still cutting. Then I was silent.

So was Luke, for a moment. Then he broke the silence.

"Ava." His voice held a warning.

My mind raced for an excuse for another delay and it found none.

Fuckity, fuck, fuck, *fuck.*

Time to get it over with.

"Um… well. You know my friend Sissy?" I asked, eyes on the melon.

"Yeah."

"She's married to Dominic Vincetti."

"I worked that part out," he told me.

"Now, they're kind of separated."

Silence.

"She's going to file for divorce."

More silence.

"She's up in Wyoming, staying with her Mom."

I looked at the cantaloupe and realized I had cut far too much for just myself. Oh well, at least Sandra wouldn't have to worry about cutting up the cantaloupe next time she was there. I put down the knife, picked up a chunk of melon and popped it into my mouth.

"Are you done?" Luke asked.

My eyes slid sideways to look at him and I swallowed.

"Um... yeah."

"That's it? Your trouble is that Sissy's filing for divorce?"

I grabbed another chunk and put it into my mouth while I turned to him and leaned my hip against the counter.

"She's my best friend. Her troubles are my troubles."

Luke stared at me for a beat then asked, "So why were you there last night?"

"She needed something and asked me to get it for her."

"She needed something out of Vincetti's nightstand?"

Hell and damnation.

I looked down at the melon and back at Luke.

"I cut too much melon just for me. You sure you don't want any?" I stalled again.

He shook his head, totally seeing through me, but took a chunk and put it in his mouth. I found watching him chew was weirdly fascinating and decided I was not a dork, I was a freak.

Once he swallowed, he said (his voice kind of scary), "Ava, I'm not gonna tell you again not to lie."

Crap.

I took another chunk of melon and chewed while glaring at him.

"You know," I told him, again trying to stall. "This is really none of your business."

"It became my business when you and I were caught in a hail of gunfire."

Hmm.

In all fairness, he was kind of right, though I wasn't about to tell him that, nor was I going to give in. I didn't ask him to be there.

I nabbed another chunk of melon and chewed it angrily, now seriously glaring at him.

"I didn't ask you to be there," I pointed out. "You weren't even supposed to be there."

"Okay, then it became my business when you walked into the offices yesterday."

"No it didn't."

"Yes, it did."

"No. It didn't."

He took another chunk of melon and threw it in his mouth calmly, then his eyes came back to me and I noticed he was totally oblivious to my glare.

"I don't need your help," I told him, switching subjects and still delaying.

"Right," he said.

"I don't."

"Maybe you would have had the presence of mind to get out of the line of fire last night, maybe you wouldn't. With the way you freaked out afterward, I doubt you would have. The way I figure it, you owe me double."

I blinked with confusion. "Double?" I asked. "I owe you double for what?"

"Saving your ass last night and not telling me you have a situation."

I shook my head, not following. "Excuse me?"

"You're standing here, right now, because of me. And yesterday, I told you if I found out you had trouble, you'd pay. You're paying."

I was not getting a good feeling about this.

"I don't... I don't even know what to say. That's just crazy," I told him.

"Nope, it isn't. Last November a friend of mine did something brave but stupid to save someone she cared about. She got a bullet to the chest and another one to the belly for her troubles."

Yikes.

I sucked in breath at his announcement and the way he shared it. He looked angry, his body was tense and I knew this event affected him in a profound way, as it would anyone.

I stared at him, but he wasn't finished talking. "I saw her on the floor, bleeding while her man tried to staunch the flow with a fucking bath towel. Before she went down, she shot a man in the head, killing him. She's got to live with two kinds of scars now. The kind you can see and the kind you can't."

Ho-ly crap.

"Luke," I had lost my glare and my anger and my voice went soft.

Luke didn't feel like responding to my soft voice. He came closer and it took a lot of effort, because his intensity was freaking me out, but I stayed where I was, even when I saw his eyes were shining with anger.

"I'm not playing this fucking game with you, Ava. You told me last night you wanted to know why I cuffed you. So now I'll tell you. You're playin' with fire and I'm not about to stand around and watch you get burned. Before Jules got shot, there was Roxie, another friend of mine's woman who was stalked by her ex, beaten, abducted right from his fuckin' house while he was out runnin', and taken on a crazed, zigzag ride through three states. We found her cuffed to the sink in a sleazy motel. Before Roxie there was Jet, whose Dad got some poker debt and his loan shark tried to use Jet to force payment. She caught the attention of a fuckwad and ended up kidnapped and nearly raped. Before Jet there was—"

"Okay, I get it," I broke in quietly.

Jeez.

I was freaked out and he hadn't even gotten to the car bombs yet. Boy, and I thought all the men I had met were assholes.

"Tell me right now what you and Sissy are up to," Luke demanded, moving back, but only slightly.

I gave in. I might as well. He wasn't going to let it go, that was easy enough to read. And anyway, I knew this extent of sharing was taking some effort for him, what with being a tough guy, macho man and all. I didn't like that he was angry and struggling with unhappy memories, and I further didn't like that I was the cause of it. It made me feel like crap.

"I don't want Sissy to come back here," I blurted, and Luke's body went still, likely preparing for what I would say next. "Dom's good at sweet-talking her back to him and he's a total jerk and no good for her. I won't get into it, but trust me, he's seriously no good for her. While she's gone, I promised to get the goods on Dom, find some evidence to use so the divorce would go well for her."

"So you were searchin' his shit last night to find somethin' on him."

"Yeah."

His body visibly relaxed and I felt my body relax in response. I didn't know his tension was making me tense, and I didn't know what to make of that. I decided not to think about it as I watched him nab another chunk of melon and throw it in his mouth.

"It's covered," he told me, mid-chew.

I stared at him. "What?"

"I'll get what Sissy needs."

Yee ha!

"Really?" I breathed.

Yay! No more breaking and entering and stupid behavior, Good Ava shouted happily.

Damn, there goes all the fun, Bad Ava pouted.

"Really," Luke said.

I couldn't help it. I smiled at him. This was good, really good for Sissy. I imagined Luke knew what he was doing, considering the loft and the Porsche showed that people paid him a lot to do it.

His eyes dropped to my mouth and watched me smile. When they did this, his face, as usual, stayed hard, but his eyes lost the shiny, dangerous anger and became soft and warm.

I ignored this because it made my knees wobble.

"What do I do?" I asked. "Do I go to the offices and talk to Shirleen? Set up an account?"

His eyes moved back to mine. "You aren't gonna pay Nightingale Investigations."

My smile widened and I had the happy thought that maybe there *were* good guys out there, and Luke was one of them.

"No, that's okay. I have money and Dom's loaded. Once Sissy nails him, she'll have more than enough to cover—"

"You aren't payin'."

"Luke, really, it's cool," I told him.

"I'll rephrase. You aren't payin' in money."

My smile died, my heart clenched and I feared that he was going to prove my earlier thought wrong about there being good guys out there.

"Excuse me?" I whispered.

"This means you owe me triple," he told me.

"Excuse me?" I repeated.

"You owe me triple."

My body stiffened.

Nope, there it was. No good guys. Of course he wouldn't do something for nothing. Of course he wouldn't do something just because he was a good guy.

Fucking hell.

"What does that mean?" I asked.

"I haven't decided yet."

"Okay then, what does *that* mean?" I pushed.

My eyes narrowed on him and I found it kind of hard not to yell or cry or go out and buy an island for just me and my girlfriends, no men allowed.

He cut into thoughts of my Girls Only Island and said, "That means tonight we're havin' dinner and I'm gonna find out what happened to the Ava I knew. Once I find that out, I'll decide."

Holy shit.

"Nothing happened to the old Ava," I told him.

He shook his head. "The old Ava was funny, smart and sweet. The new Ava acts more like Marilyn and Sofia."

It felt like he had slapped me across the face. I even felt myself flinch at his words. Seriously not a good guy, and knowing this about Luke hurt more than his words.

"That wasn't nice," I whispered.

"No, it wasn't, but it's true."

Damn, but he was honest.

Still, he didn't know what he was talking about. He didn't know the half of it about Dom and he didn't know anything about Rick, Dave and Noah. It wasn't like I was being a bitch for the fun of it. I had reasons and he didn't even bother to find out what they were before he made a judgment. I didn't care about his offer of dinner so he could get my explanation. He knew, maybe more than anyone (except Sissy and my Dad), how much it would hurt to compare me to Marilyn and Sofia.

"A lot has happened since I last saw you," I said, not about to go into detail, *never* going to go into detail. He could blow for his explanation.

"Yeah, that's obvious."

Time for an evasive maneuver. This talk was beginning to sap my strength, suck my energy and make me want to stay in bed for a week eating rolls of chocolate chip cookie dough, bags of cheese puffs and tubs of ice cream (of all flavors).

"I can't go to dinner tonight, I'm meeting some friends," I told him.

"We'll talk after you meet with your friends."

I thought about Ally and The Hornet. I figured it was a taxi night for certain, considering nearly any time I had spent with Ally ended up with me being shitfaced and sleeping with a foot on the floor so the room would quit spinning. *Not* the disposition I wanted to be in for the next brutally honest third degree.

"It's probably going to be a late night."

"I'll wait."

"It might be a wild night."

He gave me a half-grin. "That'll work."

Shit.

"Luke," I said, sounding like I was putting a line under this conversation.

He ignored my line. "I'll give you a remote for the garage and a key. You don't come here after you're done, I'll find you. You make me find you, you owe me quadruple."

This talk was not going my way in *any* way.

"Why can't I just pay money for your services like normal people?"

"You aren't normal people."

"I am."

"You're Ava."

"I'm that, too."

"I've known you since you were eight."

"So?"

"I've liked you since you were eight."

Oh! I like him again, Good Ava told me.

Jump him! Rip his shorts off! Bad Ava urged.

Luke kept talking over Good Ava and Bad Ava's blathering. "That makes you *my* people."

Whoa.

Whoa, whoa, whoa.

Stop right there.

I needed time to bury that deep before I set myself up to start thinking he was a good guy again, only to find out he wasn't.

To buy that time, I said quietly, "Luke."

"We're not talking about this anymore," Luke told me.

"We are."

"We're not."

I glared. "We are. Give me something to go on here. What's triple payment mean?" I asked, sounding kind of bitchy.

"I told you, I haven't decided."

"Which way are you leaning? Maid service? Vacation planning? Darning your socks?"

He threw back his head and laughed. I crossed my arms on my chest.

"This isn't funny," I told him.

And it wasn't.

Before I could react, his hand snaked out and wrapped around my neck, pulling me forward with a gentle jerk and my hands came up to shield my fall. They hit his chest right before my hips slammed into his.

I tilted my head back to look at him and pulled at his hand at my neck. This served no purpose. So I glared at him and pushed against his chest. This also served no purpose.

I saw, in close proximity, that his eyes were very warm.

Eek!

Danger, danger! Retreat, Ava Barlow. Retreat!

Before I could push away, he spoke, sounding lost in thought. "Maybe part of your payment is makin' you worry what your payment will be."

See? There it was again.

Not.

Nice.

I pushed against his chest again and pulled my hips away. His other arm slid along my waist and pulled me back, pinning my hands and arms so they were helpless between our bodies.

"That's really not nice," I told him, but he didn't respond so I demanded, "Let me go."

His eyes moved over my face and hair and then settled on my mouth. I pursed it angrily. The minute he saw the pursing of lips he did the half-grin.

"Gotta admit, I'm beginning to like the bitch."

"Stop calling me a bitch."

His eyes came back to mine. "Stop actin' like one."

"Men suck," I told him, because this was true.

"See, you don't feel like not actin' like a bitch."

"You suck, too," I went on, going for the gusto. Why not? I had nothing to lose.

"Babe," he said, sounding like I was entertaining him.

"Stop calling me 'babe'. It's demeaning. I'm not a babe, I'm a woman."

The fingers of his hand at my neck slid into my hair then twisted it, wrapping it around his hand. This wasn't a rough gesture. It was a sensual one and it made tingles slide across my scalp, the good kind. I stared at him, realizing belatedly we were ultra-close, and my eyes dropped back to his lips of their own accord.

"Where's Matt with my diet?" I asked, sounding desperate and kind of breathy, and not taking my eyes from his mouth. My body was going pliant and I couldn't control it even if I tried (though, I didn't).

I knew he felt me melting into him. I knew this because his arm around me drew me closer and his fist in my hair gently pulled my head back. This was not a good position to be in, plastered against him, arms pinned, head tilted back in a way that my face was an open target for anything he wanted to do. My eyes shifted to his, the warmer-than-normal warmth was still there and my knees got weak.

Shit.

I tried to pull myself together, mentally chanting "men suck" and reminding myself I knew exactly where to place the vibrator to get ultimate orgasmic pleasure, thus no fiddling around and experimenting with hitting the target like most men found difficult to do. Even so, I found it impossible with his mouth so close to me, his lips being so fantastic and my eyes dropped to them again.

They were *fine.*

I licked my lips.

"Ava."

My eyes drifted back to his and I was in a Luke Lip Fog. "Yeah?"

"You lick your lips while looking at my mouth one more time, you'll find that pretty pink tongue of yours *in* my mouth."

Ho-ly shit.

His face came closer and I watched, frozen and fascinated, mainly because that meant his lips were also coming closer. His indigo eyes had melted to pure, liquid ink, and I forgot totally that men sucked.

"You wanna taste me?" he murmured.

Yes, I wanted to taste him. I would pay every penny of Aunt Ella's inheritance to taste him.

"No," I lied.

He did a full grin this time, a full *satisfied* grin. It was hot. So hot my knees totally buckled and he took all my weight into his body.

"Liar," he whispered, knowing he had me (he couldn't actually miss it, considering I'd lost the ability to stand on my own two feet).

I watched as his lips started to get closer. In response, my eyes began to close and my lips parted in preparation for contact.

Honestly? I hated to admit it, but I could barely wait.

It was then the doors to the elevator glided open. My eyes flew open and our heads twisted to watch Matt walk out, carrying a case of Diet Coke.

Thank you *God*.

I instantly tried to pull out of Luke's arms, but he didn't let me move an inch even though his hand went out of my hair. It only did this to wrap around my back to keep me where I was.

"Hey, sorry," Matt said, grinning like an idiot, not looking sorry at all, and even with the idiot grin I wanted to kiss him for interrupting. My vibrators were going to divorce me if I kept going like this.

I looked at Luke and saw his lips were pressed together and he didn't seem happy.

"Next time, buzz up," Luke's voice proved my theory correct and made me slightly concerned about his use of the words "next time".

Matt put the case of soda on the counter.

"Will do," he replied cheerily, ignoring Luke's pissed-off voice. "I'll just be going."

"Good idea," Luke said.

Matt lifted a hand in a small wave as he walked across the room and then he hit the elevator button. I pulled again at Luke's arms. He looked down at me, still with an unhappy expression, but let me go.

I moved straight to the case of Diet Coke.

"Later!" I called to Matt as the doors started to close. He lifted his hand to his forehead, gave me a wink and a salute right before we lost sight of him.

Burying the latest episode with Luke deep, deeper, deepest, I ignored it even happened and got myself a can of pop, a glass, some ice from the fridge and poured it. All the while I was doing this, Luke watched me moving around his kitchen, his back to the counter, hips against it, arms crossed. I knew this not only because I saw him looking at me, but I also *felt* it.

"You want a soda?" I asked, pretending not to be affected by him watching me.

"No," Luke answered.

"I'm going to get dressed," I told him.

Luke didn't respond.

I took my glass of pop, grabbed my clothes and moved toward the bathroom, sensing escape and planning my grocery store dash, direct to the cookie dough.

"Ava," Luke called.

I stopped and turned to him. "Yeah?"

"I've decided your payment."

My body froze and a thrill ran up my back. It was a good thrill, maybe even a great thrill; definitely a vibrator-cheating thrill, and I stared at him.

"What is it?"

"Be here tonight when you're done with your friends."

I did not *think* so.

"Luke, just tell me."

"Be here tonight."

I would have put my hands on my hips if my arms weren't full. Instead, I hitched a hip and put a foot out in Bitch Attitude Stance.

"Tell me," I demanded.

"Tonight."

I glared at him. He watched me.

Then he turned away, threw another chunk of melon into his mouth and started to make coffee.

I made the instant decision that there was no way I was coming to his loft that night.

Fuck that.

And he couldn't make me pay him anything unless he sent me a goddamned invoice. That, I would gladly pay.

On that thought, I stomped to the bathroom, sucking back some soda, and I kicked the door shut with my foot.

Chapter 5

I Need Cookies

I was standing in the cookie section at King Soopers, searching for my motivational healthy living mojo when my phone rang. I dug through my bag, pulled it out and saw "Riley Calling". I flipped it open and put it to my ear.

"Thank God it's you. Chips Ahoy or Nutter Butter?" I asked instead of saying hello.

Riley laughed in my ear. "Neither, where are you?"

"King Soopers, and I had a shit night. I need processed cookie-type food."

"No shit night is worth processed cookie-type food," Riley told me.

He was *so* wrong.

"Last night was, believe me," I said.

"Ava, step away from the cookies."

"No."

"Do it."

"No."

"Step away from the cookies and I'll bring lunch to your place, one thirty. Deal?"

Holy crap.

What was *that* all about?

I'd never seen Riley outside of the gym. Well, not exactly. He'd been to all my birthday parties for five years and my annual Thank God It's Summer Party that I held on Memorial Day every year. Maybe we should just say I'd never seen Riley at my house *alone*.

"Deal," I said, feeling kind of weird.

"Later."

Disconnect.

Well, that's interesting, Good Ava noted.

Luke's cuter, he has better lips and he has good chest hair. Not to mention his eyes are total YUM when they turn ink, Bad Ava said and then peered across my neck at Good Ava. *Did you see his eyes?*

I saw 'em. They were YUM! Good Ava agreed.

"Shut up," I whispered and a lady standing beside me gave me a weird look. I shot her an embarrassed smile, went directly to the produce section and bought enough grapes, oranges and plums to unconstipate the French Foreign Legion.

At Luke's I had dressed quickly, came out of the bathroom, grabbed my purse and keys and gave him a "Later". The whole time he sat on a barstool, holding his coffee cup, watching me and not saying a word. I had managed to escape without him giving me keys or his remote, which I figured worked in my favor.

I went directly to King Soopers and was saved by Riley.

After I left King Soopers and was heading home, I decided I would call Shirleen at Nightingale Investigations and set up an account. I figured she would take my information and invoice me. It *was* a business and they had to keep their men in lofts and Porsches. They weren't going to turn down my trade.

What I didn't allow myself to think about was *anything* that had *anything* to do with Luke, his eyes turning to ink, the scar across his belly, his chest hair, how good a night's rest I had while lying beside him (even handcuffed), or what he might taste like.

And I definitely didn't think about getting shot at by AK-47s.

I let myself into my house, and to keep my mind busy I cleaned it. Then I took a shower and tamed my hair. I swiped on a hint of makeup (Riley was coming over, after all) and because it was warm I put on a black Foo Fighters baby doll tee, another pair of faded (but not quite as faded as yesterday) Levi's and a shitload of my silver to buoy my spirits.

After I'd done that, I had about a half an hour before Riley got there, so I got to work on one of my accounts. A deadline was drawing near, and with all the Sissy business, I was procrastinating. I had to get some work done or I'd be fucked.

The office was upstairs in my second bedroom. The walls were painted a soft salmon because I heard that orange sparked energy and creativity and there was a desk and futon in there for overnight guests. I'd made it into a funky room with cool, light wicker baskets and boxes, colorful toss pillows on the futon and a kickass, state-of-the-art swivel chair so I wouldn't mind spending time there while I worked.

I barely got my computer booted up when my phone rang.

I answered it with a, "Yo."

"You didn't call me," Sissy said, her voice sounding funny.

"Hey," I replied. "You okay?"

"The police called me."

Uh-oh.

"Sissy—" I started.

"Someone shot up my house and Dom is missing."

I blinked. "Dom is missing?" I asked.

"Yeah. They waited for him at the house and they called his cell, no answer. They went to his office and he hasn't shown up for work for two days, no calls to explain why he wasn't there. Nothing."

I knew Dom had an office. He "worked" for his Uncle Vito, but I suspected it was a front for something. I didn't ask because Sissy wouldn't tell. And anyway, I liked Uncle Vito. I met him at Sissy and Dom's engagement party and he was a hoot. He thought I was hilarious and always laughed at my jokes. I didn't like thinking he was a criminal mastermind mafia-type person. That would suck.

"Are you okay?" I asked.

"I'm freaked. Can you check my house?"

"Sure," I told her.

"Thank God you weren't there," she breathed. "They told me they used a machine gun, totally shot up my living room. Can you imagine if you were there?"

Yep, I could imagine.

"Go to the house during the day," she said. "Take someone with you."

"Riley's coming over for lunch. I'll ask him if he wants to go."

Silence then, "Riley's coming over for lunch?"

"Yeah. He called me this morning and told me he was coming over."

"What's *that* all about?"

I laughed at her saying my thoughts out loud. "Hell if I know."

"Call me the minute you find out."

"I will."

"Do you think I should come home?" she asked.

"Let me check it out, Sis. I'll let you know."

"Okay," there was a pause then, quietly, "I hope Dom is okay." I didn't speak. "I know you don't like him, and I know he's a jerk, but I can't help how I feel."

"I know, Sis. I hope he's okay too."

There it was again. Liar, liar pants on fire.

We said good-bye and I had barely put the phone down when it rang again. I picked it up. "Yo."

"Yo back at 'cha," Ally Nightingale said in my ear. "You comin' to The Hornet?"

"Hey, girl. Sure," I told her.

"Cool, but you gotta give me something early. The girls are goin' nuts. You know Luke?" she asked.

Shit.

"What girls?" I asked back.

"The Rock Chicks. Indy, Jet, Roxie, Daisy, Jules—"

My breath caught. "Jet, Roxie and Jules?" I asked.

Those were the names of Luke's friends that he told me about, and since not many people were named Jet, Roxie and Jules, they had to be...

"Yeah. Jet works for Indy and she's living with Eddie Chavez. Roxie is my brother Hank's girlfriend, they're living together, too. Jules is with Vance, one of Lee's boys."

Holy cramoly.

See, what'd I say about Denver having a small town feel?

"So... Luke?" Ally prompted.

"I've known him since I was eight. He lived across the street."

"Seriously?"

"Yeah."

"Wicked, sister. Luke is hot," she said.

Boy, did I ever know *that*.

"He works for my brother," she went on.

"I know."

"What happened yesterday?"

"I don't know. He went gonzo on me. I haven't seen him in years. I popped by and he just lost it."

Silence then, "Girl, I know Luke pretty well. He doesn't lose it unless he has a reason." She said this with only a hint of accusation, but I felt like a bitch.

Maybe I *was* turning into Marilyn and Sofia. I shivered, and I shivered because that would suck.

Time to fight back the Barlow Bitch Pull.

"It's a long story," I confided. "We have some history. I made him a promise I didn't keep and it was important to him."

"You two work things out?"

"Not really."

"You gonna work things out?"

I hoped not. I didn't know what working things out would entail, but I had a scary feeling it would entail Vibrator Infidelity.

"We'll see," I allowed. "I'll tell you about it tonight."

"Righteous. See you at seven."

"Cool."

We hung up and I sat looking at the phone with the very unhappy thought that my life was about to get pretty fucking complicated.

I had barely pulled up my files when the doorbell went. I sighed, walked away from the computer and down the stairs. I opened my door and Riley was there.

Really, he was seriously good-looking. I wasn't into blond guys, but if I was I'd likely have a crush on him.

"Hey," I said.

"Hey," he replied on a white smile and lifted up a bag. "Noodles, veggies, no processed cookie-type food."

"Damn," I mumbled to be funny, and, as usual when I was trying to be funny, Riley laughed.

As I let him in the phone started ringing.

I took the bag from him saying, "I'll see to the food, you get the phone."

"No problem."

I headed to the kitchen. Riley headed to the cordless in the living room.

I was pulling noodles and veggies out of the bag (which, I had to admit, looked good) to put on Fiestaware plates (cobalt blue for Riley, pink for me) when he walked in saying, "Sure, she's right here."

He took the phone away from his ear and said on a grin. "It's for you."

I reached for the phone. "What a surprise, Riles, you big dork."

He reached out and nabbed the back of my head. Pulling it to him, he kissed my forehead.

I went solid, phone in my hand and stared at him totally stunned.

He'd never done that before. Sure, it was kind of brotherly and cute, but it *was* a kiss.

To cover my freak out, I ordered, "Quit kissing me, Riley, you'll give me cooties."

"Fuck off," he returned, still grinning at me.

I put the phone to my ear and greeted, "Yo."

Silence.

"Hello?" I called into the silence.

"Who's Riley?"

Fuckity, fuck, fuck, *fuck*.

It was Luke.

"Luke?"

"Who the fuck is Riley?"

Wow. He sounded pissed-off. As in *extremely* pissed-off.

"Um… a friend?" It came out as a question, like I needed Luke to answer it for me.

"You didn't tell me about any friends this morning."

"You didn't ask."

"Okay, then I'm askin' now."

"About what?"

"How many friends do you have?"

"A lot of them."

"I'm talkin' about the ones who kiss you."

Someone's got the wrong end of the stick. Hee hee, Bad Ava sing-songed in my ear.

Oh dear, Good Ava said in the other one.

"I can't talk now, I'm kinda busy." I wasn't playing games. I was acutely aware of Riley watching me and the fact he had just kissed my forehead, and this was a weird situation I'd never found myself in. I honestly didn't know what to do.

I felt unhappy vibes stinging my ear through the phone.

"Why are you calling?" I asked when Luke made no response.

"You forgot the remote and keys."

"Erm…"

"You gonna be home for a while?"

"I have company."

"You gonna be home for a while?" Luke repeated.

"Um, no, we have an errand to run after we have lunch."

"We do?" Riley asked and I waved at him to shut up.

"You gonna be home after your errand?" Luke asked in my ear.

Shit.

"Yeah," I answered.

"I'll be there at four," Luke declared.

"Luke."

He didn't hear me say his name, he had already disconnected.

"My life is fucked," I told Riley, punching the off button on the phone with my thumb.

"Who was that?" he asked, his face morphing to concern.

"An old friend," I blew it off, not wanting to delve deeper and certainly not willing to share. Thankfully, Riley let it go.

"What errand we running?" he asked.

I told him about Sissy's place.

"Holy shit. Sure, I'll go with you," he told me.

"Thanks, Riles."

We ate lunch. We chatted. Riley teased me (as usual). I made him laugh (as usual). Nothing weird, nothing out of the ordinary, nothing to make this seem in any way other than our normal friendship. Nothing.

After we were done, he drove me to Sissy's and we inspected the damage using the key I still had after pocketing it last night.

"Holy shit," Riley repeated his words of earlier, looking around while standing in the living room.

Holy shit was right. The place was a mess. The front window and door were boarded, debris everywhere. I started to get the shakes, for more reasons than just seeing the devastation an AK-47 could do. Flashback City.

Riley put an arm around me and guided me out. "Let's get you out of here."

"Sissy's going to freak," I told him.

"Sissy's going to freak," he agreed.

"I think this is a processed cookie-type food moment."

"Ava, *no* moment is a processed cookie-type food moment. This is, however, a shot of tequila-type moment."

He was not wrong.

We went to Reiver's, a bar on South Gaylord that was close to Sissy's place. It had been there forever and was decorated entirely in wood. They had kickass black bean dip there, but I did not suggest this to Riley who would likely find that suggestion a disappointing testament to lack of motivation for healthy living mojo.

I had a shot of tequila, chased by a Diet Coke. Riley had a beer. Riley engaged me in a conversation that would take my thoughts off Sissy's living room, and what he didn't know were my thoughts of my own mortality and plans to draw up a will, ASAP.

Eventually, I looked at my watch and gave a little scream.

"What?" Riley asked.

"It's ten to four. Luke's gonna be at my house at four. We gotta move." I'd jumped off my barstool and was hopping around on my flip-flops, freaked way the hell out.

"Who's Luke?" Riley was watching me closely.

"An old friend."

His eyes narrowed. "You got a lot of them."

"Let's go!" I nearly shouted.

"All right, all right. Keep your pants on.'

We paid. We left. We got home too late.

I knew this because the clock on the dash of Riley's Pathfinder said it was quarter after four. I also knew this because, as we rolled up to my house, Luke's Porsche was parked there, Luke leaning against it, arms crossed on his chest. He didn't look happy, and this unhappiness increased exponentially when his head turned and he saw Riley and me pulling up.

"Crap," I whispered.

"That Luke?" Riley asked, checking him out.

"Yeah."

"You owe him money?" Riley asked, maybe trying to be funny, but his question was too close to the bone.

"Thanks for lunch, for going with me, for the tequila, everything," I said, turning to him as I saw Luke push away from the Porsche.

"I'll just make sure everything's okay. He doesn't look—"

"No!" I cried, again in a near shout.

Riley's eyes cut to me.

"I'll just make sure everything's okay," Riley repeated in a tone I'd never heard him use before. He was usually laidback. He looked not at all laidback anymore.

Crapity, crap, crap, *crap.*

Riley got out. I got out. Luke met us on the sidewalk by Riley's car, right in front of my house. Luke and Riley sized each other up. Riley was a personal trainer and Luke *still* looked like he could wipe the floor with him.

"You Luke?" Riley asked, even though he knew the answer.

"Yeah. You Riley?" Luke asked, even though he, likely, knew the answer, too.

"Yeah."

They stared at each other and I had visions of them wrestling to the ground in a tough guy death match and this made me ultra-uncomfortable.

"I need cookies," I blurted and both men looked at me.

Luke's mouth twitched. Riley's brows drew together.

"You gonna be okay with this guy?" Riley asked what I thought was a question that proved he was a lunatic.

Luckily Luke showed no reaction to this in your face question.

"Of course," I replied.

Riley looked like he didn't believe me. Then he did the wrap-his-hand-around-my-head-kiss-my-forehead thing again, but left his hand where it was and looked me in the eyes.

"See you tomorrow?" he asked softly.

I nodded.

Riley threw a scowl at Luke, who was back to looking unhappy in a way that made Riley's scowl seem amateur.

Riley got in his Pathfinder and took off. I turned to Luke.

Now he was glaring at me.

"You have something to give me?" I asked.

"In the house."

"Luke, I need to get some work done. I haven't had—"

"In the house."

Jeez.

All right, in the house, if that's what he wanted. The sooner I did what he wanted, the sooner I'd get this over with.

I stomped up to the house and let us in. I walked into the living room, threw my keys and purse on the couch and turned to Luke.

"Okay, Luke, we're in the house." I put my hand out, palm up. "You have something to give me?"

"Who's that guy to you?"

"Riley?"

"No, Jack Lemmon," he quipped, and I couldn't help it. I laughed mainly because it was funny.

He advanced so fast, I barely got my feet coordinated to retreat. But I did, all the way across the living room, until my back hit the wall and Luke came up close. One of his hands hit the wall by my head, the other arm wrapped around my waist and pulled me into his body.

I stared at him, shocked breathless at his behavior, and every thought flew from my head.

"You like playin' games?" he asked and his eyes were shining dangerously.

"No."

"You like yankin' men's chains?" he asked.

Holy crap. Where was *this* coming from?

"No!" I shouted.

"Lose weight, get contacts, dye your hair, become a knockout and make all the men pay who wouldn't look at you before?" he clipped.

At his words, I lost it. I mean, how *dare* he?

"Fuck you!" I yelled.

"Why did you come to the offices yesterday?" he asked.

"Go to hell, Lucas Stark."

His palm pounded on the wall next to my head and his face got right in mine so he was the only thing I could see, and this scared the shit out of me.

"Don't fuck with me, Ava," he warned.

"I'm not fucking with you," I whispered, totally freaked out.

"Who's Riley to you?"

"He's my personal trainer," I said immediately.

"You fuckin' him?"

My eyes rounded and I instantly answered, "No!"

"He wants to fuck you."

"He does not. We're friends."

"He does."

"No he doesn't."

"Yes, Ava, he does."

"Step back."

He didn't step back. He came closer, or more to the point, brought me closer. Both arms wrapping around me, he hauled me tight against his body.

"You just earned a preview of tonight," he told me, face so close his mouth was nearly on mine.

"I don't..." I cleared my throat, and that pissed me off because it made me sound scared. I *was* scared, I just didn't want to *sound* scared. "I don't want a preview."

"Too bad."

"Luke."

"You're gonna be in my bed, and not like last night. I'm gonna give you a taste of me and I'm gonna take more than a taste of you."

Holy... fucking... *shit*.

"Luke," I repeated.

"One thing you need to know. While you're sharing my bed, I don't share your body."

At this, I blinked, thinking I saw red film covering my eyes, but he went on before I could say a word.

"Until we're done, however long that takes, no one touches you, not even to kiss your goddamned forehead. Got me?"

Um.

One, two, three... oh fuck it.

"You are fucking *kidding* me," I snapped.

"Not even a little bit."

"What about Sandra?"

"Sandra is gone."

"Her food is in your fridge!" I yelled.

"She's gone."

"Have you told her that?"

"Not yet, but she's my next visit."

Oh my God, he was a jerk. He was beyond a jerk. He was the jerkiest jerk I'd ever met.

"You're a jerk," I told him.

His brows snapped together. "You *want* me to fuck Sandra while I'm fuckin' you?"

"You're not gonna fuck me."

"Yeah, I am."

"No, you aren't."

"Ava, you missed it when it happened so I'll clue you in. Last night, around the time you fell asleep against me, you became mine."

My eyes went huge. "How do you figure that?"

All of a sudden, his face changed. He was watching me and I could tell he was thinking about something, and by the look of him whatever it was didn't bode well for me.

"Luke, step back," I demanded.

"No," he said softly, but it wasn't to my demand, it was to himself. "I'm thinkin' you've been mine a lot longer than that."

I stopped breathing and stared at him, scared far, *far* more now than I had been when he was angry.

His eyes roamed my face and hair again then they locked on mine. "I'm thinkin' you been mine since about the time your Dad left your Mom."

Whoa.

Whoa, whoa, whoa.

This was *not* happening.

"Step back," I whispered.

"Maybe before." He was still talking to himself.

"Please, step back."

His eyes had gone far away, but they came back and focused on me. "I'm right, aren't I?"

"You're crazy and an out-of-control macho man is what you are."

"I'm right."

"You're nuts."

"Think about it."

I wasn't going to think about it. I was going to move to Wyoming and live with Sissy and her mother to get away from Luke.

That was when I realized something and my eyes snapped back to his. "How did you know my phone number? It's unlisted."

His face began to relax from its trip down memory lane intensity, but I was way behind him, still back at being pissed-off.

"Babe, I work at a private investigations agency."

"Is that how you found out where I live?"

"Yeah."

"Did you follow me from here last night?"

"Yeah."

I found that my hands were holding onto his waist and there was no way to put them between us, so I grabbed at his tee and tried to shove.

He didn't move.

"Luke, forget finding dirt on Dom. You're fired. I'll hire another investigations agency."

"First they'll have to find Vincetti, which they won't do nearly as fast as Vance's gonna do, and he's already working on it."

"Goddammit!" I shouted, foiled again.

Luke did the half-grin. I glared at him.

"Don't fight it." His voice was soft, gentle and affectionate, and I had to claw at my anger to keep it with me, I liked that voice so much.

"Please go."

The grin didn't fade, but he did let me go to move away about two inches. Then he dug in his pocket, pulled something out and shoved it in the front pocket of my Levi's.

His eyes came to mine and he said, "See you tonight. You get drunk, you call me. I'll come get you."

I didn't answer, I just glared at him. He ignored the glare, touched my nose with his finger, and then he was gone.

Oh my. I've got goose bumps. That was INTENSE, Good Ava told me.

I think I had an orgasm, Bad Ava shared.

I slid down the wall and put my head on my knees.

Yep, I was right.

My life just got pretty fucking complicated.

Chapter 6
What I Don't Get

Once I got off my ass, I called Sissy and told her about the state of her living room (and her pottery) and told her not to come home. Whatever Dom was caught up in, I wanted her to be far, far away from it.

Then, because she was my bestest best friend, I told her about Luke. Every last detail about every second, from the minute I walked into the Nightingale Investigations offices to the minute he walked out of my house, including being there during the shooting, which made her scream a little bit.

"Wow," Sissy said when I was done, sounding like she'd just run the hundred yard dash.

Wow didn't cover it.

"You don't have to worry, Sis," I told her. "I get the impression from Luke's loft and Porsche, and what I saw of the Nightingale Investigations offices, people pay a high premium for their services. They'll find Dom *and* get the dirt on him. You just stay safe with your Mom."

"Okay," Sissy replied, paused and went on. "Ava?"

"Yeah, honey?"

In a very quiet voice, she whispered, "Luke called you a knockout."

I hadn't let that penetrate until the moment Sissy repeated it to me.

"Holy crap," I whispered back.

"I think you may want to rethink your vow to hate men forever," she advised.

Not gonna happen.

"Yeah, and maybe Sandra Whoever-She-Was rethought her vow to give up on men when she got hooked up with Luke and filled his fridge with healthy food, thinking thoughts of a long and happy life together. Now she's crying her eyes out and eating her way through a three pound bag of M&Ms."

Sissy remembered what Luke looked like as a teenager. Sissy knew Sandra Whoever-She-Was was *definitely* crying her eyes out with a three pound bag of M&Ms.

"You have a point," she conceded. "We'll see how this goes."

Kristen Ashley

I didn't say anything because I knew how this was going to go. This wasn't going to go *anywhere*.

I got off the phone with Sissy and dug in my pocket to see what Luke gave me. His remote, a key and a business card with his name on it, his home and cell numbers written in black ink on the back.

I picked up the phone, called his office and shoved the card in my back pocket.

"Nightingale Investigations," Shirleen answered.

"Hey Shirleen, this is Ava Barlow. From yesterday?"

"Girl, how're you doin' today? Heard you spent the night with Luke."

I sat, stunned speechless, and stared at my computer.

Then I said, "Matt's got a big mouth."

"They all got big mouths, girl, learn that quick. These boys talk more than a pack of women. I lost fifty bucks on you."

I was stunned speechless again. This time it didn't last as long.

"What?"

"See, Lee nailed Indy the first night they were together. Not *nailed* her nailed her, but she was in his bed. Eddie, with Jet, it took a few days. Hank and Roxie, like, a day. Vance, like three, but Jules was a virgin and he had to interrupt the festivities once to go out and shoot someone."

I was blinking rapidly and feeling kind of faint at the amount and sensitivity of information Shirleen was imparting, not to mention what it might mean to me.

"So we had a pool," Shirleen carried on. "Everyone threw down money on when they thought Luke would nail you. Mace won five hundred dollars."

Ho-ly *crap*.

"So," she went on. "Did he *nail* you nail you or did you two just sleep?"

For some reason, I answered her unbelievably nosy question. "We just slept."

"New pool!" she shouted.

Oh my God.

Wyoming all of a sudden looked even better.

"Shirleen," I cut to the chase because I was beginning to feel sick. "I'm calling to set up an account. Luke and Vance are doing some work for me and I need you to invoice—"

"Oh girl, I don't *think* so. Luke already told me you'd try something like this. He says you two got something worked out and we don't want to step on *that,* do we?"

"Yes, we do," I told her. At least *I* wanted to step on it. I wanted to stomp all over it.

She laughed in my ear, loud and happy. "This is gonna be fun. First one of these I been in on, on the ground floor."

I could almost hear her rubbing her hands together.

"That means you're mine," she declared, I thought bizarrely. "See, Ally got Indy 'cause no one knew them then. Daisy got Jet. Everyone took care of Roxie 'cause that was some *serious* shit that went down. May got Jules because they knew each other beforehand, but we all kicked in, seein' as she was a virgin and all. Though I wasn't in on the cherry poppin' discussion, I've seen the tape."

The tape?

"Anyhoots," she went on. "See you at The Hornet tonight. I can't *wait.*"

Then she hung up.

I put down the phone kind of in a daze, picked it up immediately and called Sissy.

⌖

I got about an hour of work done before I started my preparation for the next nightmare of the day.

I decided to go heavy on the makeup and the silver. I spent ages on my hair, pulling it back away from my face smooth in parts, other parts in twists, and even other parts in braids, and clipped it at the back of my head with a huge silver barrette, leaving the back long.

I also decided to wear my kickass, rock 'n' roll, deep green, fitted, long-sleeved tee that had such a wide neckline, it fell off my shoulder.

This meant, since I didn't have a strapless bra (and no way I'd go braless sporting c-cup boobs), I had to wear my baby pink, satin bustier-slash-teddy-like contraption with snaps at the crotch. It fit like a glove, had beige triangles of lace at the hipbones and cups of the brassiere area and some soft boning that moved with my body. I'd bought it to wear with a strapless dress I wore to the New Year's Eve party Dom, Sissy, Noah and I went to the year before last and it was the only time I wore it. Noah loved it, thought it was hot

For my evening at The Hornet (and the rest of forever), it had only a utilitarian purpose.

I re-donned my faded jeans, ran a long, silver scarf through my belt loops, buckled on a pair of matte-silver strappy sandals and called a taxi.

By the time I got there, I was ten minutes late.

I walked into The Hornet and it was packed. It was a warm Friday in late March, so Denverites were ready to roll to summer. The bar area was shoulder to shoulder, the seating area was entirely filled and neither area had a seat with Indy's and Ally's asses sitting on them.

I went to the back room where the pool tables were and immediately to my left I saw them. Indy, Ally and eight other people, including Tod and Stevie, Indy's neighbors who I'd met several times before (gay, partners, totally fucking cool), Shirleen and the other black lady from the offices yesterday, not to mention the black-haired, violet-eyed Glamour Girl.

Holy cramoly.

"Ava!" Indy called and everyone's gaze swung to me.

"Hey," I said weakly, deciding that, yes, this was the next nightmare of my day.

I was introduced to the rest. A honey-blonde with green eyes and a fantastic smile (Jet). A dark blonde with blue eyes and a great outfit (Roxie). A platinum blonde that looked so much like Dolly Parton I thought she *was* Dolly for a minute, including the cleavage and a denim jacket with so many silver studs and rhinestones, she lit up the dim room. Her name was Daisy. The other black lady, older than the girls, with a Jacqueline Kennedy hairdo (May). And Glamour Girl (Jules).

Indy, by the way, was a tall, built, fantastic redhead, and Ally was tall, lean and gorgeous with shiny, dark brown hair.

"Sit down, sit down. Let's get to it. Someone get this girl a drink." Shirleen had a seat saved for me, right next to her, right smack in the center of the long table. She was patting it and grinning at me huge.

"I'll get you a drink," Stevie mumbled getting up. "What'll you have?"

"Cranberry juice and vodka. Let me give you some money," I told him.

"Girlie, sit! Gay men don't get to buy women drinks very often. Live it up!" Tod shouted.

Stevie moved off, I sat and Shirleen yelled after Stevie. "Hurry with that drink, you don't want to miss anything." Then her eyes moved back to me. "All right, girl, tell us *all* about it."

"Maybe we should tell our stories first," Jet suggested.

"I'm thinking that's a good idea," Indy put in.

I was happy to be off the hot seat, even if it was for five minutes, so I nodded.

It wasn't for five minutes. It was for a helluva lot longer. Two full drinks longer.

Indy told me her story. As she did, I was glad when Stevie brought my drink because Indy's story included the car bombs (yes, bombzzz, plural).

Even though Luke gave me the scary-ass flavor of Jet, Roxie and Jules's stories, he didn't get into the half of it (not even a quarter of it).

What he missed out was the part that included Eddie making Jet move in with him during her drama and she never moved out. Hank and her uncle conspiring to move Roxie in with Hank after her drama, and she did. And lastly, Jules doubling up on toiletries in about ten days between her place and Vance's place. She was still doubled up as they had her place in the city and his cabin in the mountains.

Every single one of them had been nailed and then *nailed* within a week.

"I need another drink," I whispered when Jules was done.

May patted my arm and Stevie disappeared for more drinks.

"Now, *your* turn," Shirleen said.

Instead of launching into my story, I turned to Jules, who'd been the last one to share and said, "I know you got shot and I'm sorry about that, but I think what you did was brave."

Jules stared at me.

Indy, Ally, Tod and Stevie were already my friends, and Shirleen had claimed me, whatever that meant. I could tell right off that Jet, Roxie, Daisy and May were cool.

Jules I hadn't cracked. Jules wasn't looking at me with kind eyes. She was looking at me with assessing ones. I didn't know what to make of her.

When she didn't speak, I looked away. "Sorry, not my place to say."

"What I did was stupid," she said to me, and my eyes moved back to her.

85

"Maybe, but it was brave, too, and you saved someone's life. So even if it was stupid, he's still here, and so are you. I think brave outweighs stupid in the end, don't you?"

May was smiling at me with a warmth I felt from across the table, and on a quick glance, I noticed everyone else was too. My eyes settled on Jules and I was pleased to note she was smiling, too.

Stevie set my drink in front of me and I took a gulp, looked around again and saw the expectant faces. There was nothing for it. I took a deep breath and started from the beginning. Two drinks later, I was done.

I told them the whole shebang, leaving nothing out. Not my weight. Not my Dad. Not my sisters and mother. Not my years-long crush on Luke. Not Luke punching out the boys who called me Fatty Fatty Four-Eyes. Not him sitting next to me on the stoop after my Dad left. Not our embrace at his Dad's funeral. Not my promise and breaking it with my non-return of Luke's calls. Not Rick, Dave and Noah. Not Dom. Not Sandra Whoever-She-Was. Not Luke cuffing me to him and his bed.

Not a thing.

Everyone stared at me when I was done.

"Oowee, these boys don't play games," Shirleen announced, sitting back and fanning herself with her hand.

"Holy crap," Indy mumbled.

"He even makes Lee's pursuit look old-fashioned, and Lee used cuffs on you, too," Ally said, moving her stare to Indy.

"What 'cha gonna do now, sugar?" Daisy asked.

"Yeah, are you going to Luke's place tonight or your own?" Roxie put in.

I looked at Roxie. "My place," I said without hesitation.

Everyone drew in breaths.

"Oh Lordy," Stevie whispered.

"Here we go again," Jet said.

"No, really, it isn't like that," I told them.

"It's *always* like that," Daisy told me.

"What I don't get," Shirleen said to the table, "is why you women don't just give in? It ain't like these boys aren't fine. Are they fine?" she asked Tod and Stevie.

"They're fine," Stevie confirmed.

"They are *so* fine," Tod threw in with a little jazz hand wave to emphasize his point.

"I mean, I get me a chance at a taste o' Luke Stark, I'd take a bite outta that boy faster 'n Jiminy Cricket," Shirleen said.

"You called it, sugar," Daisy giggled, and it sounded like tinkling bells.

"Men suck," I declared, not having much fight in me after four cranberry juice and vodkas and zero dinner.

"Maybe so, but Luke Stark pushed me against the wall and told me he was gonna fuck me, I'd say, 'When and what you want me to wear?' And I would not care if he *did* pull a slam-bam-thank-you-ma'am. I'd just take my orgasm and *go*. You hear what I'm sayin' to you?" Shirleen asked.

I heard what she was saying. I heard it loud and clear.

"Did you *not* hear me when I told you Noah stole five thousand, three hundred and twenty-five dollars from me?" I asked back.

"I was you, I'd tell Luke Stark about them five thousand some odd dollars. He'd find this Noah whose-ee-whatsit and nail his ass to the wall," May told me.

"That's right," Shirleen agreed.

"Okay, then Dave, Rick, *Dom*," I went on. "Men are all assholes." I looked at Tod and Stevie. "Present company excepted, of course."

"Of course," Stevie mumbled.

Tod just smiled.

"Hank's not an asshole," Roxie muttered.

"I'm glad for you. It sounds like he isn't, and that's cool." I emphasized my comment by reaching out and squeezing Roxie's hand. Then I sat back and declared, "But for me, I'll take my rabbit vibrator, thank you. It works *every* time."

"No vibrator is better than Eddie," Jet whispered to a grinning Jules. "Trust me, I know."

"Just this morning, Lee had me singing the Hallelujah Chorus, *twice*," Indy didn't whisper. "I haven't touched a vibrator in ten months."

"I didn't even bring my vibrator from Chicago. I tossed it in a dumpster," Roxie threw down. "And I do *not* miss it."

"Why are we talking about vibrators?" Stevie asked May. She started shaking with laughter.

"I've vowed fidelity to my vibrators," I told them. "I'm not going to get talked down to, stolen from, cheated on, walked all over or walked *out* on. Not like Sissy, not like myself and *not* like my Mom. No way. No fucking way."

There was a lot of grinning, some shaking of heads and at least one roll of the eyes.

Oh well. There was no convincing this crowd. But *I* knew if I could shed seventy-five pounds and go from a Fatty Fatty Four-Eyes to someone Lucas Stark would call a knockout, I could and *would* remain faithful to my vibrators.

On that thought, I got up. "I'm getting a drink. Who needs a drink?"

"We all need drinks, girlie," Tod replied.

"My shout, I'll find a waitress," I announced and then weaved my unsteady way through the crowd to the bar.

I didn't make it.

Five steps away from the bar two big, beefy guys came up on either side of me, both with a hand at each of my elbows, but only one leaned in and asked, "You know Dominic Vincetti?"

Uh-oh.

This doesn't look good, Bad Ava told me.

Eek! Good Ava screeched.

Shit.

That was when I was kidnapped.

They weren't good kidnappers.

I knew this because I got away.

They pulled me out of the bar and behind the back-to-the-alley parking area and shoved me in the backseat of the car. They weren't rough. They weren't gentle. But they were in a hurry. They didn't take my purse and they didn't ask any questions outside of the first one which, incidentally, I didn't answer, but they took me anyway.

What they *did* say was that if I didn't go with them, they would blow my head off. It didn't occur to me that it was unlikely that they would blow my head off in a crowded bar. The only thing that occurred to me was that I liked my head where it was.

Therefore, I went with them.

They were huge guys. Both dark, both Italian-looking, both wearing ill-fitting suits and, on one of them, I could see his shoulder holster and the butt of a gun. Thus, me going with them.

I sat in the back of the car wishing I had had dinner. Firstly, because I was hungry. Secondly, because I was now a lot more drunk than I normally would have been if I had only had four cranberry juice and vodkas. Thirdly, because if I was going to die, I wished I had had a last meal that consisted of more than noodles and veggies.

We drove down Broadway toward Englewood and I wondered when the gang was going to notice I was gone. They'd probably call Luke and Luke would probably get pissed. *At me.*

Fuckity, fuck, fuck, *fuck.*

"Mr. Zano wants to see you," the big guy in the passenger seat turned to tell me.

"Okay," I said, deciding to be cooperative in order not to get beaten up, shot at, chained to a sink, car bombed or the like.

"You know Mr. Zano?" he asked.

"No," I told him. I mean, I knew several Zanos, including Uncle Vito and Dom's shit-hot cousin Ren Zano, but I could call both of them friends and neither of them would kidnap me.

He looked at his friend then back at me. "Mr. Zano knows you."

"Okay," I agreed, even though I knew no kidnapping, having beefy-henchmen "Mr. Zano".

"Mr. Zano also knows you were at Dominic's house last night with Stark. Are you like The Law?" he asked.

"Law" was Jules's street name. Jules was a social worker, and months ago she'd started a rather successful one-woman vigilante operation against the drug dealers in the city. This was part of why she was shot. She also worked with Lee's boys for a few days, and did what she did with them so well it significantly enhanced her street cred. She didn't do that anymore, but apparently she hadn't been forgotten.

"No," I repeated.

"What were you two doin' there?" he went on.

"Sissy Vincetti is my friend. She left Dom and she wanted some of her stuff. We went to get it for her," I lied.

He looked at his partner as if his partner could confirm my story. His partner shrugged. The guy talking to me lost interest in our conversation and turned back to the front.

I looked out the window, trying not to hyperventilate as we pulled to a stop at a red light, and my eyes moved across the street. Brightly lit and totally still open was a Walgreens.

I looked to my door. It was unlocked.

I looked to my kidnappers. They weren't paying any attention to me.

I didn't know Mr. Zano, but I knew anyone who sent two big goons after a woman was someone I didn't really want to talk to. I'd also heard on a TV show once that it was actually hard to shoot someone, considering bullets were little tiny things, targets were usually moving and most people were bad shots.

I sighed, said a little prayer, promised myself that tomorrow I was drawing up a will, opened my door and took off like a shot.

"What the fuck!" One of the guys shouted.

I zigzagged across Broadway, throwing my arms out as I got from the southbound lane, where the traffic was stopped, to the northbound lane, where traffic was flowing. Cars honked and swerved and I ran in my high-heeled sandals as best as I could.

I hit the sidewalk and heard him pounding behind me, more cars honking and I was worried he was close.

Damn, damn, damn it!

I kept going, not looking back. The automatic door swooped open and I ran directly to the cash register.

I stopped, bent over, breathing heavily as the cashier said to me, "Are you all right?"

I looked at the doors.

The Passenger Seat Guy was stopped outside the door and glaring. He pointed at me, moving his mouth saying something I couldn't hear, and then he turned and jogged away.

I watched him go, memorizing as much as I could about what he was wearing and how he looked.

When he disappeared, I turned to the cashier and said, "I've just been kidnapped. I need you to phone the police."

In the next fifteen minutes, I met both Roxie's boyfriend, Hank (he looked like a Nightingale; tall, lean and handsome as all get out) and Jet's boyfriend, Eddie (he was Mexican American; also tall, also lean and fucking hot). They were both cops, and they were the first to the scene after the squad car.

Two minutes later, Luke's Porsche glided in and parked in the yellow lined area right at the front doors next to Eddie's red Dodge Ram.

Crapity, crap, crap, *crap*.

He strode through the doors and all the Walgreens employees took a step back after one glance at him. I figured they did this not only because he looked like he wanted to rip someone's head off, but also because he looked like he *could*.

One of the cops straightened when Luke arrived at our huddle. I was sitting (more like shaking like a fucking leaf) on one of the cash register counters and all the cops were surrounding me.

"Stark," the uniform cop greeted.

"You all right?" Luke ignored him and asked me.

I nodded.

"You know her?" the other uniform asked.

"Yeah," Luke bit off.

There were two uniform cops, one youngish-looking white guy and one handsome black guy. They looked at Luke, then at me, then at the way Luke was staring at me.

"Oh shit," the white cop said.

"This your woman?" the black cop asked.

"Yeah," Luke answered.

"I am *not* your woman," I snapped.

"Oh shit," the white cop repeated.

Eddie, standing beside me, chuckled. Hank, standing by Eddie, looked at the ceiling.

"We gotta take her to the station. Take her statement, show her mug shots," the white cop said.

"I'll take her to the station," Luke told them.

"Works for me," the black cop said.

"Wait!" I cried, jumping off the counter. "Aren't I supposed to go with you guys?"

They were already on the move.

"You can go with Stark," the black cop told me.

"What if I don't want to go with Stark?" I asked.

Kristen Ashley

The black cop looked at Luke and grinned. Then his grin swung to me, but he didn't answer. He and the other uniform walked away.

"Go on vacation," Hank advised Luke, also moving toward the door. "Seriously, Luke. Just pack her up and go. Let whatever this is blow over. Come back in a month."

"That's good advice," Eddie agreed, following Hank. "Go somewhere far away. Australia."

Then they were both gone.

I stood, still trembling, because let us not forget, I'd just been kidnapped and I watched the automatic doors close behind Eddie.

My eyes moved to Luke.

"Let's go," he said.

His hand came out, palm up, toward me.

I swear to God, I had no control over what I did next. I looked at his strong hand and walked forward, ignoring the hand. I moved right by it and kept walking until I collided with his hard body, head on. I shoved my face in his chest, grabbed fistfuls of his shirt right next to my cheeks and held on while I let the tremors overwhelm me.

Within a second of making contact with his body, Luke's arms wrapped around me.

Tight.

Chapter 7
Pink Lady Sandy

For the next year of my life (not really), I looked at seven million, two hundred thousand and forty-four (not really) mug shots. I found the pictures of both the guys who kidnapped me. My identification of them made Luke's mouth get tight when he saw their faces. I didn't ask why, mainly because I didn't want to know.

This was after I told a nice, older man named Detective Jimmy Marker my kidnapping story. This short story took a lot longer because Indy, Ally, Shirleen, Daisy and Jules all phoned me while I was telling it to find out if I was okay. I was guessing Jet and Roxie got the story from Eddie and Hank, and Shirleen, Daisy and Jules got my number from Indy or Ally.

After this was all over, Luke took me to his Porsche. We strapped in and the Porsche glided to the street (even post-kidnapping I had to appreciate the ride was sweet) and I requested quietly, "Please take me home."

Luke didn't answer. What he did do was drive through LoDo, taking Speer Boulevard all the way into the Highlands, which led to my house. In front of my house I got out of the car and made my way to the door. Luke took the keys from my hand at the door, let us in and stopped me just inside.

"Stay here, I'm gonna check the house," he ordered.

I did as I was told.

When he was done, he came back to me and closed the door.

"Ava."

I looked up at him.

"I'm spendin' the night."

I let out a breath.

Thank you *God*.

I nodded.

He watched me a beat and said, "I'm gonna do a scan of the neighborhood. Lock the door behind me."

I nodded again. He turned to leave.

"Luke?"

He turned back.

"You should park your Porsche in my garage. This neighborhood isn't good."

"Got an extra remote?"

I took him to the kitchen, dug through my junk drawer and gave him the extra remote and an extra set of keys.

He left. I locked the door behind him.

I walked upstairs and went straight to the linen closet, pulling out the bedding and extra pillows for the futon. My futon was a fancy one with armrests and everything. It was a pain in the ass to get open because it weighed a ton. I figured I'd make the bed when Luke got back. He'd probably be able to pull it out by glaring at it.

I went to my bedroom and dropped the Roman blinds. I'd painted my bedroom in a soft eggshell blue. It had a white bed stand. Solid wood, no slats, which meant no way to cuff me to it, which was not why I bought it, but that had now become an additional bonus.

There were two thin white nightstands on either side, a white dressing table with a big mirror and a tall, narrow seven-drawer lingerie dresser.

The sheets on the bed were pale green, the bedspread and pillow shams were a pattern of eggshell blue and green that matched the tile around the fireplace.

The big windows had wispy white curtains and custom-made Roman blinds.

I took one look at my room and decided I was never going to leave it, ever again, in my whole fucking life.

Unfortunately, before I could do that I had to take out my contacts.

I pulled off my silver and dropped it on the dressing table, unbuckled and flipped off my shoes, yanked the scarf out of my belt loops and pulled off my t-shirt. I took out my barrette and arranged my hair up in a messy bunch on top of my head.

I didn't know how long it took to "scan the neighborhood" and park the Porsche, but, considering Luke was likely thorough in his job, I figured it would take a while. Therefore, I thought I was safe (and alone) in the house for that while.

What could I say? I'd just been kidnapped by beefy Italian bad guys. I wasn't thinking clearly.

I walked barefoot in my jeans and teddy-type-thing to the bathroom, stood at the sink and looked in the mirror.

"Fuck," I said to myself.

You can say that again, Bad Ava agreed.

You shouldn't curse, even if you have been kidnapped. It isn't very ladylike, Good Ava chastised.

I ignored both of them, pulled open my medicine cabinet and got my contact solution. I had just readied the case with solution when I saw a movement at the bathroom door.

I whirled and shrieked (yes, girlie *shrieked*), my hand coming up to my chest.

Luke stood there.

Okay, so maybe it didn't take long to scan the neighborhood. And I was seeing that I should have probably closed the bathroom door.

Luke's eyes were on my torso, and even standing all the way across the bathroom, I could tell they were ink.

Ho-ly *shit.*

I turned back to the sink, trying to be cool. It wasn't like I was naked or anything. In fact, I had dresses that I wore out in public that showed more skin.

I leaned into the mirror and pulled open an eye with one hand, my index finger of the other up and at the ready to take out the contact.

Luke materialized behind me in the mirror. *Close* behind me.

I poked myself in the eye.

After I quit blinking, I glared at him. I was certain he'd be laughing or at least giving me a half-grin.

He was not. His mind was clearly on other things. I knew this when his hand, fingers splayed, hit my side and slid around my midriff. His eyes watched its movement in the mirror.

My knees did a little wobble.

"We need to make up the futon," I told him, deciding to pretend the wobble didn't happen.

"Why?" he asked.

"So you can sleep there," I replied, and successfully (thank God), pulled out the contact.

"I'm sleepin' with you," he said, his hand sliding further across my midriff toward my other side, which meant, to accommodate its motion, my body moved back into his.

"No you aren't."

"Yes I am."

"Luke, I don't want to argue about this."

His eyes moved to mine in the mirror. "Then don't."

Shit. How did you respond to that?

My head dropped. I started cleaning my contact in my palm and widened my net to try and pretend everything else that was happening to my body wasn't happening (rapid heartbeat, blood warming, nipples hardening). Not just the knee wobble.

I pulled at his arm to lean in to the mirror to take out the other contact. He watched me do this, which, I might add, was supremely nerve-wracking. I got the contact on the first go and leaned back, squirting solution on it in my palm to clean it. Luke's hand slid up to the side of my breast so his forearm was pressed underneath both of them.

There was the knee wobble again.

Hell and damnation.

I looked at us in the mirror and we were fuzzy. But even fuzzy I liked what I saw.

"Luke."

I watched as his head bent and felt as his mouth hit my neck.

"I like this," he said against my neck, and showed me what he meant by rubbing his thumb along the side of my breast.

It felt nice.

I closed my eyes then opened them again.

"Noah liked it, too," I told him, calmly morphing into Barlow Super Bitch, but my heart was beating so fast I thought it would tear right out of my chest and I was finding it hard to breathe. But none of the physical manifestations of Luke's touch stopped me. "He liked it a lot. So much, it's kinda surprising he didn't steal it when he cleaned out my bank accounts, took all my Auntie Ella's gold jewelry and disappeared."

I felt and saw Luke's head come up and I was pretty certain he was looking at me in the mirror.

"He should have taken it, a memento of good times," I went on, seriously Barlow Super Bitch.

"Let's go back to the part about cleaning out your bank accounts," Luke's mouth was close to my ear and I actually felt his deep voice rumble through my body.

"Five thousand, three hundred and twenty-five dollars, everything I had in savings and checking. It took him days of maximum ATM withdrawals, but you have to hand it to him, he stuck to it."

I ignored the scary, pissed-off life force emanating from Luke that filled the room as I opened the medicine cabinet. I replaced the solution and aimed for the bottle that I knew was my face soap, and as I did this Luke's arm dropped away.

Then I felt Luke's presence move away.

When I knew he was gone (and peeked to check), I put both my hands to the basin and dropped my head.

Now, that wasn't nice, Good Ava sounded disappointed.

It wasn't, Bad Ava, surprisingly, agreed.

"Shut up," I whispered.

I washed my face, brushed my teeth, slathered with moisturizer and went to my room.

I closed the door this time and changed into my pajamas (cream, silky-satin, drawstring pants and a matching camisole with spaghetti straps, gathers under my breasts and a low, straight back that cut just under my shoulder blades). I got in bed and pulled up the covers.

I didn't know where Luke was, but I told myself I didn't care, noting that now I was lying to myself.

I was planning my strategy to get all men out of my life (which included gaining back every one of those seventy-five pounds—and then some—by eating my way through the entire inventory of LaMar's donuts every day for a month, as well as firing Riley) when the door opened and Luke walked in.

The house behind him was dark and so was the room. As I watched his shadowy form move, he walked right to the bed and sat on the edge like he'd been in my room hundreds of times.

"Luke, the futon is in the second bedroom," I informed him.

I heard his boot hit the floor.

"Or, you can sleep on the couch downstairs," I went on.

I heard his other boot hit the floor.

"There's pillows and blankets on the futon. I got them out," I persevered.

He leaned forward a bit, lifted his arms so his hands went between his shoulder blades and he tugged off his tee.

"Luke!"

He stood and for a second I thought he was going to leave. Also, I had to admit, for a second I felt unbelievably disappointed.

Instead, he dropped his cargo pants and I heard his belt hit the floor.

Holy crap!

Then he pulled the covers back and settled on his back in the bed.

I came up on an elbow and glared at him, or in his general direction. "You aren't sleeping here."

"What's Noah's last name?"

I blinked in the darkness.

"Excuse me?" I asked.

"His last name," Luke repeated.

"Dexter, why?"

"He white?"

"Sorry?"

"Caucasian."

"Yes," I answered, deciding to move away from this strange turn of the conversation. "About the futon—"

"Do you know his birthdate?"

"Luke—"

"Ava, what's his fucking birthday?"

"July twenty-third. Why are you asking me this?"

"You got a social security number?"

I felt a thrill slide through me as I cottoned onto the purpose of his interrogation and I shot up to a sitting position in the bed.

"Don't you—!" I started to protest, but Luke sat up too, faster than I'd seen anyone move, giving new meaning to "abs of steel". In the blink of an eye I found myself on my back, Luke full body on top of me.

"Get off me!" I shouted, bucking my body under his.

"This Noah guy's got her."

I was back to blinking, so confused I stilled.

"Got who?" I asked.

"The old Ava."

Instantly I felt the tears stinging my eyes, all fight left me and I turned my head to the side.

His hands came to either side of my face and he turned it back.

"He took her when he disappeared, didn't he?" Luke asked, his voice gentle.

Crapity, crap, crap, *crap*.

His gentle voice got me every fucking time.

"A piece of her," I whispered. Do *not* ask me why, but I did (I knew why, The Voice).

"Who's got the other pieces?"

I shook my head against his hands. I didn't think the minuscule amount of information I shared on Noah boded well for Noah's future. Luke, I was realizing, was not the kind of guy who fucked around. I couldn't imagine that Noah was still in town, but I knew Rick and Dave were and I didn't want Luke hunting them down and doing whatever. They were jerks, but they were also history.

"Please, get off me," I said softly.

"Ava, I spent years doin' some crazy shit and gettin' paid well for it. Well enough that by the time I came back to Denver for my father's funeral, I could retire."

Ho-ly shit.

He'd been twenty-eight! What kind of "crazy shit" paid you enough to retire at twenty-eight?

I sucked in breath and stared.

Luke kept talking. "To keep from gettin' bored, because I like it, because I'm good at it and because Lee pays me a shitload of money to do it, I work. I could walk away from it tomorrow and live a good life, even takin' care of someone along the way."

Whoa.

Whoa, whoa, whoa.

I was digging deeper than ever to bury *that*.

"I'd never fuck you over, steal your money. No fuckin' way," he finished.

And even deeper to bury that.

"Please, Luke, get off me."

To my surprise he did, sliding off to my side. I immediately turned my back to him and scooted away several inches. He wanted to sleep with me fine, we'd sleep. Then tomorrow, I was moving to Wyoming.

Luke had other ideas.

His arm slid under me, hooked at my waist and hauled me back into his body. The second I made contact, his body pressed into mine and his other arm went around me.

"I want her back," he said into my hair, and his words made me shiver. I had to close my eyes tight to stop my tears and my thoughts.

He went on, "I've decided I like the bitchy Ava. The way you throw your attitude around is sexy as hell, but I still want the old Ava back."

"She's gone," I whispered again. Do *not* ask me why.

His arms tightened and his mouth came to my ear.

"She's right here."

<hr>

You would have thought I'd never get to sleep after that, but somehow I did.

Deeper in the night, when it was still dark, my body moved, again not of its own volition.

Sometime during the night we'd come face-to-face. Arms around me, Luke rolled me over his body and to his other side. Again he hooked my leg over his hip.

"Why do you do that?" I whispered sleepily as I wrapped my arm around his waist, slid the fingers of my other hand into the hair at his chest and pressed in close to his warm, hard body.

He might have answered, but I didn't hear him because I was already back to sleep.

<hr>

I woke and the light was trying to force its way through my shades.

I was back in the position I'd woken up in yesterday, tight against Luke's side, arm wrapped around his abs, leg thrown over his thighs.

Shit.

I tilted my head and looked at him to see that he was still asleep. I didn't have clear vision, but even with the mini-blur his face in sleep somehow still looked hard.

I rolled away and he moved into the space I left. I stilled and looked at him, but he didn't wake.

I grabbed my glasses (kickass, black-rimmed, oval-framed, D&G) from the nightstand, yanked my thin, yellow-green, cotton cardigan off the hook on the back of the door and got the hell out of there.

I went to the bathroom, washed my face, brushed and flossed and settled my hair in a less-messy-but-still-tangled bundle on top of my head.

I put on my glasses and shrugged on the cardigan as I went downstairs to the kitchen, grabbed myself a cold Diet Coke from the fridge and started some coffee. I cut up fruit, enough for both Luke and me, tossed his in a bowl and put it in the fridge. I dumped a couple of globs of yogurt on mine, sprinkled it with my homemade granola (delicious with tons of sesame seeds and almonds) and did what I did every morning when it was semi-warm.

I took my bowl and Diet and went to the back porch. I sat on the bright cushion of my wicker loveseat with my heels to the edge and my knees pointed skyward. Then I stared at the sun hitting my yard and, while eating, planned my day.

First up, get rid of Luke.

Second, go workout with Riley.

Third, get some work done.

Fourth, learn how to become a lesbian.

"Babe." I heard, and my head twisted to see Luke standing in the door to the porch wearing nothing but his cargo pants, belt not done (and neither was the top button) and an intriguing trail of black hair disappearing into his waistband.

God, he was fucking *hot*.

So much for becoming a lesbian.

"Hey," I said.

He gave me a sexy half-grin.

I got up and walked to him. He moved out of my way as I went into the kitchen and put my empty bowl in the sink.

"You want coffee?" I asked.

"Yeah."

He was standing, arms crossed, hip against the counter, watching me move.

Ee-yikes!

I pulled down a cup ignoring his eyes on me, or trying and, admittedly, failing. "You want some breakfast? Fruit, yogurt and granola?"

"Sounds good."

I nodded and poured coffee. "Do you take sugar or milk?"

"Black."

I nodded again and handed him his coffee without looking at him. Then I went to the fridge to get his fruit and the yogurt, all the while gabbing.

"Sofia tried to start drinking coffee at twelve, she thought it was cool," I told him just for something to say because I was flipping way the hell out. I set the bowl down, grabbed a spoon from the drawer and opened the yogurt. "Mom told her if she did she would grow chest hair." My eyes moved to his chest then lifted to his face. "When did you start drinking coffee?" I asked.

"When I was twelve."

I burst out laughing. I couldn't help it, it was funny.

I started to pile globs of yogurt on his fruit, still smiling.

"Babe," he called.

"What?" I kept my head bent to my task.

"Ava."

I turned to him, still smiling.

I should have paid attention to what was happening with Luke and not the yogurt.

His face was hard but his eyes were ink.

Uh-oh.

"Luke—"

He pulled the yogurt out of my hand, put it on the counter and then took the spoon and tossed it in the bowl.

I moved to take a step back, again reacting too late. He leaned in, his arm went around my waist and he drew me to his body. His other hand went up my back and into the hair at the base of my head.

I pulled back and his arms tightened, moving me forward.

"This isn't a good idea," I whispered, watching his lips come toward me.

"This is a fucking great idea," he muttered.

Then he kissed me.

For your information, the hard kiss Luke gave me to shut me up was *nothing* like this.

Yes, his lips were hard, but they were also effective.

Coupled with his tongue, they were ultra-effective.

It took, like, two seconds before my knees buckled. He took my weight and I lifted my arms to wrap them around his neck, the fingers of one hand sliding across his spiky hair.

At first he teased me with his tongue, playing with me, making me want it and then taking it away, so I went after it. The minute my tongue entered his mouth, he sucked it in deeper.

Holy... fucking... *shit*.

I didn't mean to, but I moaned into his mouth. I got up on tiptoe and pressed myself against him full frontal.

When I did that, his head slanted and he leaned in. His hand in my hair moved down so that his arm was wrapped around my shoulder blades, fingers at my armpit, the other one still sliced around my waist. Both arms tightened and my back arched with his lean, pressing my whole torso and hips into his.

The kiss went wild. He didn't tease anymore. He meant serious business and I liked Luke's serious business, and so did my body.

Finally, he tore his mouth from mine and stared at me, his eyes so beyond warm and inky it was not funny. They were molten. I was in an uncontrollable Luke Lip Fog, mainly because his lips had been on my lips, so I was staring at him eyes half-mast, lips parted.

"Christ," he bit off tersely, his hands going down over my ass. He lifted me up and I threw my legs around his hips and tensed my arms around his neck. Before I could think a single thought, he kissed me again and started walking.

I didn't know how someone could kiss someone while carrying them and walking through three rooms, but he did it. I thought we were going to my couch in the living room (that was where I would have headed) but he walked straight through my living room to the stairwell entry.

I didn't care where we were going. Lucas Stark was kissing me, his tongue in my mouth, my special girl parts pressed against his hard boy parts. He could have taken me to the moon and I wouldn't have given a shit.

He had one foot on the bottom stair when there was a pounding at the door. Not a knock, a *pound*.

He stopped walking, stopped kissing me and his head jerked back while mine lifted up. We looked at each other.

The pounding came again, louder and more insistent this time.

"What the fuck?" Luke muttered.

"Ava, open the door! I know you're on the back porch!" Sissy shouted and then pounded again while my mouth dropped open. What on earth was Sissy doing there? "Don't make me walk back there, I have suitcases!" she yelled.

Oh shit.

"Jesus Christ," Luke mumbled, and he dropped me to my feet.

"That's Sissy," I told him over the pounding.

"No kidding." He was joking, but he wasn't laughing.

Eek.

Someone was not happy to be interrupted.

I'm not happy either, Bad Ava complained.

Good Ava had no comment.

I skirted past him to the door, but before I could open it, he pulled me back, arm at my waist.

"What are you doing?" I asked over the pounding as he shoved me behind him, unlocked the deadbolt and the chain and opened the door.

Sissy was standing there, arm up, hand in mid-pound. She stopped dead when she caught sight of Luke, and she gawked. Full-on, mouth-opened, eyes bugged out, *gawked.*

"Holy crap," she breathed.

"Sissy, what are you doing here?" I asked, peeking around Luke's body.

Sissy (and I could see the effort it took her) tore her eyes from bare-chested Luke and looked at me.

She took in my messy hair, the glasses I wore only at home (if I could help it) and pajamas and shouted, "Holy *crap!*"

I slid in front of Luke, grabbed Sissy's still upraised wrist and pulled her into the entryway.

"What are you doing here?" I repeated.

She was looking between Luke and me and blinking slowly.

"What?" she asked in a dazed voice.

"You're supposed to be in Wyoming," I told her.

She focused on me. "The cops called, said you were kidnapped. Since it had to do with Dom and they thought whoever it was might come after me next, the Denver boys warned the local authorities in Wyoming and they came by my Mom's house to talk about protection. I packed up early this morning and hauled ass down here." Then realizing where she was and the current scenario of our lives her eyes narrowed. "Why didn't you tell me you were kidnapped?"

Uh-oh.

"Um…" I mumbled.

"I can't believe you didn't tell me you were kidnapped."

"Sissy, honey—"

"When a girl gets laid, she tells her best friend. When a girl finds a lump, she tells her best friend. When a girl finds a kickass shade of nail polish, she tells her best friend. And, I might add, when a girl gets kidnapped, *she tells her best friend!*" Sissy was shouting when she finished.

"Sissy, calm down."

"I will not calm down." She was still yelling and she turned her eyes to Luke. "Where were you when this happened, stud?"

Oh no. Sissy was channeling Olivia Newton-John from *Grease.* It was never good when Sissy channeled Sandy's Pink Lady from the finale. Sissy didn't normally lose her temper; usually sweet as pie, totally Sandy. She had not a single thread of Rizzo in her. When Sissy channeled Pink Lady Sandy, the results were disastrous.

I chanced a glance at Luke and he was smiling his sexy half-grin.

Shit.

"Luke, can you get her bags?" I asked and didn't wait for his response. I pulled Sissy into and through the living room directly to the kitchen.

I stopped and turned to her.

"Pull yourself together," I hissed.

"Pull myself… pull myself…" she stammered, eyes wide. "Pull myself together!" she shouted then, still shouting, she cried, "Last time I talked to you, you were going out on the town, had everything sorted with these shit-hot private eye guys and were sworn off men forever. Hours later, you've been kidnapped, Mr. Beefcake's in there barely clothed and you're in your pajamas and *glasses* for God's sake!" She stopped and looked around in mock confusion. "Have I entered an alternate universe?"

"I haven't had a chance to call."

"That's no excuse."

"We got home late."

"*We?*"

"Sissy!"

She glared at me. Then I watched as her face fell, the anger faded, her eyes started shimmering and Pink Lady Sandy was a memory.

"I got my best friend kidnapped," she whispered and then burst into tears.

I pulled her into my arms and held on tight. As I absorbed her shaking sobs into my body, I double-vowed revenge against Dominic Fucking Vincetti (rat-bastard).

"Sissy," I murmured into the top of her hair, and that was when I saw Luke leaning against the doorframe between the living and dining room. He'd put on a t-shirt and done up his belt. His eyes were on me and I could see the warmth in them from across the room.

Crapity, crap, crap, *crap.*

"You could have been hurt," Sissy mumbled.

"I wasn't," I said, totally unable to take my eyes from Luke.

"You could have," Sissy went on.

"I'm fine," I assured her.

She looked up at me, saw my eyes and followed them to Luke. She realized what she was about, pulled out of my arms and swiped at her face.

"Hey Luke," Sissy said in belated greeting, and I had to press my lips together not to laugh.

"Sissy," Luke replied.

"Sorry I yelled at you," she told him.

He did a single shoulder shrug.

"I'm usually not this loud," she went on.

He did the half-grin. Sissy stared, transfixed at all that was Luke. I rolled my eyes and caught a look at the clock on the roll back.

"Shit!" I shouted. "I'm supposed to meet Riley in twenty minutes!" I made a mad dash out of the kitchen and then halted and whirled. "Have coffee, get settled, I'll be back in a couple of hours and we'll talk," I told Sissy and then whirled again and restarted the dash.

I got four feet and was caught short when Luke threw an arm out as I was about to pass him, so it caught me at my waist.

I let out an "oof" and heard Luke say, "Just a minute," to Sissy. He grabbed my hand and dragged me through the living room, up the stairs and to the bedroom.

I allowed this, mainly because I didn't want Sissy to hear me struggling, and also I was mentally counting to ten.

When he'd closed the door to the bedroom, I turned on him.

Half-Grin, Amused Luke was gone, brows drawn, Pissed-Off Luke in his place.

"What was that?" I asked, foolishly ignoring Pissed-Off Luke.

"I thought I made myself clear about Riley."

"He's my personal trainer."

"He wants to fuck you."

I looked at the ceiling seeking divine intervention.

When none was to be had I looked back at Luke. "He's a friend."

"He wants to fuck you," Luke repeated.

"Okay then, he wants to fuck me. He's not *going* to fuck me. No one's going to fuck me."

"I'm gonna fuck you."

I put my hands to my hips and leaned forward. Yes, now Pissed-Off Ava.

"Luke, get it through your head. You and me, not… gonna… happen."

His brows went up. "So tell me, what was that ten minutes ago?"

Hmm. He had a point.

"Temporary insanity," I answered.

"Because you've sworn off men?"

Hell and damnation.

Sissy and her Pink Lady Sandy big mouth.

"Yes," I snapped.

We stared at each other, Pissed-Off Luke vs. Pissed-Off Ava, the battle of the century.

Then to my surprise (and discomfort), he grinned. Not a half-grin, a full-fledged one.

I did not take this as a good sign.

"What's with the grin?" I asked, wary.

"I like this," he told me.

"What?"

Instead of answering my question, looking very pleased about something he said, "I'm gonna enjoy this."

"*What?*" I snapped.

Again he didn't answer my question. Instead, he said, "We still haven't discussed your payment."

I threw up my hands

Jeez.

I couldn't take anymore.

"Oh for goodness sakes!" I cried and started to move toward the closet. "I don't have time for this. I have things to do."

He caught me and swung me into his body. Both his arms locked around my waist and he looked down at me.

"I'll take you to the gym. After you're done, I'll pick you up. I don't want you going anywhere alone, so whatever you gotta do, wherever you gotta go, either I take you or I'll arrange for someone to do it. Same with Sissy. Last night you likely pissed off some pretty dangerous people. I'm not fuckin' around with this."

"Fine," I clipped, mainly so he would let me go, but also so I wouldn't have to think about dangerous people being pissed-off at me, and so I could get to the gym. It was rude to be late.

"Tonight, we talk about your payment."

"Fine," I lied, totally not going to talk about payment or be anywhere *near* Luke that night.

He shook his head while it dropped toward mine and I knew he knew I was lying.

His face an inch away from mine he said, "If you think I'm gonna let you go back on that promise you made me in the kitchen, think again."

"I didn't make any promise."

"Oh yeah you did."

I gave up. "Luke, let me go. I'm going to be late."

He kept looking at me then his eyes got ultra-warm and he murmured, "Yeah, I'm gonna enjoy this."

Shit.

Chapter 8

Get the Business

This was my morning:

Luke took me to the gym. Sissy decided to go with, so we all trudged out to the garage. Luke took the keys to *my* car out of *my* hand and declared *he* was going to drive. Standing outside of the garage, we had a fight about who was going to drive.

Luke won.

Then Luke drove us to the gym. Luke got out when we got there and I told him he didn't need to walk us into the gym. Standing by my Range Rover, we got in a fight about whether he was going to walk us into the gym or not.

Luke won.

Then when we got *into* the gym, Luke asked to talk to Riley privately "outside". Standing in the reception area of the gym, Luke and I got in a fight about him talking to Riley privately "outside".

Luke won.

I waited until they returned, both stony-faced with the addition of Riley looking way, *way* pissed-off and I opened my mouth to give it to Luke for being a he-man, tough guy jerk when he grabbed my purse. I stared, still with my mouth open, as he dug through my purse, took out my phone and started to hit buttons.

"What are you doing?" I asked.

"Programming my numbers into your phone. Call me when you're done."

I snatched my purse out of his hand, which he allowed. Then I went for the phone, which he didn't allow, and stopped me by pinning me to his frame with one of his arms and holding my struggling body while he beeped buttons with the phone held behind my back.

He let me go and handed me my phone.

"I hate you," I snapped.

"No you don't," he replied calmly. He grabbed the back of my neck, yanked me into his body and kissed me, hard, open-mouthed and hot until my knees buckled and I melted into him.

Then he let me go, gave me a half-grin, touched my nose and left.

Jerk.

I whirled around and Sissy was standing there.

"Oh my God, you totally need to fuck him or you're going to spontaneously combust," she said.

Argh!

Needless to say, my workout nearly kicked my ass. I was so pumped up and Riley was so pissed-off, I pushed myself hard and he ran me ragged. I tried to talk to Riley a couple of times, but he wasn't in a talkative mood. He was in a kick Ava's ass mood, therefore I quit trying to talk to him when I couldn't talk at all because I was breathing too hard.

After we were done, I called Luke, saying only, "We're done," then I hung up on him.

Ha!

We showered and changed into normal clothes and I took my sweet time in the locker room in order to make Luke wait. I did my hair, my makeup and put on a pair of jeans, a cornflower-blue blouse with a silver-thread design on the front, a square neckline and cap sleeves and finished my ensemble with silvery-blue flip-flops, because seriously, Luke was in the picture. I hated him and thought he was a jerk, but I had been crushing on him since I was eight. I wasn't going to look like garbage when he was hanging around.

I breezed through the reception area, but Luke wasn't in the reception area. He was waiting outside in the Range Rover, which made my efforts at "breezing" moot.

We got in the Range Rover and Sissy suggested happily, "I know, let's get some coffee!"

I turned in my seat and glared at her. She grinned at me. Luke took us to Fortnum's.

We got there and everyone was there. Indy, Ally, Daisy, Shirleen, Jules, Jet, Roxie, Vance, some guy who looked a lot like Hank (who I found out was Lee, Indy's fiancé and Luke's boss), and even Matt.

Shirleen took one look at me and announced, "Nope. They haven't done it yet. You're out," she said to Matt and then smiled at me. "I'm still in. I got my money down that you get the business on Monday."

I felt the heat hit my face just as my stomach dropped.

Sissy, to my total disbelief, burst out laughing and asked, "Which days are free? I want in."

Oh... my... God!

"That's it!" I yelled at her. "You aren't my best friend anymore. I'm filing for best friend divorce."

Sissy just kept laughing.

"You must be Sissy. Come here, child, sit by Shirleen. I think we got Wednesday open, but that's nearly a whole *week* after this all started. It ain't good odds," Shirleen informed her.

Everyone was staring at us so I whirled on Luke who was standing behind me. "This is all your fault."

"Babe," he replied, his eyes warm, his tone gentle and affectionate.

Fuckity, fuck, fuck, *fuck*.

I like it when he calls us "babe". It's sweet, Good Ava said.

It isn't sweet, it's HOT, Bad Ava contradicted.

I dropped my head and looked at my toes. They were painted hot pink. I inspected them because if I was thinking about my toenail color I wouldn't think about how my life had gone out of my control.

This wasn't a smart thing to do, letting my guard down when Luke was close. His boots came into my vision very close to my toes and his hand wrapped around the back of my neck. His fingers started to knead my muscles and I lifted my eyes to his.

"You're tight," he said low, eyes no longer just warm but ultra-warm.

"Are you surprised?" I snapped. "My life is total shit. I'm completely stressed out."

His fingers kept kneading, but he also put a different kind of pressure there so that I leaned closer to him. I had to tilt my head back further, and so I didn't topple over, my hands went to his stomach, which, by the way, was hard as a rock.

He tipped his face to mine and murmured, "After we talk tonight, I'll give you a rubdown."

Ho-ly crap.

A rubdown from Lucas Stark. I had barely processed the kiss-and-carry through the living room. I couldn't even begin to contemplate a rubdown.

I felt my nipples tingle.

"I need cookies," I told him to move talk away from rubdowns. "Cookies are the only thing that works on stress."

That and tequila, but I wasn't going to get snockered anywhere near Luke. I lost all inhibitions when I got snockered and that would *not* be good.

The warmth in his eyes was tinged with amusement. "I'll also get you cookies."

"Nutter Butters and Chips Ahoy. Not the soft ones, the hard ones," I ordered, blathering on for some ungodly reason. "And those Pepperidge Farms Milano thingies. And Oreos with double stuff, but not dipped in chocolate, because that's too much of a good thing. And if I have Oreos, I have to have milk. I can't eat Oreos without milk."

He was laughing now, softly. I liked the sound and I liked that I could make him laugh. I'd always liked it when I made him laugh.

Boy, was I screwed.

"Anything else?" he asked.

"I think that'll do it."

His eyes moved from me to across the room then back to me. "Vance and I got shit to do. Stay here. If you go home or anywhere, go with Lee, Matt, Duke or Tex."

I knew Duke. He'd worked at Fortnum's for years and was like Indy's second father. He was an old Harley guy, long gray braid, gray beard, always wearing a black leather vest and a red bandana wrapped around his forehead. I didn't know any Tex.

"Tex?"

"Coffee guy," Luke told me. "You might have one of his coffees. It may soothe the cookie craving."

"*Nothing* soothes the cookie craving."

His face got even closer. "I know something that'll soothe the cookie craving."

Eek!

I walked right into that one.

New topic!

"What are you and Vance gonna do?" I asked.

"Hunt down Vincetti and Dexter."

My already tight muscles turned to steel. "Luke—" I started, but he touched his lips to mine to stop me from speaking.

"Gotta go," he said.

My hands grabbed fistfuls of his t-shirt so he wouldn't move. "Why are you hunting down Noah?"

Without hesitation, he gave me an answer that made the world tilt under my feet.

"He took a piece of you. I'm gonna find him and get it back."

Oh my goodness gracious. I LOVE him, Good Ava trilled.

I hope he kicks Noah's ass. Noah was a rat-bastard, Bad Ava groused.

"Luke," I whispered, not knowing what I was feeling, just knowing it felt really, *really* nice.

He squeezed my neck one last time, then his fingers wrapped around my wrists, pulled them away from his shirt and he said, "Later."

Then he was gone.

I watched the door close behind him and Vance.

"Oowee, now I'm thinking Monday's odds aren't good," Shirleen, eyes on me, declared to the room.

⚜

This was my afternoon:

Tex, the coffee guy, was a huge, blond man with a wild russet beard, even wilder eyes and a very loud voice. And Luke was right, Tex made me a skinny vanilla latte and it was so good, it totally soothed the cookie craving.

Lee and Matt escorted all the girls to Las Delicias and we had Mexican food. Lee, by the way, was absolutely gorgeous and very nice, but even so he kind of scared me. He was intense the way Luke was intense. A tough guy, bad boy so deep to the core, you just knew that you did *not* mess with him.

Luckily, all through lunch no one mentioned when I was going to "get the business". After Las Delicias, Matt followed Sissy and me home. He did a walkthrough of the house before he let us in, stood and chatted for a while, and then he left.

The minute he was gone and we'd locked the door, Sissy turned to me. "You want to talk about Luke?" she asked.

No, I definitely didn't want to talk about Luke. I didn't want to talk about him, think about him or see him ever again (liar, liar, *liar*).

"I need to get some work done," I said.

"Do you want to talk about the kidnapping?"

I shook my head and gave her a small smile. "It wasn't as bad as it sounds."

She stared at me a few beats to assess if I was lying, and since I wasn't (really) she nodded. "Get some work done. I need to call my Dad."

I went upstairs and worked for a couple of hours. Around five o'clock, Sissy walked in and started to sort through her suitcases. A few minutes later there was a knock on the door.

"That must be Dad," Sissy said.

What?

I swiveled around in my chair. "What's your Dad doing here?"

"I'm staying with him for a couple of days."

What, what, *what*?

I got out of my chair and followed her down the stairs. She was carrying one of her smaller suitcases.

"I thought you were staying with me," I said to her.

"I was, now I'm going to stay with my Dad." She was at the door and unlocking it.

"Why?" I asked.

She opened the door so I didn't get my answer. Though I knew my answer.

Shit!

"Hey Dad," she greeted.

Mr. Whitchurch smiled at his daughter and gave her a big hug. I could see straight off he looked worried because of the strain around his mouth. This meant Sissy must have told him what was going on, and I tripled-vowed revenge against Dom because he made Mr. Whitchurch worried.

I'd known Mr. Whitchurch since forever and liked him. It was a bummer when he and Sissy's Mom got divorced and Mrs. Whitchurch moved to Wyoming. Fortunately (for me), Sissy stayed in Denver with her Dad. Mr. Whitchurch and I got along great, most recently because we both hated Dom.

"Beautiful Ava," he said, kissing my cheek. He'd always called me "Beautiful Ava", even when I was Fatty Fatty Four-Eyes.

"Hey Mr. Whitchurch."

"Hear you been takin' care of my daughter."

"Nothing she wouldn't do for me," I told him.

He stared at me and sighed. "Dom's a shithead," he said.

"Dad!" Sissy snapped.

"Well, he is." Mr. Whitchurch was not to be denied.

Sissy glared at him. He took her glare in stride. He'd been getting Sissy Glares for twenty-nine years and he knew she never meant them.

"Um, Mr. Whitchurch," I interrupted the Sissy Glare, "can Sissy and I have a second?"

He looked at me a beat, correctly assessed I had something weighty on my mind and nodded. Then he took her suitcase and walked to his car.

I closed the door and turned to Sissy. "Why didn't you tell me you were going to stay with your Dad?"

"I wasn't going to stay with him."

"Well, you're staying with him," I pointed out.

"Yeah, *now*," she returned.

"Why now?" I asked even though I knew the answer.

That was when she gave me the answer I knew. "I know Noah was an asshole and Dom treats me like shit. I know Dave was weird and Rick was a jerk. I know your Dad broke your heart when he left. I know you don't ever want to get hurt again. But I also know you've been in love with Luke Stark since you were eight years old, and now he looks at you like you're lunch and he missed breakfast *and* dinner."

"Sissy—"

"No, Ava. I know about your vow and I know you like your vibrators and I know you think all men are shit, but there are good ones out there and I think Luke is one of them. I'm not standing in the way of that, and I'm telling it to you straight, girlfriend, neither should you."

Jeez.

Was no one on my side?

I'm not, Bad Ava said. *I want to get MORE of a taste of Luke.*

I'm not either, Good Ava agreed. *I think Luke is lush.*

Argh!

I focused on Sissy. "Seriously, I told you how he's been behaving since I saw him again. He's *not* a normal guy."

Her hands came to either side of my face and she looked me in the eyes. "No, he's not and that's a *good* thing." She pulled my face down to hers so our foreheads were touching. "Call me a hopeless romantic, but I want to see my

115

friend with the guy she's been pining for forever." Her voice dropped to a whisper. "I want that more than anything on this earth."

Oh crap.

Tears filled my eyes, but before I could let them loose her hands moved away. She gave me a smile and a wink, then she was gone.

I locked the door behind her and rested my forehead against it.

"My life is shit," I told the door.

The door had no response.

I went back to work. Half an hour later, my phone rang.

"Yo."

"Babe."

Hell and damnation.

It was Luke. My knees wobbled and I wasn't even standing.

"Did you get my cookies?" I asked.

I heard his soft laughter then, "Not yet."

What was I doing?

I was trying to be cute and funny. I wasn't supposed to be trying to be cute and funny with Luke. I was supposed to drive him away by behaving like a screaming shrew.

Bad, *bad* Ava.

"Why are you calling?" I asked, trying to pull up the Barlow Super Bitch, but it sounded halfhearted.

"I'll pick you up at seven. We're goin' to Lincoln's for dinner, my place to talk afterward. Sissy got anybody who'll stay with her or do I need to arrange company?"

"Sissy's gone."

Silence.

"Luke?"

"Come again?"

"Sissy's gone. She's staying with her Dad for a couple of days."

"You're alone in your house?"

"Well… yeah."

"Fuck," he clipped, sounding pissed.

"What?" I asked.

"Tell me your doors are locked."

"Of course."

"Somebody will be there soon. If it's someone you haven't met, I'll call you to tell you who to expect."

"Luke, I'm sure I'll be fine."

"Right. That's what Lee thought when he left Indy at her house before they let off a car bomb that drew her out and she was kidnapped and nearly taken to Costa Rica."

Oh yeah. I forgot about that.

Belated *eek!*

"Don't open the door to anyone but one of Lee's boys, got me?"

"Okay."

"I'll see you at seven."

Disconnect.

Oh shit.

I didn't even get a chance to argue with him to tell him I wasn't going anywhere with him that night. My mortal danger was getting in the way of me protecting myself from the carnal danger that was Luke.

I mentally shrugged it off and went back to work. I was making some good headway on my deadline, so at least *that* wouldn't be stressing me out along with everything else.

Five minutes after I put down the phone from Luke, I heard a floorboard creak in my office. I swiveled in my chair expecting to see Luke who, incidentally, I noticed pocketed the extra set of keys I gave him last night.

Instead, I saw Dom.

I shot out of the chair and opened my mouth to scream. Dom was on me in a flash and everything went black.

⌖

This was my early evening:

I woke up in the back of Dom's BMW. I'd been in Dom's BMW, like, a gazillion times, but I'd never been lying in the back unable to move my limbs (okay, so a few drunken times I'd been lying in the back, but I'd been able to move my limbs).

The inability to move my limbs freaked me right the hell out.

"Dom," I whispered.

He didn't reply. Maybe he didn't hear me; maybe he was concentrating on driving. I started to get tingling in my extremities, which I took as a good sign, while I felt the car moving, like it was going in long circles. I was getting my strength back and was just able to pull myself into a sitting position when Dom parked, got out of the car then got in the backseat with me.

"Hey, you're awake," he said, settling next to me and turning toward me. Then for some bizarre reason, he pulled my still not-entirely-under-my-control body across his lap and leaned into me.

I blinked. "What did you do to me?" I asked.

"Stun gun. Sorry, Ava, but we need to talk and I didn't want to put up with your mouth."

Stun gun?

Stun gun?

Dom stun-gunned me?

I'd never even seen a stun gun. I saw a video of someone getting Tasered on YouTube (and I might add I was not at all happy that Dom had done that to me), but I'd never seen a stun gun.

What a jerk!

"You stun-gunned me?" I asked.

"We need to talk."

I was getting back to fighting fit (read: could control my hands) and I shoved against him, but his fingers wrapped around my wrists and he held on tight.

"We don't need to talk," I told him then asked, "What are you doing here? Where have you been? The police said you were missing."

His eyes narrowed. "You talked to the police about me?"

"No, the police talked to *me* about *you*. Your living room was shot up, and for some reason a Mr. Zano sent some henchmen to kidnap me and it has something to do with you. Is this Mr. Zano related to you and Uncle Vito?"

A weird look crossed his face before he muttered, "Fuck."

"Fuck is right!" I snapped. "What's going on?"

"I got a problem at work. I'm fixing it," he said, passing it off like it was nothing. "Listen, Ava, you and me—"

"There is no you and me," I interrupted him.

His hands tightened on my wrists. "Listen!" he clipped. "I know you got a problem with the whole Sissy thing—"

118

The whole "Sissy thing"?

Oh... my... *God*.

I vowed quadruple-revenge against Dom, rat-bastard.

He went on, "I'm leaving her."

"You can't leave her, she already left you," I reminded him.

"Then I'll give her a divorce, no contest."

Well this was good news.

"Wonderful. I can't wait to tell her. She'll be over the moon."

Obviously, Dom didn't care that his wife of five years would be thrilled at his granting a no-contest divorce.

I knew this mainly because he said, "Then you and I can hook up."

I blinked again.

Was he insane? Why were men such total assholes?

"We're not hooking up," I snapped.

I watched as his face changed in a soft, sexy way, and I felt a weird moment of sadness. Mainly because he was hot and that look on his face was even hotter. If he'd been a good guy, some woman (read: Sissy) would have been very lucky. Instead, he was a rat-bastard, tore through women's lives and left devastation in his wake.

"You changed. Noah fucked you over and you changed," he said, his voice just as soft and sexy as his face, and I stared at him. "You got this... *attitude.*" His eyes dropped to my mouth. "Fuck, makes me hard just thinkin' about it," he muttered.

Ho-ly *crap*.

I pulled at my wrists. "Let me go!" I shouted.

His fingers tightened and it kinda hurt. "You and me will be good together. Explosive," he told me.

"You've got a screw loose! You're my best friend's husband!"

"Not for long."

"Fuck off!" I yelled.

He yanked me forward by my wrists and kissed me. Dom had a lot of practice at kissing. He was, I noted with some detachment, a good kisser.

I noted this right before I bit his tongue.

He reared back. "Stop doing that!"

"Stop kissing me!" I yelled and began struggling in earnest.

This didn't go well for me. Yes, I had lost seventy-five pounds, but I was not a lightweight. I worked out, was fit and did strength training. But Dom was six foot tall and all lean, compacted muscle. He had me on my back and was on top of me in no time.

This was not good.

It was then I began to panic. "Get off me!"

"Ava, you want it, I want it and I'm gonna fuckin' take it."

"No!" I shouted and bucked.

Then the door was thrown open, and to my utter disbelief, Mr. Kumar leaned in, pounding on Dom's back with both his hands clenched together to do it.

I stared, momentarily stunned.

Mr. Kumar was a Middle Eastern guy who owned a corner store about a block and a half away from my house. Pre-weight loss, I went in there regularly to get provisions. I also went there to have a good old gossip with Mr. and Mrs. Kumar. They were good people. They struggled against the odds to keep their little corner store open and they looked after the neighborhood. Post-weight loss, since the corner store was stocked mostly with junk food, pop and smokes, I went in there just for the gossip and to buy diet soda and gum.

How Mr. Kumar was in Dom's car was beyond me, but I wanted to jump for joy.

"Unhand her!" Mr. Kumar shouted.

"What the fuck?" Dom muttered, letting me go and turning to Mr. Kumar.

I got over feeling stunned and we all started wrestling in the backseat, and because there wasn't a lot of room, fell out the open door and started wrestling on the concrete. Mr. Kumar was a little guy and I guessed on the wrong side of his fifties, and I must repeat, Dom was strong. Dom took both of us on and seemed to be winning.

Dom shoved off Mr. Kumar, who went rolling, then tackled me. I was trying to get up and get some leverage on the situation when he did it. I felt my blouse tear at the neckline as I went down hard on my palms and Dom landed on top of me. I twisted underneath him and lifted my hands up, and finally, after all these years, got the opportunity to scratch his face.

His head shot back as, with satisfaction (it might not be nice, but it was honest), I saw blood form on his cheek and he shouted, "Fuckin' bitch!"

Mr. Kumar jumped on top of him. We wrestled more and I got out from under Dom. As he was trying to subdue Mr. Kumar, I gained my feet. I saw my opportunity and aimed a kick. I missed where I was aiming and kicked him savagely in the gut.

Dom grunted and curled into himself.

I immediately grabbed Mr. Kumar's hand and pulled him up. "Let's go!"

We ran willy-nilly because I had no idea where I was going and Mr. Kumar was freaked way the hell out.

"My car's over here," Mr. Kumar finally said and we ran toward his old, faded-yellow Cadillac Seville.

We stopped at his car and Mr. Kumar fumbled for his keys. "You drive," he said, his hands shaking, his hair and clothing looking exactly like he'd been wrestling with a strong Italian-American at least twenty years his junior. Mr. Kumar handed me the keys and automatically I took them.

"I can't drive, I've been stun-gunned. You drive," I handed him back the keys.

"I can't drive, I'm shaky. We'll get in an accident. You drive," he handed me back the keys.

Out of the corner of my eye I saw Dom running toward us.

"Get in the car!" I shouted, going to the driver's side.

We got in, locked our doors and belted up. Dom at my door trying to open it, I started the car (it took two goes, but I did it) and we shot forward on a screech of tires.

We were in a parking garage, a weirdly vacant parking garage, and I had no idea how to get out.

"Where's the exit? I yelled, turning in a way that seemed to be taking us deeper into the garage.

"I don't know. Let me think. I can't think," Mr. Kumar was still freaked out then he shouted, "There! It says exit! Go left."

I went left.

"No, I mean right," he said.

Shit!

I did a u-ie through some parking spots and went right. We went back up through the parking garage and past Dom's BMW that was going the other way. We went up two levels and I shot out into the street not even looking. A car swerved to avoid me, honking his horn and giving me the finger. I just put the pedal down and the big car roared.

"Where are we?" I asked, looking around, trying to get my bearings.

"I don't know. I saw him carrying you to his car and I told Mrs. Kumar to call Tex and I followed. I didn't pay attention to where we were going. I just paid attention to following you."

"Tex?" I asked.

"Tex, he lives down the block opposite the store from you. He takes care of the neighbors."

I found it bizarre that I would hear the name "Tex" twice in one day when I had never known a Tex in my whole life.

I finally figured out where we were and this made some of my panic and adrenalin subside. I did some deep breathing and pointed us home. I turned onto my block and my stomach clenched.

My street was filled with cars. Big, shiny ones (except for Luke's Porsche and a Crossfire, they weren't big, just shiny). What looked like Eddie's red Ram was there, a black GMC truck, several black Ford Explorers and a black Toyota 4Runner.

I double parked the Caddy (because there were no spaces on the street) right outside my front door and saw, over the roof of Luke's Porsche, the Bad Boy Brigade standing in my front yard, all wearing scary faces. Those faces turned to the Caddy as it stopped. Luke, Lee, Vance, Hank, Eddie, Matt, Mace and, what I realized was not coincidental, Tex, the wild-eyed coffee guy from Fortnum's.

"Uh-oh," I said.

Chapter 9

Feeling Fine, Feeling Loose

Mr. Kumar and I got out of the car as Luke detached from the Bad Boy Bunch, and I met him on the sidewalk.

I tilted my head back to look at him and said softly, "Seems I got kidnapped again."

His mouth got tight and his eyes did a body scan. I looked down at myself.

Blouse torn, scrapes on my belatedly stinging palms, and what appeared to be smears of blood on the skin of my chest (this, I hoped, was Dom's).

"You all right?" Luke asked, and my eyes moved back to his.

"Yeah," I said.

"Please tell me that isn't your blood."

It was then I did something ultra-stupid.

The something ultra-stupid I did was say, "It's Dom's."

It seemed Luke sucked in every molecule of oxygen in the Denver Metro area when he did a swift intake of breath. With one look at his face it would not have surprised me if he had walked to his Porsche in Incredible Hulk style, picked it up and hurled it down the street.

Mr. Kumar stood beside us. "I saw him carry her out of the house," he shared, and Luke and my eyes turned to Mr. Kumar as the Bad Boys gathered around us. "She was unconscious and I knew something was wrong. I followed in my car and when they stopped I wanted to wait for Tex and was about to call on my cell, but I didn't know where we were." Everyone watched him talk and he looked around, nervous at being the center of attention. "I was going to call the police, but then he started kissing her and Ava didn't like it and I knew…"

Oh shit.

Luke's eyes sliced to me.

Oh *shit!*

"I had to do something," Mr. Kumar finished.

Luke was still looking at me. Or more to the point, scowling at me in a very scary way.

"Um…" I said to him, lifting my hand to do the finger and thumb half-an-inch-apart gesture again. "There might be a *wee bit* of my troubles I haven't shared."

I watched, somewhat fascinated, as Luke pulled in his very nice lower lip and bit it with his equally nice, straight, white teeth. The Bad Boy Brigade all looked at each other with knowing, equally (almost) pissed-off in male camaraderie faces and they took a step back.

Then Luke grabbed my upraised wrist, yanked me up my walk and into my house.

"Luke!" I yelled.

He ignored me, walked up the stairs and took me to the bathroom where we stopped.

"Where's your first aid?" he asked.

I stared at him, surprised at his question, thinking he was going to lay into me. "What?" I asked back.

"First aid. Your palms."

Oh. My palms.

"Closet," I told him, motioning with my hand to the closet door.

He walked to the bathroom closet and pulled out the first aid kit. He opened it, sorted through it, found what he wanted and dragged me to the sink.

"Wash your hands," he ordered.

I did what I was told, finding his behavior somewhat intriguing. I could tell (hell, anyone could tell) he was angry, but he was controlling it and taking care of me.

Hmm.

He's very nice. And you can tell he's mad, but he's still being lovely. I like that, Good Ava informed me.

He's hot when he's all pissed-off-but-controlling-it. Jump him! Bad Ava suggested.

I blinked away my advice angels, finished with my hands and buried Luke's most recent behavior right alongside all the rest of it.

He'd gone back to the closet and nabbed a clean hand towel. He tossed it to me and I dried my hands carefully while he took a washcloth, wet it and went to work on the blood on my chest.

"Luke."

"Quiet."

I shut my mouth. I knew what Luke's "quiet" meant when said in that tone and I didn't want a repeat of Hard Angry Kiss.

He finished wiping off the blood, took the towel from my hands, threw them both in the sink and wiped at my scrapes with an alcohol swab. I sucked in breath at the sting, but he kept going, albeit gently.

He tossed the swab in the trash and then looked at me. "Now. Share."

I didn't have to ask what he meant. I took in a deep breath.

"Well..." I started and stopped, not certain how to proceed.

Luke got close, his patience visibly waning. "Ava."

"All right," I said and leaned back. Then I told him the story of Dom flirting, Dom touching, Dom cornering me in the kitchen and that being the reason Sissy left him. I told him about Dom's threat to "get what I want". I finished on a description of the last forty-five minutes.

Luke was silent after I stopped talking. His face was hard, but I saw his eyes were working. I also saw his jaw was working, too, clenching and unclenching, and I did not take this as a good sign. I held my breath while this happened.

Finally he said, "Pack a bag."

"Excuse me?" I asked on a gush of air.

"Pack a bag."

"What? Why?"

"You're movin' in with me."

My eyes bugged out. "What? Why?" I repeated.

"Just do it."

Ho-ly *shit*.

Lee had made Indy stay with him to keep her safe when she was being shot at and kidnapped. He moved into her duplex after it was over and now they were getting married. Eddie had also made Jet move in with him to keep her safe. He never let her move out and she had just bought a new blender. Roxie had stayed with Hank during her troubles because, at the time, she lived in Chicago. After she was safe, she had decided to move to Denver to be with Hank, thinking to move into an apartment for six months to "see how it went" but he had talked her into moving in with him. Now she was entering his dog into a Frisbee competition.

I felt panic seize my chest. "I'm not moving in with you."

"You're movin' in with me."

"I'm not."

He reached behind his back then his arm came forward and I saw the cuffs.

Oh no.

I started to take off, but didn't even get by him. He whirled me back around, hand wrapped around my upper arm. I yanked at my arm, but he grabbed my wrist and slapped the bracelet on me and then he slapped the other bracelet on him.

"I can't believe you cuffed me to you again!" I shouted.

"Now, *we're* packing."

"I'm not moving in with you." I pulled back, putting all my weight into it as he started walking. He dragged me, and all my weight, into the bedroom.

"This is too much," I snapped as he went to the closet and threw open the door.

He turned to me. "Pack."

"I have my office here. I have my yoga mat here. I can't move out," I babbled.

He jerked on our cuffed hands and I flew forward, slamming into him.

His arms went around me (thus taking one of my arms and twisting it behind my back) and he held on tight, his face dipping to mine.

"Since I seem to have to repeat myself every time I need to get something through to you, I'll keep doin' it." His eyes were shining dangerously and it was clear his patience was at an end.

Eek.

"First," he continued, "I'm not gonna fuck around with this shit. You've been kidnapped twice in two days and shot at. As of now that shit is *over*. My building is secure, your house is not. You're movin' in, end of discussion. Second, I want you in my bed. I want you to look at me the way you looked at me after our first kiss, but I want you to do it when my cock is buried inside you. Third, you owe me and you're gonna pay. The first one is happening now. The last two are gonna happen tonight. Do you understand me?"

I understood him. I *so* understood him.

I stared at him. My chest seemed to have expanded and my eyes seemed frozen in a wide-open position. Unable to speak after what he'd just said, I nodded.

"Good," he clipped. "Now, pack."

At that juncture, I thought it prudent to pack.

So I packed.

⌐⊫

I was drunk.

I knew it wasn't smart, but I didn't care. I'd been kidnapped (twice), wrestled with my best friend's husband in a parking garage and moved in with Luke. I needed to get drunk.

Screw the consequences.

⌐⊫

At my house I packed. Luke uncuffed me so I could do it.

This was after, still attached to him, I threw a few things in a bag and muttered, "Done."

He looked at the bag and back at me and demanded, "More."

I sighed. He uncuffed me and I packed more.

We toted my two suitcases (and my yoga mat) out to his Porsche. The Bad Boy Bunch was still hanging around outside, likely for moral support. They all looked at Luke with understanding and at me with impatience. All except Tex, who was grinning at me like the crazy guy I was thinking he was.

For some reason, even though I didn't know him (at all), he put his big hand on the top of my head and said, "Been a long time since we had some excitement, darlin'."

Luke glared at him, obviously not sharing in Tex's excitement. Tex chuckled as he took his hand from my head.

While I thanked Mr. Kumar for saving me from dastardly Dom, Luke talked to Matt, who peeled off and went back into my house.

"What's he doing?" I asked as Luke led me to the Porsche.

"Your computer," Luke said.

Shit.

He had it all covered. I was so screwed.

We went to his place and dumped my stuff. I unpacked my toiletries in the bathroom, changed out of my torn blouse and cleaned up.

Then he took me to Lincoln's Road House, a no-frills biker bar that was located on a slip road off I-25. They had great food, great atmosphere and, usually, great music. It was Saturday night and a band was playing when we got there. Luke glared a couple of guys who were hanging out but not eating away from a table. He planted my ass on a stool and got menus.

I could tell he was still pissed. I could also tell he was still controlling it.

He got me a Fat Tire beer and I was reading the menu (Luke was not, he likely knew it by heart) when Jules and Vance joined us.

I could have done a cartwheel of joy. Saved from Luke's bad attitude by my ex-vigilante current-social worker new friend and her bounty hunter boyfriend.

We all ordered food and we ate.

I was trying very hard not to think about what Luke said in my bedroom. I was scared to death about that night. No, I was scared to death about everything. Everything about Luke and everything about my life. I couldn't deal, not openly, so I buried it, and as I buried each and every word he said and all that had happened the last two days, I got more and more stressed out.

Therefore, when Hank and Roxie joined us and Daisy and Shirleen hit our party, and then Tex ambled in, I decided, fuck it.

Time to party.

So I got drunk.

"How's it goin', sugar?" Daisy asked me, blue eyes soft with concern, when all the girls were shoulder-to-shoulder in the tiny bathroom, breaking the seal and reapplying lipstick.

I knew she was likely asking if I was okay about Kidnapping Part Two, but I ignored that and got to the important stuff.

"I moved in with Luke this afternoon," I told her and she sucked in breath, her eyes slid to Shirleen and they both smiled at each other.

I was in my Good Drunk Zone, feeling fine, feeling loose, feeling *talkative,* which was, along with losing my inhibitions, another bad habit I had when I was tipsy.

"This is *not* good. You would *not* believe what he said to me," I announced.

Roxie and Jules got close, and even though I barely knew any of them, I told them about the latest incident and I did so in great detail. There was more sucking in of breath then more smiles.

"Shit. I thought some of the stuff that Vance said to you was Sexy Hot Boy Hot, but Luke's got him beat by a mile," Daisy told Jules.

"I'd *pay* a man to talk to me that way," Shirleen put in.

"He's a jerk," I said happily, sounding as if this was a good thing and applying shiny lip gloss to my lips in the mirror. "I hate him." Again, this was said with drunken good cheer and all the girls looked at each other, lips tipped up at the ends. "I'm moving to Wyoming the first chance I get. I'm moving in with Sissy's mother, even if Sissy isn't there anymore. Mrs. Whitchurch likes me and she owns a shotgun on account of the bears that are always going through her trash."

Daisy gave a tinkly-bell laugh.

Jules came up behind me in the mirror. "During my thing, I convinced myself I was moving to Nicaragua," she shared.

"Nicaragua sounds good, but it's filled with those Latin-lover types. I'm trying to get *away* from macho men."

She pressed her lips together like she was trying not to laugh and glanced at Roxie. I ignored them and turned, screwing on the cap to my lip gloss. I heard the band strike up again after a break and I instantly got the best idea, I decided at that moment, that I'd ever had *in my life*.

So of course I had to share and I shouted, "Let's dance!"

I shoved my lip gloss in my pocket and charged out the door through the bar right by the table where all the Bad Boys were sitting and straight to the dance floor. The Girl Gang followed me.

I loved music and I loved to dance. There were times in my life when Sissy and I went out and I didn't drink a drop, just danced like a lunatic. Even when I was Fatty Fatty Four-Eyes I was the kind of person who got lost in the music and didn't care who was watching. Now, especially as I was heading towards three sheets to the wind, I let it all hang out.

Of course, I'd never been to a club where Luke could see me, but I was feeling fine, feeling loose, and as the girls and I moved in our Girlie Dance Circle, I was having the time of my life.

After a few songs I shouted the latest, greatest idea I ever had in my life, "Shots!" Then I peeled off and went to the bar.

The place was packed and the bar was three deep. Two guys saw me and shifted to the side to let me through. I smiled at them huge and bellied up to the bar.

129

"Hey, thanks," I said, still throwing a smile over my shoulder.

"Don't mention it, darlin'," one of them replied.

It took a few minutes, but a bartender made it to me.

"I want…" I turned to the dance floor and counted my Girl Gang membership. "Five shots of tequila. Don't bother with the lime. We're Rock Chicks, we can hack it," I informed him.

The guy behind me chuckled. I gave him another over the shoulder grin, not exactly knowing what he found funny, but also not caring. If he was in a good mood then I thought it was rude not to share in his good mood.

"Outta my way," I heard, and the crowd around me parted without comment. This was somewhat unusual, seeing as we were at a biker bar and someone pushing through the crowd was normally frowned upon. I understood why there was no comment when Wild Man Tex moved in beside me. Not many people would stand in Wild Man's way.

"Hey Tex. How ya doin'?" I asked, as if we had known each other all our lives and he was my best friend in the whole world.

He looked at me then he commented, "Darlin', you're shitfaced."

I leaned into him. "Yeah. Isn't it *great?*"

He shook his head and grinned but said, "I don't mean to rain on your parade. You deserve a good night after a coupla kindnappin's, but you best be watchin' your step. Your man ain't likin' what he's seein' and the atmosphere is gettin' *tense.*"

I blinked at him. "My man?"

"Luke," Tex told me.

I swung my head around and looked at Luke. He was watching me and it appeared Tex was right, he didn't seem happy.

I turned back to Tex. "He isn't my man."

"Girl, it don't matter you don't think he is, *he* thinks he is. Therefore, in Badass Motherfucker Land, that means *he is.*"

I laughed and waved my hand between us, dismissing Tex's warning as the bartender set the shots in front of me.

"Everything will be okay," I assured Tex.

Tex held up a bill to the bartender for my drinks and I smiled at him. I gathered all the shots in two hands, but Tex grabbed my elbow and leaned in before I moved away.

"One more thing," Tex said.

I stopped and looked up at him. It registered in my drunken state that he looked ultra-serious.

"Yeah?" I asked.

"Long as things are under the boys' control, excitement is good, excitement is fun. We all get a buzz off it. Last time, though, it got out of the boys' control and we almost lost Jules."

Part of my fine and loose feeling slid away as Tex kept staring at me intently.

"Be smart. These boys know what they're doin' and they'll do all they can to keep you safe as long as you stay smart. Don't make it hard on 'em. They got enough to worry about on a day-to-day basis without someone one of 'em cares about doin' stupid shit and puttin' her ass on the line. Got me?" Tex asked.

I swallowed. Then I nodded.

He let go of my elbow and said, "Have fun."

Shit.

I headed back to the Girl Gang, handed out the shots, and standing in our circle, we threw them back. Mine played double duty of helping me erase my latest scary-assed conversation, most especially the part about Tex telling me I was someone Luke "cares about".

I shook it off as the band started playing "Ding Dong Daddy". Daisy threw her hands up in the air and shouted, "That's what I'm talkin' about, sister!" and I was immediately back to feeling fine and loose.

Three songs later, I was giggling at Roxie, who was pretending to dance outrageously sexy and throwing kissy-faces at Hank when a waitress came up to me and handed me a shot.

"Bass," she said, jerking her head toward the bass player.

"Thanks," I muttered and took the glass, my eyes moving to the bass player, who, I noted, was watching me. The minute my eyes hit his, he smiled at me. I smiled back, lifted my glass in a thank you salute, sniffed the shot (tequila) and tossed it back.

I no sooner had my head straightened when my wrist was seized and I was dragged across the dance floor.

"What the——?" I started to say, but Luke pulled me to a halt, grabbed my purse from the table and threw it at me. I caught it and noticed the Bad Boys were all glaring at me unhappily and I blinked at them in confusion. Luke tore the shot glass out of my hand, crashed it to the table and dragged me out of the bar.

"Hey! I was having fun!" I yelled at his back.

He stopped at the Porsche and yanked me around, my back to it, him in front of me, and he closed in until I felt car behind me and had nowhere to retreat.

Then he growled, "I noticed."

"Why'd you drag me out of there?"

"We're goin' home."

It was then I got a good look at him.

"Are you angry?" I asked stupidly, because it was clear he was not only angry, he was *angry*.

"You've got to be fuckin' shittin' me," he clipped.

"What?"

He moved around me to open the door, but being drunk and not thinking clearly (if I was thinking clearly I would have run screaming into the night), I moved into his face.

"What?" I asked again.

"Get in the car."

"What?"

"Jesus. I want to think you aren't playin' games, but I know you're fuckin' playin' games. Nobody's that stupid."

My fine and loose feeling slipped a notch, mainly because, again, it felt like he'd slapped me across the face.

He watched my face change in the streetlight.

"I'm not stupid," I whispered.

He got close and backed me against the car again. I went, my head tilted back to look at him, my feelings still smarting from his comment.

"So you're sayin' you don't know that every fuckin' guy's dick is hard from watchin' you move. Christ, give you a pole and put you in a g-string, you wouldn't have been more effective."

My mouth dropped open. Then I snapped it shut.

"I was just dancing," I told him.

"Right."

"I was."

He watched me but stayed silent.

"I like to dance," I said softly. "I was just dancing."

He kept watching me and it seemed like he did this for a long time. Finally, his hand came to my neck with his thumb out to touch my jaw.

"Jesus, you aren't lyin'," he muttered.

I shook my head because no, I wasn't lying. Instead, I was freaking out about what he said.

"I'm never going to dance again," I said quietly to myself on a little tremble, so upset at the thought of people watching me, *men* watching me and having that reaction, that I didn't even care I was quoting bad eighties music. Serious yuck.

"Ava."

My eyes had slid to the side and they came back to Luke. "Men suck," I whispered. "They take everything. *Everything.*"

Before he could respond, I slid out from between him and the car and turned to the door. He didn't say a word just bleeped the locks. I opened my door and got in. He shut it for me, got in on his side and we glided out into the street.

I watched Denver pass me as Luke took us to his loft. Neither of us spoke. I was still drunk and I wanted to be happy, but I couldn't stop the dark "all men are bastards" thoughts from flooding my head.

He parked and we took the elevator to his loft. He switched on the lamps and I went directly to the Triumph t-shirt which was sitting, folded, on the barstool where I left it two days ago. I dumped my purse on the bar, grabbed the tee and walked to the bathroom.

"I'm going to bed," I announced and then walked into the bathroom.

I shut the door, took out my contacts, got ready for bed, put on my glasses and walked out. I dumped my clothes on my suitcases and headed toward the bed.

I saw that Luke was in the kitchen. I grabbed a pillow and walked to the couch. I threw the pillow down, threw myself on the couch and settled on my side. I was going to sleep there, without a blanket if I had to, I didn't care.

On this thought, Luke's legs came into my vision. I looked up. He was holding a glass of water out to me.

"What's that?"

"Ibuprofen and water. Take it, you'll need it for the morning."

"I don't get hangovers," I informed him, again not lying. I had to be far drunker than I was to get a hangover. Sissy called it my gift. She got a hangover after two beers.

"Take it," he demanded.

I was in no mood to argue. I was in the mood to go to sleep for fifty years, wake up an old maid and live out my life in a nursing home with my only excitement being Friday Night Bingo.

I sat up, took the pills he had in his fist and drank the water. When I was done, he pulled the empty glass from my hand and put it on the coffee table. Then he came back to me, and I kid you not, picked me up (again!). He turned and sat on the couch, settling me in his lap, his arms around me.

"Luke, it really bugs me when you haul me around," I told him, sounding bitchy.

He ignored my bitchiness. "We're gonna talk."

Right then, still drunk and feeling in a shitty mood, I thought this was an *excellent* idea.

"Good. I have a few things to say," I informed him.

He stared at me a beat before he invited, "Shoot."

"First, I'm confiscating this t-shirt," I announced.

He kept staring at me. Then he asked, "Come again?"

"From this point on, your Triumph tee is now *my* Triumph tee," I declared.

His lips did that twitch thing like he was trying not to laugh.

I crossed my arms. "I'm being perfectly serious."

"Babe, I'll make you a deal. As long as you share my bed, the t-shirt is yours."

"No. The t-shirt is mine *forever*," I countered.

He shook his head. "You're not sharin' my bed, the tee stays here."

"I'll give you twenty-five dollars for it," I started to haggle.

The lip twitch came back and it looked like he was losing his battle at biting back his smile. "No," he said.

"Fifty."

"No."

"One hundred dollars!" I cried a little loudly because I had never paid a hundred dollars for a t-shirt in my life and I was worried he would accept.

"I gave you an offer, it's the only one you're gonna get."

"Okay then, I'll steal it," I blabbed.

His body started shaking and I was pretty sure it was with silent laughter. "Probably shouldn't tell me your plan to steal my tee," he advised.

"Forget I said anything," I told him.

He shook his head, still silently laughing, and when he was done, his arms got a little tighter. "Now we're talkin' about what I want to talk about."

"I'm not finished."

"We'll get back to your shit later."

I made a "harrumph" sound and glared at him.

"You owe me," he said (again).

"I don't—"

He interrupted me, "Your first payment is to tell me who else got a piece of you."

Was that it?

I thought he was going to make me clean his bathroom with a toothbrush or something else. Something that required me being naked, but I didn't want to think thoughts of being naked with Luke. Not when I was sitting in his lap, on his couch, in his loft, wearing his t-shirt. Not *ever*.

"Okay," I agreed happily.

I shuffled my bottom in his lap, settling in, and I began.

"There was Dave. He was a sex pervert. Wanted me to go to swinger parties with him and had a huge collection of porn. He tried to convince me this was perfectly normal, which, I'll grant it is, but it wasn't my scene. He ignored me telling him it wasn't my scene and he got pushy, then he got pouty. Then he got angry, then he started being mean to me so I kicked him out."

Luke was silent, but he moved. He fell to his side and stretched out on the couch. During this he took me with him. I was so intent on my story, his actions barely registered and I just stretched out, too.

"Before him, there was Rick. He was hot. Seriously. He knew it though. He cheated on me right off the bat, wasn't good at hiding it, probably because he knew I'd put up with it. I did, because I was so into him, but warned him not to do it again, full of piss and vinegar and thinking he just strayed. He did it again, I found out again we had a rip-roarin' and he promised never to do it again. Which, in like a month, he did. Three strikes, he was out."

Luke was still silent, and since I was sharing (and still drunk) I didn't notice that, even in his silence, he was communicating to me, communicating something that should have made me keep my mouth shut. He moved under me like he did in bed so that for a few seconds I was on top of him. Then he slid to his side so his back was to the room, mine to the couch. Through all this, I kept blabbing.

"Then there's Dom, you know about him. Then there's my sister Marilyn's *first* husband, who was a slimeball cheat and a drunk. I think he might have slapped her around a bit, but she would never say. I saw her once with a black eye and she said she fell down the stairs. A, they didn't have stairs at their house and B, how do you get a black eye by falling down stairs?"

Luke didn't answer. I kept gabbing.

"Then there's Marilyn's *second* husband, who made her first husband look like a choirboy. *Total* slimeball. I don't like Marilyn 'cause she's kind of a bitch, but I truly think she loved her first husband and it hurt when he fucked her over. She's my sister. Even though I don't want to hurt, I hurt when she hurts. Do you know what I mean?"

I didn't wait for him to reply (not that he would have). I was on a roll so I just kept talking.

"Then there's Dad, you know all about that. He never came back. Never called, never sent a card, nothing. Not when I turned sixteen, when I graduated from high school or college, nothing. Disappeared. Gone."

I realized belatedly where I was and what position I was in, but I didn't care. It was rather comfy, really, so I went on.

"Noah was hot, too. Really handsome, and I thought totally into me. He was super sweet, bought me flowers, shit like that. Acted like there was no other woman in the world but me. At first I wasn't into him, after Dave, well, you can guess. But he worked at it hard, convinced me he was a good guy. I fell for it. All that time, he was planning on screwing me over. Not nice. He left, cleaning me out, and still *I* felt like a moron. Rat-bastard."

I sighed, searching my memory banks for more jerks to dredge up. I found I was empty, looked Luke in the eyes and decided it was time to sum up.

"So you see, men suck. They're all jerks. I vowed never to get caught up with one again. Ever. Ever. *Ever.* That brings us to now. That's why you and I can't get together, because I'm not going through that again. Once I help Sissy get revenge on Dominic Dickhead, no more men in my life, ever. And that's also why you need to send me an invoice. I don't mind paying, really. Noah didn't get the inheritance money Aunt Ella gave me. I'm not loaded, but I'm also not hurting—"

"Babe," Luke finally spoke.

"What?" I asked.

"You can shut up now."

I blinked then I thought maybe that was a good thing. "Okay," I agreed. Then I asked, "So, are we square?"

"You owed me triple. That was the first part. I'm gonna tell you the next part, and I'm keepin' one in reserve."

"What's next?" I asked, thinking this was easy. In fact, thinking that hadn't been hard at all. I thought it would be, but after six Fat Tires and two shots of tequila, it had been totally cool.

Luke's arms, which had been loosely holding me, tightened so I was pressed to him full frontal. He also threw his thigh over my legs. Normally, I would have seen this as the warning sign it was. After six Fat Tires and two shots of tequila, I missed it.

Then he spoke. "The next part you pay is letting me cuff you naked to my bed and you stay that way while I eat you 'til you come, and then fuck you 'til you come again."

"Holy shit," I breathed aloud, which was a feat, considering the fact that my lungs had seized.

He didn't allow me to process his demand. He kept talking.

"Not tonight, not when you're shitfaced. I want you clearheaded when I do that to you. Tonight, after your rubdown, I'll fuck you normally. Tonight, I want your hands and mouth on me."

It took me a few seconds to pull myself out of the complete and utter shock his brutally honest (and unbelievably sexy, if my hard nipples had anything to say about it) words caused.

Not to mention this was Luke Stark talking to *me*, Fatty Fatty Four-eyed Ava Barlow. It was so incomprehensible he would say such things I thought there was a good possibility that Satan had ordered a fur coat.

"Didn't you hear anything I just said?" I asked.

"I heard it."

"No more men."

"I heard it."

"That includes you."

"Did you bring lotion with you?"

I shook my head at what I thought was his strange question. I tried to pull away and didn't get anywhere. So, I narrowed my eyes. "Why do you want to know?"

"Rubdown."

"Luke, you aren't rubbing me down."

His hands moved. One went up my back, his fingers sifting into my hair, one went down to rest on my bottom.

"We could go straight to the sex." His mouth came to mine, but his eyes were open and watching me. I saw the warmth there, but there was something else, something I couldn't put a finger on, something assessing. Before I could figure it out, he continued, "That will work out the kinks."

"I'm sleeping on the couch."

"You're sleeping beside me."

"I'm sleeping on the couch."

"Then we'll sleep here. And, if you want, we'll fuck here, too."

"Luke!" I yanked my body backward, found nothing but the very solid couch hampering any retreat, and realized too late I was in a very dangerous position.

"Ava, this is what's gonna happen," Luke said in a firm voice.

Uh-oh.

I can't WAIT to see what he says next, Bad Ava was nearly drooling.

Mm, Good Ava mumbled dreamily.

"You're gonna get your lotion and I'm gonna work out the stress in your back. Then, together, were gonna work out the tension of the last couple of days. Tomorrow, or however long it takes, I'm gonna deal with Vincetti and Dexter. You want a shot at Dexter when I find him, your call. We'll have him in a safe place where you can say, or do, whatever you want to him, and I'll be there if you need me when you do it. After that, you and I are gonna ride this out, see where it takes us. If you're even close to the promise you gave me this morning, or what you showed on the dance floor tonight, that's gonna take a while. We'll see how it goes. Got that?"

He had it all figured out and apparently he didn't think I had a choice.

Fuck that.

I didn't even try to count to ten, I just pushed against him. "No, I do not *have* that. You can't just pick up Noah and…" I stopped and glared at him. "What are you going to do when you pick up Noah?"

"I'm gonna tell him who I am and what I am to you, and then I'm gonna beat the shit out of him."

I quit pushing and stared. I would have said it was impossible for him to shock me further, but there it was.

"You can't do that," I whispered.

"I can."

"You can't."

"Ava, this isn't up for discussion."

"I don't even want you to do that."

"It isn't for you to say. He took somethin' that was mine. I'm gettin' it back."

Oh… my… God.

"You're nuts!" I cried. "I'm not yours. I haven't even *seen* you in five years."

"You've been mine since you were eight."

That cut right to the bone.

Crapity, crap, crap, *crap*.

To hide it, I shoved hard. He rocked back an inch, moved forward and his arms got so tight they crushed me to him.

"I'm not yours. I'm not anyone's ever again!" I shouted in his face, getting pissed instead of scared, because pissed was a whole lot better place to be. "And I'm not paying the second part of your deal. No way. No fucking way."

"All right, then you pay by telling me why you didn't pick up my calls or see me after my father's funeral. That was before all the shit went down with those fuckin' guys takin' you away, piece by piece. I wanna hear why you stood by my father's grave and made me a promise and days later you reneged."

My mouth snapped shut and my body went statue-still.

Okay, then there was really, really, *really* no way I was going to tell him *that*. I was never going to tell him it embarrassed me that he held me when I was Fatty Fatty Four-Eyes. No way I was going to tell him that I lost weight, dyed my hair and got contacts because I'd been in love with him since I was eight (he wasn't wrong about me being his, but I wasn't going to tell *him* that, either) and I wanted him to notice me.

No way in hell.

In fact, there was *so* no way in hell that I made a split-second, dangerous decision that would protect that knowledge forever.

"I'll get the lotion," I told him.

He stared at me a beat then pressed his lips together and tilted his chin up looking for patience. His eyes came back to me.

"Jesus, you're a pain in the ass," he said.

"Are we doing this or what?" I asked, sounding bitchy, which was a relief, considering I *felt* hysterical, but I didn't want Luke to know that.

His arms went loose. I pushed up, scrambled over him, got to my feet and I shot to the bathroom like a rocket.

Chapter 10

Mrs. Stark

It was the dead of night when Luke moved me, arms around me, up and over him to his other side. He hooked my leg over his hip and I snuggled in.

"You're nuts," I mumbled into his throat.

Then I went back to sleep.

⊰⊱

I woke up alone in Luke's bed.

I stared at the pillowcase, quiet, still, listening, and at the same time assessing my situation. I heard the shower. I took a deep breath, rolled on my stomach, pulled Luke's pillow into my belly and held it tight.

Last night, I'd dodged the bullet. As I lay in Luke's bed thinking back, I decided this was because I was on an adrenaline crash after Dom's kidnapping, because I was drunk, but most especially because Luke gave really great rubdowns.

I got the lotion, gave it to Luke, took off my glasses and lay down on my belly, all bitch attitude, like a rubdown from Luke was akin to torture in an iron maiden. Just to be difficult, I kept on my tee and my panties (which, thank *God,* were mocha-colored satin hipsters with a load of beige lace and not ratty old ones that sagged at the ass). Luke pushed up the tee, up, up until I was forced to do a back arch and he whipped it over my head. He warmed the lotion in his hands and went to work on me.

I wanted to stay tense, just to be contrary, but I couldn't. His hands were strong and you could tell he'd done this before (another thought I clung to, telling myself it proved he was a womanizing rat-bastard). He went right to the kinks and worked them out. This was not a sensual massage to get me turned on. He genuinely was trying to relieve my stress.

When I wasn't freaked out that I was lying, in my undies, in Lucas Stark's bed (which was, at the beginning, my prevailing thought), I found this show of kindness disturbing, but in a good way. I was trying very hard to hold on to thoughts of him being an ultra-pushy, unbelievably blunt, tough guy, macho man, and Sandra Whoever-She-Was crying into her M&Ms. But it was hard when underneath everything Luke did it seemed like he truly was a nice guy trying to protect me and keep me safe, but in an ultra-pushy, unbelievably blunt, tough guy, macho man way.

Then again, I thought that about Rick when he promised not to cheat on me. And Noah, when he worked so hard to win me before screwing me over. And mostly my Dad, when I thought it was him and me against the Barlow Super Bitches and he left me.

Slowly, as Luke worked at my back, all these thoughts sifted out of my head and I fell asleep.

That was it.

Except for Luke's weird habit of rolling me to the other side of the bed every night, all we did was sleep.

I pulled the covers to my neck and was about to move to my second mental topic, how to successfully flee to Wyoming, when the bathroom door opened. That was when I realized my mistake. I should have gotten up and got dressed.

Instead, like the big dork I was, I lay in bed and let my mind wander, so much so I hadn't even heard the shower go off.

Fuckity, fuck, fuck, *fuck*.

When was I going to *learn?*

I reviewed my options, waited for Good Ava and Bad Ava to give their input (they were still sleeping, which figured. Always chattering away when you didn't want them to, and never there when you needed them) and decided to pretend that I was still asleep. In fact, if I was good at it, maybe Luke would get sick of waiting and go out and hunt down my ex-boyfriends and beat the shit of them while I escaped and drove to Wyoming.

I was putting this plan into action, eyes closed, when I felt the bed depress as Luke sat on it.

Uh-oh.

I continued to feign sleep. The covers slid down my body.

Ee-yikes!

Luke may have felt gentlemanly enough to let me sleep after his rubdown, but he hadn't been gentlemanly enough to put my tee back on me. Therefore, I was wearing nothing but my satin panties.

First, I had a silent freak out that I slept next to Luke mostly naked. Then I had a silent freak out that he could see most of my body. I didn't know what Jennifer Aniston looked like naked (and didn't want to know) and I was probably far off that mark, but Riley hadn't done badly with me. Still, I wasn't ready for this.

Un-unh.

No way.

Luckily, I had the pillow pressed to my belly so all he could see was my naked back. Covers gone, the bed moved and I felt heat against my back as Luke settled in. This was not getting any better.

Then I was turned.

Seriously not better.

I held the pillow close to me like a shield, still pretending to sleep. Luke tugged it gently, and I had to make the decision whether or not to let it go. If I held on to it for dear life like I wanted to, he'd know I was awake which would foil my plan.

I let it go.

Second string defense, I moved my body into his to cover myself, pressing my chest to his, tucking my face into his throat and snuggling in, in the hopes that he would think I was giving him a sleep cuddle.

This was a bad idea. I knew it the minute my mostly naked body hit his bare chest. It felt nice, as in ultra-nice.

Shit.

"Ava," he called my name softly, his arms around me, one hand sliding up my back, fingers of the other hand trailing across the top, lacy edge of my underwear.

I kept pretending to sleep. This was hard. The trailing touch at my underwear felt good.

His fingers went into my hair at the back of my head. "Babe, wake up."

Hmm.

I couldn't ignore him much longer. He would think I was dead.

I was realizing my plan was going south, way south, when his fingers sifted through my hair a few inches then twisted around it. I felt his hand fist and my head was pulled back gently.

Not good.

I felt his mouth against mine.

Worse!

"Babe," he said against my lips, and I couldn't pull it off anymore. Slowly, I opened my eyes.

As his lips were against mine, I was close enough to see, even without my contacts, his eyes were ink.

"Hey," I whispered, and luckily my voice sounded sleepy.

"Hey," he said against my mouth, and something about that soft word, said by Luke, in his bed, in the morning, against my mouth made me melt.

When my body pressed deeper into him, his eyes went molten and that was it. No more stall tactics. I was going to be screwed, literally.

He kissed me. Maybe I should have pushed it, torn away and stood firm to my vows. But he was a seriously good kisser.

Added to that, our mostly naked bodies were pressed up against each other. His chest hair felt sexy-rough against my breasts and his hand at my underwear was keeping up the lovely torture.

And this was Lucas Stark and he had always, in my heart, been my special guy.

I gave up the ghost and kissed him back. When I did, he groaned into my mouth, rolling me to my back, him on top of me. The groan sounded and felt good. So good I wrapped my arms around him and started to explore with my hands, wanting to make him do it again.

This was when I discovered he was naked, mainly because my fingers drifted over his tight ass.

Holy cramoly.

Nice.

His head came up and I focused on him, barely. I was half in a Luke Lip Fog and half in a Luke Tight Ass Fog. I knew my eyes were hooded and I was already breathing heavily.

"Christ," he muttered. "You look like that after I kiss you, what are you gonna look like when I make you come?"

My hands slid up his back and I answered him, even though his question wasn't one you answered.

"I don't know," I whispered.

"Let's find out," he murmured against my mouth.

I found myself thinking that was a *great* idea.

Then Luke got down to "giving me the business".

I discovered in short order that Luke's lips were not just good at kissing. They were good at a lot of things. They were good at my neck, behind my ear, trailing down my chest and they were *especially* good at my breasts.

In what seemed like five minutes (but was longer; time flies when you're getting so turned on you feel like you're going to explode) he had me wild. I gave Bad Ava what she wanted and I tasted more of Luke, my tongue and mouth moving to any piece of skin that came near it, my hands drifting, my nails dragging. I wanted all of him, every rock-solid inch I could get (and every one I encountered was just that), and for some reason I wasn't scared that he knew it.

He released my nipple after a delicious tug and a finishing swirl of the tongue and came back over me, kissing me again, hard, wild, his tongue teasing me and making me follow it which I did, gladly. Then his hips slid to my side, his mouth still kissing me and his hand went into my panties. I gasped against his tongue, as with no fooling around, no fumbling, no exploration, no hesitation, his finger hit the target.

"Holy crap," I whispered against his mouth, my eyes flying open.

He was watching me, his gaze so hot I felt the heat of it through my body.

"You're dripping wet," he told me, his voice sexy-hoarse. Before I could react to this statement, his mouth came to mine again. My eyes stayed open and so did his. "I can't fuckin' wait to get a taste of you," he said against my mouth in a fierce way that I knew he *really* meant it, and his finger did an unbelievable roll that was so good my neck arched and I sucked in breath.

My arms were around him, the fingers of one hand at the back of his head, but at the roll my other hand went to his wrist, holding it steady, telling him I wanted more.

"Ava," he muttered and my chin dipped to look at him.

"Do that again," I murmured.

He did as I asked. I couldn't help it, even though my eyes were mostly closed I felt myself smile.

"Fuck," he muttered against my mouth, and his finger slid inside me.

My hips moved, pressing against his hand, and his finger slid out, then in, then again and again. My hand stayed wrapped around his wrist as his finger worked me, my other hand still at his head. I pressed up not just my hips, my whole body, seeking contact with his, and he didn't disappoint me, pressing his body into me.

His finger slid out of me while he kissed me, his tongue sliding in my mouth as his finger did another roll, right on target, followed by another one then another one. I stopped kissing him, ready, close, my mouth against his panting. I opened my eyes to see him watching me, I knew he liked what he saw and I found that I liked that he liked what he saw.

"Show me," he murmured, his voice a deep rumble, and at the sound, I felt it coming, my tongue wet my lips.

And it was then the fucking door buzzer went.

His finger stopped rolling, his head jerked up and my body stilled. The door buzzer went again, this time for longer. This was difficult to ignore. It became worse when Luke's phone rang. Both of these were impossible to ignore. But then my purse started ringing.

"You have got to be fuckin' *kidding* me," Luke snarled.

The buzzer silenced then started again immediately.

Luke's hand moved away, his arms wrapped around me and he rolled, taking me with him and knifing to a sitting position on the side of the bed, me in his lap. He snatched the phone out of its cradle and growled into it, "This better be fuckin' good."

I was still out of it, trying to wrap my thoughts around this terrible turn of events, when Luke said, "Ma?"

Oh... my... *God*.

I was sitting, nearly naked (Luke *was* naked) in Luke's lap, post-nearly-having-a-Lucas-Stark-induced-orgasm (something I'd wanted since I was sixteen and learned what they were) and Mrs. Stark was on the phone.

This was *not* happening.

I tried to tug away, but Luke's arm went tight and his eyes sliced to me.

"I'll buzz you in," he said, looking at me.

My mouth dropped open and my eyes bugged out, totally affecting a Sissy Gawk. He put the phone down.

"My mother's here," he told me, totally calm, though his eyes were still ink.

I didn't have time for inky eyes. I flew into a tizzy.

"Holy crap. Oh my God. Holy crap," I chanted as I pulled out of his lap and threw myself on the bed, crawling over it to the other side where Luke tossed the Triumph tee last night. I nabbed it from the floor and whipped my legs around into a sitting position, my back to Luke, and tugged it on. Then I snatched my glasses off the nightstand and slid them on my nose.

I jumped up, ready to sprint to the bathroom, and ran headlong into Luke, whose arms closed around me.

"Ava, calm down."

I tilted my head to look up at him. "Mrs. Stark is here!" I shouted.

He grinned. What there was to grin about, I did *not* know, but I didn't have time to ask.

"Let me go. I need to get dressed. *You* need to get dressed."

I looked down and saw he was wearing his cargos.

Thank God for that.

I gave another tug, but his arms went tighter.

"Babe, seriously, calm down. Ma likes you. She's always liked you."

I stared at him again in a gawk.

I knew this, of course. Mrs. Stark had always been nice to me. She was a nice lady. I sometimes wondered why she was friends with my Mom, but then again, she was friends with everybody.

"I know that, Luke, but she doesn't want to catch me up here with you going commando in your cargos and me in nothing but a Triumph tee and a pair of panties."

"She'll do fuckin' cartwheels. She's hated every woman I've ever dated."

Whoa.

Whoa, whoa, whoa.

That had to go so deep I needed to bury it next to the molten core at the center of the earth.

I tried to pull away, but it was too late. The elevator doors were opening. My head snapped toward the doors and I froze, still standing in Luke's arms as Mrs. Stark walked out of the elevator.

This is interesting, Bad Ava said, sounding sleepy.

Good Ava yawned. *What'd I miss?*

Mrs. Stark turned. She had a small smile on her face, but it went wonky when she caught sight of us standing across the room. Luke didn't drop his arms and as I was frozen, my hands resting on either side of his chest under his shoulders, I didn't move.

Luke looked like his Dad. His Mom was petite and kind of round. She had blonde hair, but now it was mostly gray and she left it at that. She was a motherly-type mom who dressed like a mom, talked like a mom and acted like a mom. Therefore she stood there wearing a pair of slacks with a neatly pressed crease, a flouncy blouse, a set of classy but mom-like pumps with short heels, appropriately-sized earrings and her hair had obviously been recently set.

"Oh my," she said softly, her eyes moving to her son. "Luke you should have—"

"Hey Mrs. Stark," I broke in nervously, taking my hands off Luke's chest and turning. One of his arms dropped away from me, the other one kept me close to his side by slicing across my waist, his fingers putting pressure at my hip.

Mrs. Stark blinked.

I hadn't seen her since her husband's funeral. Considering her son's reaction to the new me, I felt it was a good idea to cut to the chase.

"It's Ava," I said.

"Ava," she repeated and kept looking at me. After a beat, the light dawned and she whispered, "Ava." Then her eyes moved to Luke, then back to me, then to Luke. Then, I kid you not, she looked like she was going to burst into tears.

"I just need to..." Her head swung around, for some reason frantically. She spied the bathroom and started toward it. "Freshen up." She disappeared into the bathroom and closed the door.

I whirled on Luke, and completely at a loss for words, leaned forward, hands straight down to my sides in fists and *glared*.

He took one look at me and burst into laughter. I lifted up both hands and gave him a big old shove. He didn't move back with the shove (of course). Instead, his arms closed around me and he pulled me close. His face went to my neck and he was still laughing so I could feel it against my skin.

"Babe," he said against my neck when he finished laughing.

"I hate you," I whispered.

His head came up and he was full-on smiling, which made my knees do a wobble, even though I was angry.

"No you don't," he whispered back.

I pulled out of his arms, ran to my suitcases and had a pair of jeans on by the time Mrs. Stark got out of the bathroom.

"Well, sorry about that. Nature calls," she said, blushing, even though the toilet didn't flush and her eyes were looking funny.

I walked up to her, lips pressed together. "Mrs. Stark, I'm sorry if I upset you—"

Her head did a little jerk to the side. "Upset me? Oh, Ava, dear, you didn't upset me."

Then she walked right up to me and gave me a tight hug. Automatically, I wrapped my arms around her, confused. I thought she'd escaped to the bathroom to burst into tears of devastation that her handsome, tough guy, macho man, shit-hot, rich enough to retire at twenty-eight (now thirty-three) son had the likes of Ava Barlow in his loft.

Apparently this was not the case.

She pulled back and her hands went to squeeze my upper arms.

"Well, look at you." She smiled at me. "You always were a pretty little thing, but now," she leaned in, "you aren't even giving Marilyn and Sofia a run for their money. You've left them in the dust," she told me quietly.

I blinked.

"Well!" she exclaimed as she patted me on the arm and walked into the room, leaving me stunned and immobile in her wake. "I came by to see if I could take my son, who, by the way, never sees his mother so she has to show up unannounced at his house on a Sunday morning, to breakfast. Now, I'll take you both," she declared, clapping her hands together like this was her most fervent wish.

My eyes went to Luke who was standing there, arms crossed and still smiling, this time at his mother.

"Lucas, put a shirt on. You'll get a chill," Mrs. Stark ordered.

I couldn't help it. At her words, it was my turn to burst into laughter.

⚜

We went to Le Peep in Cherry Creek. This, I thought, was good as they had granola pancakes there. I wasn't in the mood to search for my healthy living mojo. I was going to ask for extra butter and syrup and a double side order of bacon.

We took my Range Rover, Luke driving, Mrs. Stark making a big thing out of me sitting in the passenger seat by Luke. Of course, I had to give in. When we got to the restaurant, I hung back, intent on sitting at the table next to Mrs. Stark, when she made a big thing out of Luke and me sitting side by side. Again, I had to give in.

I knew this would be bad, but it got worse when Luke moved his chair closer than was seemly in front of Super Mom Stark, sat back and draped his arm across the back of my chair. He took it away to eat, but even part of the time he was eating, he left it there. Worse than that, him being close meant his thigh was pressed full length down mine the whole time.

Argh!

To counteract the effects of Luke's thigh, I ordered a triple side of bacon. I couldn't eat it, so Luke did. Seeing Luke eat off my plate made Mrs. Stark sigh in motherly contentment.

Throughout all of this, Mrs. Stark blathered on, eyes shiny happy, about everyone in our old neighborhood; all of them she was still in touch with, I wasn't surprised to note.

She also asked me a gazillion questions. So Luke found out I was a self-employed graphic designer. That my sisters hadn't inherited as much from Auntie Ella because I was a favorite. That I fixed up my own house. And that I was allergic to cheap brands of cosmetics.

On the second pot of coffee, she announced, "Nature calls," and got up, throwing a warm smile at the two lovebirds (which was what we looked like, seeing as Luke, now done eating, had leaned into me, arm around my shoulders, fingers playing with a lock of my hair).

Once she disappeared in the bathroom, I turned to Luke, flipping my hair off my neck and out from between his fingers.

"Stop it," I hissed.

"What?" he grinned.

"She's going to think we're together."

"We are together."

"We're not."

"We are."

I made a noise in the back of my throat and leaned into him so I was close, or, I should say, closer.

"When she comes back, I'll go to the bathroom and you tell her this isn't what it seems."

"And what should I tell her it is?"

"That I've got some troubles, you're helping me sort them out and I'm staying at your place until it's sorted. That's it, nothing more."

He shook his head. "I'm not gonna do that."

"*Why?*" I cried.

"First, because she'll worry if she thinks you're in trouble. Second, because she'll wonder what you're still doin' at my place when it's all over. Third, because that would be a lie because that's not all it is, it's a fuckuva lot more."

My heart did a stutter and I ignored it. "It isn't."

His hand came to the back of my neck. "I'm not sparrin' with you about this, Ava."

"You aren't being very nice to your mother. She actually *likes* the idea that we're together. You let her go on thinking we are when we aren't, it's just mean."

I should (again) have realized what it meant when his hand came to the back of my neck. I should have read the warning sign. I didn't.

It was when his eyes got shiny dangerous, I read the warning sign. Too late.

"Tell me, after what happened in my bed this morning, how you figure we're *not* together?"

"That was nothing. I was asleep," I lied. "You took me off-guard."

Uh-oh.

His hand tightened on my neck and brought me even closer so we were ultra-close closer.

"You're too fuckin' much. Throughout breakfast you've been decidin' how to lie to me, and yourself, about what happened. That same time I've been strugglin' with the urge to walk away from my mother, drag you back to my bed, rip your fuckin' clothes off and bury myself so deep inside you, you feel me in your throat."

Ho-ly *shit*.

Did Luke just say that to me?

He did.

"Luke—"

"Save it," he clipped. "I figure next time you're ridin' my hand is the next time I'll get the truth out of you. I don't trust a goddamn thing that comes out of your mouth, but your body, *that* I trust."

There they were again, the words "next time".

Shit.

"I can't believe you just said that to me," I snapped.

"Believe it," he bit off.

"You're way too blunt."

"Deal with it."

"You're a jerk."

His fingers went tighter on my neck. "Ava, one more word—"

I opened my mouth to give him one more word. Luke kissed me.

It started as a hard, angry, shut-Ava-up kiss, but then his tongue slid inside my mouth and it ended up as an Ava holding on to Luke's shoulders for dear life kissing him back kiss.

"Children," Mrs. Stark whispered, and my whole body jerked as my head whipped around to see Mrs. Stark sitting across from us, her lips tilted up in a mini-smile. "The other patrons can see you," she warned us, but you could tell she didn't care, not even a little bit.

I was *so* screwed.

Luke and Mrs. Stark fought over who was going to pay (Luke won). We got back in the Range Rover, went back to Luke's loft and Mrs. Stark came up to the loft with us.

His loft, I might add, magically now had a black lacquered desk in the corner with my computer and two of my wicker baskets filled with work files sitting beside it.

I made a (somewhat desperate) demand that she stay for a cup of coffee and Luke shook his head at this, totally knowing my game. Mrs. Stark agreed happily. I made a full pot and she and I drank and chatted while we both cleaned Luke's kitchen. Through this, Luke made a number of phone calls while I tried to ignore him. Then she and I sat on barstools and kept chatting.

Eventually, she cried. "Oh, look at the time!" and I felt my stomach pitch because it was then I knew I was seriously screwed.

"We're auctioning a homemade quilt at the church. I'm supposed to sell iced tea and cookies. I'm going to be late." She was flying around in a dither, grabbing at her purse and rinsing her cup to put in the dishwasher.

She came to me and touched my cheek. "Ava, so lovely to see you," she said softy.

Then Luke walked her to the elevator doors. They slid open, his arms moved around her and he bent to kiss her cheek as I watched, feeling, I had to admit, something warm spreading inside me as I did so.

Luke had never been close to his Dad, but he'd always been close to his Mom.

How Mr. and Mrs. Stark ever got together was beyond me. He was a macho man, like his son. She was Mrs. Cleaver. Why he and Luke didn't get on, I never asked and I didn't know. Maybe too much alike, or maybe Mr. Stark knew his son would be more than him and he didn't like it. Mrs. Stark must have felt like she was living in the depths of hell and it was a testimony to her quiet strength that she'd not only made it to the other side, she was auctioning quilts.

I was so caught up in these thoughts, just like the *screaming* dork I was, that I didn't realize I should have either thrown myself out the window or locked myself in the bathroom.

Again, I was too late.

The elevator doors closed and Luke and I were alone.

He turned to me.

Eek.

I made a dash toward the bathroom. He caught me around the waist, swung me up in his arms and walked toward the bed.

"Luke, put me down," I yelled, legs kicking and arms pushing.

He did. He threw me on the bed. I rolled and scrambled. He caught my ankle, yanked me back and pinned me with his body.

"Get off me," I shouted.

"This latest bullshit maneuver bought you punishment."

Oh crap.

Considering "payment" meant me handcuffed naked to the bed while he had his wicked way with me, I wanted no part in "punishment". Hell, I wanted no part in "payment" (although I found the idea intriguing).

I shook my head to clear my thoughts. "Get off."

He stared at me. His eyes weren't shiny dangerous. They were something else far more scary.

"I knew I was gonna enjoy this, but it just keeps gettin' better and better."

"Get off," I repeated.

He shook his head but said, "I gotta go out. Talk to Vance and Ike about what's happening with Vincetti and Dexter. Then Lee and I scheduled a meet with Vito. When I get home, we'll see to your payment *and* your punishment."

I blinked at him, not processing his last words as I was stuck on an earlier one. "Vito?"

"Vito Zano, Vincetti's uncle and his boss. The guy who had you kidnapped."

Vito *Zano?*

Uncle Vito Zano?

Uncle Vito had me kidnapped?

"Uncle Vito?" I asked.

Luke stared at me.

"Oh my God," I put my hands to my face then took them away and smiled at Luke. "This is *great.*"

Luke kept staring, but he was now doing it in a way like he thought maybe I'd slid over the deep end.

"Uncle Vito *loves* me," I told Luke. "He's hilarious. We're always partners during euchre games after Thanksgiving dinner. We kick *ass.* I didn't know it was Uncle Vito who kidnapped me. No wonder his henchman said he knew me."

"Ava."

"This is good news, Luke." I swiped my hand on my forehead. "Shoo."

"Ava, Vito Zano is not a good guy," Luke told me.

"Maybe not, but he'd never hurt me. He loves me and he really loves Sissy. He was always saying to me he had wished Sissy had married his other nephew, Ren. Ren is a good guy, and he's even hotter than Dom."

Luke's face grew dark. "Ren Zano isn't a good guy either. And Vito would torture his grandmother if he felt it served a purpose."

"Oh, Luke, seriously."

"Seriously."

"I've played euchre with the man. Have you played euchre with the man?"

"No, I've been in a vacant warehouse staring at two men with bullet holes in their foreheads. Hits ordered by Vito."

I stopped smiling.

He watched the smile fade and his eyes moved to mine. "Shit," he said quietly. "I don't know what's more disturbing, you playin' euchre with Vito Zano on Thanksgiving or thinkin' Lorenzo Zano is 'hotter' than Dominic Vincetti."

"Dom's a mean, cheating, scum-of-the-earth, rat-bastard, but that doesn't stop him from being hot."

Luke stared at me a beat then dropped to his side, taking me with him, all the while saying, "And you think I'm nuts?"

"You *are* nuts."

His hands slid up my back and his chin tipped down to look at me. "I'm goin' out. Do I have to cuff you to the bed?"

"No!" I pulled back, but his arms went tighter. "I've got a shed load of work to do and with all this nonsense, I'm way behind. You cuff me to the bed, I'll miss a deadline and lose a client."

His eyes narrowed on me. "Can I trust you not to do anything stupid?"

"Of course."

Without hesitation, he asked, "Can I trust you not to lie to me about not doin' anything stupid?"

"Luke!"

His hand went into my hair, his head slanted, and he kissed me, hot and deep. Then he did it again, hotter and deeper. When I'd pulled his tee out of his cargos and was running my hands up the muscles of his back and pressing myself full frontal into him, his lips detached.

I stared at him in a total and complete Luke Lip Fog.

"That's how I like it," he muttered against my mouth. He moved up to kiss my nose then he was gone.

Chapter 11
That Didn't Go Too Good

After Luke left, I had, what I found out much later, was a very stupid idea.

After that, I had what Luke would consider a very stupid idea (if he knew about it, which I was not about to tell him). I had to admit, the way it turned out, if he had known about it and given me his opinion, he would have been right.

⌖

See, I figured if I took care of myself then I wouldn't get so hot and bothered all the time when Luke kissed me. I hadn't had an orgasm in a while, and I thought if I had one then no way would Luke affect me so much. I'd be oblivious, unmoved and I could resist him.

Not to mention, after Luke's wakeup call and his recent kiss, I was way turned on.

So I lay in his bed and waited for a while to make certain he wouldn't come back. Then I unbuttoned and unzipped my jeans and slid my hand inside.

What I did not know was that was when, not far away, a guy named Jack, sitting in the surveillance room at Nightingale Investigations, leaned forward and flipped *off* the switch that activated the cameras in Luke's loft, that Luke just called him and told him to switch *on*.

⌖

As I mentioned, it had been a while, and it was helped by the fact that I was in Luke's bed, so my self-gratification didn't take long to achieve.

After, as I was lying in bed, pleased with myself (very pleased), a thought came to me. A way out of this mess.

Uncle Vito.

If I got to Uncle Vito first, before Luke, taking Sissy with me, and told him what was happening with Dom, he'd deal with it. He'd even probably help

Sissy out in the divorce. He was Italian, he was Catholic, but he also thought Dom was a dickhead (like everybody else). And since he loved both Sissy and me, if we double-teamed him we couldn't go wrong.

That way I wouldn't owe Luke and I could move out of his house. All my problems solved!

I don't think this is a good idea, Good Ava commented, wringing her hands.

I think it's a GREAT idea, call Sissy right now! Bad Ava yelled, jumping up and down with excitement.

I called Sissy.

"Hey," she said.

"Yo. Listen, you know who kidnapped me?"

"Mr. Zano," she answered.

"*Vito* Zano," I said.

"Uncle Vito?" she sounded shocked as if there were five thousand "Mr. Zanos" in Denver. However, I didn't blame her. I would have been shocked, too, if at the time I knew Uncle Vito kidnapped me. He loved me. "Who told you that?" she asked.

"Luke."

"I don't believe it. Uncle Vito wouldn't kidnap you. He loves you."

See!

"I have a plan," I said then I told her the plan.

"I'm in," she agreed immediately, as bestest best friends do.

"We have to hurry. We have to get there before he meets with Luke."

"Come get me. I'll be ready."

I was in the Range Rover, just blowing out of Luke's parking garage, when my phone rang.

It said, "Shirleen Calling".

I flipped it open and put it to my ear. "Yo."

"Yo mama. I called this morning early 'cause I *know* these boys like their mornin' piece of ass. You didn't answer. Please tell me you didn't lose me another fifty bucks," Shirleen begged.

"I didn't."

"All right, girl." She sounded pleased. "You got to hold out until tomorrow, then you and Luke can do the nasty. It *has* to be tomorrow."

"Shirleen, Luke and I are *never* going to do the nasty."

"Unh-hunh." Now she sounded like she didn't believe me.

I rolled my eyes and came to a stop at a red light.

"He there now?" she asked.

"No, I'm on my way to pick up Sissy."

"He let you out?" Now she sounded surprised.

"Not exactly."

"Oh Lord." Now she sounded worried. "What're you and Sissy plannin' to do? Daisy's over and we're gonna watch a *Days of Our Lives* marathon. Now that I got a day job, I got to DVR *Days of Our Lives*. I watch the whole week solid every Sunday afternoon. It's a ritual. You and Sissy could come over, we got popcorn."

"Sissy and I are going to talk to Vito Zano."

Silence.

"Shirleen?"

"Girl, why in *the* hell are you and Sissy goin' to talk to Vito Zano?" Now she sounded kind of mad.

"He's Dom's uncle. Sissy and I both know him. We're going to ask him to help us out. He loves us. He's Uncle Vito."

"Uncle Vito my ass. Are you crazy?" Now she sounded like she thought I was crazy.

"Relax, Shirleen, I have it all figured out."

"Shee-it, girl. You're cracked."

She took the phone away from her ear and I heard her talking to Daisy, then I heard Daisy screech, "*Is she crazy?*"

Jeez.

Shirleen came back to me. "Tell me what chance I got of talkin' you out of this fool idea."

"Zip," I informed her.

"Tell me where Sissy's stayin'. We'll meet you there."

"Shirleen, there's no need."

"There's a need. There's so much of a need I'm missin' my *Days of Our Lives* ritual. Tell me the address."

"Shirleen—"

"Tell me." Now she sounded like she wasn't going to take no for an answer.

I told her.

✴

Sissy, Shirleen, Daisy and I rolled up to Uncle Vito's house in Englewood.

He lived in what looked like your normal, average, everyday house in a normal, average, everyday neighborhood. It wasn't until you got inside and saw the Picasso scribble framed on the wall and swam in his indoor pool off the back room that you found out he was loaded.

We all trooped up to the house and knocked on the door. Uncle Vito's wife, Aunt Angela, opened the door.

"Sissy! Ava! What a wonderful surprise!" she cried and gave us big hugs.

Uncle Vito was nearly bald, very round and about an inch taller than me. Aunt Angela was slim, trim, stylish and disappeared once a year to a "spa" where she came out looking five years younger. Her forehead never moved. Botox city.

Still, she was sweet.

"Aunt Angela, these are our friends Daisy and Shirleen," Sissy introduced as we walked into the foyer and Angela greeted Daisy and Shirleen.

She was such a premier hostess, she seemed not to have any reaction at all to Daisy and Shirleen. Not that there was any reaction to be had about them, except Daisy was wearing skintight faded jeans with silver rivets up the sides, pink platform boots and a baby blue v-necked shirt that showed so much cleavage most mothers would cover their children's eyes at the sight of her.

Then again, we found out quickly that Aunt Angela knew Daisy. They moved in the same social circles.

They gave each other cheek kisses that came nowhere near the cheek.

"Come in, come in. Can I get you coffee? I have some cannoli from Pasquini's," Aunt Angela offered

"That sounds good," Shirleen said.

I gave Shirleen a look and then turned back to Aunt Angela.

"Sorry, Aunt Angela. We're here to see Uncle Vito, it's important."

She looked at me and said, "Vito's just about to head out to a meeting."

No!

My gaze swung to Sissy, screaming mutely, *do something!*

Sissy to the rescue. "We have to see him before he goes. It's important," Sissy told her then her voice lowered. "It's about Dom."

Aunt Angela's mouth got tight as she looked at Sissy. Angela also thought Dom was a dickhead.

Angela made a decision and said, "Come through to the family room. I'll get Vito."

She led us to the family room and then hot-footed it out.

"I don't see why we couldn't have a cannoli and a coffee while we're waitin'," Shirleen groused.

"We don't have time," I told her.

"Have you ever *had* a cannoli from Pasquini's? There's *always* time for a cannoli from Pasquini's."

In my fatty fatty four-eyed days I'd practically lived at Pasquini's. I'd had more cannolis, chocolate candles, napoleons and profiteroles at Pasquini's than the entire population of Denver.

I decided not to answer. Luckily, I didn't have to. Uncle Vito walked in.

He threw out his arms toward Sissy and me. "Sissy! Ava! Come give your Uncle Vito a hug."

Okay, so I was a little weirded out that Luke told me Uncle Vito had ordered hits where guys ended up with bullets in their brains. Not to mention he'd kidnapped me a couple of days earlier. Still, if Sissy and Dom divorced, I'd likely not be invited to the huge family Thanksgiving dinner again. This was probably one of the last times I'd ever see him. Anyway, if he was a man who could order a hit, it was probably not prudent to dis him on a hug. So, with Sissy, I moved forward for a big Uncle Vito hug.

"How're my girls?" he asked, leaning back and dropping his arms.

"Not good, Uncle Vito," Sissy answered.

Vito's eyes came directly to me.

Eek!

What'd *I* do?

"What's Dom done now?" he asked.

Oh, okay, freak out cancelled. I was always telling on Dom to Uncle Vito. He knew I'd give him the truth.

Sissy and I looked at each other. Vito moved into the room. We found that he knew both Shirleen and Daisy. With Daisy, it was understandable if Aunt Angela knew her. Shirleen was a wildcard.

Shirleen had also morphed into a badass Shirleen I'd never seen before. Her eyes were sharp, her face was serious and she didn't look like someone you messed with. She certainly didn't look like someone who had just been talking about cannolis. It was also clear Vito took her seriously. You could see this, but it wasn't spoken. I found this intriguing, but decided not to ask. I had more important things on my mind.

We all sat and Sissy and I told our stories about Dom. We both discreetly avoided Vito kidnapping me because that was likely not a topic for polite conversation.

When we were done, Uncle Vito said, "That boy. I told my sister. Told her time and again. Now, listen to you two."

Sissy and I looked at each other again.

"I'll handle it," he finished.

Yippee!

"Really?" I asked.

"You won't have any troubles with Dominic anymore," he assured me.

"That's great," Sissy replied. "Thanks Uncle Vito."

"I need to have a talk with Dominic myself. When we have our chat, I'll also tell him to get home, take care of his wife, treat her right, give her some babies, keep her happy," Vito said to Sissy.

Uh-oh.

His eyes turned to me. "As for you, I'll talk to Lorenzo. He's a good boy, but he needs to settle down and he likes you. You're with Lorenzo, Dominic won't get any ideas. I'll get him to give you a call."

Uh-oh.

"Uncle Vito, we were um… hoping you'd help Sissy out with her divorce," I shared.

"Vincettis and Zanos don't divorce. Marriage is life," Vito replied with finality.

This was not good.

"But—" I started.

"Listen to your Uncle Vito, Ava. Angela and me have been married thirty-three happy years. You gotta work at it. I know what I'm talkin' about. We just gotta worry about gettin' you settled. I like you with Lorenzo. I see happy things."

Uh-oh, uh-oh, uh-oh.

Vito grinned huge. "You're unhappy. All attitude. You need a man. Lorenzo will put a smile on that pretty face."

No, no, no.

"Big wedding and lotsa beautiful babies," Uncle Vito went on.

Oh... my... *God.*

I told you I didn't think this was a good idea, Good Ava reprimanded, arms crossed.

Oo, lots of Ren's babies. That means we'd have to sleep with Ren lots, and Ren's HOT! Bad Ava gushed, arms crossed, rubbing her hands up and down her biceps with glee.

"I don't think—" I began.

"It's settled. I got a meeting." He got up and looked at Sissy. "I'll take care of Dominic." He looked at me. "Lorenzo will take care of you." Then he clapped his hands together, held them out in front of him and walked out of the room.

"That didn't go too good, did it?" Shirleen asked.

"Sugar, you can say *that* again," Daisy answered.

⌐╫═

"Ren Zano calls you and asks you out on a date, Luke Stark is gonna have a shit hemorrhage. He's gonna lose his motherfuckin' *mind*," Shirleen said from the back of my Range Rover.

I figured she was not wrong.

"Maybe we should take Ava to Wyoming. Maybe we should stop by Zip's Gun Emporium and load up on weapons and *then* take Ava to Wyoming. Hole up in a cabin somewhere and shoot at anything that moves," Daisy suggested, sitting beside Shirleen.

"I ain't shootin' at Luke Stark. First, that boy is fine. Second, if I missed, he'd beat the shit out of me," Shirleen said.

I glanced at Sissy. She had her fingers to her temples and was rubbing in circles.

"This is unprecedented. A Bad Boy pursuing a Rock Chick with competition on his ass," Daisy noted. "I'm not thinkin' good thoughts, I'm not gettin' good vibes, I'm not seein' good things. We gotta get Ava out of here now. Luke is gonna blow his top. Blow... his... top. Comprende?"

"Would you two stop talking? You're freaking me out," I told them.

"Girl, better to be freaked out then cuffed to a bed for the next month. Which is exactly where you're gonna be when Luke finds out you orchestrated this fiasco," Shirleen told me.

Ee-yikes!

I stopped at a red light. "Maybe this is a moot point. Maybe Ren won't call me. Have you thought that maybe Ren's not interested in me?" I asked, somewhat hysterically and also loudly.

"He's interested in you." Sissy said quietly.

My head jerked to her. "What?"

"Ren's interested in you," she repeated.

"How do you know that?" I asked.

"He told Tony, Tony told Carla, Carla told me."

"Why didn't you tell me?" I asked, beginning to sound more hysterical and definitely louder.

"I don't know. Maybe because you'd sworn off men, stating you'd never, never, never, *never* get involved with another one again. I like Ren. He's a good guy. You can be a bitch to guys. Ren doesn't deserve that. He deserves a woman who hasn't vowed fidelity to her vibrators."

I had to ask, why me?

It was on this thought that we were bumped from behind. Not a big bump, but we all jerked forward and snapped back.

I looked in the rearview mirror. It was another SUV. I couldn't tell the make because it was too close. The person driving it was a man. He had dark hair, but that was about all I could make out before he started to reverse.

"We've been rear-ended," Shirleen stated the obvious.

I watched him reverse thinking that was weird then he came forward again.

"Holy crap. He's gonna—" I started to say.

BAM!

He rear-ended us again, this time a lot more than a bump. Everyone jerked forward harder and snapped back.

Shit!

"What the hell?" Daisy asked.

I watched as he reversed. I looked forward and the light turned green. I slammed the Range Rover in gear and I put the pedal to the floor.

"Oh my God! What's going on?" Sissy cried, looking behind her.

"I don't know. Is everyone buckled in?" I asked.

"Do you know that guy?" Daisy was looking to our rear as well.

"No. Now, I asked, is everyone buckled in?" I shouted, driving like a demon.

"I'm in," Shirleen answered.

"Me too," Daisy said.

"Yes," Sissy added.

I saw the light in front of us turn red.

"Shit!" I shouted as I braked, looked in the rearview mirror and saw the SUV behind us wasn't slowing. "Brace!" I yelled.

We had a split second to brace, then, *BANG!*

"*What's going on?*" Sissy screeched.

"Go! Go, go, go!" Shirleen shouted.

The guy behind us was reversing again.

"I can't. It's red," I pointed out.

"Lay on your horn, girl, and *go!*" Shirleen yelled.

The guy started coming again. I laid on my horn and went. As I entered the intersection, cars screeched and swerved. To avoid one, I pulled a left into the heavy, three-lane traffic on Hampden Avenue.

"Don't stop, just go, keep honking and drive," Daisy advised.

I did as I was told, weaving in and out of traffic. I went fast. Cars honked, swerved out of my way, threw me gestures, and the whole time the SUV followed me.

"I can't shake him!" I cried.

"Keep drivin'," Shirleen told me.

"I've done this before, I got experience. Go to a police station," Daisy said.

"I can't!" I yelled.

"Why not?" Sissy screeched.

"If I go to a police station then Luke will know I've been out and he'll freak."

"Better Luke freaks than we die," Shirleen put in.

Easy for her to say, she wasn't facing "payment" and "punishment" tonight.

Hell and damnation.

"Hold on!" I shouted and then I drove faster, weaved more and on the overpass to I-25, at the last minute I swung a huge, tight, very illegal u-ie.

It was not good at all to swing a huge, tight u-ie on a highway overpass in an SUV.

SUVs rolled easily. Very easily.

We teetered on two wheels, visions of us flipping over the overpass onto the busy highway below flying through my head. Every last one of us screamed at the top of our lungs. We slammed back down on four wheels and I motored.

The SUV following us missed the u-ie and I kept driving like a madwoman, bent over the wheel, eyes glaring at the road.

I drove this way for a while then Sissy said quietly from beside me, "Ava, you're kind of scaring me."

I slowed.

"I think we lost him," Daisy murmured, looking behind her.

"Shee-it," Shirleen breathed.

"I need cookies," I declared.

I dropped a shaking Sissy off. She wandered into her Dad's house looking dazed.

Shirleen and Daisy followed me to Luke's. I went in and they drove off, Daisy behind the wheel of my Range Rover.

The back of the Range Rover was damaged. Shirleen and Daisy were taking it to "a friend" so he would fix it, thus hiding the evidence from Luke that I'd been out, doing stupid shit and getting into trouble.

I went up to the loft, directly to my computer, flipped it on and decided to work and not think about any of this.

I had no idea who this new person was who was after me, and I was going to pretend it didn't happen. I was going to find a happy place in my mind and live there forever. I was going to forget about hot guy, macho man Luke Stark wanting to get in my pants, about Dominic Dickhead being a jerk, Uncle Vito ordering people to be murdered and me to be kidnapped, and the upcoming call from Ren Zano, which would lead to a big wedding and lotsa babies.

I had walked into Nightingale Investigations on a Thursday. It was Sunday, and my life wasn't just pretty fucking complicated. It was completely out-of-control.

I managed to quit shaking. I did this not with cookies, because, after a very thorough search of Luke's kitchen, I found that Sandra Whoever-She-Was hadn't stocked Luke's cupboard with cookies, only healthy eating crap which didn't do anything to stop the shakes. I did it by alternately working, tidying Luke's loft and drinking Diet Coke liberally mixed with splashes of Sailor Jerry.

I finally was able to focus and was coming close to finishing my deadline project when I heard the elevator doors slide open. I turned in my chair. Luke walked in silently, eyes on me.

Or, I should say, his dangerously shining, dark blue eyes were on me.

Uh-oh.

I slowly stood and turned to face him. He walked directly to the semi-circular bar and dropped a pair of cuffs and what looked like a weird gun on it.

I stared at the cuffs and the weapon, thinking upsetting thoughts.

He rounded the bar and came into the kitchen area. He stopped, put a palm on the counter and leaned into it. The whole time he did this, he kept his eyes on me.

"Hey," I said, trying for innocent and casual. "You have a good afternoon?"

"Come here," he replied and he did *not* use his soft, gentle, affectionate voice.

Eek!

"Everything okay?" I asked, still clinging to innocent and casual with all I had.

"Come here," he repeated.

Okay, innocent and casual weren't working.

"What's going on?"

"Ava, if you make me say it again..."

I went silent.

He moved, just slightly, but it was enough to make me jump. This made him smile. Not a Sexy Luke Smile, a Dangerous Luke Smile.

"Luke, tell me what's going on!" I demanded, beginning to freak out.

This was not smart. He bit his bottom lip with his teeth and looked away from me. When his eyes came back to me, my body went still.

Oh dear, Good Ava muttered.

Holy SHIT! Bad Ava exploded.

One could say I knew Luke pretty well. I hadn't been around him in a long time, but I had watched him grow up (with avid interest). His Mom was friends with my Mom. He and I had shared some laughs and some intense moments. Still, you didn't have to know Luke to know that grown up, tough guy, macho man Luke was barely controlling what appeared to be a very scary fury.

"Was it good?" he asked.

I blinked, not expecting that question, not even understanding it.

"What?" I asked back.

"When you touched yourself, was it good?"

My mouth dropped open and my lungs seized.

Ho-ly crap.

"How did you——?" I breathed.

"Cameras," he told me and my body jerked. My eyes swung around the loft, but Luke started speaking again and they went back to him. "You won't see them. I had the place wired, surveillance put in, so when I wasn't here with you, the boys could watch out for you. When I'm not here, they're monitoring the loft."

Ho-ly *crap*.

"Did they see——?"

"Jack turned it off. He knew I'd break his neck if he watched you do that. He gave you some time. Apparently too much time. By the time he turned on the cameras, you were gone."

I was certain I was going to die. I actually *wanted* to die. The very idea of the Nightingale Investigations men knowing what I'd done was mortifying.

"Where'd you go?" Luke asked, breaking me out of thoughts of how best to off myself.

"I spent some time with Sissy," I told him immediately, and that wasn't a total lie.

"And Shirleen and Daisy?" Luke pressed.

I didn't know how he knew this, but I thought it was safe to say, "Um... yes."

"Spent some time being pursued by a dark blue SUV down Hampden Avenue? Your back bumper completely fucked up. Losing him after nearly rolling onto I-25?"

Holy crap!

How did he know this shit? It was just bizarre.

I kept my mouth shut. I thought that was the sensible way to go.

Luke didn't. "It was reported to the police by about two dozen other drivers. In detail, with license plates and descriptions of the people in the vehicles."

Crapity, crap, crap, *crap*.

"Luke—"

"Come here," he said quietly, and his voice was not affectionate, it was lethal.

"I don't think I want to," I told him.

"That may be the smartest decision you've made today," he said back.

Okay. Hang on a second.

Firstly, he was not the boss of me. Secondly, I was a free woman. I could do what I wanted, when I wanted, where I wanted, with whom I wanted. I didn't need his permission for one goddamn thing. Thirdly, no one asked him to be Mr. Over-Protective. He'd given himself that role. He even put cameras in his house, cameras he didn't tell *me* about, which was a serious invasion of privacy beyond making me move in with him, sleep beside him and the list could go on (and on). Fourthly, he was not the boss of me.

I'd had enough.

"You're not the boss of me," I told him.

"Ava, I'll give you one last chance to get your sweet ass over here."

"No!" I snapped. "I'm not going to be freaked out by you. I'm not going to be pushed around by you. And I'm not going to be told what to do by you. I'm alive. I'm breathing. So are Sissy, Daisy and Shirleen. I don't know what happened, and I don't care. I'm ignoring everything, including you having your buddies watch me when I didn't know they were doing it. I'm ignoring *everything*. I'm going to live my life and let all this shit blow over."

"You haven't clued in yet but this shit is not gonna blow over. Who was the guy in the SUV?"

"I have no idea. I've never seen him before. Maybe he had road rage. Maybe I pulled out in front of him and didn't notice it. Who cares?"

"I care."

"Well I don't!" I snapped.

"Why are you all of a sudden the focus of some seriously scary shit?"

"How should I know?"

"Maybe because it's happening to you?"

"Well, I don't know!" I yelled. "I don't even want to know!"

He glared at me. I glared back.

We were locked in another Luke vs. Ava Glare of the Century Contest when my phone rang. I was kind of glad it did because I was about to back down from the glare and this gave me an excuse.

To save face, I made a "huh" sound, grabbed my phone from the desk, flipped it open and put it to my ear. "Yo."

"Ava?"

"Yes?"

"It's Ren."

Oh *fuck*.

My eyes snapped to Luke. "Hey," I said.

"Hey, Uncle Vito told me about Dom. You okay?"

"Yeah."

"You okay after Uncle Vito sent his goons after you?"

I blinked in surprise at his question and turned away from Luke. "What?"

"Santo and Lucky are idiots. They were supposed to be cool, tell you it was Vito who wanted to see you. Not scare you half to death and send you running through traffic on Broadway."

Wow. That was news.

"Sorry about that," he went on, like he apologized for mistaken kidnappings every day.

I moved away slowly and went to the window at the side of the loft. All the while, I was very conscious of Luke watching me. "Um, that's okay."

Did I just tell Ren it was okay that his uncle had me kidnapped? Maybe I *was* nuts.

"Listen, Ava, don't worry about Dom. I'll take care of him," he assured me.

Oh no.

My eyes went back to Luke. He was still leaning on the counter, still watching me and now his eyes were narrowed.

I looked away again.

"I think someone's already working on that," I told him.

"I know. You got Stark doing it. Tell him to back off. We want to take care of this in the family."

Oh shit.

No way was I going to tell Luke that Ren Zano was going to take care of Dom for me and he could back off. No way in hell.

I would never have expected my life could get more complicated, but there it was.

"Ren," I said softly and stupidly, for the minute I uttered his name, the air in the room changed and *not* in a good way. It took all my efforts to keep my eyes looking out the window and ignore the scary air.

"I'll take you out to dinner tomorrow night, apologize properly for all this shit."

"I'm busy," I said immediately.

"Tuesday."

I felt Luke get close rather than seeing him do it. I felt this, because the not good air in the room started pressing on me.

"Erm…" I mumbled, too focused on the scary air to come up with another excuse to avoid a date with Ren.

"I'll take you to Carmine's on Penn. You love it there."

I did love it there, and I thought it was kind of sweet that Ren remembered. We'd all gone out, Sissy and Dom, Noah and me and Ren and one of his women, I forgot her name (Ren had a lot of women). We'd had a good time and the food was orgasmic.

"Seven o'clock. I'll pick you up at your place. See you then."

Before I could say a word, he disconnected.

Okay, there were a lot of not-good things happening in my life at the moment, but this was *seriously* not good.

I flipped my phone closed and turned.

I was right, Luke got close. Real close.

And I was also right about the not good air.

If Luke had been barely controlling fury before, he was visibly losing his battle with controlling rage now.

Eek.

Chapter 12
Pins and Needles

Luke's hand came up to rest on my neck, his thumb under my jaw.

"Why is Ren Zano phoning you?" he asked softly.

I needed to make a split-second decision and I made it. I wasn't going to live in fear of tough guy, macho man Luke Stark. He was nuts and he was a badass, but he wasn't going to hurt me. Sure, most of the way he behaved, and nearly all of the brutally honest shit that came out of his mouth, was shocking, but he would never hurt me. Maybe he would cuff me to the bed again or do some other macho man shit, but I could handle that.

I was in control of my mind and my body. Okay, the last one wasn't really true but I did have a pretty magnificent orgasm not too long ago, so I should be topped up.

I wasn't his woman. It was time to stop acting like I was.

"He says you should back off from Dom. He'll take care of it," I told him, instantly going back on my pledge never to tell him that, ever.

Luke's fingers tensed at my neck. "That it?"

I took hold of my liberated woman and shared further. "He's taking me out to dinner on Tuesday to apologize for everything."

I felt Luke's body go still as he stared at me. "You're tellin' me you made a date with Zano while you were standing in my living room?"

I was *not* going to think "Eek!"

"It isn't a date. I don't date. I've sworn off men. This is an apology dinner."

Luke stared at me, one beat, then two. Then surprisingly he dropped his hand from my neck and walked away. I watched as he lifted his hands to his shoulder blades, pulled off his tee and dropped it to the floor (incidentally this annoyed me, considering I'd spent ten minutes that afternoon gathering his clothes and throwing them in the laundry hamper in the utility area that was tucked behind the bathroom). Then he sat on the bed and yanked off his boots. He stood and started to unbuckle his pants.

Oh crap.

I turned and sat back down at the desk, ignoring what his actions might mean to me. I heard drawers opening and closing then rustling. When I heard the elevator doors slide open, I twisted in my chair and saw Luke walk into the elevator, wearing running clothes (all black, except his shoes). The elevator doors closed and he was gone.

Weird.

Way weird.

I took a deep breath, got back to work and tried not to wonder about Luke (and failed).

About an hour later he came back. I watched from my chair as he walked directly to the bathroom without a word to me. I heard the shower running while I closed down my files and shut down the computer. I decided to move away from Sailor Jerry because I needed to be drunk for whatever was going to happen next like I needed a hole in the head. I found a box of Sandra Whoever-She-Was's peppermint tea and was boiling the kettle when Luke came out of the shower, wearing nothing but a silvery-gray towel around his hips.

Seriously, he was worse than Captain Kirk. Luke hardly *ever* had a shirt on.

I looked away from his body, bit my bottom lip and watched the kettle boil. I felt him behind me and tensed. My hair was swept off my shoulders and his lips touched my neck.

Um.

What?

His arm slid around my waist and he pulled me into his body. "You want to order Chinese or pizza?" he asked.

I blinked at the kettle.

What was happening? Where was Pissed-Off Luke? He sounded completely calm, normal, un-pissed-off.

"You have tons of food in your fridge. You don't eat it, it'll go bad," I told him.

"You wanna cook?" he asked.

"I could cook," I answered.

"Works for me," he said and let me go.

Holy cramoly.

What was going on?

I made tea. Luke put on black sweatpants with a thick line of dark gray running up the sides and a black tee with a black insignia you could barely see on the front that looked like a set of wings. I made dinner, Sandra's long and happy life with Luke healthy living options of salmon fillets, broccoli and cous cous. I brought the food to the couch where Luke was watching TV. I sat down and we both ate silently. Then I took the plates back to the kitchen and did the dishes. When I was done, I came back and sat on the couch.

This was freaking me out. He didn't carry me around, making grand statements about how he was going to fuck me, how I belonged to him, demanding I not go out with Ren. He seemed relaxed and mellow. I didn't like it and I didn't trust it one bit.

I started to watch the game, my mind sliding from thought to thought when Luke's arm came out and pulled me against his side. He was slouched into the couch, feet up on the coffee table. I decided not to poke the sleeping tiger by struggling. I slouched pressed next to him and put feet up on the coffee table by his.

After a while I could take it no more. I wanted to allow myself to sit next to Luke, pressed to his side, in a happy, pretend world of what it could be like with Luke. Instead, I was freaking out wondering what he was playing at.

I got up announcing I was going to bed. Luke let me go without a word. I went to the bathroom, got ready for bed, spent some time trying to decide if the Triumph tee was the way to go (I went for it, it was snuggly) and I came out of the bathroom.

Hmm. Conundrum.

I *should* sleep on the couch, make a statement. But Luke was watching the game on the couch. I figured I could move to the couch later and I got in bed.

Half an hour later, Luke switched off the TV and I heard him moving around the loft. He turned off the lamp and he took off his clothes (probably dropping them to the floor, argh!). The bed moved and he got in.

I tensed. He didn't touch me.

I kept tense. He still didn't touch me.

This made me tenser.

My mind whirled. Maybe he'd given up. Maybe he thought I wasn't worth the effort.

I didn't know what to think of that. I should have been relieved, but I had to admit I was not.

You really messed things up this time, Good Ava sounded angry.

That's okay. Ren's taking you out to dinner on Tuesday and Theresa Bianchi said he was a GOD in bed, Bad Ava was moving on to new game.

We don't want Ren, we want Luke. We've ALWAYS wanted Luke, Good Ava snapped at Bad Ava.

We'll take what we can get. Ren Zano is hardly sloppy seconds, that man is FINE, Bad Ava informed Good Ava.

I forced my body to relax and my mind to go blank. I was drifting off to sleep when Luke tagged me around the waist, turning me to my back.

"What are you doing?" I asked, finding myself instantly alert.

He didn't answer. He covered me with his body and before I knew it his hands were in the Triumph tee and it was up and over my head. He didn't pull it off. He stopped it when my arms were up, the tee bunched at my elbows.

I was taking this as a sign he hadn't given up.

"What are you doing?" I screeched.

He twisted his torso, nabbed something off the nightstand and came back to me. I heard a clink and realized what was happening.

"No you don't!" I bucked, twisted, struggled against his heavy weight and tried to shove off the tee.

Luke "helped" and the tee was gone in a flash. Wordlessly, he seized my wrists, slapped a bracelet on one and then, without apparent effort, and clearly with a good deal of experience working with struggling people, the other, and I was cuffed to the bed.

I stilled, a tremor of fear (and excitement, I had to admit) ran through me and I glared at him in the dimly lit dark.

"Uncuff me," I demanded.

He ignored my demand and declared, "Now, payment."

Ho-ly *shit.*

Definitely not giving up. His mouth came to my neck and ran the length of it. A shiver shuddered through me.

At my ear he said, "We'll save punishment for later. Coupla days," he informed me conversationally before his lips moved along my jaw then to my mouth. "You gave me a fuckin' great idea."

Uh-oh.

I didn't think that *I* would think it was a great idea.

He went on, proving me irrevocably correct. "I'm thinkin' I'll watch while you make yourself come."

Oh… my… *God*.

Me and my bright ideas. I was *such* a dork!

"Get off!" I cried.

He kissed me. I bucked and twisted, these being the only options for me. He didn't budge.

I tore my mouth from his. "Seriously, Luke, this is *not* cool."

His hands ran down my sides, and I couldn't help it. My body trembled because his hands on me felt nice. I knew he felt it. He had to have felt it.

Hell and damnation.

"No?" he asked, sounding satisfied.

Yep, he felt it.

"Go to hell!" I snapped.

He touched his mouth to mine, then he moved lower, his mouth on my neck, my throat. Then lower, spending some time at my breasts. Then lower, at my belly. By the time his tongue traced the top edge of my panties, it was like I hadn't had an orgasm a few hours ago. It was like I hadn't had one in ten years.

He went lower and my legs opened immediately in invitation.

Damn it all to hell.

He kissed me over my panties. I moaned and lifted my hips, more than ready for him. His hands slid under my ass and that was it. All vows to vibrators and swearing off men were history.

This was quite simply hot. His mouth moved on me over my panties and it felt good. Even better, it felt naughty and slightly pervy not being able to touch him. I wanted to touch him, needed to put my hands to his head in encouragement, keep him there and not let him stop. Not being able to do that, having no control over the situation, was sexy as all hell.

He moved away and I made a sound of protest low in my throat. But he only moved to pull my panties down my legs. Then he was back and he hit the target immediately.

"Oh my God," I breathed, bucking now to get closer to his mouth. I was out-of-control moaning and panting. I couldn't help it and didn't try.

It was better than that morning. It was better than my self-gratification that afternoon (*far* better). It was better than anything I'd ever had.

It was exquisite.

I was there, *right there* and I gasped, "Luke."

Then his cell rang. His mouth stilled. Then his head came up.

Oh no. No, no, no, no, *no*. Not again.

"No!" I cried aloud.

He moved up and over me. "Fuck," he muttered, sounding pissed and full of regret at the same time.

It was the regret that penetrated my pre-orgasm fog.

I stared at him. "Go back. Don't stop," I whispered.

He kept his body on me but reached to the nightstand.

"Luke, please," I begged, and I didn't care what I sounded like, this was not going to happen to me again.

"Sorry, babe. That's Lee's tone," Luke whispered, hand at my jaw, thumb running along my lower lip. One thing you could say, he did sound sorry. *Very* sorry. But I didn't care that he sounded sorry. I didn't care at all.

He flipped open the phone. "Yeah?"

This was *not* happening.

He listened for a few beats then said, "I'll be there in ten."

What?

He flipped the phone shut.

"You have got to be kidding me," I breathed, half-still turned on, half-totally pissed-off, not just at him, but at myself.

"Lee's workin'. He's in a situation where he needs backup. The boys on call are busy with somethin' else. I gotta go," Luke told me.

I glared at him, not knowing what to think.

He looked at me, likely sensing my mental battle to decide how I felt that he'd leave me in this state to go do backup for Lee so he said softly, "No way I'd leave, Ava, but Lee needs a man at his back. He knows you're here and wouldn't call unless it was important. I have to go."

Fuck *that*.

I kept glaring at him. He ignored the glare, touched my mouth with his and moved away.

Then things, already bad, got worse.

He pulled the covers over my body, but left me cuffed to the bed before he got up and started dressing. In stunned, angry silence, I watched him pull on his pants then tug on his shirt. He sat on the edge of the bed to put on his boots.

Finally I called, "Luke?"

"Yeah?"

"Did you forget something?" I asked.

"What?"

"Uncuff me."

He tugged on his second boot, twisted toward me and put his lips to my jaw. "Quick, three things," he said there.

I got the feeling that these three things weren't going to be good for me. My body, already solid with fury, felt like it was going to shatter in a million pieces.

He lifted his head but kept his face close to mine, his hand at my belly over the covers. "One," he started. "Leavin' you cuffed means you can't do anything stupid."

One, two, three, four...

"Two," he continued. "I like thinkin' of you cuffed naked to my bed."

Five, six, seven, eight...

"Three," he went on. "This won't take long and we'll finish when I get back."

Nine, ten, eleven, twelve, thirteen, fourteen, fifteen, sixteen...

Nope, it wasn't going to work.

"You leave me cuffed, I'll never speak to you again," I told him.

"Babe," now he sounded amused, "that's a good thing. You got a mouth on you."

Then, to my utter disbelief, he was gone.

<hr />

Luke had been wrong. It *did* take long. So long, I had time to let it penetrate that Luke was off somewhere being the man at Lee's back during a "situation". I didn't want to care, but I got worried. Then I got scared. The longer it took for him to come back, the more scared I became. I should have been scared about being cuffed to a bed if something happened to Luke, and thus, who knew how long it would take for someone to find me, if ever (I had, in my state, forgotten about the cameras). Instead, I was just scared for Luke.

Then I got angry. Angry at Luke for leaving me the way I was, angry at him for having a scary-as-shit job and switching my anger to Lee for existing at all.

Finally, tiredness overwhelmed me. I was forced to roll to my side, find a somewhat comfortable position and I fell into a fitful sleep.

I woke up when the bed moved and I felt hands working efficiently at my wrists. Then I was free. I pulled my arms down and pins and needles attacked them viciously.

I bent my elbows and circled my hands at my wrists. Luke pulled me up to a sitting position in the bed, moved his body so his legs were around me, his front pressed against my back. Both of his hands worked at my arms, his fingers pressing in, forcing out the angry tingles.

"Babe," he said softly against my neck.

I was silent, and even just awakened, absolutely furious.

"It took longer than I expected," he continued.

No kidding, I thought, but kept my mouth shut.

"I got away as soon as I could," he told me.

Rat-bastard, I thought.

"Christ, Ava, I'm sorry."

I don't care. Go to hell. I hate you. I kept my silence.

The pins and needles subsided and I leaned forward, pulling away from his hands.

His arms went around my waist and kept me there, his mouth at my neck. "Ava," he said against my skin.

I jerked my neck away from him.

"Shit," he muttered and moved away from me.

I scrambled and got my panties and the Triumph tee (let us not forget, I was naked as a jaybird). I noticed he'd come straight to the bed fully-clothed to release me and now he was taking off his clothes. I tugged on my stuff and walked directly to my suitcases. I rummaged through them, found what I wanted and went to the bathroom. I yanked off the Triumph tee and put on a pair of pajama pants striped in yellow, green and pink and a fitted tee in matching pink. I walked out, threw the Triumph tee on the bed, not even looking to see where Luke was. I grabbed a pillow and stomped to the couch.

I threw the pillow down, lay on the couch, tucked myself in a ball and wrapped my arms around my knees. I'd barely got in this position before Luke was there, lifting me up and carrying me to the bed. I didn't struggle and I didn't say a word.

He put me in bed. I scooted as far away from him as I could and settled. He yanked me to him, my back to his front, and held me close. I didn't struggle against that either.

"I'm thinkin' you givin' up my tee isn't a good sign," he said into my hair.

He was *so* right.

I didn't answer.

I was giving him the Ava Barlow Silent Treatment. I was famous for my silent treatment. Once I didn't talk to Noah for a week after he'd done some stupid thing to piss me off. It drove him crazy and in the end he begged me to talk to him. This was one of the very few happy memories I had after he cleaned me out. I was figuring, cuffing me naked to the bed and going out to do backup during some dangerous situation, not to mention leaving me at all during my second on-the-verge-of-having-a-Lucas-Stark-induced-orgasm in one day, was worth at least twenty-seven years of the Ava Barlow Silent Treatment.

Luke just held tight. I stayed tense. After a while, I felt his bodyweight relax into me as he fell asleep.

I didn't fall asleep. I needed advice, and not from Good Ava and Bad Ava. I needed someone to talk to about my life and what I should do. I had people kidnapping me, rear-ending me and pursuing me in car chases down busy streets. I had Luke thinking we were together and what we had was a "fuckuva lot more" than nothing.

I couldn't talk to Sissy. She wanted me with Luke. I couldn't talk to my Mom. She was shit at advice and usually didn't spend much time listening before she turned the conversation to herself. I couldn't talk to my sisters because I tried not to talk to my sisters if I could help it. I couldn't talk to Uncle Vito because he was scary. I couldn't talk to Mrs. Stark because she also wanted me with Luke.

I could have talked to my Dad. He was a great listener and even better at advice.

I felt trapped, scared, sad and because of all that, tears slid out of the corners of my eyes.

I pressed my lips together. Luke's arm went tight around me and he buried his face in my hair.

"Babe," he said softly, and I knew he wasn't asleep, and he knew I was crying.

Hell and damnation.

I kept silent but took a deep, broken breath to control the tears. When he heard the breath, his arm went even tighter, but he didn't say anything else.

After a while, I fell asleep.

☙

Sometime in the middle of the night, Luke moved me, rolling under me, situating me at his other side.

I tried to turn my back to him, but he didn't allow that. He caught my leg behind my knee and hooked it over his waist.

I didn't struggle nor did I say a word.

Luke's hand ran from my knee, up my thigh, over my ass, halting at my hip. "Ava babe, you awake?"

I told him I was by pressing my forehead to his throat but also told him, even so, I wasn't speaking to him by keeping silent.

"Jesus, you could bring a man to his knees," he muttered, but his tone didn't sound angry. It sounded resigned, as if he knew this was to be his fate. Worse, it sounded like he didn't really mind. Worse than that, I found this moved me in such a profound way, it was so big I couldn't bury it. I had to carry it with me and that I didn't like *at all*.

It took a while but I fell back to sleep.

☙

I woke up in the same position as ever when I was in bed with Luke and I immediately remembered I was in the throes of my Silent Treatment.

Without a word and without looking at him, I rolled away. I threw my legs over the side, went directly to the kitchen to nab a diet, got my stuff and went to the bathroom. I didn't come out until I was dressed and ready for my day.

When I got out of the bathroom, the bed was empty. Luke was in the kitchen making coffee, chest bare (of course), wearing his sweatpants from last night.

I went about the business of making myself toast and calling Sissy to ask her to come and take me to the gym (she decided to come with me). All the while I acted as if Luke didn't exist.

I was wiping my hands on a kitchen towel after rinsing my plate when Luke tagged me around the waist, backed me against the opposite counter and moved in, hands on the counter on either side of me.

I tilted my head back to look up at him (silently).

"How long you gonna keep this up?" he asked.

I just stared at him.

His hands moved from the counter to either side of my neck, thumbs of both hands stroking my jaw. This felt nice and the warm look in his eyes was so killer, my dedication to the Silent Treatment took a direct hit.

Sucking it up, I recovered.

He kept talking, "I fucked up, Ava. I apologized. Not much more I can do."

I kept staring at him.

One thumb slid along my lower lip and he watched it go then his eyes came to mine.

Gently he said, "Someone apologizes and they mean it, you should accept. Doesn't say much about you if you don't."

I swallowed because he sounded disappointed in me and I never wanted Luke to be disappointed in me. In fact, I spent six years of my growing up life twisting myself into pretzels so that I would make him anything but disappointed in me. Not to mention an entire year of my adult life changing my appearance to make sure, when he saw me again, he wouldn't be disappointed in that either.

It wasn't like a slap in the face, but it didn't feel good either.

Right after I had that thought, I got angry because *I* wasn't the one who cuffed me to his bed and left me there way longer than expected with nothing to do but worry and freak out. *I* didn't want or ask to get kidnapped, shot at, manhandled, ordered about, taken to the verge of orgasm *twice* to be left wanting. In fact, I'd made it perfectly clear I *didn't* want any of those things.

Furthermore, he had a scary job where he got called late at night to do scary things. And that scary job or the old "doing crazy shit" one got him that vicious scar slicing across his belly, because he sure as hell didn't have it when he left the neighborhood (I would have noticed, or his Mom would have told my Mom). I wasn't going to ask about it because I *really* didn't want to know. Even if I wasn't sworn off men, I didn't know if I could hack being with who Luke had become. But I had to remind myself, I *was* sworn off men.

I just kept staring. The buzzer went. Sissy.

I slid away from him, grabbed my workout bag and headed to the elevator.

When I got in, hit the button and turned, he was leaning against the bar, arms crossed on his (bare) chest, eyes on me.

The doors slid shut.

I spent the rest of the day seeking advice.

Sissy (next to me on a stair machine in the gym):

"I've already told you what I think about Luke. In regards to Ren, just tell him you're with Luke, he'll back off. In regards to scary guy trying to run us down, just talk to Luke, he'll take care of it. Simple."

Okay. No.

Next!

Riley. After my workout and I cornered him, even though he still looked pissed-off at me. Which, I might add, if Luke lost Riley as my friend I'd tack another ten years onto his Ava Barlow Silent Treatment Sentence:

"Jesus, Ava, what the fuck?" he breathed when I shared most of the story, leaving out all of the sex stuff and Luke's brutally honest proclamations. Then his face went gentle and I saw for the first time that Luke was right. Riley wanted to fuck me.

Jeez.

What was going on? How on earth did this happen?

"Do you want to stay with me?" Riley asked.

Hell no!

"Thanks, Riles. That's sweet of you, but I can't," I said softly.

Next!

Shirleen, at Fortnum's, where Sissy and I went after the gym to get one of Tex's unbelievably divine coffees:

"Child, tune out your head and follow your heart." Her tawny eyes had gone soft.

Following my heart meant holding on to Luke and never letting go. That was, until he got tired of me and scraped me off, or he got filled with bullets and killed in a gunfight.

Not gonna happen.

"What are you doing here? I thought you had a day job?" I asked Shirleen. She was relaxed in one of the couches at the front of Fortnum's where the espresso counter was.

"I'm pickin' up orders for the boys in the surveillance room," she said, tossing back another gulp of her cappuccino.

I hoped "the boys" weren't hankering too much for their coffee. By the looks of Shirleen they were going to wait awhile.

Next!

Tex, while handing me my skinny vanilla latte:

"Go on vacation..."

Hmm. This had merit.

"With Luke," he finished.

I did not *think* so.

Next!

The Rock Chicks:

Jet: "Don't fight it."

Next!

Ally: "I don't get it. Luke's hot."

Next!

Indy: "Do you want me to talk to Lee about this guy who chased you in his SUV?"

No!

Next!

Daisy, over the phone while Sissy was dropping me back at Luke's:

"Sugar, take it one minute at a time. Life will lead you where you need to be."

That was what I was afraid of.

She went on, "And don't worry about whoever is after you. When one of the Rock Chicks finds trouble, every one of the Hot Boy Brigade kicks in. Whoever-it-is will have to take 'em down one by one to get to you, and that's just not gonna happen."

Eek!

Next!

Jules, after Sissy dropped me off. I had a shower, picked up Luke's newest clothing additions from the floor, started a load of his laundry and sat at my computer to research all-inclusive vacations in Jamaica:

"Give him time, Ava. There's more to Luke than you know."

"I've known him since I was eight!"

"I know, but you want the truth?"

No, I did *not* want the truth.

She gave it to me anyway. "I don't think you know who he is now. If you did, there would be no question."

Shit.

I finished my deadline project, e-mailed it off and was working on clearing all my other projects in order to send them in well ahead of the due dates which would cause client-wide strokes as I always worked right up to deadline.

I had a plan. I intended to clear my workload and disappear to Jamaica for a month, taking Sissy with me. By the time we got back, all the macho men in my life, undoubtedly needing to give *someone* the business, would have moved on to a new girl and I'd be off the hook. Then it would be back to just me and my vibrators.

The elevator doors slid open and I knew it was Luke just because. It might have been a long time since I'd seen him, but my Sixth Luke Sense was instinctual and kicked in immediately, like riding a bike.

And anyway, these days, I'd been getting lots of practice.

I ignored his presence, kept my back to the room and kept clicking through holiday getaway packages.

I heard his keys hit the bar and then he came up behind me.

"Goin' on vacation?" he asked.

I stayed silent and kept clicking. He waited a beat before he pulled my chair out at least four feet, me still in it.

My head shot up to look at him. My mouth opened and I almost cried, "Hey!", but I just stopped myself.

He bent low, took a wrist and threw me over his shoulder. It took a lot of control, but I didn't struggle and stayed completely limp. He carried me to the bed, tossed me on it and followed me down. He settled part at my side, part on top of me, and his hand came to my jaw.

"You don't want to talk, Ava, we'll do something else. We don't have to talk to fuck."

186

Uh-oh.

Escape!

I pulled out from under him and rolled away. He caught me and brought me back.

I glared at him. He ignored the glare and his face (and I might add his fantastic mouth) started to come closer.

"You scared me," I blurted in a whisper, do not ask me why. He still had twenty-six years, three hundred and sixty-four days left on his Silent Treatment Sentence.

His head stopped moving and he looked from my mouth to my eyes.

Go on, Ava, share. Pour out your heart, Good Ava said quietly in my ear.

Quiet! Shut down, Ava. He'll just use it to hurt you eventually, Bad Ava was sounding desperate.

"You were gone a long time. I was worried something happened to you." Now why did I say that? Why was I talking at all?

Still in a quiet voice, I kept sharing, unable to stop myself. "I don't know you anymore. I don't know who you are, what you do. But I know that scar on your belly isn't from an appendectomy."

Oh... my... *God.*

Someone shut me up.

He rolled me to my side facing him, and both his arms came around me as he said, "Ava."

"No, Luke. I thought I was protecting myself against all things men. After last night, I'm protecting myself from something a lot scarier. I'm not one of those women who can hack that kind of life. I don't want any part of it."

"So this is your new excuse?" he asked. Instead of being accusatory, his voice was soft, gentle, affectionate.

"It's not an excuse, Luke. I figure you'll screw me over or leave me, one way or another, and I'll end up alone. I'm alone now and I'm happy with it. Why go through the pain of losing someone again?"

"Someone you care about," he said.

"What?"

"Go through the pain of losing someone you care about."

Whoa.

Whoa, whoa, whoa.

We were *not* going to go there.

Time to change the subject.

"What's the scar from?"

"Bullet to the gut," he shared without hesitation.

I closed my eyes tight, visions of Luke with a gaping, bloody wound at his belly danced unhappily through my head. I didn't like the visions. They scared the shit right out of me so I opened my eyes again.

"When?" I asked.

"Last summer."

"How?"

"Babe," he said softly and with a hint of regret. "I can't tell you that. The cases we work are confidential."

"Right," I said.

"I'm good at what I do."

"I'm sure you are."

His hands drifted up my back, pulling me closer. "You're hangin' on to this to hold me back. You're a lot stronger than you're sayin' and you know it," he told me.

"How did Vance feel when he was trying to staunch the blood pouring out of Jules?" Luke's body went still at my soft words and I knew it was wrong to use this against him, but I kept at it. "I get the impression from both you and Jules that you two are close. You were there. How did *you* feel, seeing her lying there bleeding?"

His face changed. To my shock he let me see the pain slice through it and it hurt like hell to watch.

Then he said, "Quiet, Ava."

"You *want* me to go through that?"

One of his hands slid up my neck into my hair, twisting it gently in his fist. "You wanna know what I want?" he asked.

Um. No. I definitely didn't want to know what he wanted.

Before I could get a word in, he told me. "I want the old you to come back and make me laugh. I want the new you to toss your attitude around and make me hard. I liked comin' home tonight to you, even knowin' you were pissed at me. I liked leavin' last night for work, knowin' you were in my bed. I might like it for a week or I might like it for a lot longer. I can't make any promises. All I know is, I want you now and you want me, even though you won't admit it. And I'm gonna do whatever it takes to give us what we want for as long as it lasts until however it ends."

"You never listen to me," I told him, beginning to get angry, because I was right. If his latest speech was anything to go by, he didn't.

"I listen to you," he said.

"Then you don't hear me."

"Ava, I hear you," he was beginning to sound impatient.

I stared at him. He stared at me. This went on for a while.

He sighed and touched his lips to mine then said, "I'll take you to dinner."

"I don't want dinner," I shot back.

His eyes started to melt. "All right. I'm hungry, but I'm happy to eat somethin' else."

Ee-yikes!

"I've just realized, I'm hungry. Let's go to dinner."

He gave me a half-grin.

We went to dinner.

Chapter 13
Solid

It was the middle of the night again when Luke rolled, taking me over the top of him, settling me on the other side of the bed.

"Why do you do that?" I mumbled sleepily.

I was about to fall back to sleep, feeling his hand tag the back of my knee and pull it over his hip when he murmured, voice husky, "You're on the wrong side of the bed."

I cuddled into him, sliding into dreamland. "Then I'll sleep on this side."

I was so out of it, I didn't realize all that my words said nor what it meant when, upon hearing them, Luke's arms went tight around me, pulling me deep into his body.

"This side's the wrong side, too," he told me.

That got my attention because it made no sense.

I tilted my head back and looked at him in the dark. "What?"

"I can't sleep on one side too long. The wound still gives me some pain."

For some reason, I felt imaginary pain in my own belly at his words.

To hide my reaction, I stated the obvious, "Then just roll over."

"If I roll over, you won't be in arm's reach."

I blinked, then sleepy or not, I started to get angry. "Luke, I'm not going to sneak out of your bed in the middle of the night and do something stupid."

"That's not why I want you in reach."

Whoa.

Whoa, whoa, whoa.

Stop right there.

Time to go to sleep.

I dipped my chin and closed my eyes. Then, because I had Barlow Bitch Blood pumping through my veins, I muttered, "You do that with all your women, they'll think you're nuts."

"I've never done it with another woman."

Really.

Stop.

Time to nap for fifty years.

"Babe?"

"Yeah?"

"If you're awake..."

I cuddled into him again. "Very sleepy," I whispered, feigning a sleepy voice.

I felt his body start shaking with silent laughter, and somehow, while he was laughing, I fell back to sleep.

⌘

My eyes opened and I saw a wall of chest.

My first thought was, *Crap, Luke's not in the shower.*

Okay, so that was actually my second thought. My first thought was, *Hmm. Yum.*

Last night Luke and I walked from his loft to Wynkoop's Brewery and had beer and dinner. During dinner, he took a call that made his mouth go tight and his eyes move to me. I had an Eek Moment, thinking he'd found out about my visit to Uncle Vito through his varied tough guy, macho man, bounty hunting, private eye sources.

Relief flooded through me when he got off the phone and said, "Sorry babe, something's come up. After dinner I gotta meet Hector. I don't know how late I'll be."

Therefore the mouth tightening meant, for Luke, him missing another opportunity to "give me the business", and for me, relief that I'd dodged the bullet again.

"That's okay," I told him breezily.

He gave me a half-grin, totally knowing my thoughts.

He had walked me home and left me in his loft after giving me a hot and heavy kiss that left me in a Luke Lip Fog.

Looking at my face he said, "If you take care of yourself again, you'll owe me."

All righty then, I could scratch *that* off my list of Things to Do While Luke's Away.

I wasn't big on watching TV so I'd putzed around his loft all night. I spent my time calling Sissy to chew over the latest Luke episode, doing more of Luke's laundry and tidying his magazines and mail into neat piles to the extent of putting notes on top: "To be opened", "Deal with this", "This needs to be filed", etc. What could I say? I was an organizer.

Then I went to bed. Later, Luke woke me up by shifting me and we had had our scary chat.

Now, morning.

Ee-yikes.

I tried to slide away without him noticing. He rolled and his arms came around me.

"Babe," he said, sounding very awake.

Foiled!

I looked up at him and he had his chin dipped toward me so I looked right in his eyes.

"Hey," I mumbled.

"Hey," he replied.

"I need to brush my teeth."

His arms got tighter. "Later."

"No. Now. I can't face the day without brushing my teeth."

"Your day can start later," he said, his eyes turning inky and his thigh sliding between my legs to rest at the heart of my special girl parts.

"Luke—"

His mouth came to mine, his eyes still open, so I kept mine open, too, captivated. Then he pressed his hard boy part into my belly.

Wow.

"I'm not waitin' to get inside you any longer, Ava. This is happening now."

Before I could say a word, he kissed me. It became very clear he was quite intent on *this happening now*.

I wore the Triumph tee to bed and it was gone within seconds. Then his hands were on me, all over me, all the while his mouth on mine. It didn't take long for me to fall into a Luke Lip Fog and fall I did, headlong.

In fact, he was *so* serious it didn't take long for me to surpass his dedication to the cause to the point where I tried to shove him on his back to get more of him. He stayed firm, mouth at my neck, hand trailing down my belly, his destination clear.

I planted a foot in the bed and heaved, rolling him to his back and dislodging his hand.

"Babe…"

He thought I was going to move away.

I didn't.

Instead I straddled him, bending over to use my mouth on him. I put my lips against his neck using my tongue, my teeth. I went down his chest, running my nails through his chest hair and over his nipples while my mouth explored. I went lower to his abs, then lower and stopped. I sat up astride his thighs and got my first full look of all that was Luke.

Yowza.

Nice.

So nice, he should be cast in bronze.

I reached down and wrapped my hand around him, my half-mast eyes on his inky ones, my thumb moving over the tip.

I stroked. Then I was done.

He knifed up, sliced an arm around my back, lifted me clean off him and I was in the air for a moment before I was on my back. He tore my panties down my legs, settled between them and that was it.

It was going to happen. I was going to do the nasty with Lucas Stark.

And I could not *fucking* wait.

His lips on mine, both our eyes open, his fingers went between my legs. When he touched me, I did a happy gasp against his mouth and I felt his smile.

"Dripping," he said against my lips.

Then he kissed me, his hand went away from between my legs. Both of his hands went to my hips, he positioned, lifting his head. I saw as his eyes went molten when he watched my tongue wet my lips in anticipation.

Then the buzzer went.

No! My brain shouted.

But whoever was out there was serious. They didn't take their finger off the buzzer.

"Ignore it," Luke muttered.

"What if it's someone needing backup?"

"Fuck 'em."

Yippee!

He lifted my hips and he was right there, I could feel him and I wanted him more than my next breath. The buzzer died, I lifted my mouth to press against his and that's when we heard the scream.

194

We both froze.

Then it came again.

"*Ava!*"

My blood turned to ice.

"That's Sissy," I breathed, but Luke was already off me, off the bed, grabbing his cargoes.

I rolled to the side, nabbed the Triumph tee and pulled it over my head then I hopped into my panties. By the time I did this, Luke was already clothed and headed to a door at the side of the loft. I saw that he was shoving a gun in the back waistband of his pants.

"Luke," I called as he unlocked the door. My voice, I could hear, was filled with fear.

He turned to me. "Stay here. Lock yourself in. Don't go anywhere. I don't care what you hear."

I ran to him, he went out the door and I watched as he went down the fire escape.

I closed the door and ran to the drawer where I found a bunch of keys in my search for cookies the night before. I grabbed a key ring full, ran back to the door and found the right key on the third go. I locked the door, tossed the keys to the bar, ran to my suitcases and grabbed my jeans, pulling them on.

Then I didn't know what to do.

Sissy, my bestest best friend was out there, screaming my name.

I put my hands to my forehead, fingers sifting into my hair. I shoved the heels of my palms in and I stood solid, listening.

"Luke, get to her, please, Luke, get to her," I whispered to no one.

Breathe, Ava, in, out, in, out, Good Ava spoke quietly in my ear.

Snap out of it, girl. Go to the bathroom, brush your teeth, get your glasses, put your bra on. Be ready for anything, Bad Ava advised.

I listened to both of them. Breathing deeply in and out, I went about the business of being ready for anything to the point of putting on a bra and deodorant, changing into my Tom Petty and The Heartbreakers tee and putting on flip-flops.

I'd flipped the switch to a fresh pot of coffee (don't ask me, I wasn't thinking clearly), when the elevator doors slid open. Luke and Sissy came in and I rushed to them. Sissy was bleeding from the nose and shaking visibly.

Luke looked like Luke. Once I ascertained that he was okay, it was all about Sissy.

I put my arm around her waist and the minute I did she started crying.

"Shh, Sissy, shh." I sat her on a barstool and Luke went to the phone. I ran to the bathroom, wet a washcloth and carried it into the other room.

"I got a woman bleeding in my loft. Where the fuck is Bobby?" Luke snapped into the phone as I stopped by Sissy and whispered to her, wrapping my fingers around the wrist of her hand at her nose and pulling it away.

There was blood everywhere and I gently wiped at it, constantly whispering in a soft soothing voice as great, shaking sobs tore through her.

"Calm, Sis. Calm, honey. You're safe. We're here. No one can hurt you here. Let's get you cleaned up and see about your nose."

"He... he punched me, Ava. Right in the nose," Sissy told me

"Who, honey?" I asked, wiping.

"I don't know. I don't know. I've never seen him before. He wa... was so big."

My eyes slid to Luke. He had a fist to his hip, head bowed and he was listening to the phone at his ear.

"Do you think it's broken?" she asked.

My eyes came back to Sissy. "I don't know, Sis. Wait until Luke gets off the phone, he'll look at it."

Hearing his name, Luke's head swung around and his eyes came to me.

"Right. Out," he said. He beeped the phone off and walked to us, the whole time his eyes on me.

"Can you look at her nose?" I asked, shocked to find my voice sounded normal, not shaky and hysterical like I felt inside. "She's worried it's broken."

Luke's eyes stayed on me a beat. They were intense. Partly angry, partly hyper-alert and partly something else. Then they turned to Sissy and I watched his always-hard face grow slightly soft. I was holding the washcloth to her nose, but pulled it away as Luke put his hand to her forehead, gently pressing it back. He looked at Sissy's nose and then turned back to me.

"She's okay. We'll take her to the hospital to make sure."

I nodded.

"Darius will be here in five minutes with an Explorer. He'll take you to the hospital. I'll follow later," Luke went on.

I nodded again.

He took the washcloth from me and gave it to Sissy. "Head back, gentle pressure. Ava and I need to talk. You okay with that?"

This time Sissy nodded.

I followed him to the utility recess behind the bathroom, and once there, he turned to me.

"I had a man on her. That man's off the radar," he told me.

He was standing close and I had my head tilted back to look at him. I made no sound or other physical reaction to this statement. Internally, however, my lungs forgot how to work.

"Darius will take you to the hospital. He'll also stick around. Matt's off duty, but he's right now gettin' a call. He'll relieve Darius. We're going to find Bobby. You don't leave that hospital unless it's with me or one of the boys. We can't get Matt, you'll get Jack or Ike. Jack's white, light brown hair, six two, built like a Mack truck. You're concerned about his identity, you ask him what he saw you doin' on the monitors Sunday, only you, me and him know about that. Ike's light-skinned black, bald, about two inches taller than you and has a tattoo up the left side of his neck. You can't mistake Ike. Darius won't leave unless he has relief. *Anything* happens to Darius, you get to a safe place and call the police, got me?"

I nodded but asked, "You had a man on her?"

"Why did you think I let you leave the loft on your own yesterday? I knew you were covered. Bobby followed you two all morning."

"Why didn't you tell me?"

"You weren't speakin' to me, remember?"

Oh yeah. Right. I forgot about that.

Moving on.

"Do you think Bobby's okay?" I asked.

"Gonna find out."

I nodded.

When he didn't say more, I asked, "Anything else?"

"Yeah, show me your hands."

I blinked at him. "What?"

"Babe, lift up your hands."

I lifted my hands, palms up.

His eyes dropped down to them and he whispered, "Solid."

"What?"

His hands closed over mine and he gave them a jerk so I fell into him, our hands up between our bodies.

"You're solid. You aren't even shakin'."

I stared at him, not knowing what he was talking about, and he took one hand away, wrapped it behind my neck, brought me to him and kissed my nose.

He pulled back and looked me in the eyes. "Proud of you, Ava." I felt happy heat spread through me at his words before his eyes went ultra-warm and he continued, "Not one of those women who can hack this kind of life? Bullshit."

He said it in his soft, gentle, affectionate voice, and I knew I had just screwed myself royally. I couldn't have exactly run around like a raving lunatic, not with Sissy bleeding and crying. Still, I should have at least affected a minor hissy fit to save my own hide.

Shit.

⚒

Darius was a quiet, handsome, black guy with twists in his hair.

I figured the Nightingale Investigations job application form had the question "Are you hot? Yes. No. If you answered no, please exit the building."

He took us to Presbyterian/St. Luke's and we found out Sissy didn't have a broken nose.

Darius had been relieved by Matt by the time Sissy was done. Luke had not arrived and I had not had word from him. Matt ushered us to another Black Explorer and we belted in, me in the back.

Matt turned to Sissy. "Where do you want to go?"

I leaned forward and gave her an around-the-seat hug. "You want to go back to your Dad's?" I asked softly. "I'll give him a call at work."

I saw her head shake. "I need coffee."

I was thinking more along the vein of cookies, but I had no say. I wasn't the one who got punched in the nose by a huge stranger.

I let Sissy go and turned to Matt. "Fortnum's."

He grinned. "Gotcha."

Matt took us to Fortnum's and stuck around. I figured he did this because he was told to. He seemed wired though, like he needed to do something. I didn't ask, but I guessed he was anxious to find out about Bobby. Then again, I didn't even know who Bobby was and I was anxious to find out about him.

When we walked in, Tex took one look at Sissy and his eyes didn't leave her.

Then he said to the two customers in line, "Stand back. VIPs comin' in." When they didn't move fast enough (even though they moved), he pointed the espresso filter at them and boomed, "Back!"

They jumped out of the way and Sissy and I went to the front of the line. We got our coffees, sat on the couch in front of the store window and the Rock Chicks crowded around. Indy, Ally, Daisy, Jet and Roxie were all there.

"What on earth happened, sugar?" Daisy asked, taking in Sissy's swollen nose and blackening eyes.

"I'm so stupid," Sissy whispered.

I was sitting next to her on the couch and I slid my arm around her shoulders and pulled her into me.

"Tell us," I urged.

She looked at me and then at the girls.

She took a deep breath and said, "My day's Wednesday."

Everyone looked at each other. Then our eyes went to Sissy.

"What, honey?" I asked.

She looked at me. "In the Ava and Luke do the business pool. My day's tomorrow. I knew you didn't do it yesterday. But men like morning nookie. I thought I'd come by early, before anything could happen, take you to the gym. Keep you busy all day. I was protecting my fifty bucks."

Oh, for God's sake.

I just stopped myself from doing an eye roll when she continued, "I was trying to be funny. I was going to tease you about it," she whispered to me. "I didn't mean anything—"

I interrupted her softly, "I know."

She nodded and went on, glancing around the Rock Chicks. "I was buzzing up when some big guy came up to me, saw which buzzer I was pressing and asked if I was you. I said no, I was Sissy Vincetti." She shook her head and looked like she was going to cry again as her eyes moved back to me. "I'm so stupid. I shouldn't have told him my name. Why did I do that?"

I shook my head, too, mainly because I didn't know why she did that, and squeezed her shoulder as she took a calming breath.

She carried on, "The minute I said my name, he grabbed me. Didn't say a word, just grabbed me. I started struggling. He pulled me out of Luke's building and I saw he was taking me to the SUV from Sunday. That's when I screamed and he punched me in the nose. Then I called your name. He almost had me in the car when Luke got there. He took one look at Luke and ran, leaving his car and everything. Luke told me to wait in the building and took off after him. A few minutes later, Luke came back and we went up to the loft. You know the rest."

All the Rock Chicks looked at one another.

"I hope Vance doesn't hear that some guy hit you. If he does, that guy's fucked," Ally said.

"Yeah, Vance isn't a big fan of that kind of thing," Jet put in.

"Who is?" Daisy asked.

Jet gave Daisy a look. "I'm just saying, Vance is *really* not a big fan of that kind of thing."

"You can say that again," Roxie muttered.

Sissy turned to me. "Which one is Vance again?"

My purse rang before I could answer Sissy. I pulled out my phone, flipped it open and put it to my ear.

"Yo."

"She okay?" Luke asked.

I really wanted to smile when I heard his voice, but stopped myself just in time.

"Her nose isn't broken," I told him.

"I know that. Is she okay?" Luke asked again.

I had to admit, I liked not only that he asked the question, but that he knew to ask it.

I looked at Sissy and said, "Yeah, she's hanging in there. You find Bobby?"

"Not yet, we're still lookin'."

Shit.

Luke went on, "You get her story?"

I was beginning to realize that I couldn't live in a pretend world of happiness and ignore everything that was going on around me. It was one thing when it was happening to me, it was quite another when it was happening to Sissy. Luke had been right again, this shit was not going away.

I got up with my latte, walked to the book counter, leaned a hip against it and told him Sissy's story. I finished on, "Do you know what's going on?"

"I'm piecin' it together, but none of what I've got is leadin' back to you."

"What do you have?"

"I'll tell you when I get home tonight."

It was then I remembered I had a date with Ren that night.

Oh crap.

Why was my life so complicated?

"Erm, Luke?"

"Babe, I gotta go," he sounded distracted.

"No, Luke, wait."

"What?" Now he sounded impatient. Not a good way to start.

"Um, I have plans tonight. I'll be... out."

Silence.

I took this silence as Luke remembering my plans.

Then he said, his voice quiet and lethal, "You come to me when you're done."

Ee-yikes.

Luke kept talking, his voice quieter and more lethal. "He touches you Ava, there'll be trouble."

Yep, he remembered my plans.

"I'm sworn off men, remember?" I told him.

I heard muffled movement and I should have realized that he was somewhere he couldn't talk and he was seeking privacy. I should have also realized that this was one of the many warning signs Luke gave me before rocking my world. Instead, like a dork, I just stood there waiting for him to talk.

Then, still in the ultra-quiet, lethal voice, he said, "I keep hearin' that line coming from you and then the minute I get my mouth or hands on you, some- thin' different happens. Ava, you're the hottest fuckin' piece I've ever touched. I find out that heat isn't just for me, I'm still takin' my fill. Zano can have you when I'm done."

I felt pressure crawling up my throat because what he said was just not nice.

I was, of course, forgetting that tough guy Luke Stark was simply giving what he considered were the ground rules for "his woman" going out to dinner alone with another man. The fact that he wasn't throwing a he-man shit fit was practically a miracle.

Still.

"Lucas Stark, you better watch your mouth," I hissed.

"You come to me when you're done," he repeated.

I did not *think* so. "I'm staying the night with Sissy and her Dad."

"You do, it'll be embarrassing for you when I drag your ass out of there."

My heart stopped. "You wouldn't dare," I breathed.

"Try me."

I wasn't going to try him. No way. He'd do it and I knew it.

"You're a jerk," I snapped.

"Tonight, you're mine."

Disconnect.

Argh!

I turned back to the Rock Chicks and they were all looking at me.

Finally Roxie said to Sissy, "Doesn't seem like Wednesday's looking too good."

"Lee's got today, he's going to be bummed," Indy said.

"I got in on the pool late, my day's Friday," Jet put in. "The way this is going, I'm thinking of buying a KitchenAid mixer to match my blender."

"Oh! I love those!" Daisy exclaimed, turning to Jet. "Which color you gonna get?"

I looked to the ceiling as the Rock Chicks discussed Jet's forthcoming KitchenAid appliance purchase.

Then I thought, *my life sucks.*

Chapter 14

You Missed It Again, Babe

After I got off the phone with Luke, I planned my day carefully.

I hung with the Rock Chicks, Tex and Matt at Fortnum's all afternoon and I made a call to Shirleen. Duke, Indy's second-in-command, came in, and even though I hadn't seen him in months, I smiled at him and yelled, "Hey Duke!" He scowled at me and disappeared in the books.

"What's that all about?" I asked Indy.

"He's not a big fan of the 'during' part of a Badass Motherfucker Courtship. He prefers the 'after'," Indy explained.

I couldn't say I blamed him.

Detective Jimmy Marker stopped by at Luke's request. Sissy and I told him about the car chase and the recent kidnapping attempt, and I took that opportunity to explain that my first kidnapping was a "misunderstanding"—news that made him stare at me hard.

He gave me a lecture about talking to the cops next time I nearly rolled my car over onto I-25 while being pursued by a bad guy. Then he and Duke carried on a loud conversation about "how these boys need to get their heads examined". Then Detective Marker left.

Matt and I dropped Sissy at her Dad's and we both stayed while Sissy told her Dad the latest story. Then we stayed while Sissy's Dad hit the roof. We left after he calmed down.

Sissy walked us to the door and gave Matt a look. Matt correctly interpreted this look and stepped outside of hearing distance.

I turned to Sissy. "What?"

"Remember when you pretended not to care when you didn't have a date to the senior prom?"

Oh no, where was she going with this?

"Yeah."

"Well, tonight you're going out with one of the hottest guys we know and then you're going home to *the* hottest guy *ever*. How's them apples?" She gave me a big smile, so pleased for me she didn't seem to remember she got punched in the face that day for the first time in her life (and hopefully the last).

I shook my head. "You're a dork."

"And *you're* a *knockout*."

I shoved her shoulder. She shoved mine back.

After a few more shoves, Matt and I left.

Matt took me to Luke's loft and I held my breath until the elevator doors slid open and we saw Luke wasn't there. As the place was under surveillance, Matt didn't stick around. He was itching to get into the search for Bobby. I spent a few moments sending good vibes to Bobby and encouraging vibes to the Nightingale Boys to find him, and fast. Then I called Shirleen as scheduled.

"Shee-it," she answered instead of saying hello. "You still gonna do this?"

"Yes," I told her.

She sighed. "I'll be there in ten."

I'd called her from Fortnum's, and as she was my Rock Chick and Badass Motherfucker Courtship Mentor, she was bound by Rock Chick Law to help me (yes, it was weird, but at that point it worked for me).

She picked me up in her Lincoln Navigator (seriously, Lee had to pay his employees well if his receptionist had a Navigator) and took me to my place. She hung out watching TV while I got ready for my date with Ren.

Halfway dressed, my phone rang.

I looked at it, scared to death it would be Luke. It said, "Dom calling".

What the hell?

"Yes?" I answered.

"Ava, don't hang up," Dom said quickly.

"You're a dickhead," I told him.

"Our last thing didn't go too well…"

I wanted to shout "Ya think?" but he kept talking.

"I'm sorry about that but, Ava, you gotta listen to me. There's some serious shit goin' down. You and me, we gotta get out of town. You gotta meet me at—"

"Fuck that, Dom. You're nuts."

"No, this is some serious shit."

"Yes, it's *your* serious shit. Keep me out of it," I snapped.

"That's what I'm tryin' to do," he snapped back.

"Can you please tell me why I'm *in* it?"

"They're tryin' to get to me."

"No kidding. They're trying so hard, they nearly kidnapped Sissy this morning. Punched her in the nose, blood everywhere. We thought it was broken. She was a mess."

Silence.

"Dom?"

"What'd you just say?"

"Some big guy in a dark blue SUV *punched* your wife in the nose this morning while trying to kidnap her."

Silence again.

I was losing patience, and time, quickly.

"Dom! I don't have time for this."

"He hit Sissy?" Dom asked quietly.

Something about the way he said it made my mind still.

"Yeah," I told him.

"He's got at least a foot and probably a hundred pounds on her."

"Do you know this guy?" I asked, but he ignored my question.

"And he *hit* her?" Dom was sounding a bit scary.

"Dom, tell me, who is this guy?"

Dom still wasn't listening. "You say her nose isn't broken?"

"She's fine. It's swollen, her eyes are black, but she's okay."

Was I reassuring Dominic Vincetti about his wife's well-being? Was it me who'd stepped into an alternate universe?

"I'll call her," Dom told me.

Oh no.

"Dom, don't," I said.

"Later."

Disconnect.

Fuckity, fuck, fuck, *fuck*.

I looked at my alarm clock on the nightstand and it was already seven o'clock. I wanted to call Sissy, but I didn't have time. As it was I rushed through my final preparations.

I had decided to go gung ho for the night. I was telling myself this wasn't an in-your-face to Luke after his last tough guy speech. I was telling myself this was for me. That even though I had sworn off men, it didn't mean that I couldn't look cute.

I was wearing a black skirt, so tight it fit like a glove and cupped my ass. Its hem hit me at the top of the knees and had a front slit that went to mid-thigh. I topped it with a black, ultra-wide, low scoop-necked, long-sleeved, stretchy t-shirt that also fit like a glove and had a long hem so it came down well over the waistband of the skirt and gathered around my waist. I put on tons of silver bangles and charm bracelets on my right wrist and hoops at my ears, but didn't add rings and necklaces (in the latter area, I was going to let my cleavage do the work). I finished with pointy-toed, pencil-heeled, sling-backed, black pumps. I left my hair long and wild, had done my makeup in "Drama!" and spritzed with my expensive perfume.

I walked into my living room and Shirleen was lazing back on my couch, eating yogurt out of a container. Her eyes bugged out when she saw me.

"Girl," she muttered low. "You are playin' with fire."

"I'm just going out to dinner."

"And I'm just sayin', you best pop by here before you go back to Luke, change your clothes, wash your face and hope he never finds out you went out with another man wearin' that outfit."

"It'll all be fine," I assured her.

"Yeah, that's what you said about our visit to Uncle Vito. Now he's plannin' your weddin' to his nephew."

This, I had to admit, was true.

There came a knock at the door.

Shirleen looked to the heavens. "Here we go," she said as if warning God to brace.

I went to the door and opened it. Ren stood there.

Ren was just like Dom in the tall, lean-hipped, broad-shouldered, thick, dark hair departments. Ren's hair had no wave like Dom's did, though. His eyes were a fantastic espresso color, and even though I pretty much knew that he knew he was hot, he didn't strut like his cousin. He was just... cool. Way cool. Yumalicious cool.

He was wearing a well-cut, dark-brown suit, a light-brown shirt and his muscular throat was on show. I'd always loved his throat. There was something about it that made you just want to *taste* it.

"Ava," he said.

My eyes went from his throat to his face. "Hey Ren."

He was looking in my eyes. Then he did a body sweep and his gaze came back to mine.

When it did and I caught the hungry look in his eye, I had to stop myself from putting my hand to the door to hold myself up.

Boy was I screwed.

⌖

Carmine's on Penn had a cozy atmosphere, was always packed to the gills, had white paper over the tables so you could draw on it with crayons they provided and didn't have menus. Their dishes were listed on blackboards on the wall, but none of the items made any sense unless you'd been there before. The waiters explained the dishes then wrote your order in crayon on the white paper on your table.

I didn't need the waiters to explain the dishes. I knew exactly what I wanted. I just hoped it was what Ren wanted because the food was served family style.

Ren and I had chit chatted on the ride there in his black Jaguar (seriously sleek ride, totally super-fly). He valet parked and we were seated at a cozy table a deux. We chit chatted before ordering and chit chatted while eating the delicious garlicky rolls.

Ren was easy to talk to. He might have been hot as well as way cool, but there was something mellow about him, laidback, and he gave the impression he gave a shit about what you said.

Our big bowl of caesar salad was put on the table when Ren asked, "So how are you doin'?"

Considering we were into the salad stage, I didn't figure this was an opening remark.

I looked at him and tried to judge how safe he was. Luke had thrown a new light on the Vincetti-Zano family. Still, I'd spent a lot of time with them. When they took in Sissy, they took me in and they were always really nice to me. There were a lot of them I liked, and one of the ones I liked the most was Ren.

"Do you know what's been happening?" I asked.

He sat back ignoring the salad, eyes serious. "Tell me."

I served up the salad and told him. Then I told him more while eating the salad. Then I told him some more while eating a second serving of the salad.

While I talked, I could feel Ren's laidback mood slipping into something a lot scarier.

The big salad bowl was taken away and I just stopped myself from nabbing one last crouton as the server took it when Ren asked, "Why didn't you call me?"

I looked at him a little surprised. We knew each other, but weren't exactly close. He wasn't like a bestest best friend who you called when you found a great fingernail polish or when you got kidnapped, especially when his family was doing the kidnapping.

"Why would I call you?" I asked back.

"This is family business."

"I'm not family."

"Sissy's family."

I couldn't argue with that.

He sat back and said with finality, "I'll take care of it."

I leaned forward. Time to get down to business.

"What, exactly, are you gonna take care of?" I asked.

"Don't worry about it," he returned casually, and I could tell he was ready to move on to another subject.

I didn't think so. "Well, considering the fact that, for some bizarre reason, I'm involved, I can't help but worry about it."

He just looked at me.

"Why am I involved?" I went on.

"Because Dom's a dickhead," he answered.

I couldn't argue with that either, but still. "That doesn't give me a lot to go on, Ren."

My hand was resting on the table and Ren put his over mine. I looked at his hand and noticed it was nice, strong and well-veined. His hand didn't look like the hand of a man who wore a suit.

I looked back to him, shrugging off thoughts of his hand, when he started speaking.

"Dom's been talkin' about you a lot. I won't repeat it and I'm sorry to have to tell you this because I know it's gonna piss you off, but he's made it pretty clear he's moved on from Sissy, and even more clear who he'd like to move on to." At this news, my fingers curled in and fisted angrily under his, and he twisted his hand so that our palms were facing and his fingers were laced in mine. I was hoping that Luke didn't have cameras installed in Carmine's because I was pretty certain if he saw Ren and I holding hands, especially like that, there'd be hell to pay, and I'd be the one paying.

Ren kept talking. "He has some troubles with some not-so-good guys. Fucked with the business, fucked with the family. Vito's pissed, but he's trying to sort it out because Dom's family. In the meantime, Dom's disappeared. They want Dom and are tryin' to flush him out, so I suspect that's why they've gone after you. And today, finding Sissy available, her."

I gently pulled my hand away and sat back, looking to the floor at the side of the table as I vowed quintuple-revenge against Dickhead Dom.

"You'll be safe," Ren was saying and I looked at him. Laidback Ren was history, his eyes were sharp, and he even looked angry. I'd seen a lot of Ren's looks, but this was a new one, and I had to admit, even if it made me a freak, it was hot. "I'll assign Santo to you and Lucky to Sissy," he finished.

I blinked at him as our family style meal was served. Ren let me pick; Chicken Montana with asparagus, sun dried tomatoes and Gorgonzola sauce. I'd let the healthy living mojo have the night off.

"What do you mean, assign—?" I began to ask.

Ren interrupted me, "Bodyguards. Santo and Lucky will look after you two."

Oh shit. This was not good.

"No, really, that isn't necessary. I'm covered."

Ren's eyes caught mine. "By Stark?"

Hmm.

He seemed very interested, his eyes no longer angry, but still sharp and very alert.

"Um… yeah," I answered.

Ren went in for a direct hit. "You seein' him?"

Well there we were, the moment of truth.

Was I seeing Luke Stark?

Was I seeing Luke Stark?

Crap.

"Kind of," I hedged.

The tips of Ren's lips went up slightly and I knew he found this amusing. "Stark doesn't strike me as a guy who would 'kind of' be seein' a woman like you."

"What's that mean?"

Why did I ask? Why, why, why?

"A man like that has a woman like you, there's nothing 'kind of' about it."

"Do you know Luke?"

"I know him. Not well, but I know him."

"If you don't know him well then how would you know? He might be perfectly happy with having a relationship that's not exclusive. In fact, he might do it all the time."

Just ask Sandra Whoever-She-Was, she'd tell you, I thought, but did not say.

"I bet he does, just not with a woman like you," Ren said.

"What's that mean?"

I did it again! Why?

He leaned toward me. "Ava, you should know Stark and me don't get along. We don't because we find ourselves on opposite sides of the fence a lot of the time. We also don't get along because we're a lot alike. Therefore I know a man like that doesn't 'kind of' see a woman like you because *I* wouldn't 'kind of' see a woman like you. A man like that gets hold of a woman like you, all ass, legs, hair and attitude, protecting a soft spot you can just about see but she won't let you touch... Fuck." His voice lowered in a sexy way and he leaned in further. His eyes got that hungry look again and I found I was having trouble breathing. "A man like that gets hold of a woman like you, it automatically becomes exclusive."

Holy cramoly.

I decided I didn't want to know any more and started spooning up the Chicken Montana.

I also decided that, even though I couldn't stay in my pretend happy place for very long, there were certain times I was going to go visit.

This was one of those times.

"Ava," Ren called.

I looked at him.

He still had that hungry look, but it had intensified. Chicken Montana slid off the spoon and plopped on the white paper as my belly did a plunge.

"Do you understand what I just said to you?" he asked softly.

"I'm in my pretend happy place," I told him.

He leaned back and smiled and I had to admit it was *hot*.

It was also predatory.

I was *so* screwed.

For some reason, when Ren and I left the restaurant and I told him he had to take me to Luke's, Ren found this amusing.

Discovering that Ren found this amusing, I found I needed cookies. Therefore I asked Ren to detour to King Soopers so we could buy cookies.

Ren found this even more amusing.

While we were at King Soopers, I bought a whole bunch of other stuff, probably because I was stalling about going back to Luke's. Ren seemed not to care even a little bit that we were grocery shopping at ten o'clock at night with our end destination being Luke's.

This made me uncomfortable. Seeing as I was a dork, I again didn't read the warning signs. When Ren parked outside of Luke's and I got out and went for the bags, Ren came around to help me.

Not good.

"I've got it," I said, struggling with five bags, two of which contained cookies.

"I'll carry them."

Oh no. No, no, no, *no!*

Ren was *not* walking into Luke's loft with me.

He took the bags away from me firmly and started to walk to Luke's building.

Crap!

Ren was walking into Luke's loft with me.

Alert! Alert! Danger! Danger!

"Ren, really," I said, catching up and beginning to sound desperate.

He turned to me and I stopped dead at the look in his eye. "I'm makin' sure you're safe in the building, Ava."

And that, apparently, was that.

I couldn't exactly get in a rip roarin' on the sidewalk with him, not with Luke (maybe) upstairs. I had to be cool, calm and composed. I'd sworn off men. It was my decision and I was sticking to it.

So what? One hot guy who wanted to get in my pants was orchestrating a faceoff with another one. It didn't touch me. I was immune. I was removed.

I'm a little scared, Good Ava was trembling, holding close to my neck.

I can't WAIT to see what happens! Bad Ava was trembling with excitement.

I called the elevator and then used my key to the button to Luke's floor. The whole time, even if I was immune and removed, I hoped that Luke was out doing scary shit (but not too scary) and not at home.

The elevator doors slid open and all hopes were dashed.

The loft was softly lit, Tom Petty was singing "American Girl" on the stereo and Luke was standing behind the semi-circle bar, phone to his ear.

His head snapped up when we entered. His eyes did a body scan of me, his mouth tightened then his eyes moved to Ren and his jaw clenched.

Shit.

I turned immediately to Ren. "I'll take them now," I said, grabbing the bags. "Thanks for helping me," I went on, as if it was all my idea.

He let me take the bags. Luckily cookies didn't weigh that much in cookie form. Their weight multiplied significantly once they'd processed themselves onto your ass.

Ren smiled down at me. "Nice night, Ava," he said softly.

Don't touch me, don't touch me, don't touch me, I thought.

"Thanks for dinner," I replied.

His hand came up, I held my breath and he tucked my hair behind my ear. All the while he did this, he was looking into my eyes, his carrying that look that made me feel like I was going to pass out.

He walked into the elevator, turned, his eyes moved to Luke then back to me, he smiled and the doors slid closed.

Alone again with Luke.

Shit.

I walked into the loft not looking at Luke and planning my defense.

He'd mostly touched my hair, *not* me. I was going to argue that hair didn't count.

I put the bags on the counter at the back wall not looking at Luke and heard Luke say into the phone, "Call me when you have an update on his condition."

At his words, I turned to him woodenly and heard him beep the phone off. My eyes moved to his and I wished they didn't.

He was *way* pissed-off. Super-pissed. Ultra-pissed.

Still, I had to know. "Bobby?" I asked.

"Found him," Luke answered. "Fractured skull, major head trauma."

I closed my eyes and opened them again. "Is he going to be okay?"

"We'll know more tomorrow."

"I'm sorry, Luke," I said quietly, meaning every word.

"You didn't smash him in the head."

This was true. I still felt like shit. Bobby got hurt looking after Sissy and me.

"I don't know what to say," I told him.

"Nothin' to say."

He was likely right about that.

"You wanna tell me why you brought Ren Zano to my loft?" he asked. His voice had changed from matter-of-fact to lethal and I tried to find my immune and removed zone (and failed).

I turned away from him and started to unload cookies. "I told him about my troubles. He wanted to make sure I got in safely." I tried to pretend it was nothing when I knew it was anything but.

"Ava, turn around and look at me."

Not gonna happen. "I'm putting away the groceries. Some of it has to get in the freezer." Like the three containers of ice cream.

"Ava, turn around."

"Luke, no. I know you're angry, but you're just going to have to get over it." I shoved the ice cream in the freezer and slammed the door, all the while avoiding his eyes. "We just had dinner. We talked. Nothing more. That's it. The end."

I started unloading cookies. Double Stuff Oreos, Chips Ahoy, Nutter Butter, regular Milanos, Mint Milanos, orange-flavored Milanos…

"You stood right in front of me, wearin' a fuck-me skirt and fuck-me shoes, and let him touch you," Luke said to my back.

All right. Enough.

I whirled on Luke.

"He touched my *hair*." There, I used that as my defense. It didn't sound good, but I was going to go with it. "He just took me out to a nice dinner. I could hardly bean him with a grocery bag full of cookies for touching my hair!" I snapped.

That was when Luke moved.

One second, he was three feet away, the next second he was on me. Or, I should say, I was in his arms and he was giving me an angry, shut-Ava-up kiss.

Then (I swear I couldn't help it) my mouth opened under his. My tongue touched his fantastic lips, his mouth opened, my tongue slid inside and the kiss exploded.

In fact, it kind of felt like *everything* exploded.

After that we were all over each other. My hands pulled his tee out of his cargoes and up. His mouth disengaged and he took over, yanking the tee off and throwing it aside. His hands went to my ribcage then up, over my breasts, one hand pulling down my shirt and one of the cups of my bra, exposing me to him. I did a swift half-shocked half-turned-on intake of breath and his hands slid around my back, pressing in, arching it. His head came down and his mouth closed around my nipple and he sucked deep.

I gasped then moaned, shock gone, now only turned on. My hands went to his head, holding him to me when he did the same to the other side.

His lips started gliding up my chest and I went for his buckle, yanking at it, losing patience, wanting a feel of him *now*. I gave up and slid my palm down his hard crotch. When I did, his mouth came back to mine, kissing me hotter, deeper than before and pushing me into the back counter. He tore his mouth from mine, leaned to the side, did an arm swipe at the counter and cookies went flying.

He captured my lips again, his hands going down, tugging my skirt up to my hips then yanking down my panties. I shimmied out of them and he lifted me, hands at my ass, and planted me on the counter. He spread my legs and moved his hips between them, all the while his lips on mine, his tongue in my mouth.

His hand went between my legs, hit dead on the target and it felt so good my back arched, my head dropping back, losing contact with his lips. His mouth went down my neck, my chest, back to my nipple as his hand worked me, thumb rolling on the target while a finger slid inside.

"Luke!" I gasped, close, oh so close, I was nearly there and I knew it was going to be good.

Upon hearing my gasp, his hand and mouth instantly went away. I gave a small cry of protest as his other hand fisted in my hair.

"No you don't," he growled and picked me up, one hand at my ass, the other one still in my hair. I wrapped my arms and legs around him as he carried me to the bed with his face buried in my neck, his tongue sending shivers sliding straight from the skin under my ear on a no-fail trajectory to my special girl parts. He set me on my feet beside the bed and released me.

At that point, it was all go, go, go. Not because I thought we would get interrupted but because I wanted him inside me and I wasn't going to wait one fucking second longer.

My hands went back to the buckle of his pants. As I worked it, I got up on tiptoe and my mouth went to his neck, tasting him with my tongue. He tasted great, he smelled great, everything about Luke was *great*. I got the buckle free, undid the button and slid down the zip as he unzipped my skirt at the back and shoved it down so it fell at my feet.

My mouth now at his throat and working my way around, he pulled my shirt up, foiling my plan to stick my hand down his pants. Without a choice I leaned back, lifted my arms and he whipped it over my head. He picked me up, hands at my ass again. My legs went around his hips and he put a knee to the bed, planted me in it and covered me with his body.

Now we were getting somewhere.

During this maneuver, wanting to be ready for anything, I slid his cargoes over his tight ass. I dipped my chin and looked at him, my eyes hooded, his molten. His hands went to my hips, lifted them. I felt him there, and eyes on mine, without hesitation he slammed inside me, burying himself to the hilt.

I closed my eyes, arched my neck and breathed, "Yes."

He felt good, he felt hot, he felt hard.

He felt *right*.

I lifted my knees and pressed them against his sides as he drove in again and again and again, hard, hot and totally out-of-control. While he slammed into me, he kissed me. When I started panting, his mouth went to my ear and I lifted my head and pressed my lips to where his neck met his shoulder, wrapping my arms tight around his back, my legs around his hips like I was never going to let go.

I was there, *right* there when I heard him say, his voice hoarse, "Ava."

I dropped my head back and tried to focus on him but couldn't because it hit me. I came and it was toe-curling, world-tilting *amazing*.

I didn't know it but when I came, I gasped Luke's name, and shortly after, I smiled.

And he watched the whole thing.

⌖

Luke rolled to his side, taking me with him. Still inside me, his hand behind my knee to keep my leg wrapped around his hip.

I'd just done the nasty with Lucas Stark.

I'd played the scenario in my head dozens of times, *hundreds* of times, and never, not once, was it as good as what just happened.

Shit.

I was so screwed.

Luke gently slid out of me, tugged at the bottom of the comforter and pulled it over my body. Then he rolled over on his back and bucked his hips, pulling up his cargoes. He moved away and I watched as he silently sat at the edge of the bed. He put his elbows to his knees, forehead in the heels of his hands in a masculine position of defeated reflection.

I stared and felt my throat close as if in slow motion.

Of course. Fatty Fatty Four-Eyes Ava Barlow had just done the nasty with ultra-hot, tough guy, macho man Lucas Stark, which meant Lucas Stark just gave the business to Fatty Fatty Four-Eyes.

He must be mortified.

I rolled, taking the comforter with me. All I could think of was escape. I had to get out of there, get away from him. Wyoming wasn't far enough. I had to buy myself onto one of those spaceships that they let rich people take a ride on and never, *ever* come back to earth.

I neared the end of the bed. I was still wearing my pointy-toed, pencil-heeled sling backs and they kept catching on the covers hampering my movement. I was just about to crawl over the footboard when he tagged me with an arm around my waist and I landed on my back. He pinned one side of my body with his and looked at my face. I saw, somewhat surprised, that his eyes were still ink.

"Where you goin'?" he asked, voice soft, slightly husky and very sexy.

"I'm going to spend the night with Sissy and her Dad," I told him, voice quiet, slightly husky and very scared.

I watched in total shock as he gave me a sexy half-grin then touched my mouth with his. His mouth moved away, but his face didn't and he kept looking in my eyes.

"You missed it again, babe," he said in his gentle, affectionate voice.

"What?" I whispered, transfixed by his inky eyes and caught up in The Voice.

He lifted his head a bit and shook it. His hand came up and he sifted his fingers through my hair at my temple. He watched his hand's movement then his eyes came back to mine.

"I'm not gonna clue you in this time, Ava. This time you're gonna have to figure it out for yourself. One thing I'm gonna tell you is that you're not goin' *anywhere.*"

The way he said it, I knew he didn't just mean tonight.

Guess he wasn't mortified by giving the business to Fatty Fatty Four-Eyes.

Seriously, I was screwed.

Chapter 15
Together in A Way You Can't Deny

In the dead of the night, Luke tugged me over the top of him to his other side. I started to settle into him face-to-face, but with pressure at my hip, he rolled me so my back was to him and he leaned in so we were bent at the waist.

I didn't say a word. I didn't mind this new position. It was nice.

And anyway, I was tired.

I started to fall asleep again when his arms wrapped around me. One of his hands went north and one went south.

I sucked in breath and came awake when one of his fingers hit the target between my legs and the thumb and finger on his other hand did a delicious nipple roll.

Um... *wow*.

"Luke?" My voice sounded sleepy and quiet.

"Quiet, Ava," Luke murmured into the back of my neck, and then I felt his lips there.

For some reason, I snuggled my ass into his crotch, feeling him hard against me. He did another roll at the target and I made a small noise in my throat as heat shot through me.

His body shifted, and I kid you not, he slid inside me.

Oh... my... *God*.

None of my lovers had been adventurous, weirdly, not even Dave, the sex maniac. He might have been a perv, but he wasn't imaginative. I'd never been cuffed to a bed and I'd never done it in any position but the two top sellers (him on top, me on top).

This was nice. Very nice, ultra-nice. Moaning, panting with mouth open nice. His hands kept at me as he moved inside me and I pressed into him, wanting more.

"Luke," I breathed, nearly there.

His hand went away from my nipple, came to my jaw. His thumb slid across my opened lower lip and I came. Hard.

Minutes later his arms tensed. He drove into me one last time, his mouth in the crook of my neck, where I heard (with deep satisfaction, I had to admit) his low groan.

Moments after he finished, his arms came around me tight, one at my waist, the other one slashed diagonally across my torso. He stayed inside me and his mouth moved up my neck.

"Wow," I whispered, somehow moved by the experience, feeling, for some strange reason, it was the most intimate moment with another human being I'd had in my life.

I felt a movement of his lips at my neck and I was pretty certain he smiled. Then I snuggled my behind into him and I heard him groan again. I smiled to myself in the dark, and believe it or not, wrapped tight in Luke's arms, Luke still inside me, I immediately fell back to sleep.

⌖

I was in my usual morning position, tucked into Luke's side, arm around his abs, leg thrown over his thighs, when Luke woke me by tilting up my chin and kissing me.

Then he rolled me to my back. Then his mouth moved down my body. Then it was between my legs.

After he made me finish, he came up over me and he finished.

All of this was done without a word.

When it was over, Luke stayed where he was, his bodyweight pressing me into the bed. One of my legs was bent, foot on the bed, inside thigh pressed against his hip. The other leg wrapped around his thigh, my arms around him, hands idly sliding across his skin and muscle.

His face was buried in my neck, his mouth moving there with no purpose or intent. Just a post doing-the-nasty affectionate touch. A *sexy* post doing the nasty affectionate touch.

My hands slid up his back. "I have to brush my teeth," I whispered.

His head came up and he looked down at me, eyes ink. He stared at me one beat, two, then three, then more. I didn't know why he kept looking at me.

What I did know was that his face looked less hard than normal. Partly with satisfaction, partly with something else I couldn't decipher.

Okay, to be perfectly honest, I didn't *want* to decipher.

Goddamn.

Finally I said softly, "Luke."

He gave me a half-grin, and even in a lying position I felt my knees wobble.

There I was, lying in bed, Luke on top of me, still inside me, my limbs wrapped around him.

Hell and damnation.

How did I let this happen?

What happened to my vow?

How was I ever going to go back to my vibrators now?

I took my arms from around him and shoved his shoulders. "Get off."

The grin turned full-fledged. He bent his head, touched my lips with his and rolled off.

I hightailed to the bathroom.

Crapity, crap, crap, *crap.*

Now how was I going to get out of *this* mess?

I couldn't just get on a spaceship and float around the earth. That was too close. I needed to beam to another galaxy. Since Star Trek technology wasn't possible in the non-TV realm, I decided I needed to find a plastic surgeon and have my face altered so I was unrecognizable *and* move to Guadalajara for good measure.

Then I realized I was naked in the bathroom and had nothing with me to put on.

I was *such* a dork.

A black zip-up sweatshirt was hanging on the back of the door and I fell on it like a starving man at a feast. I zipped it on and looked in the mirror.

I'm happy, Good Ava told me, grinning like a loon. *This is what we've AL-WAYS wanted.*

Bad Ava had her arms crossed, She was scowling and she was strangely silent. But I knew what she was thinking.

I did my morning business and walked out of the bathroom. Luke, naked (and looking *fine* by the way), was heading toward it as I walked out. He nabbed me at the waist, pulled me in for a quick, hard kiss then, let me go and went into the bathroom.

I stared at the door in a mini-Luke Lip Fog for a few beats. Then I found my underwear, pulled them on and wondered what to do.

I needed to get out of there, and soon. I needed to find a quiet place to let my head explode. I needed to shove all this down, bury it, forget it happened.

Bad Ava's unspoken advice was the only thing I could think of. I needed to find a way out before this all turned to shit. Like it always turned to shit.

Always.

Instead of doing any of that, I went to the kitchen, nabbed a diet, tidied the cookies, put away the forgotten-in-the-sex-a-thon-last-night groceries and started to make toast.

Luke came out when I slid down the lever on the slices of bread. I heard him moving around, but I stared at the toaster as if I was certain it would animate and start dancing around like all the stuff in the Beast's house in that Disney movie and I didn't want to miss the show.

He came up behind me, wrapped his arms around me and touched his lips to my neck. This felt good. Sweet, nice, intimate and wonderful.

Ava, Bad Ava's sharp voice was a warning.

What? Good Ava asked innocently. *As far as I'm concerned, Luke could hold us all day.*

Fuckity, fuck, fuck, *fuck.*

"You want toast?" I asked, not moving my eyes from the toaster.

He moved closer. I pressed against the counter. Luke pressed against me.

"Yeah," he said against my neck.

"Okay, I need to get the butter."

He let me go. I got the butter and put it on the counter. I did all of this without looking at him.

I was going for a knife when he moved in again, getting in front of me. He pressed my bottom to the counter, this time full frontal, arms sliding around me. I tilted my head back to look at him. He was smiling down at me, amused about something.

"What's funny?" I asked, not thinking anything was funny, at all, in the whole universe.

"I don't know yet," he answered.

I stared at him, blank-faced. Then I asked, "What?"

"Just waitin' to see what you're gonna say next."

"Why does that make you smile?"

"'Cause I'm thinkin' whatever it is, it's gonna be good."

"Why?"

"You've had a full ten minutes to think about how you're gonna get out of this now that you and me are together in a way you can't deny. I'm lookin' forward to hearin' what you've come up with."

My blank look turned into a glare.

One, two, three, four, five, six... there, temper under control.

I took a deep breath and I blurted out the first thing that came to me, "Simple. We stop seeing each other immediately."

He burst into laughter, his arms got tighter and his face went into my neck. He laughed into my neck for what seemed like a long time as my body went stiffer and stiffer in his arms.

"I wasn't being funny," I pointed out what *I* thought was the obvious.

His head came up and he looked at me, still grinning. "Babe, you're hilarious."

"It's just sex. We're not 'together in a way you can't deny'," I told him.

"Ava, after I made you come, you fell asleep with my cock inside you. That's about as together as two people can get."

I did do that.

Shit!

"It's just sex," I pushed it.

His face got closer, but he didn't look any less amused.

"It isn't just sex and you know it," he returned, his voice soft, gentle, affectionate.

He was right. It wasn't.

And he was using The Voice a lot these days.

Crap!

Then I hit on a plan. It was a stupid plan, but it was all I could come up with at the time. I knew he'd never go for it, but at least it was something.

"We'll be fuck buddies," I told him.

His grin disappeared, his chin jerked down and his brows drew together. "Come again?"

"Fuck buddies. You know, like they talked about on *Sex and the City*. Guys you know that you sleep with. Just sex. No entanglements, no relationship, just mind-blowing sex."

The grin came back as his face relaxed. "Mind-blowing sex?"

223

Oops. I probably shouldn't have used that adjective.

"Or, you know, good sex," I tried to cover.

His body started shaking with laughter.

I started getting angry again. "Luke!" I snapped.

His hands pulled the sweatshirt up over my behind and went in, sliding across the skin of my back.

"I could do fuck buddies," he said, and I blinked.

I thought he'd say no. In fact, I was certain he'd say no. That was why I suggested it.

"You could?" I asked.

"Yeah." His hands started moving up my back (taking the sweatshirt with it, by the way).

"Seriously?"

"Yeah."

Okay, *now* what had I gotten myself into? I'd just become fuck buddies with Luke Stark.

Worse than that, it was my idea!

I like that idea, I think it's fab, Bad Ava had lost her warning vibe and now sounded dreamy.

I hate it. It stinks, Good Ava had lost her happy vibe and now sounded pissed.

"With rules," Luke said.

Uh-oh. Here we go.

"Fuck buddies don't have rules. It's like being in a fight club. The first rule of fuck buddies is... there are no rules." I was making this up as I went along. I had no idea if fuck buddies had rules. I'd never had a fuck buddy. I'd never even *wanted* one.

Hell, I didn't want one now!

Especially not Luke.

The inky went out of his eyes and they got scary shiny. "We're gonna have rules."

I thought, considering his scary shiny eyes, it was probably best I at least listen to his rules.

"What are the rules?" I asked on a sigh.

"First, we're the kind of fuck buddies who spend time together not fuckin'."

224

"Luke, that defeats the purpose of fuck buddies."

Again, I was making it up.

He ignored me. "Second, we're exclusive fuck buddies. No one else touches you while I'm fuckin' you."

That one wouldn't be hard.

"Let's go back to the first one," I said.

"Ava, that's the deal, no discussion."

"What kind of time would we spend together?"

"Ava—"

"No, I want to know."

His eyes dropped to my mouth and his arms wrapped around me so his fingers were resting on the sides of my breasts.

Then he muttered, "Maybe we'll just fuck."

I felt my knees wobble as my lungs expanded. "I could spend time not fucking," I blurted.

He grinned.

Foiled again!

I glared.

He caught the glare and his body started shaking with laughter again.

"Honestly, I hate you," I told him.

"No," his mouth came to mine, his eyes not leaving my own, "you don't."

Against my will, I started sliding into a fog. My head tilted back further, his slanted and he started to kiss me when the buzzer went. He disengaged from my lips, but kissed my nose and walked away.

In another fog, I watched him move. He'd put on another pair of sweat-pants, these black with three black-on-black stripes up the sides.

Not surprisingly, his chest was bare.

I noticed, not for the first time but with my Luke Sense significantly more honed after our sex-a-thon, that he moved well. He moved like he was in absolute command of every centimeter of muscle, sinew and bone in his body, and there were a lot of them. I sighed at the sight, and even I had to admit it was a contented sound.

Damn it all to hell.

He picked up the door phone and said, "Yeah?" Three seconds later, his eyes cut to me.

Whatever it was, I knew by the look of him was not good.

He listened for another couple of seconds, then without a word he put down the phone. I watched him walk back to me, and since he had a funny look on his face, as if he didn't know whether to laugh or yell, I didn't watch the way he moved; just his expression. I was waiting for him to decide.

He came into the kitchen and leaned his hips against the counter opposite me, putting his palms on it at his sides.

"Santo Mancini wants you to know he's ready, just in case you wanna go somewhere," he told me calmly, neither laughing nor yelling, which was a relief.

I stared at him. "Who?" I asked.

"Santo Mancini."

"Who's San...?" Oh shit. Ren's bodyguard.

Again, I wanted someone to tell me: why me? My life was so complicated, I couldn't even keep track of all the fucked up shit that was happening.

His voice started sliding into the "going to yell" zone. "You wanna tell me why the guy who kidnapped you a few days ago is buzzin' up to the loft tellin' me he's waitin' for you downstairs?"

No, I actually didn't want to tell him.

"Um..."

"Ava," he said low.

What the hell? I'd tell him.

"Well, I told Ren what was happening, and he kind of arranged for Sissy and me to have bodyguards."

He stared at me a beat then his head dropped, and he might have been staring at his feet, or he might have closed his eyes. I couldn't see which one and it didn't matter, really. He was in another masculine position of reflection, this time likely wondering what in *the* hell he'd gotten himself into when he got mixed up with me.

I thought it best to carry on with breakfast. The toast in the toaster had long since come up and wouldn't be hot anymore so the butter wouldn't melt. I hated non-melted butter on toast. I decided to let Luke have the non-melted butter ones, exchanged toast for bread and pressed down the lever.

"Ava," Luke called from behind me.

I turned. He was now sitting on the counter, eyes on me.

"Come here," he demanded softly.

Don't ask me why, but for some reason, I went. He opened his legs and I walked between them. He closed his thighs against my sides, wrapped a hand around the back of my neck as I tilted my head back to look at him and his face came close.

"You're lucky," he told me.

"I am?" I asked.

"Yeah. You're lucky I've fucked you. You're lucky it was mind-blowing. You're lucky I think it's fuckin' sweet-as-hell that you would nestle into me and fall asleep with me inside you. You're lucky I like you movin' around my kitchen wearin' my sweatshirt. You didn't have all that, babe, I gotta tell you, I would likely be pretty fuckin' pissed Zano assigned one of his thugs to be your bodyguard."

"Well, I didn't——" I started to say in my own defense (really, I *didn't*, it wasn't my idea for Ren to give me a bodyguard), but Luke's lips touched mine and I stopped talking.

"Don't try your luck," he warned.

I thought about trying my luck. I did this while looking in Luke's eyes. I decided not to try my luck.

"You want toast or what?" I asked, kind of bitchy.

He did a half-grin. His hand slid in my hair and he gave me the kiss he meant to give me five minutes before.

In the end, my toast had non-melted butter too.

⚛

Luke and I went to the hospital to see Bobby.

Santo Mancini followed us in a black Volvo. Glancing out the back window of the Porsche, I noticed he was one of my kidnappers. The driver.

Well, at least it wasn't the other guy. I didn't think the other guy liked me.

My phone rang on the way to the hospital. It said, "Sissy calling."

I flipped it open and put it to my ear. "Yo," I greeted.

"Some big, beefy guy is here," Sissy informed me, sounding kind of breathless. "Says his name is Lucky and he's my bodyguard. He doesn't look like one of the hot guys. I just screamed in his face and closed the door. He's outside, standing by his car. What do I do?"

Damn, damn, damn.

"Ren set it up," I told her. "He's not one of the Hot Bunch. He's one of Ren's um… people."

"Oh. So he's okay?" Sissy sounded less panicked.

That was a question I couldn't answer. "I think so," I said.

"Did they find the Hot Bunch guy that was missing?" she asked.

I bit my lip and watched Luke drive for a few beats.

"Ava?" Sissy called in my ear.

"Luke and I are going to visit him at the hospital now."

Silence then quietly she said, "Shit."

She could say that again.

"Dom's a dickhead," she whispered. "He started all this and now someone is in the hospital. Someone we don't even *know.*"

"Did Dom call you?" I asked, remembering my conversation with Dom last night.

"Yes, like, five times," she said, now sounding pissy. "I didn't answer."

Shoo. At least that crisis was averted.

"Well, don't answer if he calls again. We have to talk. I'll call you after we get done at the hospital."

"I want to know everything. What a date with Ren is like. How Luke was when you got home. *Everything.* I'll meet you at Fortnum's," she replied.

There was something about Sissy calling Luke's loft "home' that freaked me out. I didn't feel like freaking out in Luke's Porsche with Luke in it (again, or ever, really). I needed to freak out privately with lots of bags of cookies available.

"Sounds good," I said instead.

I was about to say good-bye when I heard her call, "Ava?"

"What?"

"Did Luke give you the business?" she asked.

I looked at Luke again. He was driving. Calm, casual, practiced, eyes on the road, seemingly oblivious to our conversation.

I looked away. "Yeah," I answered quietly.

She screamed so loud I had to pull the phone away from my ear. I glanced at Luke when I heard him chuckle.

Fuckity, fuck, fuck, *fuck.*

I stood outside Bobby's hospital room, facing the wall, forehead resting against it.

Just a minute before, I saw that Bobby was a big guy and looked like a younger Tex, except less crazy. Though how would I know if Bobby actually was less crazy, considering he was lying in a hospital bed in a coma? I couldn't help but feel the blame that Big Bobby was lying in a hospital bed. Still, I vowed sextuple revenge against Dominic Dickhead.

I felt a strong hand slide under my hair and rest at the back of my neck then, "Babe."

I straightened, turned and looked at Luke, but he didn't take his hand away. Lee had been with Bobby when we got there, and now he was standing by Luke, but his eyes were on me.

"What's in that head of yours?" Luke asked quietly.

"I just vowed sextuple revenge against Dickhead Dominic Vincetti," I told him.

One side of Luke's lips went up. Lee's eyes did an amused crinkle.

"And I feel it's my fault," I went on.

Luke's grin faded and so did Lee's eye crinkle.

"If I hadn't walked into your office——" I started to continue.

"Quiet, Ava," Luke ordered softly.

Lee spoke more words. "Ava, most of the time, my men volunteer for their Rock Chick assignments and do them on their own time. Bobby was on his own time, a favor to Luke. He knew what he was doing and he wanted to do it. It isn't your fault that some shithead brought you trouble. Don't take it on your shoulders, it doesn't belong there. What happened to Bobby belongs on the shoulders of the guy who hit him in the head with a baseball bat."

Well, that was honest, succinct, to the point and made sense.

Still.

I closed my eyes and Luke turned me into his body by putting pressure on my neck. I put my hands to his waist and rested my forehead on his chest.

"Later," I heard Lee say to Luke.

"Yeah," Luke replied.

After some time slid by, I lifted my head and looked at Luke. "I need cookies," I told him.

His face got that almost-soft, still-hard look, his eyes going warm, and he bent his head to kiss my nose.

Sissy had spread the word and by the time Luke and I (and Silent Santo) got to Fortnum's, everyone had congregated. Everyone being Indy, Ally, Daisy, Jet, Roxie, Shirleen, Sissy (and Silent Lucky, her bodyguard and my other kidnapper), Tod and Stevie.

The minute Luke and I (and Silent Santo) walked in, all eyes swung to us.

"Babe," Luke muttered, sounding amused.

I turned to him, my back to the Rock Chicks (and gay guys). "Don't leave me here. Take me to Australia. Now."

He looked down at me. "Don't think I'll find Dom Vincetti in Australia." A shiver slid through me as Luke got close, and his hand went to my jaw, thumb stroking my cheek, and fuck buddies or not, it was nice. "I don't want you leavin' here, not even with Mancini. You gotta go somewhere, you call me."

I nodded. Not because I was giving in to Luke's tough guy, macho man demand, but because I didn't want to be kidnapped again.

He kissed my nose then he was gone.

No sooner had the door closed behind him when Tod squealed, "Girlie, get *over* here. Spill. We want *details*."

Again, I had to ask: why me?

I walked to the Rock Chicks and flopped on the couch by Shirleen. Ally peeled away and got me a skinny vanilla latte. When my coffee arrived, I sipped and told them about Dom calling, Ren's date and Luke giving me the business.

I didn't go into detail.

Shirleen narrowed her eyes on me. "Girl, so far I've lost a hundred bucks on you. I gotta get *somethin'* outta that hundred. I want it blow-by-blow. You don't give it, I'll cuff you to somethin' my damn self."

I stared at Shirleen. She looked serious, as in *seriously* serious. I didn't want Shirleen to cuff me to something so I sighed and gave them a blow-by-blow.

When I was done, Sissy said, "Oh my."

Indy said, "Holy crap."

Roxie said, "Wow."

Ally said, "Righteous."

Stevie said, "Lordy."

I said, "I know."

"Oowee," Shirleen said, getting off the couch and pulling her blouse in and out at her chest. "I need to go home and get me a cold shower before I go back to work. Child," she said to me. "You did good. You held out. Then you got nailed. You're a real Rock Chick now."

Everyone watched her leave, but it was probably only me who was, for the first time, wishing I wasn't a Rock Chick.

"My favorite part is the cookie swipe," Tod shared with the congregation.

"The cookie swipe was good," Roxie agreed.

"That ain't *my* favorite part," Daisy put in.

"Mine either," Ally concurred.

"I can't believe you're fuck buddies with Luke Stark." Sissy's tone was accusing and she was glaring at me. Obviously fuck buddies wasn't where she thought this was heading. She likely had visions of wearing a bridesmaid's dress and was planning my bachelorette party.

"I can't believe it either," Indy put in, but she didn't sound accusing, she sounded amused.

"I wish I was fuck buddies with Luke Stark," Tod told everyone and got a scowl from Stevie.

"Me too." Ally's voice sounded far away.

"Ally!" Roxie and Jet cried in unison.

Ally snapped back into the room. "I'm just saying." She looked at Roxie. "Has Hank ever done a cookie swipe?"

Roxie looked away. "No," she mumbled, obviously liking the idea of a cookie swipe.

"Eddie?" Ally's gaze had moved to Jet.

"We did it against the wall once." She hesitated. "Or twice," she said in a low voice then her voice got lower. "Or maybe four times."

Everyone stared at her.

Daisy gave a tinkly-bell laugh. "The wall is good."

"So what now?" Jet asked, moving attention away from wall sex with Eddie.

I shook my head because I didn't know what now.

What I knew was that I'd always, since I was eight, wanted Luke Stark to want me to be his girl then his girlfriend, and now I was "his woman". I knew I'd had the best night and morning of sex in my whole fucking life. I knew that I liked moving around in Luke's kitchen wearing his sweatshirt and kissing him while he sat on the counter, probably more than he liked it.

I knew Luke was right. I was lucky, but not for the reasons he said. And I felt lucky. I felt like the luckiest girl in the world.

I also knew I was screwed.

Because worse than never getting what you always wanted was having it and losing it.

"Uh-oh, I don't like the look on your face," Tod said to me.

"What?" I asked, knowing exactly what he meant.

"I'm thinkin' we're not in the straightaway here, am I wrong, sugar?" Daisy put in.

She was not wrong. "I need more coffee," I declared to deflect conversation from me, mainly because I could take no more. I needed peace and quiet and alone time, something I hadn't had in days.

Everyone looked at everyone else.

I got up and went to the coffee counter. "Set me up, Tex."

He stared at me. "Darlin'..." he started, and I just knew he was going to impart some sage piece of wisdom on me that I couldn't cope with, not then, not ever.

"Set me *up*, Tex," I repeated.

Tex ignored my demand and said, "He won't let you do it."

Whoa.

Whoa, whoa, whoa.

I was *not* having this conversation.

"Set me up," I repeated.

"He'll wear you down."

"Set me up."

"He'll get through whatever defenses you put up."

"Set me up."

"He won't give up."

"Tex! Set me up!" I shouted.

Duke walked up beside Tex all the while watching me.

Tex turned to Duke. "Tell it to her straight, brother."

Duke shook his head. "Not yet my time. I'll lay the honesty on her when the time's right."

Tex nodded as if he understood this completely. I didn't want to understand it. I wanted to get to a phonebook and start calling plastic surgeons to get quotes on a total face makeover.

"Can I *please* have some coffee?" I snapped.

Santo walked up beside me and said his first words of the morning to me. "I don't get it. I thought you were Ren's woman."

Someone! Please tell me!

Why me?

Chapter 16

Milano Interruptus

After the Rock Chicks made plans to go see Stella Gunn's gig the next night (Stella was a friend and The Premier Rock Chick, on account of she was lead singer and lead guitar in a kickass local cover band called "The Blue Moon Gypsies"), Sissy took off with Lucky to inspect her house. She'd been delaying it due to grieving her Stephen Kilborn pottery.

I got a call from Jules saying she'd be over around lunchtime to hear the dirt on Luke firsthand. She warned she was bringing May.

I decided to hang at Fortnum's because it seemed safe. I wasn't all fired up to move from the "Kidnapping and Getting Nailed Portion" of my Rock Chick in Trouble Experience to the "Shot At or Car Bombed Portion" just yet.

I was standing behind the book counter when I saw Jules and May walk in. I gave them a smile as my phone rang. Seeing as I was on edge (and the ultimate dork), I jumped, knocked over a can of pens, a pot of paper clips and, unfortunately, a jar of pink and purple bouncy balls, which seemed a weird item to have at a bookstore, but who was I to say? Indy had always been a bit crazy.

They went all over the floor, balls bouncing everywhere. I dropped to my hands and knees, fumbling with my ringing phone and scooping up balls, pens and clips.

I put my phone to my ear. "Yo," I greeted.

A low laugh then, "Ava."

It was Ren.

I froze on all fours then said stupidly, "Yo Ren."

"Hey," he replied softly.

Ren, too, had a sexy soft voice.

Crap.

Where were these guys during my senior prom, I ask you? No need to answer that, I knew. They were nowhere near Fatty Fatty Four-Eyes. They were dating Skinny, Easy Cindy Too Much Lip Gloss.

"Hi," I said and my voice sounded too high.

"Babe." I heard from what seemed like far away. I jerked, dropped the phone from my ear and it clattered to the floor.

I did not want Luke to see me on all fours on the floor. It had grown somewhat chilly outside so I was wearing jeans, a pale pink thermal under a faded brown tee that had pink script on the front that said "Sah-weet" across my boobs and I was wearing pale pink Croc Mary Jane's. I wasn't flashing my ass or anything. Still, it wasn't the best position to get caught in by Luke Stark.

I looked behind me, grabbing for the phone, but Luke wasn't there. So I slowly lifted up and, eyes peering over the counter, I saw him and froze. He was standing a few feet inside the front door facing Jules, body close to hers.

Ultra-close.

He had his hand up to her jaw, like he had with me just hours before, thumb stroking her cheekbone. Worse, his face wasn't semi-soft, still-hard. It was all-soft, totally soft in a way I'd never seen him look before *in my life*.

He was smiling at her, his eyes warm. *Ultra*-warm.

He hadn't called me "babe". He didn't even know I was there.

He'd called Jules "babe".

What's THAT all about? Bad Ava demanded.

Don't jump to conclusions, Good Ava warned.

I jerked back down to all fours and started breathing deep, feeling bad feelings. In fact, the worst feelings *ever*.

Shit.

Shit, shit, *shit!*

I heard Ren's voice coming from my phone on the floor. I grabbed it, flipped it shut and my mind screamed, *escape!*

I listened to my mind, thinking at that point it knew what the hell it was talking about.

I started motoring, cell in my hand, scrambling on all fours, sliding on bouncy balls and pens as I went, crawling down the side aisle of books that ran the length of the store perpendicular to the eight rows of fiction. I got to row four when I saw movement at my side. I stopped and my head whipped around.

Jet and Eddie were making out in the M-N-O section. Eddie had Jet pressed against the books, one of his arms around her, hand under her shirt, the other hand up on the shelves by her head. It looked like they were two minutes away from bookshelf sex.

They broke off kissing but didn't move away from each other and both of their gazes swung to me on all fours on the floor. Jet's mouth dropped open. Eddie's brows went up.

"Erm... sorry," I mumbled.

I gained my feet and ran through the front section into the middle section where there were more books and a big table topped with dozens of milk cartons filled with old vinyl, through that room and to the back room which was more books.

I went to a corner (Women's Studies) and started hyperventilating.

Get out of here, now! Bad Ava screeched.

Go talk to Luke! Good Ava cried.

I didn't listen to either of them.

All I could think was that I knew Jules and Luke were close. I could tell by the way she talked about him and the way he talked about her. I thought about the pain that moved through his face when he thought of seeing her bleeding on the floor and I didn't get it at the time.

Now I got it.

I'd never seen that in Luke, that vulnerability, not outside of what little he showed whenever I was around him after he was in a rip roarin' with his Dad. Never for one of his girlfriends, never for anyone, not even me.

He'd never looked at me with a full-on soft look. Not when my Dad left, not when he saw one of my sisters be bitchy to me, not even when he was inside me.

I leaned against the bookshelves.

He was in love with her. He would, of course, be in love with her. She looked like a movie star. And I was just Fatty Fatty Four-Eyes, the girl across the street holding onto a screaming crush.

Okay, so I wasn't really Fatty Fatty Four-Eyes anymore, but... I *was*. Worse, I always would be.

My phone rang in my hand and I jumped. The display said, "Ren calling". I flipped it open and put it at my ear. "Hey," I greeted breathlessly.

"What the fuck?" Ren clipped into my ear. "Are you okay?"

No! I thought.

"Yeah," I replied, but that one word didn't even convince me.

"Ava—"

I closed my eyes and blurted in a whisper, "I need to get out of here."

"Where are you?" Ren asked, now he was sounding concerned.

"Fortnum's."

"Where's Santo?"

"I don't know."

"Fuck," he snapped. "Don't go anywhere. I'll be there in ten."

"No! Ren, no."

Santo walked into the back room, his head swung around and his eyes caught mine. Then he walked to me.

"Santo's right here," I told Ren.

"Come to me," Ren ordered.

"What?" I asked.

"Have Santo bring you to me."

My heart stuttered. "Ren—"

"Do it. I'll be waiting."

Disconnect.

I stared at Santo, my mind racing, my heart beating so strong I thought it'd jump out of my chest. That was my only thought. My mind didn't have the capacity to process any more.

Then Santo's phone rang, he flipped it open, listened for five seconds and said, "Right." He flipped it shut and looked back to me. "We're going to Ren," he stated firmly.

I just kept staring at him. Then, I didn't know why, I nodded my head.

We walked through the books, the vinyl and down the center aisle of the front room. Luke was walking toward us. His eyes were warm when they caught mine, then, immediately, they went on alert. I looked away as I approached him and went to move by him. He caught my upper arm. I came up short and lifted my eyes to his.

"What's happening?" he asked, brows drawn.

"I have to be somewhere," I told him.

His gaze moved from me to Santo. I pulled my arm from his hand and kept walking (albeit a lot faster), Santo following.

I was at the passenger door to the Volvo when I heard the scuffle. I turned and saw Luke holding Santo back with a hand at his chest. He gave a shove, barely a movement of his arm but Santo fell back several paces. Luke turned to me and advanced, pinning me against the Volvo.

"What's goin' on?" he asked, his voice low and lethal.

"Nothing, Luke. I have to be somewhere. I'll see you later at the loft," I replied, my voice small, my eyes skidding away from his.

I tried to slide away but he got even closer, his hand went to my jaw, his thumb splayed on my cheekbone and I looked at him.

"Babe," he murmured, eyes warm on mine.

At that word, pain sliced through me. Against my will and to my total mortification, I felt tears well in my eyes. He saw them and got ultra-close. His face softened but not completely. Not even close.

And that hurt even more.

"Talk to me," he whispered in his gentle, affectionate voice.

I jerked my face from his hand, slid out from in front of him and quickly got in the car.

Santo jumped behind the wheel and we took off.

I didn't look back.

Ren's offices were a lot like Lee Nightingale's, except the wood was darker, and instead of a cowboy motif there was a lot of fancy glass and modern art.

Also, he didn't have a black lady receptionist with a huge afro and a messy desk. He had an ultra-gorgeous blonde receptionist with an obsessively tidy desk.

Her head snapped up when she saw us enter and her eyes narrowed on me in immediate and unconcealed hate, which I thought was kind of weird. Considering the fact that I was freaking out, I didn't have time to confront a bitchy receptionist.

"Ren's expecting you," she told Santo, and she didn't sound pleased about it.

"Yeah, Dawn, I know," Santo muttered, sounding like he thought she was a bitch, too, and leading me into an open doorway and down a hall. Santo stopped, and so did I. He knocked on a door and when we heard Ren calling us in he opened it.

Ren was already moving around his desk. His office was huge and his desk was not obsessively tidy. It was covered with papers and files in a way that it looked like he was really busy.

I walked in with Santo, saw Ren give a jerk of the chin, and without a word Santo took off.

Ren stopped in front of me, put his hand to my neck, tilting my chin up with a gentle thumb in the soft spot between my jaws and he looked in my eyes.

"Jesus, Ava," he murmured, and I knew at his words that I was clearly not hiding my emotional freak out, which was kind of a bummer.

I stared at him then started blabbing. "I need quiet space. I need to be alone. No bodyguards. No tough guys. No imminent threat of kidnapping and car bombs. I need to think. I need to get my head together. I haven't been alone for days. I need to be alone." Before I could stop myself, I leaned into him and put my hand on his (it must be said, rock-hard) abs. "Ren, please, can you arrange that for me?"

He watched me for a beat, his eyes scanning my face. Then he said softly, "Yeah, honey, I can arrange that for you."

I sagged into him.

"Let's go," he finished.

I felt relief flood through me. So much, I didn't notice he took my hand and held it as we walked out of his office, down the hall, through the reception area, to the parking garage and to his Jag. I did, however, notice Dawn glaring at me.

We drove through downtown where his offices were and I stared word-lessly out the window. My phone rang. I looked at it, saw it said, "Luke calling" and flipped it open.

Then I flipped it shut. I opened again and turned it off.

I knew Ren watched this and I didn't care. I was beyond caring. About a lot of things.

He took me to a house in Cheesman Park, a big, old, graceful one. He expertly parallel parked in front (and I had to admit, I was impressed; I could never parallel park) and walked me to the door. Inside it was a big, house-wide front room, side dining room to the back and left, kitchen on the other side, behind a wall, lots of windows with some stained glass. A split, sunny staircase in the middle where Ren led me up and to a bedroom.

Ho-ly crap.

I halted and turned to him. "Ren——" I started.

He gave me a gentle shove inside but took a step back, hand at the door-knob. "If you need anything, call," he said.

Then he left, closing the door behind him. I stared at the door then turned and looked at the room.

More big windows, hardwood floors, dark wood furniture with a big bed, four high, spiked posts, wine-colored sheets and comforter.

I sighed. Nothing for it.

I threw myself on the bed, bounced a couple of times and curled into a ball.

You're just latching onto this to protect yourself, Good Ava accused in my ear.

Yippee! We're in Ren's bed! Bad Ava yelled.

You need to talk to Luke, Good Ava advised.

You need to touch yourself in Ren's bed. Mm, yum, Bad Ava advised.

Good Ava glared around my neck at Bad Ava. *Stop talking about Ren!*

Bad Ava glared back. *Ren called us "honey", we've been around Ren with LOTS of other women. He's never called ANY of them "honey" like he did to us.*

Good Ava had no comment because Bad Ava was right.

I closed my eyes tight and decided instead of sorting through my rampaging thoughts, I was going to try to think nothing at all.

That didn't work so I started to sort through my rampaging thoughts.

In the end, I realized I had two choices.

Be sloppy seconds to Jules for as long as it lasted, and who knew how long it would last? Jules was with Vance. *Very* with him, no way Luke was going to get in there. He might need sloppy seconds for a good, long while if his sexual appetite last night was anything to go by.

Or I could get the hell out and fast.

Since I couldn't get the hell out and fast, which was my preferred choice, (considering my life was totally fucked up, and Luke had made it clear he wasn't done with me) I'd have to take the first.

At least until I got my sextuple revenge against Dominic Dickhead. Then I was off to Jamaica for the longest vacation in history.

On that unhappy thought, I slipped into a wee nap.

I woke up when the bed moved. I saw a thigh and looked up. Ren was sitting on the bed looking down at me. *His* face was totally soft *and* gentle.

Wow.

"I didn't mean to wake you," he said quietly.

I got up on an elbow. "That's okay," I replied, my voice still sleepy. "What time is it?"

"After five. You hungry?"

I had missed lunch. I still wasn't hungry.

"Yeah," I lied.

He took my hand, helped me out of his bed and we went downstairs. Ren made spaghetti while I watched and drank red wine. Considering I was coasting on the dregs of morning toast (with unmelted butter), the red wine hit my head like a shot.

Therefore by the time we sat down at his dining room table with bowls of (delicious, it must be said, Ren could cook) spaghetti, I had had two glasses of wine and was working on my third. I wasn't quite drunk, but I was in a talkative mood.

Unfortunately, Ren asked what was happening. So, seeing as I felt like talking, I told him.

Everything.

From Luke moving into the house across the street; me being Fatty Fatty Four-Eyes (that last part, Ren knew; I met him pre-weight loss and he'd been nice to me then, too); having a crush on Luke since time began; all the way to the cookie swipe. Though I just said we did the business. I didn't go into detail, thank goodness. His eyes got a little scary just hearing the "we did the business" part.

He listened without comment to all of this.

When I was done he asked, "Did you get your head together?"

I nodded.

"What'd you decide?" He seemed very interested in my answer.

Yikes.

I sat back and took a sip of wine. This was going to be the hard part.

"I need you to take me back to Luke's," I told him in a quiet don't-freak-out on me voice.

His mouth got tight, but to my surprise, without a word or a freak out, he nodded.

That said a lot about him. All of it good.

Hell and damnation.

We did the dishes and he took me back to Luke's. He walked me into the building and when the elevator doors slid open, his hand came to my neck before I could walk in.

He brought me close, his face dipped to mine and I saw the hungry look in his eyes. This time it was more intense because I could see it was mingled with anger or frustration. Or both. I figured whatever he was going to say was going to complicate my complicated life significantly.

I was not wrong.

He started talking and I vowed that if I ever got caught in a man pickle again, I would choose a man who was *not* a straight-talker.

"After he gets done with you, screwin' with your head while he's fuckin' your body when he knows you have serious feelings for him. Or you get done with bein' with a guy who would do that. Done with a guy who's thinkin' of someone else when he fucks you. When you decide you wanna be with a guy who's thinkin' of nothin' but you when he fucks you, Ava, you call me."

Ho-ly *shit!*

What did I do with *that?*

I just stared. I couldn't do anything else.

"Do you understand me?" he asked.

At that, I just nodded.

I understood him. Ee-yikes but I understood him.

"Good," he said and he sounded pissed-off. Even pissed-off, he still brushed his lips against mine. I registered that the lip brush felt nice while he walked away.

I shrugged off the lip brush, got in the elevator and used the key to Luke's floor. I did my now familiar holding-of-the-breath-until-the-doors-slid-open-to-Luke's-loft and I let it out on a gush when they did.

He was sitting at a stool in front of the bar, the kitchen garbage can a few feet in front of him, sorting through one of the piles I made for him (tossing most of it in the garbage, I might add) and eating one of my Milano cookies. He was still in his Tom Petty mood. I knew this because Tom was singing "Mary Jane's Last Dance" on the stereo.

His head swung around when I walked in.

I opened my mouth to say "Hey" when he spoke.

"Where the fuck have you been?" he bit off.

Hmm.

Someone was in a bad mood.

It was about to get worse. I knew it would because I was going to make it get worse.

And I did it on purpose.

Barlow Bitch Blood was pumping so watch out!

"At Ren's," I answered.

The air in the room went scary as I walked in, got close to Luke, put my phone down on the bar and grabbed the bag of Milanos. I shoved my hand in the bag, studiously avoiding the scary air and Luke's gaze and nabbing a cookie.

"Ava."

I looked at him. He was in his controlling-fury mode, I knew it with one look.

"Yeah?" I asked, sounding unconcerned, and a little surprised at myself that I could pull it off.

"You wanna tell me what you did at Zano's?"

Not really.

Still, I answered, "I needed space to get my head together. He gave it to me. I spent the afternoon at his place, alone, and took a nap. When he got home from work, he made me dinner and brought me back here."

I'd gone from lying through my teeth every other second to being honest when it was definitely not good for me. I should have stuck with lying. Even though all this was perfectly innocent, I could tell Luke didn't like it, not one bit.

"Now that you answered that question, you wanna tell me why you couldn't get your head together and take a nap here?"

I shrugged, being Queen of Calm. Barlow Bitch Blood was apparently latent. I'd lived twenty-nine years hardly ever being a bitch. Now it was coming out in spades.

"Okay, then you wanna tell me what your drama was about at Fortnum's?"

I was starting to bite into my cookie, I took it out of my mouth and said (back to lying), "I didn't have a drama."

"Then what was that?"

"It wasn't a drama."

"Eddie said he saw you crawling on all fours."

Jeez!

This was *so* annoying. Luke had sources everywhere.

"I dropped a contact," I lied.

Luke glared at me and then said, "Ava," in a very low, very lethal voice.

"I told you, I had somewhere to go. I had to meet Ren so he could help me out."

"When did Ren Zano become the one who helped you out?"

"Yesterday, at dinner," I told him breezily, shaking my cookie in the air for effect.

Not a good answer. I knew this because the scary air started pressing in.

Surprisingly he let it go and asked instead, "Where did you sleep?"

Again I was about to bite into my cookie, but stopped and asked, "What?"

"At Zano's, where did you sleep?"

Uh-oh.

Before I could fight back the Barlow Bitch Pull, it popped out of my mouth. "In his bed."

Eek!

Red alert! Red alert! Scary air hitting danger zone! Evacuate the premises immediately!

Then Luke growled in a voice so low, I barely heard him, "You've got to be fuckin' shittin' me."

"Luke, it was no big deal. He wasn't there," I decided to go back to breezy.

I was standing a few feet in front of him, between him and the garbage can.

He leaned in but kept his seat. I leaned back. I did this mainly because his intensity was kind of scaring me.

"You wanna call Zano right now? Ask him, shoe's on the other foot, he fucked you three times, you fell asleep with his cock inside you, how *he* would feel about you takin' a nap in *my* bed?"

It was then I saw his point.

Then again, if it was Ren fucking me, he would have been fucking *me*. Not some fill-in until he sorted out his feelings for another woman.

On that thought, I lost interest in my Milano and threw it back in the bag. I put the bag on the counter and sifted my fingers through my hair, leaving my hands on top of my head.

My eyes moved back to Luke.

He was holding his body perfectly still and I got the impression he was doing that so he wouldn't strangle me.

Time to defuse the situation.

I controlled the Barlow Bitch Pull and took a deep breath.

"Luke," I began softly. "Give me a break. It's not like, in my life, I've ever been in this situation. I've no fucking idea what I'm doing."

"What you do is you let me sort it out for you. That's why you came to the fuckin' office in the first goddamn place," he clipped, no less angry for my soft voice.

I dropped my hands and looked at him direct in the eyes. "That's not the situation I'm talking about," I said, voice still soft.

"Give me a clue."

Nope, no less angry. I looked away, closed my eyes tight and licked my lips.

Could I do this? No, I couldn't do it. Still, I did it so I guess I *could* do it.

I looked back at him and on another deep breath, I admitted, "You *know*, Luke. You know that most of the time I couldn't get a guy to look at me. Much less a hot guy. Now I have four. Four, all after I'd sworn off men. I don't know what to do." My voice went ultra-quiet, barely even a whisper. Even so there was an accusation to it. "You know. You, of all people, *know*."

That was when his body unstuck. Before I knew what he was about, he leaned forward. His arm snagging me around my waist, and he pulled me around the garbage bin and to him, between his legs, our torsos tight together. His other arm closed around my upper back, pinning me against him.

"I'll tell you what to do," Luke stated. "You come to me when you gotta sort shit out. I'll take care of you. You come to me when you need somethin'. I'll take care of it. I'll also tell you what *not* to do. You don't have dinner with another man. You don't sleep in his bed, I don't care that he's not in it with you. You don't leave me standin' on the sidewalk while you take off with a guy who, days earlier, kidnapped you and threatened to blow your fuckin' head off. You don't—"

"Okay, I get it," I broke in quietly.

His arms tightened and he gave me a mini-shake. "You better get it, Ava. I'm not goin' through the last six hours again."

I looked at the piles of stuff on the bar. I had left him several, now there was only one. I had come home and he was sitting, sorting through it and eating a cookie.

I looked back at him, confused. "Organizing your paperwork?" I asked.

He stared at me a second as if three identical noses had just popped out on my face then his head dropped back. I could almost hear him asking for patience from the divine. His chin came back down so he could look at me.

"I mean worryin' where the fuck you were and if you were okay, considerin' the last look I had of you, you had tears in your eyes."

Oh. That.

"I'm over that," I lied, *so* not over it and *so* never going to tell him what I wasn't over. Not in a million years. "It was a girl thing," I lied again for good measure. In my experience, men hated to talk about "girl things". I was hoping even the brutally honest ones would shy way the hell away from any discussion of a "girl thing".

He stared at me and I got the impression he totally knew I was lying.

Finally, and thankfully, he decided to let it go. "Zano fed you?" he asked.

"Yeah," I answered.

"Good. Now I can fuck you."

My knees did a little wobble. "We didn't have dessert," I stalled.

His head (and, I must remind you, his fantastic mouth) started coming toward mine.

"Glad he left that to me," he said before he kissed me.

※

It wasn't like last night where it was all go, go, go or shocking-but-world-tilting surprise or all about Luke giving then taking.

This time Luke went slow and we took turns. He let me touch him, taste him, stroke him, take him in my mouth, and I liked it, a lot. He had an unbelievable body, and let me tell you, it was fun as hell to explore.

When he was through letting me, he flipped me over, spread my legs and settled between them. I felt one of his knees come up for better leverage and I was certain he was going to slam into me again. I was ready for it. I wanted it and I stared at him in a fog, my body burning, nearly begging for it.

He didn't slam into me. Instead, I felt him right there, ready to come inside, when his hands came up to either side of my face. Slowly, centimeter by centimeter, he slid inside me, watching my face the whole time. My lips parted and I held my breath as he slowly filled me until he was buried deep.

I waited for him to move.

He didn't. He just kept watching me.

"Luke," I whispered, pressing my hips into him.

"Be still, Ava," he ordered then his mouth came to mine and he asked, "Do you feel that?"

Yeah, I felt it. It felt *great*.

"Yeah," I told him.

I felt him smile against my mouth, but he muttered, "You don't feel it."

"I feel it."

"Then you don't get it."

I *wanted* to get it, but he wasn't moving.

I licked my lips, and since my lips were close to his lips, I licked his lips, too.

His eyes went molten and he moved, slowly at first then faster, then harder until we both came, breathing heavy in each other's mouths. It was the first time in my life that I climaxed with a partner at the same time. If I thought the other sex was mind-blowing, I was wrong. Reaching orgasm with Luke was mind-blowing, mind-altering and world-tilting all at the same time.

I was so screwed.

After, his mouth at the skin behind my ear, he murmured, "You ever run away from me with tears in your eyes again, Ava, I'll hunt you down. Do you understand?"

I didn't move. This wasn't sweet, after sex talk. His voice was low and husky, but he was being perfectly serious.

"Do you understand?" he pushed.

I decided it was best to nod. I was unable to process this after a big time orgasm when Luke was still on top of me, when Luke was, at that moment, my whole world.

Mouth still at my ear, he said in The Voice, "I'm bein' patient, babe, but pretty soon you're gonna have to let me in."

No way in hell. He was already in as far as he was going to get, literally and figuratively.

"Don't call me babe," I said to take the post-sex conversation away from me letting him in.

I meant it this time in a way I didn't mean it before. I didn't want him to call me "babe" and Jules "babe". It made it less special. In fact, it made it not special at all.

248

His head came up and he looked down at me. His eyes searched my face and then he dropped to his side, taking me with him.

When we were face-to-face and he had my leg wrapped around his hip, he asked, "What's this now?"

"Nothing, just don't call me babe. I don't like it," I lied. I had really loved it before, if I was honest with myself. Now, I hated it.

His fingers sifted through the hair at the side of my head. He kept his hand at the back and twisted my hair in his fist.

"You mean it," he said.

"Yeah," I told him.

"I'm not even close, am I?" he asked, what I thought bizarrely.

"Close to what?"

"To gettin' through to you."

Whoa.

Whoa, whoa, whoa.

Stop right there.

Or, wait. Maybe, not.

"No, Luke. You're not. I tried to tell you, but you won't listen to me," I pressed closer to him and lied through my goddamn teeth. "You're never going to get close. Trust me, it's not gonna happen."

"It'll happen."

"It won't."

"Yeah, it will." He sounded sure of himself.

Holy cramoly!

Why me? What did I do?

I dipped my chin and tried to pull away, but his arms got tight. I struggled a bit, just in case he wasn't in the mood to overpower me. I found, as ever, he was very much in the mood to overpower me.

Tom Petty (obviously Luke had Greatest Hits on random) started singing "Learning to Fly". I gave up the struggle and listened to Tom.

After a few minutes, I asked to Luke's throat, "You want some ice cream?"

I tilted my head back to look at him.

He tipped his chin down to look at me and answered, "Yeah."

He let me go and put on his sweatpants. I put on my underwear and his zip up sweatshirt.

We ate ice cream out of the tub, two spoons. Luke holding the tub, me dipping in while we sat on his kitchen counter.

And I realized on the third spoonful of peanut butter cup ice cream that I was sitting on the countertop in my pretend happy place.

And I was going to stay there.

For now.

Chapter 17
Missed You

Seeing as I had a three-hour nap that afternoon, Luke fell asleep before I did.

I spent some time trying to fall asleep, but I couldn't. So, carefully, I slid out from under his arm (we were spooning, his face in my hair, his arm around my waist) and I got up.

The Triumph tee was in the laundry so I went to the dresser where he took me to get it that first night, opened the drawer, grabbed whatever was on top and put it on. I slid on my panties, my glasses then shrugged on the sweatshirt and zipped it up.

I went to the floor-to-almost-ceiling window, sat down on the floor beside it, knees to my chest, the side of my shoulder to the window. I pulled Luke's tee and sweatshirt over my knees and hugged them, staring at his view.

Luke was on the fourth of five floors in a LoDo loft. I couldn't see the mountains, but I could see LoDo, its lights and brick buildings. There were still some people milling about on the streets though it was way late.

I rested my temple against the cold window and lost myself in thought.

I wondered what Marilyn and Sofia would think if they knew I was with Luke (they were never going to know; I would never hear the end of it when it was over). I wondered for the gazillionth time where my Dad might be. I wondered how the Rockies were doing in spring training.

I heard a movement and my head jerked away from the window as Luke settled behind me wearing his sweatpants. It was just plain old weird how a big guy like him could be so quiet.

Without a word, he settled with his legs around me, wrapped his arms around my chest, pressed his front against my back and rested his chin on my shoulder.

I felt a shiver slide through me, not from cold.

"Did I wake you?" I asked in a whisper, like he was still sleeping.

"Yeah," he told me.

"Sorry."

His arms got tighter.

"You can go back to sleep," I offered.

"Prefer you were with me, babe."

I closed my eyes and wondered if he would also prefer to be with Jules, sitting on the floor in the dark by his window. I figured he would.

I mentally pushed away those thoughts and told him, "I can't sleep. The nap."

"I'll wait."

I was afraid he would say that.

We sat there, me looking out the window. I didn't know what he was doing.

After a while, I slid into my pretend happy place. Sitting on the floor in the dark with Luke, his arms around me.

I slid in so deep, I whispered, "I wonder where my Dad is."

His arms got tighter and his head shifted, his chin moving my hair out of the way so he could bury his face in my neck.

Mouth at my ear, he said, "You don't have to wonder."

My body went still. "Why not?"

"You want, I'll find him for you."

Oh... my... *God.*

"Really?" I whispered so low it was barely audible.

"Yeah."

Then it hit me. "What would I owe you for that?"

He kissed my neck and his chin went back to my shoulder. "I would do that for free."

I tried to put the brakes on it, tried to call "whoa" but I couldn't. My body relaxed into his. His chin came up as he took my weight and the back of my head went to rest on his shoulder.

After a while I said, "I don't want you to find him for me. I don't need another man fucking up my life."

"Your call," he replied softly.

I didn't say any more. We sat there for a good, long while. Then he moved, pulling away, standing up. I looked at him as he leaned down, putting an arm around my waist, one at the back of my knees. He lifted me up and carried me to bed.

Once there he set me in it and followed me down, stretching out beside me. He took off my glasses and put them on the nightstand. Then he unzipped the sweatshirt and I pulled it off, throwing it on the floor by the bed. Then he lifted the tee over my head and threw it aside. Luke, I was learning, liked sleeping naked. He would tolerate panties, but that was about it. Seeing as I liked the feel of his skin against mine, I didn't mind. He pulled me over his body, settled me on his other side and yanked the covers over us. He turned to me, hooking his hand behind my knee to wrap it around his hip.

"You could have put me in bed on this side," I told him.

"That's not as fun."

I smiled in the dark.

"You're nuts." Finally feeling sleepy, I cuddled closer.

His arm closed around my waist and he pulled me deep into him, but he didn't respond.

When I was inches away from dreamland, I heard him call, "Ava."

I was too close to sleep to respond. I just pressed closer.

And I was sure I fell asleep because, I swear, the next thing he said was, "Missed you."

And I knew that had to be a dream.

⌁⦙⌁

I was sitting at my desk at the loft trying to get some work done. Sissy was lying on Luke's couch, preparing to see Stella and The Blue Moon Gypsies by listening to the Black Rebel Motorcycle Club singing "Ain't No Easy Way", one of Stella and her band's coolest covers. The crowd always went wild when Stella sang that, but her signature song was "Ghostriders in the Sky". She ended every gig with "Ghostriders" and people always went nuts.

It was early afternoon and I was beginning to feel like a Rock Chick Fraud. Nothing bad had happened to me in a while outside of finding out Luke was in love with Jules, something that I didn't even tell Sissy about because I knew she would give me Good Ava-esque advice. But no getting beat up, kidnapped, shot at or cuffed to a sink.

The morning had been relatively normal. That was, if you didn't count Luke waking up in an energetic mood. Luke's energetic mood translated into us having sex, during which he gave me the business in three different positions.

One I'd done before, one I'd heard of but never done, and one I didn't even know was possible.

If you asked me which was my favorite, I couldn't tell you. I liked them all. A lot.

He'd left me facedown and drained in bed while he showered. I fell into a doze, but eventually felt the sheet slide down to my hips then Luke's mouth at the small of my back sliding up my spine to my neck.

"Gotta get to work, babe," he said there.

"Mm," I mumbled.

I felt him smile against my neck before his hands rolled me and he lifted me up until I was sitting and my chest was pressed against his. His hand went into my hair and twisted.

"Luke, I'm still sleepy," I protested, not sleepy at all. I was spent, in a good way.

"I want a kiss before I go," he demanded before he kissed me, not giving me a choice in the matter. Not that I would have said no. It wasn't hot, hard and deep. It was hot, soft and sweet.

When he was done I stared at him in a new kind of Luke Lip Fog.

"I always want a kiss before I go to work, Ava," he told me quietly.

"Okay," I agreed.

I would have agreed to anything at that point, too much in a fog to let his words and their meaning penetrate.

So in a fog, still in my pretend happy place and having been given the business rather successfully (these were my excuses and I was going with them), I lifted my hand to his cheek. I let my thumb trail the sharp edge of his 'tache that grew down the side of his mouth, my eyes so focused on watching my thumb's progress (and studying his mustache and mouth) that I missed the look on his face when I did this.

It was really too bad I missed the look on face.

Before I could catch it, he kissed me again. This time it *was* hot, hard and deep. In a true blue Luke Lip Fog, he put me back in bed, covered me up and then he was gone.

Later, Sissy and Lucky came over and we headed to the gym, Santo joining our party at the entrance to Luke's building.

I thought it prudent, so as not to earn another Luke Confrontation where I would be forced to bare part of my soul, to phone him the minute we settled in the car.

"Yeah?" he answered.

"Going to the gym," I told him.

"I'll send a man over."

"No, I mean I'm on my way with Sissy right now."

Silence.

"Lucky and Santo are with us."

"Babe," was all he said before he disconnected and, I will note, he hadn't stopped calling me "babe".

Argh!

At the gym Riley was in a better mood. Back to the old Riley, mostly. He looked askance at the two, beefy, suited Italian-Americans following Sissy and I around the weight machines. I was relieved until he caught up with me on my way to the locker room.

"You okay?" Riley asked. His eyes slid to Santo, who was standing three feet away before coming back to me.

I nodded.

"That guy, Luke, he still in the picture?"

I nodded again.

Riley's jaw clenched.

Then he asked, "The minute he's out of the picture, you'll tell me?"

Oh jeez. Here we go again.

I decided just to nod.

Riley walked away and I thanked my lucky stars he was not a tough guy, macho man, brutally honest, straight-talker.

Santo got close. "You're hot, but this is ridiculous," he told me, his eyes on Riley's departing back.

Santo was not wrong.

On the way back to Luke's loft, I called him again.

"Yeah?" he answered.

"We're gonna hit King Soopers and then back to your loft. Don't worry, Santo and Lucky are still with us."

Silence but no disconnect.

I forged ahead through the scary silence. "You need anything from the store?"

"No."

"Any word about Bobby?"

"He's out of the coma. Talking, but functions are slow. They're worried about brain damage. Can't know 'til the brain swelling goes down."

"Shit," I whispered.

"He'll be okay."

"What if he's not?"

"Then he'll be okay. Me and Lee will take care of him."

I felt a weird whoosh of warmth spread through me. This was said matter-of-fact but I knew he meant it, and for some reason I had the urge to hug him and then kiss him all over.

Before I could share that thought (luckily), Luke said, "Vance says you and the Rock Chicks are goin' to a gig tonight."

"Stella and The Blue Moon Gypsies," I confirmed.

"I want you protected. Not Zano's thug, one of Lee's boys."

"Luke." I used his name as a protest.

"Shit happens too frequently when the Rock Chicks do the town. Indy got shot at while performing with a drag queen. Jet's sister caused pandemonium on her opening night at a strip club. Roxie was held hostage at a society party. Jules took down three bitches when one of 'em insulted Stevie. I want you covered."

I sighed because he wasn't wrong. I'd heard all these stories.

"All right."

"You get separated from your man, you stick close to Jules. Not many people can mess with Jules."

This time I felt a not-so-weird pain slice through my belly. There was no denying the respect in his voice.

"All right," I said, but my voice (damn it all to hell) betrayed me. It sounded small and hurt.

"Babe?" He heard and read my voice.

"Later," I said.

"Babe." His voice went low and I knew he wanted me to share.

"We're at King Soopers, gotta go." I shut it down, not about to share.

"Jesus, Ava," he said, his voice strangely part curt, part amused, like he found dealing with me frustrating, but he found that frustration enjoyable. "It's a good thing your sweet body and the fuckin' things you don't even know you're doin' give you away or you'd be a serious pain in the ass."

I had no idea what he meant (okay, I knew what part of it meant) but I still snapped, "I'm so sure!"

"Later," he replied, now fully amused. Then he disconnected.

Santo was driving, Lucky in the passenger seat, Sissy and me in the back. I looked at Sissy when I flipped the phone closed and she was grinning at me, eyes shiny happy.

"You are *so* not fuck buddies," she declared.

Santo and Lucky glanced at each other.

Argh!

We'd trolled through King Soopers and I bought some food to supplement the anti-healthy living mojo provisions that I bought with Ren. Sandra's supplies were running low.

Sissy and I carried them up to Luke's loft (Santo and Lucky stayed downstairs) and put them away. We gabbed while I did laundry and changed the sheets on the bed and she swept the floors.

Then I went to work and Sissy went to the stereo.

I was finishing up a marketing leaflet for a client when we heard "Sissy!" shouted from outside.

My eyes swung to Sissy and found hers on me.

"Sisssss-eeeeeee!"

"Holy crap," Sissy breathed and ran to the window.

I nabbed my phone and followed her.

"Sissy, I know you're up there!"

I made it to Sissy at the window, flipped open my phone at the same time and hit the green button.

I looked down and saw Dom standing in the middle of the street, stopping traffic. Santo and Lucky were approaching him, but he dodged them, running around in the street while he shouted. "Sisssss-eeeeeeee!"

"Holy shit, he's like Stanley Kowalski without the rain and with two guys chasing him," I breathed.

"Babe," Luke said in my ear, making me jump.

"Dom's here," I told him.

"We're on it. Stay in the loft."

Disconnect.

I flipped the phone shut and watched as Dom kept yelling for Sissy and Santo and Lucky kept trying to catch him.

All of a sudden, Sissy whispered, "I have to go to him," and then she started to take off.

My stomach plummeted. "Sis, no!" I yelled and ran after her.

Catching up, I threw my arms around her waist trying to hold her back. We started stand-up wrestling, then we fell to the floor with a somewhat painful thud. Sissy was so determined to get to Dom, and I was so determined she would not, we immediately started lying-down wrestling, rolling around on the floor, each of us trying to get the upper hand. All the while cars honked and people were shouting outside, including Dom.

"Ava, he's my husband!" she screamed, still struggling.

"I know! Let Luke deal with it," I told her, trying to capture her hands.

Then we both froze as we heard gunfire. Three shots… bang, bang, *bang!*

And let me tell you, it was a terrifying noise.

I rolled off her. She and I got up and ran back to the window. We made it there just in time to see the blue SUV peeling away, its front end damaged from rear-ending me. No sign of Dom. Santo was running to the Volvo, Lucky running into the building and a Black Explorer was in pursuit.

I ran to my cell, which I'd dropped in the Sissy Wrestling Match, and phoned Luke.

I heard the connect, and before he could say a word I screeched, "Gunshots!"

"I know, babe. Stay in the loft. Buzz Lucky up now. I want him with you until I can get a man on you. Got me?"

"Yeah."

"Stay calm. Darius and Hector are in pursuit. They've reported in. Tell Sissy Vincetti's okay. They didn't hit him."

"Okay."

"You good?"

"I'm good." And I sounded good, calm and rational after my initial "gunshots" squeal, which was way weird because I was *not* good. I hated Dom but I didn't want people shooting at him, especially not with Sissy in hearing distance.

"Solid," he said in a soft voice then he disconnected.

Shit!

I did it again, exposing my strong woman-in-a-crisis. When was I going to learn?

I told Sissy Dom was okay (for now, though I didn't share that part). Luke was going to call when they knew something and I buzzed Lucky up.

While we waited, Lucky called Ren. Sissy paced. I went to Luke's utility room to take the clothes out of the dryer, switch them with the clothes in the washer and throw some more clothes in to wash. While I was there I tidied up the utility room. Seriously, how Luke could find anything was a mystery. There was stuff all over the place and it appeared he hadn't done laundry since the beginning of time.

I was putting away the last newly cleaned pair of Luke's socks when the elevator doors opened. I expected to see one of the Hot Bunch, but instead Luke walked in with a guy who looked a lot like Eddie Chavez, except rougher around the edges. He may have looked rough, but you could tell it was because he liked it that way. And I had to admit, looking at him, I liked it that way too. *Yum.*

"Dom," Sissy breathed, pulling me out of my mini-perv for Rough Hot Guy, and I shut Luke's sock drawer. She was in a state and I found myself wishing that Dom was a better guy and deserved this kind of devotion.

Why Dom was out in the street screaming her name, who knew? It was clear he didn't like the idea of someone hitting her, but I wasn't a big fan of "better a husband loves and protects his wife, especially when she's my bestest best friend, late than never". I felt more that a husband should love and protect his wife *always.* Not after she got punched in the face by a big, burly, bad guy while in the throes of a kidnap attempt.

Nevertheless, seeing as this was Sissy, I walked over to her to provide moral support.

"They got him," Luke announced, and Sissy pursed her lips together, taking a deep breath through her nose at the same time and nodded. Luke went on, "The police got the boys who grabbed him." Luke's gaze moved to Lucky. "Hector and Darius handed Vincetti over to Santo. Santo is taking him to Vito."

It was Lucky's turn to nod and he started to walk toward Sissy.

"No." Luke stopped Lucky's progress on that one word, mainly because it was said in a tone where you could tell he really meant it, and Luke wasn't the kind of guy you ignored when he really meant something, even if you were a beefy henchman. "Hector's taking Sissy to the police station. She needs to ID the guy who punched her."

"Vito wants her," Lucky returned, and I looked at Lucky, then at Luke, in an effort to understand why Vito would want Sissy. Luke was blank-faced so I couldn't read him. Lucky was always blank-faced.

"She needs to ID the guy," Luke repeated still in his firm tone, his eyes moving to Sissy. "You'll go with Hector."

She nodded at Luke and I put my arm around her shoulders. "I'll go with you," I promised.

Luke's gaze swung to me. "A minute," he said to me (I will note, he did not ask). Then he walked to the utility room without waiting for me to respond. Since I wanted to know what was going on, I squeezed Sissy's arm reassuringly then followed Luke.

When I got to the utility room, Luke was looking around like he'd stepped off our world onto another planet. His eyes came to me, and even considering the borderline scary and definitely crazy situation we currently found ourselves in, his eyes were amused.

"Babe," he said, as if that one word spoke volumes.

"What?" I asked, because that one word didn't speak volumes.

Like a flash, his hand came out and nabbed me behind my neck, giving me a jerk forward so I slammed into his body. He bent his head and kissed me. Not a hot and hard, open-mouthed tongue fest, but it *was* hard, and it communicated something that I did not quite get. He let me go but kept his hand at my neck, and his eyes on mine were ultra-warm.

"What?" I asked again when he didn't speak, but this time I asked it softly.

"I'll get into 'what' later. Tonight, after the gig, when you're home, drunk and naked."

Ho-ly shit!

"Right now, we got a problem," he went on.

His eyes became serious and he certainly sounded like we had a problem, so much so I let the "drunk and naked" comment go.

"What?" I asked (again!).

"At the meet with Vito on Sunday, Vito, Lee and I agreed if we get Vincetti before the bad guys find him, we hand him over to Vito. We got him, we handed him over to Vito. Problem is these bad guys are *bad guys*. The two Darius and Hector just nailed are foot soldiers, two of dozens. This is a big problem for Vito, an ongoing problem, because no matter what Vito offers, they don't feel like negotiating and they got a lot of men to throw at it. Losing two is not going to deter them. What they want is simple: just Vincetti. To make this problem disappear, Vito needs to make Vincetti disappear, and that's what he's gonna do."

My mouth dropped open, my heart stuttered to a halt and I stared.

Then I whispered, "Uncle Vito is going to make his own nephew sleep with the fishes?"

Luke's lips pressed together, but even so, they were still twitching like something was very, *very* funny, and he didn't want to laugh out loud.

When he got himself under control, he said, "I don't think they say that anymore, Ava, if they ever did outside the movies."

Oh well. So I didn't talk wise guy. Sue me.

I leaned in. "What you're saying is, they're going to whack him." I was still whispering.

Luke shook his head, let my neck go but his hand slid to my jaw. "No, where Vincetti's goin', he'll still be breathin'. Your problem is, Vito wants to send Sissy with him."

All my body systems froze solid.

No!

No, no, no!

No!

"That can't happen," I declared when my mouth was moving again.

"Vito's determined, says marriage is life. Wants them back together."

I'd heard that before.

"But Dom's a dickhead," I replied, sounding slightly desperate (which I was). "He's mean to her. He doesn't let her serve leftovers. He tells her what to wear. He doesn't know what a woman should wear! One time he told her to put on these pink Capri pants with this purple gypsy shirt. Apart they were kickass items of clothing. Together she looked like a fool. I know it sounds stupid, but it's not. It's bossy and not in the tough guy, kinda sexy, bossy way that *you're* bossy. It's just plain old mean bossy. He's a jerk!"

Oops.

Did I just tell Luke his tough guy, bossy ways were "kinda sexy"?

His face was coming closer to mine. His hand had flexed on my jaw and he had a full-on grin happening, so I guessed I had.

"I take that back!" I cried, a bit loud and sounding like a third grader. His head stopped its descent, but his grin didn't go away. "I don't know what I'm saying. I'm just freaked out. I don't want Sissy to go back to Dom."

Lucky for me, Luke decided to let it go. "I know that, babe, but Matt saw you two wrestling when Vincetti was out on the street. You were trying to stop her from getting to him. You have to talk to her, give her the option, because Sissy might not agree."

Unfortunately, Luke was right. She might not.

I closed my eyes. With my eyes closed, I felt Luke kiss my nose.

Just as an aside, a closed-eyes-you're-about-to-lose-your-bestest-best-friend-to-Uncle-Vito-oblivion Luke Nose Kiss was very, *very* sweet.

I opened my eyes again and saw his face was partly soft, but his eyes were fully warm, like he knew what losing Sissy would mean to me. This caused another warm whoosh to power through me.

"You've got to the police station to talk to her," Luke informed me softly. "Find out what she wants to do. She decides she wants to divorce him, we'll take care of her, put her in the safe room until Vito cools it and Vincetti is out of the picture. She decides she wants to go with him, we'll deliver her safe to Vito."

I needed more information. Tons more.

"What does 'disappearing' mean?" I asked. "Is she going to be gone for everyone, her Dad, her Mom? And if so, for how long? Will she come back? Will she phone? What do I tell them? Can we visit her? Are we talking another state, another country, another *continent?*"

"Right now, disappearing at all is Sissy's decision. We delay a lot longer here, babe, Vito's gonna cotton on to what we're doing and it will be Vito's decision."

I decided I didn't need any more information.

"Time to go," I said abruptly, turning on my heel and walking into the other room. "Sissy, let's go ID some bad guys," I announced, hightailing it through the loft, sparing Lucky a glance. "Lucky, later."

"Vito says—" Lucky began, but Sissy and Hector were already at the elevator. Hector had tagged the button and the doors were sliding open.

I joined them and we moved into the elevator as Lucky started to come our way. He was too late. Luke had already moved to block the path between Lucky and us.

The doors started closing, Luke looked over his shoulder at us, and for some bizarre, unhinged, insane reason, I mouthed, "I owe you."

I just caught his sexy half-grin and the so ultra-warm it was hot look in his eyes before the doors closed.

Hell and damnation.

Now I was screwing myself!

⋈

"Are you mad at me?" Sissy asked.

I looked at Hector. He was standing three feet away talking to Hank. We were at the police station and Sissy had just ID'd a bad guy.

On the way over I told Sissy about what she was up against with Uncle Vito. I told her Luke would keep her safe if she didn't want to "disappear". I also told her that I wanted her to take Luke up on his offer. Then I told her I *really* wanted her to take Luke up on his offer and I didn't even care if it meant I owed him.

Sissy nodded but she didn't say anything. We rolled into the police station. It took forever for them to sort out the lineup, and Sissy had ID'd the bad guy.

Then she turned to Hector and demanded, "Take me to Dom."

I sucked in breath and wished there was something to bang my head on. A wall, a floor, a very hard rock.

Sissy took my hand. "I know you think I'm crazy, but there are times when you aren't there when he can be really sweet. A lot of times, Ava."

I just stopped myself from rolling my eyes. "I know, you've told me that before." And she had.

"He's not perfect."

She could say that again. I kept my lips zipped.

"I love him," she said quietly.

Shit.

"Don't be mad at me," she went on.

I unzipped my lips. "He kissed me," I reminded her.

She looked away.

"In your kitchen," I continued.

She sighed.

263

"While you were in the house." I kept at it.

She looked back at me but she didn't reply.

I went for the killer diller. "Sissy, his crazy shit got Big Bobby put in a coma."

She moved, just slightly, but I caught it, like a flinch.

Then she said, ultra-quiet, "Ava, honey, you don't get it. I'm never gonna find my Luke. Some hot guy who calls me a knockout, chases me like I'm the greatest thing since sliced bread and shields me from bullets with his body."

I didn't want to say anything, but that last part wasn't exactly fun.

She kept going. "Dom's the closest thing I'm going to get. I'm twenty-nine and going to be divorced. That's just sad. I'm just sad."

"Shut up," I broke in, beginning to get pissed. "You're not sad."

"I'm sad."

"You're sweet and funny and loyal and everyone loves you."

"I'm sad."

"You're beautiful. You look like a happy, pretty human fairy."

"I do not. I'm not beautiful. I'm not happy-pretty. I'm just Sissy. I even have a shit name. What kind of name is Sissy? Ava's the name of a knockout. Sissy's the name of a sad, twenty-nine year old, silly-fairy divorcée."

Before I could retort, Hector got close. "In an effort to speed things up since, Santo and Lucky both just entered the building…" Hector said his first words since we had been with him. Okay, maybe second. When we arrived at the station, he said, "This way." He turned to Sissy. "You're right. Your friend's a knockout. Lotta guys go for tits, ass and attitude. Lotta guys also go for the sweet, pretty women they feel they gotta protect, who don't realize they're all that. My brother's livin' with one. You're another one. You don't think you're all that, which makes you even more all that. Trust me, you're pretty. You're your own brand of hot. You're gonna find a good man who appreciates that and you shouldn't waste your time on some asshole who doesn't. Does that help?"

Both Sissy and I were staring at Hector, speechless.

"Well?" he demanded, sounding impatient.

"I think I'll go to the safe room," Sissy breathed, still staring at Hector.

Yippee!

"I'm gonna kiss you all over," I told Hector.

His eyes cut to me and I immediately regretted my words because he looked like he was happy to take me up on that offer. Guess Hector was all about tits, ass and attitude.

Eek! Not another one.

"Let's go," I announced, ignoring Hector's happy to be kissed all over look.

I grabbed Sissy's hand and we started motoring.

Hector took Sissy to the safe room at the offices and I went with them. It was my first time back to the Nightingale Investigations offices after my first and last crazy adventure there.

We arrived and Shirleen was on the phone, handset in the crook of her neck, peering into a hand-held mirror, plucking her eyebrows.

She dropped the mirror and the tweezers upon seeing us. "Dorothea, gotta go, my girl's here with her girl. We gotta lock old Sissy down so the Italians don't get her. Long story, I'll tell you later." Then she hung up and raced around the desk to Sissy and me and she told us, "I was getting worried. Nothing was happening. I thought maybe I got the Bum Rock Chick. But we got you guys wrestling on tape and you should see it. It was great. You went down, *whomp*, and neither of you even noticed, just kept right on wrestling."

I turned to Sissy (who was, by the way, looking pale). "Um, forgot to mention, Luke's got the loft wired with cameras so the boys can keep an eye on me."

Sissy went paler.

Shirleen was walking with us as we followed Hector. "I put clean sheets on the bed and when I found out that we might have a girl coming over, I went out and bought that movie *300* to add to the library in the safe room. That movie is great. I've watched it at least ten times. Hot, white boys in leather jockey shorts and red capes. And sandals! How those boys can make sandals hot, I do not know, but those boys kicked *ass* in those sandals. Blood everywhere. Heads flyin' off. Have you seen it?" she asked Sissy.

Sissy shook her head and Shirleen linked her arm through Sissy's.

"We'll watch it together, like, right now. Part of my job description includes lookin' after the prison... I mean, our guests. Lee won't mind I watch a little leather jockey shorts action."

Hector had disappeared behind a door. Shirleen pulled ahead of me, dragging Sissy with her, clearly keen on getting to her movie. Sissy looked over her shoulder, her face kind of scared. I smiled at her and waved as she and Shirleen disappeared in the door where Hector had gone.

At that moment another door opened and Luke was there. He looked at me, gave me a grin and I stopped.

"Hey," I said when he made it to me.

"I see she made the right decision," he replied.

"Yeah."

His grin went into a full-fledged smile, and not only because he was happy my bestest best friend was not going to disappear.

"So, this means you owe me again," he noted.

Uh-oh.

"Actually I owe Hector more than I owe you. She was going to go back to Dom, but he talked her out of it," I tried.

He shook his head, clearly not agreeing with me.

Foiled!

I knew it was a long shot, but he never gave me anything.

"Tonight, I call this marker or your punishment marker. Your choice," Luke stated.

"Luke," I said softly, not about to let him call *any* markers, and definitely not letting him call the punishment one. I was never going to touch myself while Luke watched. I'd already gone way past my sexual adventure boundary. Okay, sure, one could argue that I liked leaping over that boundary. In fact, this morning, about a nanosecond after Luke flipped me into the second position and slid inside me I decided that I was never going to have sex in any other position but that one ever again. Until he did the third one, of course.

Still.

"Babe." Clearly, Luke was not about to be denied, and I could swear by the amused look on his face he knew my thoughts.

I crossed my arms on my chest. He gave me a half-grin.

"Lucas Stark, don't you think that you—"

He interrupted me. "Don't you have a gig to get to?"

I looked at my watch. It was well past six o'clock. We were meeting at My Brother's Bar at seven for dinner and drinks before we went to the gig, and I had at least an hour's worth of Rock-Chick-On-The-Town prep work to do to my face, hair and wardrobe.

"I need to get home, like, now!" I exclaimed, bouncing in my Crocs.

Luke's body shifted. His arm curved around my shoulders and he walked me down the hall, murmuring, "Let's get you home."

"Bye Sissy!" I shouted.

"Enjoy Stella," she shouted back.

"Bye Shirleen!" I shouted.

"Don't get shot at!" Shirleen shouted back.

"Bye Hot Bunch Boys!" I shouted.

No answer.

"Hot Bunch Boys?" Luke asked, pushing through the door into reception. His arm moved from around my shoulders to curl around my neck.

Oops.

In the immortal words of Britney Spears (or whoever wrote that song for her), I did it again.

Prudently, I decided after that to keep my mouth shut.

Luke let it go. We got in his Porsche and he took me "home".

Which, by the way, was the loft.

Chapter 18

Fight

We were listening to Stella and The Blue Moon Gypsies playing "Jessica" by The Allman Brothers Band. Indy, Ally, Jules, Daisy, Roxie, Jet and I were up front, right at the stage, shaking our booties like the crazy Rock Chicks we were.

Luke had taken me back to the loft, and the minute the elevator doors opened I flew into my getting-ready-to-rock preparation. Mace came over while I was in the bathroom laying on my Rock Makeup.

Before he left to do "Secret Luke Things in the Night" (his planned activities, I will note, he didn't share with me, but then again, I didn't ask, probably because I didn't want to know), Luke walked into the bathroom. He grabbed my hips, twirled me around, pressed me back against the sink and laid a hot and heavy one on me.

When he lifted his head, I asked, or more like mouthed, but with a bit of sound coming out, "What was that for?"

He framed my face with his hands, which for Luke was a weird thing to do (a *sweet* weird thing, but weird nonetheless) and stared at me, a strange look on his face that made my stomach feel funny, but in a good way. A scary good way. What he didn't do was answer. He simply kissed my nose and left me with Mace.

I decided it was best for my peace of mind not to think about what was on Luke's mind when he touched and kissed me like that. It was even better for my peace of mind not to think about what *I* felt when Luke touched and kissed me like that.

Instead, I focused on rock 'n' roll—my constant, my touchstone, the only thing other than Sissy that could get me through anything.

I pulled on my supremely faded jeans and a thick tan belt, the leather tooled with flowers and vines that had been painted. I topped this with a fitted, chambray cowgirl shirt, complete with pearl snap buttons at the breast pockets, down the front and four up the cuffs. I wore this over a white tank top and finished the outfit off with tons of silver and my fawn-suede cowboy boots.

It was cowboy chic, not rock 'n' roll chic, but I was in Denver and Denverites swung both ways.

Mace wasn't Mr. Talkative. In fact he was actually kind of broody, but like all of the Hot Bunch, this character trait worked for him (in a big way). I did find out that his name wasn't actually Mace. His name was Kai Mason, he was from Hawaii and he wasn't talkative. I found out the last bit because the first two bits took me a gazillion questions to get out of him so eventually I gave up.

The girls (and Mace) did dinner then we all went to the gig at Herman's Hideaway on Broadway.

Santo had disappeared, which I decided to take as a good sign that the bad guys were no longer after me. However, I wondered what this meant regarding my tenure at Luke's loft since, if the bad guys weren't after me anymore, I wouldn't need to stay with Luke anymore.

Another thought to put on the list to consider later.

We sent word to Stella that we were there, but other than that we didn't bother her pre-gig. As always, she'd have a drink with us during a break.

Stella and the Gypsies came out only fifteen minutes late (they were usually half an hour late or more).

They looked pissed-off but ready to rock.

This wasn't unusual, either. The band fought all the time. They were constantly in danger of breaking up, but somehow, likely using all of the piss and vinegar she had (which was a lot) Stella kept them together. She was like the mother of a dysfunctional family and I knew, because she told me, it took all her energy. If she wasn't practicing guitar or the band wasn't rehearsing, she was caught up in some band member's mess. She did this because the Gypsies played so well together they were worth the struggle. She also did this because she cared about them, from what I knew, probably more than they deserved.

Stella started the set with serious head-bouncing energy, including the guitar riffs and piano of The Doobie Brothers' "China Grove", and didn't give herself a breather before she slammed straight into Molly Hatchett's "Flirtin' with Disaster". She didn't make us wait for the famous "black" portion of her set list, starting with Ram Jam's "Black Betty", sliding straight into The Black Crowes' "Kickin' My Heart Around", taking it easy a bit for the Doobie's "Black Water" and Alannah Myles's "Black Velvet" then twanging through the Black Rebel's "Ain't No Easy Way". She gave us a break from screaming out lyrics and bouncing around like lunatics by slowing it down with The Marshall Tucker

Band's "Can't You See", one of the few songs she didn't sing herself but handed off to her bass player, Buzz. It was after that Stella and the Gypsies started the "Jessica" jam.

Stella didn't often pull out "Jessica", but when she did the crowd ate it up. This was no exception, and the Rock Chicks at the front were acting like it was our last meal.

Stella was rocking into Melissa Etheridge's "Bring Me Some Water" when Mace and I peeled off from the rest of the Rock Chicks for a beverage break, getting Fat Tire orders from the girls before we went to the bar.

I was standing amongst the crush at the bar when I looked up at Mace and noticed his eyes were locked on Stella. I followed his eyes to the stage and watched for a few seconds while she rasped out Etheridge's lyrics.

Stella was definitely Rock Chick Hot. Tall, built and wearing low slung, faded Levi's with a heavily tooled and riveted black belt with a kickass buckle that was a wide set of wings. She had on a faded black, fitted tee with the rebel flag mostly peeled but still discernible on the front and finished with scuffed, black cowboy boots. She had long, thick, dark brown hair that she held off her face just at the top with a clip at the back and she wore even more silver at her neck, ears and fingers than I did.

"You like Stella?" I screamed at Mace over the music and his eyes cut to me. His face was closed, and I knew right off he wasn't going to answer me and I was not invited to question him further.

Before I could push this, because I felt the need to be ornery as we were at a rock gig, and something about Mace invited being ornery just to see if I could get a rise out of him (not to mention Mace was staring at a friend of mine like he wanted to carry her to a deserted island, build a hut out of palm fronds and never leave), I felt his body got tense. His eyes focused on something and he stepped close to me. Real close.

I turned and my mouth dropped open when I saw Ren had materialized out of nowhere, right in front of me. He was real close, too. Ultra-close, but his eyes were on Mace.

I looked over my shoulder. "It's okay Mace, I know him," I shouted.

Mace's eyes didn't leave Ren, nor did he move away from me, but he answered in an unhappy voice. "I know."

Ee-yikes!

I stood there, the meat in a hot guy sandwich. Normally one would savor a moment like this, but the bad vibes flowing weren't conducive to savoring.

I looked back to Ren. "Hey Ren," I greeted, trying to be cool.

"Where's Sissy?" Ren replied, shattering my always tenuous hold on cool.

Uh-oh.

I stared at him. He was a Zano and Uncle Vito wanted Sissy. I didn't want Ren to turn into a bad guy. I didn't want Ren to be the man Vito sent after Sissy to make her "disappear". That would mean that Ren was on the wrong side (read: not my side) and that would suck.

I decided it was best not to answer.

Mace got closer, so much closer I could feel the heat of his body at my back.

"Back away," he warned Ren.

Ren didn't move. Not good.

Ren ignored Mace and asked me, "Does Stark have her safe?"

I kept my mouth shut, but my heart was beating double-time.

I'll be really disappointed if Ren turns out to be a bad guy, Good Ava said.

I won't, Bad Ava returned. *Bad guys are HOT.*

Ren's hand came to the side of my neck and his face came to mine. I felt Mace against my back and Mace's hand came to my waist, his fingers pressing in.

Eek!

"Both you boys, move back," I ordered, using a tone I hoped would be obeyed without question.

Neither moved.

There you go, guess they questioned my tone.

I had visions of being crushed in a hot guy sandwich, splodges of Ava squirting out the sides like too much mayo. I didn't want to be Ava mayo splodge so I snapped, "Move back!"

Ren stayed in my face, his intensity scaring me, but what scared me more was that he didn't seem at all worried about Mace. Mace wasn't as frightening a tough guy, macho man as Luke, but he was no slouch, and the broody was definitely scary.

Ren started talking to me. "Ava, if Stark doesn't have Sissy safe, tell him to keep her safe. A lot of shit is going down with Dom. Part of it is that he wants her back."

I closed my eyes in despair. I was worried about that.

Ren went on when I opened my eyes again, "I'm talking to Dom and Vito. When I work it out with them, I'll tell you. If Stark can't keep her safe, you gotta let me know so that I can."

I felt my heart stutter.

"What?" I asked stupidly, staring him in the eyes.

"If Stark isn't hiding her, tell him to hide her and keep her hidden. If he isn't willing to do that then I will. I'm workin' on Vito and I'll talk him around."

He got even closer, so much closer his forehead came to rest against mine, and when he did this I sucked in breath.

It felt weird because it felt nice and sweet and I knew it shouldn't. Firstly, I was supposed to be sworn off men. Secondly (yes, I knew it was contradictory to my first point but I was ignoring that fact), I was sleeping with Luke in an exclusive fuck buddies arrangement so I shouldn't be thinking anything about Ren felt nice and sweet.

"Ava, honey," Ren said softly, breaking into my thoughts, and since he was so close I could hear him over the music. "What I'm tellin' you is that you don't have anything to worry about, and neither does Sissy."

My tension melted and I found myself in the position (again) to want to kiss another hot guy all over for taking care of my friend, though I'd learned my lesson not to share.

When my tension left me, I felt Mace move slightly away, his fingers disappearing from my waist.

"Ren," I said softly as my way of saying thanks, and his face lost some intensity.

"Dom doesn't deserve her," Ren said back, and at his words and the way he said them, like he really meant them, I moved into him.

I couldn't help it. I agreed with what he said. I believed he wanted to keep Sissy safe and I was happy he was a good guy. There weren't a lot of them in this world, but I was beginning to think Ren was an exception to that rule. So now, by my count, there was one, maybe two if you counted Luke (though the jury was still out on him), or maybe about a dozen if you counted the Hot Bunch, Tex and Duke.

It was on that thought when Stella started to sing Hank Williams' "I'm So Lonesome I Could Cry" and all eyes turned to her.

Stella was in rare form that night. It was like she was intent on giving the performance of a lifetime, as if the King of the World had stepped in to see her set and she had to impress him or have her head chopped off. She rarely ever pulled out "I'm So Lonesome I Could Cry" and when she did the audience became transfixed, as it was right then, and I was no exception. Even though I was stuck by the heart-wrenching lyrics and the way Stella delivered them, I could swear her eyes were on Mace. It was as if she was singing right to him, and somehow, in a weird way I didn't get, that made it even more poignant.

Hmm.

Another thought to ponder at a later time and peck over with the rest of the Rock Chicks.

I was so lost in Stella and what was going on with her and Mace (because something was *definitely* going on with her and Mace, not to mention the song) I didn't pay much attention when Ren moved around to my back. I did notice his arms going around my waist and him pulling me into his body. I also noticed his chin resting on my shoulder, his cheek pressing against mine. Further, I noticed his body felt warm and hard, and he smelled really good; a hint of spicy, expensive cologne mixed with Hot Guy, and the combination of all of that was heady stuff.

I also noticed that Mace didn't see Ren move. He was staring at Stella like he was never going to stop watching her. The song was so sad, so beautiful, and Stella sang it with such emotion, it felt good having strong arms around me. I crossed my arms over Ren's at my waist and melted back into his torso.

Then, as it was with that song, especially the way Stella sang it, Ren and I seemed somehow to stand alone, even in the massive crowd, while we let Stella's singing and Hank's lyrics wash over us.

Therefore it was a shock when I felt Ren go rock-solid, not to mention at the same moment the air went dangerously electric. I turned my head to see what was causing the tension and I saw Luke standing close, wearing his customary black with the addition of a killer black leather motorcycle jacket. His face was stony, his eyes so focused on Ren they didn't even flick to me for an instant.

Uh-oh.

I straightened in Ren's arms, blinking rapidly at Luke and trying to catch one of the feelings coursing through me. The most prevalent of these included a bit of fear and a helluva lot of panic.

"Outside," Luke growled to Ren, his voice a low, angry rumble.

Ho-ly *shit*.

Ren moved from me as panic took firm hold. I tore my eyes away from Luke to look at Ren and he was grinning like he was very happy about something.

Fuckity, fuck, fuck, *fuck!*

"Rock Chicks!" I shouted toward the stage and Daisy was the only one who heard me, but a load of people gave me pissy looks for shouting during Stella's "Lonesome".

Daisy looked away from Stella to me. I pointed at Ren and Luke moving away as I jumped up and down, following the boys and motioning with hand gestures that could only describe, "Danger! Danger! The end of the world is nigh!"

Daisy's eyes moved from me to Mace, who was trying to block me, to the departing Ren and Luke. She cottoned on quickly to the situation and started tagging Rock Chicks.

I was multitasking, communicating with the Rock Chicks and following Luke and Ren, when I hit something solid and stopped to look up at Mace.

"Mace, you have to get out of my way," I told him.

"You're stayin' in here," Mace replied.

Ha!

As if!

I wasn't going to stand inside Herman's drinking a beer and listening to Stella while Luke and Ren ripped each other apart.

"No way! I've got to stop them," I cried.

Mace shook his head.

I didn't have time for this. Luke and Ren were going to tear each other to shreds in the parking lot, all on account of me being a big dork.

When was I going to learn? When, when, when? If one of them got hurt… shit!

"Out of my way," I snapped.

I dodged to the left, to the right, back to the left then ran around him on his right, giving him a wide berth and looking like a lunatic because he didn't give chase. He just watched me while he turned in a slow semi-circle, still shaking his head.

I didn't worry about looking like a lunatic. I took off out the door. By this time, the whole Rock Chick posse was on my heels.

I hit the parking lot and saw them. Luke had taken off his jacket and was in the act of tossing it on the hood of his Porsche when we got there. Ren was rolling up the sleeves of his jeans shirt.

"Lookin' forward to this," Ren said low as I stopped, the Rock Chick posse gathering around me.

"What's goin' on?" Daisy asked from beside me.

I ignored her. "This is crazy. Luke, let me—" I started but Luke's eyes cut to me and I froze in mid-speak at his look.

His eyes sliced to Mace. "Keep her back."

Before I could react, I felt an iron arm clamp around my waist as Mace grabbed hold of me. I leaned into it with all my bodyweight and tried to push his arm away with my hands, but I was held fast. I was beginning to wonder if Riley wasn't leading me down the garden path with his so-called "workouts" and "strength training".

"Shit, I don't think this is good," Jet whispered from somewhere close and I looked her way. She was pale and staring at Luke and Ren. I did a scan and noticed that all the Rock Chicks were pale.

"No, this is not good," Roxie agreed.

"No, this is really, *really* not good," Indy put in.

They were not wrong.

I decided to try another tactic and looked to Ren. "Ren, please, don't do this. This is crazy. Someone's going to get hurt. Just go, I'll call you later."

"Boys, listen to Ava, stand down," Ally threw in.

Ren ignored Ally and me.

"Ava told me about you," he said to Luke.

Uh-oh.

I went still and stopped struggling against Mace's arm so I could focus my attention on freaking about what was going to come out of Ren's mouth next. I had told him about Luke under the influence of three glasses of wine and a major flip out. I hadn't expected he'd ever have the opportunity to share, and even if he did, I never expected him actually *to* share.

"Ren," I said, but it came out breathy and quiet and I knew he didn't hear me.

I looked to Luke who was silent and watching, his body looking both relaxed and prepared at the same time.

"Ren, please. Don't," I went on, sounding louder, but not loud enough, because to my horror, Ren continued.

"I get a good shot in maybe I'll knock some fuckin' sense into you. Then maybe you'll be thinkin' of Ava when you fuck her, not some other man's piece you can't have."

The Rock Chicks collectively sucked in breath at Ren's words and all their gazes swung in my direction.

Oh shit.

Luke's eyes sliced to me and my breath left my lungs in a whoosh.

His eyes were cold, hard, furious and lastly and most frighteningly, disbelieving. Somehow his look made him seem like he'd already suffered a blow before a punch had been thrown and that blow had been delivered by me.

I wanted to say something, anything to take that look off his face, but I didn't have a chance. Luke looked back to Ren and it began.

At first I didn't move, I watched in shocked, horrified fascination.

It was brutal, powerful, and in a weird way, beautiful and even awe-inspiring. Luke and Ren knew what they were doing. They were strong, fast, light on their feet and so angry neither of them was holding anything back.

Then the sound of flesh thudding against flesh, again and again and again, got through to me.

"*Stop it!*" I screamed, my voice not sounding like my own, it came out as a screech.

They kept going.

"*Stop it!*" I shrieked again, unable to think of something better to say.

Luke's fist smashed into Ren's mouth and Ren's lip opened up, blood flying, and Ally started to scream "stop" with me.

Then I saw Ren throw a punch that Luke didn't dodge and I watched a cut open on Luke's cheek.

At that I started struggling like a she-cat and screaming like a banshee, not using words, just yelling. I pressed my back against Mace's body, lifting my feet clean up in the air to power kick out of his arms. This didn't work so I planted my feet and leaned forward, trying to take him with me or break the contact. Neither of these worked so I yelled at the top of my lungs. "*Goddammit, stop it!*"

Of course, they did not stop.

I used the move I used with Luke at Sissy and Dom's and elbowed Mace in the side with all my might. I added an additional touch at the same time, and kicked him in the shin with the heavy heel of my cowboy boot. This worked. His arm loosened just enough for me to get away.

Even though both Daisy and Jules made a grab for me, shouting at me at the same time to stay back, I evaded them and ran straight into the fight just as Luke reared back for a punch. I didn't have a chance to dodge him, his elbow slammed into my forehead and stars exploded in my eyes. I went back two steps and then down, hard on my ass.

"Stop!" Daisy screamed, running forward. She got low next to me, holding her arm out to the boys as if to shield me from them. "Stop it, right now," she snapped but they'd already stopped.

Luke was moving to me and I was shaking my head because I could swear I saw two of him.

"Sugar, you okay?" Daisy asked as the Rock Chicks lost patience with holding back and took their positions.

I put my hand to my forehead but didn't answer.

"Ava, talk to me," Daisy urged.

"Is she all right?" Jet got low beside me.

"Holy crap, Ava, say something, honey." Indy got down next to Daisy.

"I'm fine, I think." My other hand came up to my forehead and I touched it gently.

"You fucking guys!" Ally snapped from somewhere else. I couldn't see her, but then I couldn't see much of anything because I was staring at my lap and blinking a lot. I looked up and saw she was in Ren's face, blocking him from approaching me. "Why didn't you have a pissing contest?" Ally went on, getting way close to Ren. "Look at Ava, she's on her ass in a parking lot!"

"Well," I whispered to Indy, Ally and Jet. "Now I have something to write to my Mom about."

Jules materialized at my feet as the girls looked at each other, not responding to my lame effort to make light of the moment. Jules wasn't laughing either. She was looking at me in a funny way. For obvious reasons I couldn't hold her eyes so I looked back at my lap just in time to hear Roxie throw down. My head came up again and I saw Roxie quickly approaching Luke in order to get in his face and I could hear her high-heeled boots hitting the pavement in an unmistakable pissed-off woman staccato.

"Seriously!" she snapped. "It's okay if you make each other bleed, but what did you think Ava would do? Just stand there and watch you beat each other to a pulp? Men! I don't get it!" she shouted to the sky, throwing her hands out to her sides.

"I'm okay," I said, pushing unsteadily to my feet with Jet and Daisy helping me.

Once I got to my feet, I watched as Luke set Roxie aside, and he did this by picking her up by her upper arms and literally *setting her aside*. Then he was there. I could see his black t-shirt in front of my face.

"Look at me," he ordered, and he definitely used a tone that one would obey without question. Because even though I didn't want them to, my eyes lifted to his. He stared at me closely. I still felt a little funny, a bit woozy, but even so I noticed the cut on his cheekbone, blood streaming from it, and it made my stomach churn.

"You okay?" he asked.

I nodded, staring at his cut and all the blood, and wondering when I'd ever learn my lesson.

Repeat after me.

No men. No men. *No men.*

The second I nodded, before I could ask if Luke or Ren were okay or I could throw an insane, out-of-control hissy fit of my own, Luke took my hand and started toward the Porsche. I looked back at the Rock Chicks and they were watching me, all except Ally, who was kind of angrily wiping blood with a tissue from Ren's face, all the while giving him lip, which he deserved. Next time I talked to him I was going to verbally *kick his ass*.

Without thinking (I really should have thought), I got in the passenger side of the Porsche, Luke holding the door open for me and then slamming it shut behind me. He nabbed his jacket off the hood and shrugged it on. He slid behind the wheel, and with no further ado we took off like a shot.

It was then that being dazed by a tough guy, macho man elbow to the forehead wore off and I remembered Luke was angry. I remembered this because he drove like he was angry. He drove like he wanted to take me straight to the gates of hell and he wanted me to get there yesterday.

I was angry, too, but not angry or stupid enough to go up against the heat of fury rolling off Luke.

"Luke, please slow down," I said while I chanced a glance at him. I saw his jaw clench but felt the car slow.

I decided that was all I should say for now. I didn't want to start the conversation we were inevitably going to have in the Porsche with Angry Luke at the wheel. Instead, I planned my defense for whatever was going to come next

One thing that was sure and certain, and the blood proved it (not to mention Luke told me straight how he felt on several occasions) Luke was *not* the kind of guy who liked to walk into a bar and see his woman in another man's arms.

How I was going to get out of Luke finding out that I told Ren about how he felt about Jules, I didn't know, but I was going to have to come up with something.

He parked in the garage, and wordlessly we went up to the loft. I still wasn't thinking clearly. It was the first time two guys had fought over me, both getting bloody in the process. I again found myself in a situation where I didn't know what to do and I was beginning to get a little sick of feeling clueless.

Sure, one could say, considering I was practically living with Luke, I shouldn't have relaxed into Ren and let him hold me during one of the sweetest, saddest songs ever written.

But on the other hand, it was one of the sweetest, saddest songs ever written.

It was lame, but I was going to use that as my defense.

Then there was the fact Luke had a thing for Jules. It wasn't nice that Luke was with me when he felt strongly for another woman, but I probably shouldn't have told that to Ren. However, who would have ever thought in a million years Ren would have shared.

However, Ren shared.

I was going to give in on that point and would likely have to apologize, even though that would suck.

But I did have the whole fistfight thing to throw in his face. Being a tough guy, macho man was one thing, getting in fights in bar parking lots was something else. Who did that kind of thing? It was juvenile and took the whole tough guy thing a shade too far.

The doors to the elevator opened, we walked in and Luke flipped on the lights.

280

I turned to him to say something, I didn't know what, when he calmly walked to the bed, picked up the lamp on the bedside table, yanked the cord out with one vicious tug and threw it with a savage side arm throw across the room.

I watched it sail then smash against the semi-circular bar, its pieces flying.

All righty then.

One thing I knew, I wasn't going to bring up my Sweetest, Saddest Song Ever Written Defense.

He turned to me. I took one look at him and saw he was so beyond controlling-fury mode that it wasn't funny.

"Luke," I started, in order to try to defuse the situation, and I was going to do it by shifting the focus and seeing to his cut. Priorities first, and blood was pretty much always a priority. "We need to clean that cut."

"Pack," he responded.

I blinked. "What?" I asked.

"Pack. Now."

Then, without another word, he shrugged off his jacket, tossed it on the bed, walked by me and into the bathroom. I turned in a half-circle, my eyes and body following him. I watched him turn on the bathroom light, nab a washcloth and then he started to clean his cut.

Something was happening to my throat. I couldn't quite understand what it was, but I was kind of thinking it was panic mingled with fear again, this time significantly magnified.

I went to the bathroom door. "Luke, I..." I started and then trailed of because I didn't know what to say. Further, he didn't even glance at me.

It was then I realized there really wasn't anything to say.

Bottom line, now he knew that I knew he was in love with Jules. The jig was up and obviously we were over.

I didn't understand why he was so angry about it, but I'd think about that later, when Dom was gone and Sissy was with me and we had lots and lots of tequila, which always helped women understand how men's minds worked.

And this, I told myself, was a good thing. Not the angry part, the jig being up part. I told myself this but I wasn't very convincing.

I turned away from the door (by the way, he never looked at me; it was like I ceased to exist, which made my throat feel all the funnier) and went to my luggage.

281

I'd been keeping my things pretty tidy. I just had some stuff in the laundry room, the bathroom and a few things on the nightstand.

I went to the laundry room and separated my clothes in the dryer from Luke's. This activity made my throat stop feeling funny and start feeling tight. I hurried as fast as I could, taking my clothes back to my luggage and shoving it all in without folding it, which was hard to do. I didn't like to iron, but this was definitely not the time to be obsessively tidy.

I grabbed my toiletries bag and went into the bathroom. I walked by Luke, who at this point was putting those little white strips on his cut to hold the edges together. I pulled back the shower door to get my shampoo and conditioner.

Just like he'd done to me, I tried to ignore him.

This became hard when I'd nabbed my stuff, shoved it into the bag, turned back around and Luke was standing dead center of the bathroom, feet planted, arms crossed on his chest.

Clearly, Luke was done ignoring me.

"Which one?" he asked.

I shook my head because I wasn't following.

"Which one did you convince yourself I was thinkin' of when I was fuckin' you? Was it Roxie?"

I stared at him, my tight throat getting even tighter because he was *guessing*.

Why on earth was he guessing?

No time to dwell on that without tequila.

Time to move on, fast.

"I'll, um…" I stopped, deciding to ignore his question and get on with packing so I could get out, get to the store, buy an enormous amount of food that had no healthy living mojo whatsoever, go home and start the painful process of getting over Luke (which I assumed would take me approximately one hundred and fifty years, therefore, I had to get started, pronto). After making this decision, I started speaking again. "Give someone a call to come and pick me up."

I leaned to the side, reached to get my toothbrush and his hand shot out, fingers wrapping around my wrist and he yanked on it, bringing me closer to him.

My head tilted back and I looked at him. I was beginning to lose it, beginning to let all those things I wasn't thinking of, all those things I'd buried, seep into my head, and they were overpowering.

I wanted to be angry. It wasn't *me* who was in love with someone else. It wasn't *me* who had a fight in bar parking lot like a testosterone-fuelled idiot. However, for some reason, I was having trouble holding on to anger and instead felt something far, far worse.

"Which one?" he repeated.

"Luke, let me go," I said quietly, mainly because my throat was closing even more and I couldn't get more than a quiet sound out of my mouth. I swallowed as I felt the tears hit the backs of my eyes and I looked down at his fingers wrapped around my wrist. When he didn't release me, I repeated, "Please, let go."

"Look at me," he returned, his tone low and vibrating with fury.

"Please let me go," I whispered again, and I felt the wetness in my eyes start to spill over just as he used my wrist to give me another yank. I really didn't want to cry, but I didn't have a choice. It was either that or let my throat close completely, making me suffocate, which, I thought distractedly, might not be a bad thing.

His fingers were beginning to get painful and I continued in a whisper. "You're hurting me."

He let my wrist go immediately, tore the bag out of my other hand and threw it in the sink. Then he advanced, pushing me back against the wall, his body coming in close, his heat hitting me.

I kept my face down and to the side and pressed my lips together, trying to control my thoughts and tears. His anger filled the room, but it didn't frighten me. All I could think was getting out, slicing off this part of my life and starting over, as soon as possible.

"Look at me, Ava," Luke pressed. "Which one?"

"Step back, Luke," I said in a small voice, but he just pushed closer.

"I'll take you to Zano myself the minute you fuckin' answer me."

I flinched as uncontrolled pain sliced through me at Luke offering to take me to Ren. I hated the idea that he was so through with me that he was ready to hand me off to another man. But there it was.

"Move away, please," I begged.

He pressed even closer, his body now full frontal with mine, and I was looking at his shoulder.

"You didn't feel it at all, did you Ava?" he asked, and I could tell by the sound of his voice that this was an important question.

I didn't know what he was talking about and I wasn't going to ask.

I lifted my hands to his waist, grabbed fistfuls of his tee and pushed, pressing my bodyweight into his to move him back. The tears were streaming down my face and I was going to make sob noises soon, I just knew it. I didn't want him to see me cry, but I really didn't want him to hear me make a sob noise.

"Move away," I repeated.

"Who the fuck was it that you told Zano I was thinkin' of when I was fuckin' you?" He was back to his original topic, which was and was not a relief, considering I knew what he was talking about this time, but I still didn't wish to participate in the discussion.

"Move away."

"Answer me."

That was when I lost it, mainly because I couldn't take any more. It was actually surprising I'd lasted this long. I looked up at him, not caring that he could see me cry.

I had to get out. Now.

I felt the sad desperation start to subside and anger start to take control and I held fast to the anger.

"Luke, move away!" I snapped, but unfortunately my voice hitched on the end.

"*Answer me!*" Luke thundered and I'd had enough.

"Jules!" I yelled in his face. "Jules! All right?" I shoved at his shirt, but he didn't move an inch (per usual). Of course, it was then that I made the humiliating sob sound in my throat, but I powered through it. "I heard you call her 'babe'. I saw you standing close, holding her face, stroking her cheek, *just like you do to me*. You were looking at her, like… like…" I couldn't say it and I didn't have to. It finally hit me that he couldn't hold me pinned to wall not for another second, not one more fucking second.

"Move, the fuck, back! *Right now!*" I screamed.

He didn't move. Instead he stared at me, straight in the eyes with that scary, fury-unleashed look.

284

Then his gaze wandered, down the tracks of tears and something happened. Just like when he was angry at me when he thought I was yanking his chain and he ended up declaring I was his. At first it flickered in his eyes and then his face began to soften, the fury melting, the electricity sliding out of the room, and I had the distinct feeling I was in more trouble than ever.

It was too late for me. I didn't care what was happening with Luke. I was done. I'd buy more whatever it was I'd leave behind in his loft. I was going. Immediately.

With a mighty, superhuman push, I moved Luke back an inch, slid out from in front of him and ran from the room. I kicked the lid closed on my bag and bent double to zip it, but didn't even get my hands on it before I was lifted in the air.

Foiled.

Always, always, foiled. Even when it mattered the most.

Luke settled me in his arms, carrying me like a groom carrying his bride over the threshold. I was still crying, pushing against his shoulders, kicking my legs and struggling like the bride from hell. My struggle didn't last long. He planted a knee in the bed, dropped me on it and, before I could move an inch, he covered my body with his.

Shit!

"Get off!" I shoved at his shoulders, arching my back, bucking my hips.

It was like I didn't move. His face was in my face and one of his hands came to my jaw. I jerked my head away and looked anywhere but at him.

"Did you tell Zano I was thinkin' of Jules when I fucked you?" His voice was quieter, softer, and even though his complete change in tone took me off-guard, I still kept my face averted.

I decided to answer his question. As far as I was concerned, the sooner this conversation was over, the better.

"Ren came up with that on his own. I just told him you were in love with someone else."

"Ava, I'm not in love with Jules."

Bullshit, I thought but did not say, and kept looking away.

"Fine, great, sorry for the misunderstanding. Now if you'll get up, I'm going home."

285

"Babe, look at me." Now he was using his gentle, affectionate voice and I had to bite my lip. The tears were still coming, but they were subsiding. The Voice would make them come back full strength, I knew it.

"Please get off," I repeated. "I need to go home."

His weight settled full on me and his hands came to frame my face, forcing me to look at him.

I was too caught up in my drama to notice the look on his face. I just focused on the next second, which would take me to the next second and the next, which would eventually take me home, where I could be safe, renew my vows to my vibrators and never leave my house ever again.

"Jules is pregnant, Ava."

In a flash, thoughts of vibrators and a lifetime of being a hermit flew out the window and my eyes focused on his.

"What?" I asked.

"Vance told me yesterday morning. It's early. She doesn't want anyone to know until she's further along. Vance didn't agree. He's fuckin' beside himself. He told everyone but Shirleen."

I realized I wasn't breathing. Then I realized I forgot how.

Luke kept talking, "That's why I was standin' close to her, touching her face. She's got no blood family left and Vance isn't close to his. They've been through a lot and they both want this. I'm happy for them. This is a good thing."

Okay. It was official. I was The A-Number-One Dork of All Time.

I told you that you should have talked to him, Good Ava admonished.

Bad Ava was silent.

Good Ava looked around my neck at Bad Ava. *Nothing to say?*

Bad Ava looked around my neck at Good Ava. Then she put her thumb to her nose and wiggled her fingers at her.

I let out my breath and my eyes slid to the side. "Sorry," I whispered.

Luke's thumb slid across my wet cheekbone. "Babe, please look at me."

It was the "please" that got me and my eyes slid back to his.

"I'm guessin' that was the drama yesterday, why you needed to get your head together."

I didn't answer. I didn't need to. It was obvious.

He continued, "What I want to know is why you came back to me last night, considerin' you thought I was in love with Jules."

I forgot how to breathe again.

Oh... my... *God.*

I'd given it all away. I didn't even mean to but I did. I didn't expect him to find out I thought he was in love with Jules.

Fuckity, fuck, fuck, *fuck.*

I bucked my hips a bit, a tester to see if he was off-guard (he wasn't).

While I did this, his face came closer, his lips came to mine and he said, "That's what I thought."

"Whoa. Whoa, whoa, whoa. Stop right there."

Shit! Did I say that aloud?

I did.

Hell and damnation.

I was going to have to go with it.

His head came up an inch.

"I didn't have anywhere else to go," I told him. "Bad guys were after me, remember?" That wasn't bad, it was even the truth.

"You could have stayed with Zano," Luke replied.

Shit, shit, *shit.*

He was right. I could have.

Why hadn't I thought of that?

I started to think of something else, a lie, a fib, anything. Luke's body started moving like he was laughing and I knew he read my face.

I didn't think this was funny. Not even a little bit.

"Please get off me. I need to go home," I whispered.

The amusement faded from his eyes when he heard my tone, but he didn't move his body from mine. Instead, his finger traced my hairline. His eyes watched this and then they came back to mine.

"Beautiful, I told you that you were going to have to clue in yourself, but tonight I'm gonna give you a little help."

This did not sound good.

I didn't want any help. I wanted this to be over. It was much better to be over now than over later when he left me because he was bored or done with me or whatever. Or worse, when I had to identify his bullet-ridden body at a morgue.

"First..." he started, interrupting my thoughts.

Oh no! It had multiple parts.

"I'm gonna fuck you until you feel it. Until I know you feel it. 'It' being what we have between us. I thought I was gettin' through last night, you talkin' about your Dad, and today, you callin' me when there was trouble or when nothin' was happening at all. We'll see if that took, but either way, I'm gonna get through to you, I don't care what it takes."

Okay, maybe lying wasn't the way to go, maybe begging was. "Luke, please, please, just let me go home."

His hand came back to my jaw, his thumb sliding along my lower lip, and he ignored my pleas. "The second part you gotta get, babe, is that I'm not lettin' you go. I'm not lettin' you push me away and I'm not giving up. I'm gonna keep working until I piece together what your Dad and those assholes tore from you. I'm gonna keep at you until you let me in. I'm not gonna stop until you tell me you're mine, until it comes straight from your mouth, preferably when I'm deep inside you and you're lookin' at me like you look at me when I'm close to makin' you come."

Against my will, I felt my insides melt as his fingers sifted into the hair at the side of my head. His eyes got ultra-warm and his mouth came to mine.

"I love it when I make you come," he muttered against my lips, his hand sliding all the way through my hair then down my back as his arm closed around me. "Every time, you say my name and you smile this unbelievably sexy little smile."

Oh crap. I didn't want to believe I did that, but I could believe I did that. I mean, this was Luke we were talking about, which would have been enough, but there was also the fact that I'd never climaxed as hard as I did when I was with Luke and that would make anyone smile.

Then he said what sounded like a vow to a sacred quest. A sexy, modern-day vow, but a scary one for me because Luke was the kind of guy you just knew would find the Holy Grail. I was pretty certain he'd make old Lancelot look like a putz.

"Ava babe, I'm tellin' you, you're gonna admit you belong to me because *you belong to me.*"

Ee-yikes!

I tried one more time. "Luke, please, let me go home."

His lips brushed mine then he lifted his head.

I noticed his eyes had gone ink right before he smiled.

"No fuckin' way."

Fuckity, fuck, fuck, *fuck.*

Chapter 19

Cornered

He kissed me.

I tried not to let it penetrate, but he was good with his mouth. He was an amazing kisser and my melty insides intensified.

Unfortunately, my outsides turned melty too and my body relaxed under his. He felt it and rolled, taking me with him so I was on top.

Something about this cut through the Luke Lip Fog, reminding me I was still in escape mode. I lifted my knees like I was going to straddle him. Instead, I broke my lips from his, pushed up swiftly and started to exit the bed.

I got one foot on the floor before he tagged me. Twisting me, I fell into his lap and one of his arms closed around me tight. I struggled, of course, and since he wasn't paying attention I thought I had a chance. Still, he managed to hold me to him, which was *way* annoying. He wasn't paying attention because he had the drawer of the nightstand open and he was rummaging in it. I was too busy trying to get away to notice what he was doing until I heard the clink of handcuffs.

I stilled, my head jerked around and I shouted, "No!"

That was when I really started to struggle. I didn't want to be cuffed to the bed, not ever again.

I pulled away, gained my feet and ran to the elevator, slapping the button, stopping and realizing too late that it sucked Luke had an elevator. It was cool until you had to make a quick exit. If you had to make a quick exit, you were screwed.

Foiled...fucking... again.

I whirled to face him while I waited for the elevator and watched as he approached me, shoving the cuffs into his back pocket.

"I'm leaving," I told him.

"No you're not," he replied, calm as could be.

"I am. You can't keep me here," I went on, not calm at all.

"Yes, I can."

I didn't want to admit it, but I was pretty sure he could.

Shit!

He got up close just as the elevator doors opened. I had started edging back when he moved, faster than I'd seen anyone move before. One second, I was heading backward toward the elevator, the next second I was pinned against the wall by the side of the elevator.

Once again, I had to ask.

Why me?

"Luke, don't!" I shouted, sounding desperate and not caring anymore. "Please don't cuff me to the bed again."

He moved away an inch, and with a quick tug at my shirt, the buttons down the front unsnapped all the way up.

Shit again!

I moved out the inch he moved away, but he pressed me back to the wall with his body while his hand went inside my shirt at my midriff and then slid up my side, sending happy tingles in its wake.

His lips came to mine, his eyes open and not leaving my own.

"Relax, beautiful, I'm not cuffing you to the bed," he said before his hand came around, and he slid the shirt off my shoulder and down my arm.

"I'm not going to relax. I'm going to go home," I told him while I wriggled my arm to get away from his hand. Unfortunately, this also had the effect of assisting my shirt to fall off one side.

"You aren't goin' home," Luke replied, and I had to admit to the secret, private place buried deep down where I buried everything else that I loved it when he talked against my mouth.

"I have to go home," I went on, still sounding desperate, still not caring and searching for an excuse, *any* excuse. "I have to check my mail and water my plants." The last part was a lie. I didn't have any plants. The first part was a lie, too. I never got any good mail.

His head came up and he grinned at me, and let me tell you, the grin was *good*. It was unlike any grin he'd given me. It was sexy and warm and there was something about his face, something I'd never noticed before, but I was too freaked out to put my finger on it.

"You can water them tomorrow," he told me.

"Tomorrow will be too late, they're really thirsty," I returned.

I lifted both my hands and pushed against his shoulders. This, per usual, had no effect, but I still kept at it.

"They die, I'll buy you new plants," he replied.

"I don't want new plants. I like the plants I have," I lied again.

"Then we'll go tonight, after I make love to you."

I stopped pushing, my heart stopped beating, my lungs stopped working, my knees wobbled and I stared at him.

"What did you say?" I whispered.

His mouth came to mine again. He brushed his lips there and then they trailed down my cheek to my ear. I tried not to do it, but this made me shiver.

"I'll take you home tonight after I'm done with you. You can water your plants and we'll sleep at your place."

My heart kicked in as did my lungs, but I didn't resume the struggle.

He didn't repeat what I wanted him to repeat, the "make love to you" part. He'd always called it "fucking". He'd *never* called it "making love".

Still, I was pretty certain he said it.

For my safety and for my sanity I had to try one last time.

I took my hands from his shoulders and moved my head back so it was fully pressed against the wall. His head came up when I did this. I placed my hands on either side of his neck and looked into his eyes.

"Luke," I said softly. "Please, let me go home."

He dropped his forehead to mine just like Ren had done.

With Luke, it was different. It was better, so much better it wasn't funny. In fact it was so *not* funny it was world-tiltingly not funny. He came in so close, his nose rested along the side of mine and he took that opportunity to run his tongue along my bottom lip.

There were only two words to describe the feeling this whole maneuver gave me and those words were: *Oh my.*

I felt my eyelids get heavy as my knees got weak. I saw his inky eyes smile and I knew that he knew that he had me.

Damn.

"Babe, I told you I'll take you home." His face shifted and his mouth came to mine. "Later," he said there, right before he kissed me.

⚅

Luke and I had wall sex.

I'd never had sex pressed against the wall, and let me tell you, wall sex was very, *very* good. In fact, wall sex was so good, it was my new favorite position. In fact, it was so good, I couldn't believe that Eddie and Jet had only done it four times. They'd been together months!

After wall sex, as promised, we got dressed and Luke took me to my place.

This freaked me out since we were going to my place so I could water plants that I didn't own. The whole way there I tried to figure out how to get out of the new mess I made for myself and decided that I was just going to have to wing it.

First, I tried to get him to leave me at the door by barring his way, but as was becoming his custom, he just leaned down, and hands at my ass, he picked me up.

I should have known I wouldn't succeed at barring him from my house, but I told myself at least I wasn't a quitter.

As was becoming *my* custom, my legs went around his hips and my hands went to his shoulders (by the way, this was Wall Sex Position, but in clothes). He stepped in, kicking the door shut behind him, ignoring my hands pressing against his shoulders. He turned and locked the door (still ignoring my pressing hands) and walked us up my stairs.

I gave up on the shoulder press and tried another strategy.

"I have to see to my plants," I told him. I decided I'd *pretend* I had plants, maybe get him to wait for me in the bedroom and hope he didn't follow me around while I watered my non-existent plants.

"You don't have any plants," Luke returned.

Shit, shit, *shit* Did he know *everything?*

I narrowed my eyes at him. "You're annoying," I told him when he made the turn at the top of the landing toward my bedroom.

"At least you aren't tellin' me you hate me anymore."

Hell and damnation!

I forgot my own kill line.

I made a frustrated noise in the back of my throat.

Luke chuckled. Yes, he actually chuckled.

"Okay, *now* I hate you," I told him, sounding bitchy.

We'd made it to the side of my bed and he let me go in a way that my soft body slid down his hard one until my feet hit the floor. This felt nice, as in *ultra*-nice.

"No you don't," he replied on a grin, his gaze scanning my face, and I knew he could see I liked the body slide. I powered past the body slide. "If you knew I didn't have any plants, why'd you bring me home?"

"Two reasons," He answered. Then he bent his head and touched his lips softly to mine. The lip touch was ultra-nice too, might I add. He continued speaking when his head came back up. "One, because I've wanted to fuck you in your bed since that night we spent here. Two, because it amuses me to watch you when you're cornered."

My body got stiff, also for two reasons. One, because he was back to using the word "fuck", and two, because he thought it was amusing to watch me when I was cornered.

"That isn't nice," I snapped.

His arms were around me and they tightened, bringing me closer. I watched as his face got serious.

Uh-oh.

I wasn't getting a good feeling about his serious face.

"We should be straight about somethin', beautiful."

Oh shit.

Luke was straight enough about everything. I wasn't sure I could cope with him being straight about being straight.

Before I could stop him (not that I could stop him), he kept talking.

"To get through to you, I don't intend to be nice. I intend to keep you cornered. You try to get out of that corner, I'm gonna push you back in. I'm gonna keep you pinned there until you give me what I want. You aren't gonna like hearin' this, but I gotta tell you, I think you're damned sexy when you're bitchy. I've also decided to think it's adorable rather than fuckin' annoying as hell when you're lyin' to me and yourself about what we've got. I decided this mainly because you're incredibly sweet when you forget to fight it, not to mention you're a shit liar and I find that hilarious. Considerin' this is how you act when you're cornered, babe, you gotta know, I'm enjoyin' almost every minute of this, even the parts when I'm pissed at you or fightin' for you, and I'm not gonna be sorry that I am."

Yep, I was right. I couldn't cope with him being straight about being straight.

I decided not to tell him I hated him again as this had no effect. Instead, I glared.

After scorching him with a good long glare (well, I liked to think of it as scorching him, but if I wasn't mistaken, his lips started twitching toward the end), I pulled out of his arms, walked to my dresser, got a nightgown and stomped down the hall to the bathroom.

I took out my contacts, cleaned and moisturized my face with travel-sized bottles I kept in the bathroom closet and changed into the nightgown. The nightgown was a Christmas present from my Mom. I'd never worn it before because it was ugly as all get out. It was white with little flowers on it, dowdy, high-necked and old-maidish, just where I was sure my Mom thought I was headed. When I was done, I stomped back to the bedroom.

The lights were out, the blinds still up and the streetlights filtered in through the windows.

Luke, of course, was on his back in bed, hands behind his head, relaxed and Zen.

Argh!

I dumped my clothes on the wicker laundry hamper then I walked back to the door.

Before I reached it, I heard Luke say, "You get near the couch or that fuckin' futon, there'll be consequences."

I turned to him and felt my hold on my temper slip.

This wasn't surprising. I'd had a rough night, a tough day and a killer of a week. I didn't have any control of my life. None, zip, nada, and Luke was scaring the shit out of me. Not in a way where I feared for my safety. In a way where I feared for my heart.

And that was worse.

My temper-hold slipped so much, my hands went to my hips, my foot came out and the Barlow Bitch Blood started to flash through my veins.

"You were straight, Luke, so I'll be straight, too, and this time I want you to listen," I told him, voice chockfull of attitude. "I've had a pretty hectic day, what with Dom's *Streetcar Named Desire* antics and you fighting with Ren in a parking lot, though I still cannot *believe* you fought in the parking lot of a *bar*. And ended up bloody in the process! Then throwing a light across the room, for God's sake. I mean, who does that? Now you're going to have to go out and buy a new lamp, and that was a nice lamp. And I want to know, who's going to clean it up? Not me, I'll tell you that right now. Next time *I* throw a lamp, *I'll* clean it up. New rule, the person that throws the lamp *cleans it up*."

I took a deep breath, mainly because I'd run out of oxygen, and kept on going.

"Not to mention all your straight talk. No one talks like you. It's nuts. And you should know it freaks me way the hell out."

I watched as Luke threw the covers back and got out of bed. For the first time, I took this as the warning sign it was, but I was pissed-off enough that I held my stance even as he walked toward me, his naked, and (even though he was fuzzy without my contacts in, it must be said) magnificent body illuminated by the streetlights.

I ignored the thrill of fear, and the thrill of something else entirely, running down my spine and kept ranting.

"So I'm out of patience with all this," I told him in my best bitchy tone. I tilted my head back to squint at him when he stopped within a few inches of me. I lifted my finger and started poking him in the chest repeatedly to make my point. "Get it through that skull of yours, Lucas Stark. We're fuck buddies, end of story. Nothing more. Furthermore," I went on, warming to my theme and still poking him. "I'm going to warn you that if you keep me cornered, *you'll* have to face the consequences."

I had no idea what consequences he would face, but I thought it sounded good.

I stopped ranting and Luke just looked at me.

Finally, he asked, "You through?"

I thought about it a second then said, "Yeah."

His hand shot up and his fingers wrapped around my wrist. I thought he'd jerk me to him, but instead he lifted my hand, his thumb sliding across my palm to open my fist and he brought my hand to his mouth.

I watched in fascinated silence as he kissed my palm, and I felt, with a definite knee wobble, his tongue touch me there.

Ho-ly *crap*.

That was nice.

Just as quickly as I lost control of my temper, I lost control again. This time it was my temper that slid away.

When he took my hand from his mouth, he used my wrist to pull me toward him slowly.

As I moved toward him, he asked me, "You wanna do it against the wall again?"

I blinked to try to clear the Luke Palm-Tongue-Touch Fog and, even though I seriously liked wall sex, I answered, "No, absolutely not."

"The floor?" Luke asked, still pulling me to him, and I felt my breasts brush against his chest just as I felt my stomach pitch deliciously.

"I'm sleeping on the futon," I persevered, valiantly ignoring my stomach.

In turn, he ignored my declaration and asked in a soft, sexy voice, "You wanna take a bath together?"

Hmm, taking a bath with Luke. Wow, I figured that would be nice, his skin all wet, soapy and slippery.

Get a hold of yourself, girl! neither Good Ava nor Bad Ava said. Instead this came direct from my brain.

I shook my head sharply to clear it and stomped my foot on the floor.

"No!" I snapped.

I was nearly full frontal with him when his other hand came up to toy with a short, Grandma ruffle at my high collar.

"You buy this?" he asked, changing the subject, and I found myself blinking in confusion again.

"No. Mom bought it for me for Christmas."

"You like it?" he went on.

For some reason, I answered honestly, "Not particularly."

Before I knew what he was about his hand fisted on the collar. He gave a rough yank and the material tore from collar to waist.

I sucked in a stunned breath and stood stock-still as his other hand came to the tear and he used both hands to rip it again, straight to the hem.

"We'll fuck in your bed then," he finished calmly, sliding the material off my shoulders and it fell on the floor at my feet. Then his fingers hooked into my panties and he slid them down until they joined the torn nightgown on the floor.

I didn't make a move or a noise. I couldn't. I was in shock.

He picked me up and still I didn't move to resist, mainly because I was in the throes of such a huge freak out it had to be the hugest freak out I'd ever experienced. In fact, it might have been the hugest freak out in the history of the world.

Luke Stark, the boy from across the street, just literally tore my clothes off.

"You just..." I cleared my throat and I didn't care what that betrayed, "tore my Mom's nightgown right off me."

He set me in bed and followed me down. "The nightgown was ugly as hell and your mother was makin' a point," he said as he pulled the covers up over us. I tried to sit up, but he shifted me into his arms, pulling me down so we were on our sides, face-to-face. "I see your mother hasn't changed."

He was right, she hadn't changed, but he still *ripped a nightgown off my body.*

"I think you may just be crazy," I blurted. "People don't act like you. They don't handcuff people to themselves or to beds. They don't fight in parking lots. They don't carry people around everywhere. *They don't tear clothes off women's bodies.*" When I finished, my voice was pitched two octaves higher than normal.

"I only carry you around when you're always tryin' to get somewhere I don't want you to be or doin' somethin' I don't want you to do."

I pushed against his chest but his arms just got tighter. "That doesn't make it any better!" Now I was kind of shouting. "In fact, that makes it worse!"

"You scared of me?" he asked, still calm as could be.

"No," I snapped, and in a way it was the truth. I wasn't scared of him because he tore a nightgown off my body. I was scared of him for other reasons, reasons I wasn't about to share.

"You feel cornered?"

"Fuck yes!" Now I was yelling and *totally* telling the truth.

I saw the white of his teeth flash. "Good," he murmured.

Then he kissed me. It was long, hot, heavy, and even though he'd given me an against-the-wall orgasm less than an hour ago, I started to get turned on again.

Shit!

When his lips detached, I thought he was going to take things further. Instead, he turned me so my back was to his front. His arms came around me tight and I felt his lips at the back of my neck for a quick kiss before he buried his face in my hair.

I thought we might have spoon sex, and I had to admit I was kind of looking forward to it, but as the moments slid by he just held me.

I told myself it was being in my own bed again that made the tension flow out of my body so that I relaxed into him. I told myself it was not his warmth, his arms around me, his breath against my neck and the fact that he was Luke Stark, the man I'd loved since I could remember.

I was beginning to fall into dreamland when his hand came up and cupped my breast. I lost any drowsiness I had and held my breath. Even though his thumb idly stroked the inside curve from nipple to chest, it was clear this was just an affectionate touch and he wasn't taking it anywhere.

"I'm guessin' from your behavior you didn't feel it when I fucked you against the wall," he noted softly to the back of my head.

Whatever "it" was, I didn't feel it. I also didn't share this. I kept silent.

He accepted my silence and just held me, stroking my breast.

After a while, he spoke again. "You wanna tell me why you were standing in Zano's arms?"

Eek!

No, I most certainly did *not* want to tell him, mainly because I didn't really know myself. Therefore, I kept my silence.

He waited then his voice came again. "All right, we'll let that go. Instead, maybe you wanna tell me why you didn't call me after my Dad's funeral."

Any relaxation I felt left my body in an instant and it went solid. I also kept silent.

Luke waited again. His thumb stilled then he sighed.

"I'll take that as a no."

I bit my lip as his hand moved away from my breast and both his arms wrapped around my midriff, pulling me deeper into him as I felt his head move, his mouth coming to my ear.

"This starts to go bad, Ava, what we have, we'll talk about it. We'll work on it. I'm not your Dad. I'm not one day just gonna up and leave you."

"You already did, for eight years."

Oh no. Did that just come out of my mouth? And did it sound like an accusation?

"Babe," he murmured before he buried his face in the side of my neck. The murmur was soft, gentle and affectionate, and there was what sounded almost like a growl running through it, and his obvious emotion made me tremble.

Yep, it just came out of my mouth. Over and over, I kept giving myself away.

Time to go back to silence.

Luke didn't feel like silence. He turned me to face him again and I didn't fight it. I wouldn't win anyway.

Once he got me in position, as a defense mechanism I buried my face in his throat. I didn't want to look at him and I didn't want him looking at me. I didn't want to have this conversation either, but I wasn't going to resist. Resistance would just make it last longer and I needed to sleep, to get this night over with and take up the fight again tomorrow. He eventually had to leave. He had a job, even if he didn't need it. When I was alone again, I'd figure out what was next for me. I was still leaning toward plastic surgery and creating my own disappearance in the depths of Mexico.

"Jules asked me once why I was working for Lee," Luke shared, interrupting my thoughts.

I licked my lips and then pressed them together. I didn't want to talk about Jules, but I wasn't about to share that.

"I didn't tell her," he went on.

This I found surprising.

"She didn't have the right to know," Luke continued.

This I also found surprising.

"*You* have the right to know," he finished.

Oh... my... *God*.

My body went still at the meaning behind his words and he kept talking. "I was recruited by an organization. I can't tell you who, no one knows but Lee, Mace and Monty, and I'm sorry babe, but it has to stay that way."

My body stayed still. I stayed silent and he kept going. "They trained me and sent me on assignments, mostly out of the country. I made a shitload of money and was good at what I did, but I wasn't proud of it. The minute my contract was up, I got out. On one of the assignments, I met Monty. He tracked me down when I got out and he and Lee talked me back to working. What I do now is local, it's a helluva lot less risky and I'm proud of it."

I couldn't believe he was telling me this. I didn't even want to *know* this. On the one hand, it scared me. On the other hand, I was moved that he'd share.

I kept silent.

"Beautiful, you listenin' to me?" he asked.

I stayed silent but I nodded. I had to nod. Even if I didn't want to be having a heart-to-heart with Luke, I knew through to my soul it would be way out of line if I didn't acknowledge his sharing.

His hand went up my back and twisted in my hair. With a gentle tug he pulled my head back so I was looking at him.

He started talking again, his voice such a low rumble I felt it against my skin. "During those eight years, Ava babe, I wasn't someone you'd want to know."

Kristen Ashley

I couldn't stop myself. I didn't even try. My hand went to his cheek and my body pressed against his.

"Luke," I whispered.

I wanted to tell him there was nothing he could do, no one he could be that I didn't want to know, and I didn't even care what scary shit he did or who he did it for. That was how much he meant to me.

But I couldn't. I couldn't open myself up like that.

Luke went on, "A few weeks after I left that life, my Dad died. I tried to reconnect with you, then *you* left *me* for five years."

My heart lurched because there was definitely accusation in his tone.

I closed my eyes and tilted my head forward so my forehead was resting on his chin.

He kissed me there and kept talking. "Ava, I need you to tell me why you didn't pick up the phone."

"I can't." My voice was so soft even I had trouble hearing it.

"You will," he replied in a voice nearly as soft as mine and it made me shiver.

Luke felt the shiver. His hand left my hair and his arms wrapped around me.

I waited for him to say more but he didn't. Instead, he held me while I processed all he said, tied it in a bundle and buried it deep. He kept holding me until the tension ebbed out of me again.

And he kept holding me until I fell asleep.

～✕～

As usual, sometime deep in the night, Luke pulled me over his body.

Not as usual, he stopped when I was on top of him.

His hands went over my bottom, down the backs of my thighs to my knees and then he pulled my legs up so I was straddling him. As his hand went between our bodies, my head came up.

"What's going on?" I mumbled in a sleepy voice.

He didn't answer. Instead he did an ab curl, sitting up, taking me with him at the same time he guided himself inside me.

"Oh my God," I whispered at the shock and thrill of it.

One of his arms hooked around my waist, the other one went into my hair and tilted my head down to his.

"I want you to feel it," he told me, his voice husky.

The husky voice mixed with him filling me worked like a charm. I was instantly *way* turned on and I started to move. His arm went from around my waist, his hand slid down my arm, taking hold of my hand and pulling it between our bodies.

I kept moving, sliding up and down on top of him, my lips on his as he brought our hands between us and his fingers pressed mine to where we joined.

I had to admit, I liked the feel of us. We felt sexy and hot and wet, and having my fingers touch our physical connection opened something inside me, something I really wanted to stay closed.

"Luke," I breathed.

"Quiet, beautiful. Just move."

I did as he asked and moved, slowly, rhythmically. All the while he held our hands between us, his other hand in my hair, tilting my head down, slanted so my mouth was on his. Every once in a while, he'd kiss me, softly, touching his tongue to mine briefly and pulling away.

It didn't take long before I felt it—what he was talking about, what he wanted me to feel.

It was our connection. Not just our bodies but more. It was about history, it was about understanding, it was about the fact that we fit together and the fact that everything was just, simply *exactly* as it should be.

It was right.

When I felt it, it overwhelmed me, shot straight through that opened part of me right to the soft, vulnerable spot I kept guarded, and even *that* felt right.

The tears came to my eyes, spilling over silently, falling down my cheeks, but I kept moving.

"There it is," Luke whispered. His voice had gone from husky to hoarse.

"I can't do this, Luke," I whispered back.

"You can."

I pulled my hand from his, but only so I could wrap both my arms tight around his shoulders and I kept moving. "I can't."

"So you can't. We'll do it together. That's the point, babe."

I knew that. Now, I knew it.

"You don't get it," I told him, still moving.

Kristen Ashley

"Tell me," he replied gently, his hand sliding up my back making me tremble.

I slid down and stayed down so he completely filled me. I loved the feeling of Luke deep inside me.

I took a moment to memorize it before I said, "This can't go bad."

"It won't go bad."

"It can't."

"Ava—"

"Luke, you have to know, it won't be like the other guys. If it's you, it'll be worse." My voice went softer, lower, barely a whisper. "If this goes bad, it'll destroy me."

His hand stilled on my back and I waited, holding my breath.

The moment of truth.

No man wanted that responsibility. I knew it, I'd seen it time and again.

They liked to be in the chase. Luke didn't want me actually to belong to him. He wanted to *make* me belong to him. Once he did, I was like his lamp, easily disposed of. Admitting to him that he had that power over me, I knew would be the ultimate turn off. Guys wanted girls they couldn't have, so they could win them and then destroy them. Guys didn't want girls who pined for them, loved them most of their life. That was just too easy.

His hand in my hair fisted. "You sayin' you belong to me?" he asked. His voice had gone from hoarse to gruff.

"No, I'm saying if this doesn't work out—"

I didn't finish. He whipped me around so I was on my back, he was on top and he ground his hips into me.

Ho-ly *shit* but that felt good.

"Luke," I breathed, my voice catching on his name as the slow burn started sprinting.

"Admit it, Ava, you were sayin' you belonged to me."

"No."

He pulled out, slammed back in and started grinding again.

Yes! My brain screamed.

"Do you feel it?" he asked.

I nodded and whispered, "I feel it."

"Then you belong to me."

"Luke."

He pulled out and slammed back in again and my breath hitched as my body jolted.

"Say it," he demanded.

I held on to my denial. "No."

He did a repeat of the pull and slam.

"Say it."

"No!" I shouted.

I lifted my head, pressed my lips to his and kissed him, sliding my tongue in his mouth.

That was when it went wild. He didn't stop between the pull and slams, just kept pounding into me again and again and again, and it must be said, I loved every single mind-blowing stroke.

I lifted my legs at the knees, pressing them into his sides as my hands roamed, my nails scratched. I kissed, licked, and I may have gotten out-of-control and given him an actual junior high school love bite at the base of his neck.

With his hands at my ass lifting my hips to take his thrusts, I finally got so close, I called his name, ready to finish.

And he stopped.

I'd arched my neck in preparation for climax, but my chin jerked down and I stared at him. "Don't stop!" I shouted.

"Do you belong to me?" he asked.

Even in the throes of pre-orgasm, my mouth dropped open. Then I snapped, "I hate you Lucas Stark!"

I saw his white grin.

"Yeah," he murmured. "You belong to me."

Then he started moving again. And he didn't stop this time.

And he left me believing that regular position sex definitely had its merits.

⋈

We were face-to-face, my hands pressed against his chest, my leg wrapped around his hip, his fingers stroking the back of my thigh.

I had my eyes closed and even though I'd come down from my post-getting-what-was-between-us orgasm, my heart hadn't stopped beating too fast. In fact, it was pounding so hard I was certain Luke could hear it *and* feel it.

"You scared?" he murmured.

Yep, he could feel it.

"Yes," I whispered, and do not ask me why, I told him the truth.

I was scared. I was scared out of my mind.

"Of me?" he asked.

"Yes," I answered honestly again, and I actually started trembling.

He stopped stroking my leg. His fingers slid over my bottom, his arm wrapped around my waist and he pulled me closer to the heat of him.

"Finally," he muttered, "I'm gettin' somewhere."

I was so screwed.

He certainly is getting somewhere and I like where he's getting! Good Ava said dreamily.

I don't think your fuck buddies idea is working, Bad Ava told me on a huff.

I ignored Good Ava and Bad Ava and Luke held me tight until the tremors slid away.

Then I called, "Luke?"

"Yeah, babe?"

"What was with the handcuffs?"

His arm got even tighter. "If I had to, I was gonna cuff you to me again." His head came up and he kissed my shoulder then he settled again and said quietly, "I didn't have to."

Hell and damnation.

I just kept giving myself away.

Chapter 20

Straighter

It had been a long and emotional night, so when I woke up, I still felt asleep and thought I was dreaming. Either that or I was in my pretend happy place. Those were my excuses for what I did and I was going with them.

See, I woke up before Luke. I woke up happy (yes happy; it was morning, I hadn't had the chance to put my defenses up yet), warm and post-night-of-mind-boggling, life-altering sex, relaxed, curled into his side, and the first thing my eyes saw was the wall of his chest. There were a lot of things about Luke I liked (read: pretty much everything), but I liked his chest especially. So since I liked it so much and I was living a dream, I leaned down and kissed it.

I decided I also liked his neck, so once I was done kissing his chest, I shifted up and kissed his neck. Since I was at his neck, I saw that I had, indeed, given him a hickey the night before, and even though that was silly, juvenile and highly embarrassing, secretly I liked my mark on him so I kissed that, too.

You also like his jaw, Good Ava reminded me.

She was right. I *did* like his jaw. Luke had a great, strong jaw.

So I kissed Luke's jaw.

You also like his... Bad Ava started, but Good Ava threw her halo at Bad Ava. It bonked off Bad Ava's head so Bad Ava snapped at Good Ava, *Hey!*

"Babe," Luke said, his voice husky with sleep, his arms coming around me.

I lifted my head to look at him, planting my hands on his chest, moving closer to his face, and still in my dreamy, pretend happy place, I smiled and whispered, "Good morning."

That's when I noticed his face. It was soft and his eyes were sleepy, warm, inky and completely unguarded.

Whoa.

Whoa, whoa, whoa.

Stop right there.

Before I could react, retreat or even take the moment to memorize that look leveled at me, his hands came to my hair, pulling it off my shoulders to

Kristen Ashley

bunch it the back of my head. One hand shifted my hair to his other hand and the fingers of his free hand drifted down my back. His head came up and he brushed his lips against mine.

He settled back into the pillows and his warm, unguarded eyes roamed my face as I lay there frozen.

Good Ava was twirling with delight, a la Maria in the mountains at the beginning of *The Sound of Music,* while Bad Ava had her face in her hands and was shaking her head.

Luke's eyes settled back on mine and he murmured, "Christ, you're beautiful."

At his words my blood turned to ice. The pretend happy place around me exploded and I found I was in the polar arctic, surrounded by snow and wasteland.

What was I doing? What on earth was I doing? How had I let it get this far?

No.

No, no, no.

This was wrong. It wasn't right, it was very, very *wrong.*

What I was, and forever would be, was Fatty Fatty Four-Eyes.

What I was not was beautiful.

Without a word, I jerked away from him and rolled to a seated position on the side of the bed, nothing but escape on my mind. I had no idea where I was going, but I was going there, and fast. I almost had my feet on the floor when his arm sliced around my waist and I was yanked back, across his lap.

"Where are you—?" he started, but I was struggling, out-of-control kicking and hitting, my fists connecting with his flesh.

I had struggled against Luke before, but not like this. It was like it was life or death. And in a way it was life or death because what I just learned about Luke was just like dying and all I knew was I had to get away.

"What the fuck?" Luke clipped, getting hold of my wrists and forcing my back to the bed using his torso. My hips still in his lap and my legs useless, he half-pinned me, pressing my wrists against the bed at the sides of my head.

"*Get off me!*" I shrieked, desperate, panicked and out of my mind.

"Jesus," he muttered, staring at my face.

I bucked and pushed against his hands at my wrists. "Get off!"

"Ava, talk to me," Luke demanded. "What the fuck's going on?"

306

"*Off!*" I cried, my voice hitching as tears clogged my throat. I choked them down and started fighting again. Surprisingly, I got a wrist free and somehow slid away, but he yanked me back, rolled full on top of me and caught my wrists again, jerking them over my head.

"Let me go," I ordered.

"Talk to me."

"Let… me… *go!*" I yelled and bucked viciously.

"*Talk, dammit!*" he barked in my face.

I stilled at the fury in his voice, and for some reason, talked.

"This game… or whatever it is you're playing with me… is bad enough, but don't you ever lie to me, Lucas Stark."

At that point, I was ignoring the fact that I lied freely to him.

But mine were fibs. This was huge.

His body went solid and his fingers tightened on my wrists.

"Woman, you better fuckin' explain yourself," he warned, and even though a chill went through me at his tone, I forged ahead.

"I know I'm a challenge, I know how you guys like that. You even told me last night you were enjoying this." I closed my eyes tight at the memory, opened them again, and then went on. "I am *such* a dork. I should have just given in right off so you could get your fill and get rid of me."

I stopped talking and shook my head in disbelief, *at myself*, too caught up in my own drama to feel the dangerous, angry electricity emanating from Luke and hitting the room.

I kept going, "You have what you want, Luke. You like to be straight, okay this is straight. We'll stop playing this game. You win. You and I both know I'm not going anywhere, no matter how much I fight it. Take what you want and then leave me alone when you're done with me, but in the meantime, don't fucking lie to me."

When I was done, he spoke and his words came through his teeth. "We got a lot to go over here, babe. We'll start with when you thought *I* lied to *you*."

I didn't make him wait for an answer. "You just called me beautiful. We both know that isn't true. You want *me* to clue in? *You* clue in, Luke. Hello? I've had a crush on you since I first saw you. I wish it wasn't true, but the fact of the matter is I'm a sure thing. You don't have to lie and tell me I'm beautiful."

"You've got to be fuckin' shittin' me." He was still talking through his teeth.

"Oh yeah? And why's that? Luke, you've *seen* me. You've known me since I was eight years old."

"Yeah, I have, and you've been beautiful since you were eight years old."

My eyes went instantly wide and my mouth dropped open. Then I snapped it shut.

I couldn't believe he was still playing that game.

"Fuck off!" I yelled and bucked again.

Luke didn't go anywhere. He just stared at me.

If it was possible, he sounded even angrier when he said, "Shit, they really did a number on you, didn't they?"

"Who?"

"That mother and those fuckin' sisters of yours."

I rolled my eyes. "Oh please," I said, and then made a noise that sounded like "foof".

"Do I have to drag you in front of a mirror?"

"I know what I look like, Luke," I snapped.

"Doesn't sound like it to me, babe."

I bucked again. "Get off."

Luke didn't move. "My Ma said it, your Dad said it. Jesus, even *my* Dad said it. You were always the prettiest one of that fuckin' cat's den. Why do you think they were all so goddamn mean to you?"

"Hardly," I snapped. "I was fat and ugly. I had bad hair and I wore glasses, for God's sake."

"You were never more than chubby, babe, not until you grew older, and they had plenty of time to get under your skin. And you had beautiful hair, fantastic eyes and the best fuckin' smile I'd ever seen in my life. You still do."

I stopped struggling and stared at him, mainly because he sounded like he meant it, and I couldn't believe that. Even though I couldn't believe it, *nothing* about him was suggesting he was feeding me a line.

He went on, "Worse for them, you were smarter, funnier and nicer. People liked to be around you."

Ho-ly *crap*.

He sounded like he meant that, too.

"My Dad used to say that the man who got you would be the luckiest and unluckiest man alive because he'd have you for a lifetime, but he'd also have to put up with them."

All of a sudden, I was finding it hard to breathe.

"Your Dad said that about... about... *me?*" I asked breathlessly.

"It was the only thing he and I ever agreed about."

Okay, it was then I totally forgot how to breathe.

"Now let's talk about the rest of the shit that came out of your mouth," Luke continued.

Uh-oh.

I wasn't even finished dealing with all he'd just said. I didn't want to get into me blurting out that I'd had a crush on him since forever, I was a sure thing and that he'd won.

I was *such* a *fucking* dork!

Immediately, I said, "I need to brush my teeth."

His eyes narrowed.

"No fuckin' way," he clipped.

"I need quiet space," I tried.

He shook his head.

"Luke, you told me any time I needed something—"

"Quiet, Ava."

I decided, from his deathly tone, it was prudent that I be quiet.

Luke stared at me while I mentally zipped my lips and then he started talking.

"I've been straight with you since the beginning. Something, I might add, you haven't been with me. But I'll be even straighter 'cause it's obvious you are just not fuckin' gettin' it."

Oh no, not this again. Luke being "straighter".

Ee-yikes.

"I want this..." he said and he let go of my wrists. His finger touched me on the forehead then slid across it and down the side of my face. "And I want this..." He fell to the side, his hand moved down my body and I sucked in breath when he cupped me between my legs. His hand stayed there a second before it glided down the inside of my thigh, pushing it open so he could roll on top of me again, settling between my legs. "I'm not stupid. I know your heart's involved in this, and I've never, not once in all the time you've known me, given you the idea that I won't handle it with care."

Oh... my... *God.*

Someone, shoot me, kidnap me, cuff me to a sink, anyone! My mind screamed.

"Luke—" I interrupted.

"I'm talkin'," he bit off.

I shut up.

"I don't put up with the shit you've handed me the last week because you're some fuckin' piece I want to conquer. I put up with it because I've liked you since you were eight years old. You made me laugh. You understood me. You looked out for me when no one else fuckin' bothered and you acted like you thought I could move mountains, and I needed someone who thought that about me because my Dad sure as fuck didn't."

"Please, stop," I whispered, because now I *really* needed quiet space in order to process this latest episode with Luke, from waking to now. All of it.

He ignored me. "I never expected I'd want you in my bed, but I always knew I wanted you in my life. The fuckin' second you looked at my mouth in the office, though, I knew I would stop at nothin' to get you in my bed. And I thought then, too, that for the first time in my life I might do somethin' both my Dad and I would be proud of, and that's bein' with you."

My throat went so tight, the breath I sucked in sounded ragged.

He didn't just say that. Did he?

"Get this into your head, Ava. I'm not gonna do anything to fuck it up between us, but I'm also not gonna let *you* do anything to fuck it up either."

"Luke, I have to get out of here," I said, and it sounded like a desperate plea, mainly because it was one.

"I told you once, you're not goin' *anywhere*. And now I'll tell you the rest, too."

Oh shit.

There was more.

I didn't want to know the rest.

Unfortunately, Luke was on a roll.

"This is the way it is for us right now. I know you fixed this place up, but I'm not givin' up the loft so we're gonna have to work somethin' out about where we live, eat, sleep and fuck. We last, you're gonna have to give up the Range Rover. They're dangerous because they roll easy and I don't like you drivin' it. We go the distance, we're havin' a small wedding. I'm not fuckin' dancin'. And I want three kids, all boys, but if we have a girl she's not datin' until she's twenty-five, *especially* if she looks like you, got me?"

I didn't answer. Couldn't answer. I'd lost the ability to speak.

His face got closer. "Do you still think I'm playin' games?"

I shook my head. One thing was for certain, Luke was not playing games. And now I didn't know how to feel about *that*.

Great, like I needed something new to worry about.

He rolled off of me and onto his back, putting one hand to his forehead. "Jesus Christ," he muttered to the ceiling. "All those times I sat in the office laughing my ass off at stories of Lee, Eddie, Hank and Vance. They should have fuckin' medals."

I thought that was kind of insulting, not only to me but to my friends. However, I thought it best at that juncture not to share that opinion. Instead, I pulled the comforter around my naked body, got up on an elbow to look at him and decided, since he seemed to be done, to find some quiet space as soon as possible.

In order to do that, I asked softly, "Can I brush my teeth now?"

His eyes cut to me.

Eek!

Maybe he wasn't done.

"No, Ava, you can't fuckin' brush your teeth."

All righty then. There you go, he wasn't done.

I shouldn't have had to ask permission to brush my teeth, but I was going to give in on that considering the air hadn't yet lost any of its dangerous electricity. Not to mention Luke just announced he was already deciding where we were going to live, what car was safe for me to drive, what kind of wedding and how many children we were going to have.

And all of this, I had to admit, made my stomach feel melty.

"Come here," he ordered, voice gruff and still pissed-off.

That made my stomach feel even more melty.

Even so, I hesitated. "Are you still mad at me?" I asked.

"Fuck yeah," he answered.

"Maybe I should give *you* some quiet space," I told him, trying to be helpful, but with the ulterior motive that quiet space for Luke meant quiet space for me.

His hand shot out and grabbed my forearm, giving it a yank. I toppled onto him and he rolled, taking me with him so I was on the bottom. Then he shifted his hips until my legs opened and he fell between.

It was at that moment, all hope of quiet space died.

"You caused it, you're gonna help me work it out. And that's what I intend to do, by fuckin' you so hard you'll still feel me inside you even when I'm gone."

"Wow," I whispered, yes, out loud.

His head bent, his lips came to mine and he muttered, "You better fuckin' believe it."

And he did exactly what he said he would do.

And when he was done, it was so good I thought if we "went the distance" (as Luke put it) pissing him off every morning might be the way to go.

⚜

I was sitting on my wicker loveseat on my porch, my heels on the edge, finishing up a toasted sesame bagel with cream cheese, drinking a diet and trying (and failing) to get my head together.

This was partly because everything that happened last night and this morning was too much to get together, and partly because, between my legs, I could still feel Luke even though he was gone, and let me tell you, it was a nice feeling.

There was a chill in the air, but I had a space heater going. I'd also thrown on some fleecy sweatpants, wooly socks and a hoodie, so I was comfy, snugly warm even though I was feeling thoroughly fucked, both literally and figuratively.

Oo, I'm happy, Good Ava sighed.

What I want to know is, Bad Ava asked. *Does this mean we're not going to get to sleep with Ren?*

Oh for crap's sake.

Bad Ava was such a slut.

Luke was upstairs taking a shower while I was on the porch freaking out. I was freaking out because I believed everything Luke said. He was too brutally honest to be lying. Which meant I had to rethink everything about my life and who I was, and that was an impossible task without cookies and Sissy.

What I did know was that I was someone special to Luke, and I always had been, just like he was and always had been to me. And that knowledge made my word tilt so much, I was certain I was going to fall off.

"Babe."

I looked to the side and Luke was standing in the door, fully dressed, watching me.

God, he was good-looking. Even with the angry cut on his cheek, or maybe especially with the angry cut on his cheek, he was unbelievably hot.

"Hey," I said, thinking I'd not had nearly enough quiet space to ponder all that was tumbling around in my head. I needed at least an hour or maybe two hundred and seventeen of them.

He walked in, sat down beside me and rested an ankle on his opposite knee. He put his arm around my shoulders, pulled me into his side and kissed the top of my head.

"You okay?" he asked.

"No," I answered, staring straight ahead through the window to my yard. "Are you okay?"

His arm got tighter. "I'm fuckin' great."

Well, he would be.

Not to be conceited or anything, but I got a little carried away thirty minutes ago and I knew Luke liked it. He'd got me so turned on, I made him lie back and let me have my way with him for a good long while. If I didn't miss my guess, considering the low growl he made when it happened, I'd assisted in his having an even more mind-blowing orgasm than the one he gave me.

And, I had to say, I was pretty proud of that.

He plucked the soda out of my hand and set it aside. Then he pulled me into his lap and turned me to him, his arms loose around me.

"Gotta say, babe," he said in The Voice, but it was The Voice mixed with a kind of sexy rumble. "You're good with your mouth."

See! I told you.

"When you aren't usin' it to speak," he finished.

I glared at him. He grinned at me.

I stopped glaring at him when I noticed his grin was like the grin he'd given me last night. It was sexy and warm, and in the light of day, I could put my finger on what was different.

His face had lost its hardness. It was completely soft and unguarded.

Oh.

Wow.

His hands came to either side of my head and he tilted it toward him, close, closer, until our foreheads were touching and our noses were alongside each other's.

He looked me in the eyes. "We straight?" he asked softly.

I nodded.

"You cool with everything that's gone down?"

I shook my head.

He touched his lips to mine. "You'll get there."

I didn't share his positive attitude. He noted this on my face, I knew, because he chuckled. I ignored the chuckle and lifted my head away from his. His hands moved. One went to my neck, the other one sifted into the hair at the side of my head, going through it, down my back, then his arm came to rest around my waist.

I carefully touched my fingers just below his cut.

"Does it hurt?" I whispered, my eyes on the cut.

"No."

"Do you think someone should look at it?"

"No."

"Will it leave a scar?"

"Doesn't matter."

My eyes moved to his and my hand opened on his face, cupping his jaw, my thumb trailing down the side of his 'tache.

"It was the song," I said quietly.

"Come again?" Luke asked.

I took in a breath, scared of sharing, not wanting another episode, but thinking, because he had bled for me and might even carry a scar for me (even if it really was his own damned fault, it was also partially mine, I knew better) that he deserved an explanation.

"Ren had just told me if you weren't keeping Sissy safe, he would. I was grateful to know he was a good guy, there aren't many out there."

When I saw Luke's eyes turn intense and felt his body go still, I rushed on. "Then Stella sang 'I'm So Lonesome I Could Cry'. It's a beautiful song. Ren put his arms around me and I didn't even think."

Luke's mouth got tight, which I took as a warning sign (finally, I was learning) so I continued. "Anyway, something weird was happening. It seemed like she was singing it to Mace. What with the song being so pretty and my mind on Mace and Stella—"

"Mace had a thing with Stella," Luke told me.

My gossip antennae perked up.

"Really?" I asked.

"Yeah."

"What happened?"

"None of my business. None of yours, either, unless Mace or Stella want to share."

One thing I knew for certain, Mace was never going to want to share. That meant Stella's name was scratched on my list of people to call that day.

"Babe."

My unfocused eyes refocused on Luke and he hadn't lost any of his intensity.

"Let's get back to Zano."

"I still feel you," I blurted in an effort *not* to talk about Ren.

Luke just looked at me.

Crap.

In for a penny...

My thumb moved to trace his bottom lip and I watched it go, my eyes on his fantastic mouth, and it hit me that I knew, intimately, how that mouth felt on practically every part of me. That knowledge made my stomach feel funny and my voice sound lower and kind of raspy when I spoke again.

"Between my legs," I whispered, my gaze lifting from his mouth to his eyes. "I still feel you."

His eyes turned to ink, right before he muttered, "Jesus."

"I really love your mouth," I told him. Do *not* ask me why, I was having a moment.

"Ava." Now *his* voice sounded lower and kind of raspy.

I took a deep breath and pulled back a bit, dropping my hand from his face and purposefully breaking my moment before I said something ultra-stupid.

"Just thought you'd want to know," I finished.

Luke didn't feel like having the moment broken. He brought me back to him and gave me a quick but hard kiss.

"Beautiful," he started when he was done, his eyes on mine, and his intensity had changed to something that made me shiver in a good way. "You just

315

demonstrated exactly why I would fight and bleed for you. Zano knows that's what I've got and he wants it, and I'm not gonna let him anywhere near it. I'm askin' you to help me with that, and I'm askin' you to help Zano by not giving him mixed signals."

Was I giving Ren mixed signals?

I *was* giving Ren mixed signals.

Shit!

"I'm such a dork," I mumbled.

Luke shook his head. "You're beautiful, you're sweet and you're funny. You're also bein' loyal to your friend and tryin' to take care of her when she's in a bad situation. You're dealin' with this at the same time you're dealin' with a lot of other shit, internally and externally."

It must be said, I loved it that he understood. It made me feel all comfy, snugly warm, but on the inside.

This I didn't share.

His hand tightened on my neck and he brushed his mouth against mine again. "Let me deal with the external shit. You just focus on sorting out your head. Deal?"

I nodded.

He kissed my nose then his hand went away from my neck. His arms went around me again and, thankfully, he changed the subject.

"The bad guys know they gotta work out their issues with Vito. That's why Zano's called off Santo. You're in the clear, but I don't trust it yet. I still want you callin' in to me regularly."

I nodded again. I had enough dealing with the emotional trauma of Luke and the possibility of bearing him three sons. I didn't need to get kidnapped again.

"What are your plans for today?" he asked.

"Sort out my Range Rover. Go see Sissy. Workout. Shop for groceries. Maybe Shirleen and I'll go see Bobby. And I need to go to your place and get my stuff."

"No."

I looked down at him. "What?"

"Leave your stuff at my place, you can go there to unpack, but leave it."

"A lot of stuff I need is there."

"You're goin' to the store. Double up."

Shit.

Doubling up on necessities between my house and Luke's. Okay, so maybe I needed *five* hundred and seventeen hours to cope with all this shit.

"Luke, maybe we have more talking to do." I made a suggestion that I didn't think was a suggestion, as such.

His arms became tight. He leaned in, kissed my neck and then got up, taking me with him. He turned, set me back in the seat and put a hand on the seat on either side of me so his face was close to mine.

"Life's too short. I'm through talkin'. This is happening, we both know it, we both feel it and you even admitted it. Ava babe, stop fighting it."

I sighed, because in the heat of one of my many freak outs, I *did* admit it.

I was such a dork.

This meant I was with Luke Stark. I was Luke Stark's girlfriend. Worse, I was Luke Stark's woman. There was a nuance of difference between being a man's girlfriend and a man's woman, but that nuance was pretty fucking significant.

Fuckity, fuck, fuck, *fuck*.

This should have made me happy. In fact, everything that morning should have made me doing-cartwheels-of-joy ecstatic.

Instead, what I felt was scared. Shit scared to the depths of my soul.

I sighed again and told him. "I need my computer."

"I'll get Matt or Jack to deal with it."

"Luke."

He leaned in and kissed me, hot and heavy, proving he was indeed through talking.

When done, he lifted up and lightly kissed my nose.

"Call in," he ordered softly.

He moved away as I watched, my stomach still melty, my heart in my throat.

I wanted to be excited. I wanted to think Good-Ava-twirling-in-the-mountains-like-Maria thoughts, but all I could do was think about what it would feel like when he walked away for good.

When he was at the door, he stopped and turned back to me.

"One more thing."

Shit, I didn't think I could handle one more thing.

"What?" I asked, deciding it was best to get it over with quickly.

"I'm gonna get serious shit about this hickey today, beautiful. You owe me."

Crapity, crap, crap, *crap*.

He gave me his sexy half-grin and I knew he didn't care, not even a little bit, about the shit he'd get or the hickey.

"Lucas Stark, I do *not* owe you," I shouted at his back, but he was gone.

Chapter 21

Earning Retribution

After Luke left, I made coffee and poured myself a cup, then I went to get my phone and walked back to my porch.

First up, I called Shirleen.

"Oowee, girl!" Shirleen yelled in my ear. "You are workin' on bein' the Premier Rock Chick, what with Luke Stark fightin' in a parking lot over you. I heard there was blood. Was there blood? Oh wait..." She stopped and I listened as she shouted, "Oowee!" again, but not in my ear, to someone in the office. She came back to me. "Luke just walked in. Girl, you *are* the Premier Rock Chick. Even with that nasty gash, that boy looks like the cat who just got his cream. He musta got the cream if that hickey is anything to go by. A hickey! I love it!"

Shit!

Why did I give Luke a hickey? Why? I was never going to live it down.

Shirleen kept on in my ear. "Did he get his cream? If so, how many times. I want details."

I wasn't going to talk about Luke getting his cream, not any of the three times he got it.

"Shirleen, I'm calling about Bobby. Any updates?"

"Fit as a fiddle, except that fractured skull. Functions coming back, two and two make four again. If all keeps goin' good, they're releasin' him tomorrow to finish recuperatin' at home."

"Thank God for that," I said, and I meant it.

"Now, details," Shirleen returned.

"No, now I want to know what's up with my car."

"Car's bein' delivered this mornin', any time now."

"Do they expect payment on delivery or are they going to invoice me?"

"Luke's taken care of it."

I went silent.

"Ava, you there?" Shirleen asked.

"What do you mean Luke's taken care of it?"

It was Shirleen's turn to go silent. Then she muttered, "Uh-oh."

"You say he's there?" I asked.

"Uh, yeah."

"Can you please put him on the phone?"

"Maybe you need to deep breathe," Shirleen advised.

"Please put him on the phone."

She sighed and put me on hold.

For some reason, of all the shit that had gone down between Luke and me, this was something I could not allow. I'd let him be a pretty pushy, tough guy, macho man with me, but I could pay my own goddamned way.

"Yeah?" Luke said as greeting.

"It's Ava," I told him, sounding snippy.

"I know, beautiful," he replied, sounding like he was smiling.

I ignored the melty feeling in my belly at his calling me "beautiful" when he sounded like he was smiling. I liked it even before I knew he meant it in every way it could mean. It was *way* better than "babe".

"Did you pay for the repairs on my Range Rover?" I asked him.

"Yeah."

"Why?"

"Why not?" he answered.

I felt my hold on my temper slip. "Luke, it's *my* car."

"Ava, you're *my* woman."

I ignored the melty feeling that gave me, too. "So?"

"So you're my woman, I take care of you."

"Luke—"

"This isn't up for discussion."

"It sure as hell is!"

"I'm thinkin', as payback for the hickey, I want you in that pink teddy thing tonight."

Was he for real?

"Luke!"

"Later."

Disconnect.

Argh!

I fought the urge to throw my phone through the window, but instead I called Ally.

"Hey," she answered.

"Yo," I said.

"You okay after last night?" Ally asked.

"I'm officially Luke's woman after last night."

"Yep, that's the way since the dawn of time. Two men want the same thing, they fight over it and winner takes all."

"What with struggling with Iron Man Mace, I wasn't keeping close track, but it didn't seem like anyone was winning."

"Luke won when he behaved like a Neanderthal, elbowed you in the head and still, without a peep from you, you got in his car with him."

Yikes.

I had to admit, that was true.

"What was that about Luke thinking about someone else when he was with you?" Ally asked.

Shit.

I knew I'd have to get into that.

"Luke explained I had the wrong end of the stick," I told her.

"Well, chickie, just to warn you, the girls have been chewing over that all night and all morning. Roxie thinks you think it's her. Jules is pretty certain you think it's her. Who was it?"

"Jules," I answered. "I saw them together and got the wrong impression."

"That's what I figured. Listen, Jules and Luke had a thing. It was brief, she thought Vance had broken up with her. Once she found out that Vance—"

My stomach plummeted.

"What?" I whispered, interrupting her.

Silence for a beat then, "Oh shit."

"What did you say?" I asked.

"Ava—"

"What kind of 'thing' did Jules and Luke have?"

"It was nothing."

Oh... my... *God.*

"What kind of thing?" I repeated.

"It only lasted a couple of days."

My heart was racing and I was pretty certain I was going to throw up.

"Ava? You there?"

"I have to go."

"Ava."

"Later."

I disconnected then I punched in Luke's cell number.

"Babe," he answered, sounding amused. "I want you to call in, but you don't have to do it every five minutes."

I didn't dillydally. "You had a thing with Jules when she thought Vance broke up with her."

Silence, then he hissed, "*Fuck.*"

He didn't deny it.

Shit!

I felt an ugly feeling slide through my body, a feeling I'd felt once before in my life. It was the day my Mom sat Marilyn, Sofia and I down, and while crying and carrying on, she informed us Dad had left us.

I pulled myself together and said, "You forgot to mention that last night."

"Ava—"

I heard a knock at my front door. "My car's here. I have to go."

"Leave it, we have to talk."

"Life's too short, Luke. I'm through talking."

Then I disconnected.

I ran to the front door and got the keys to my car from a black guy wearing greasy, blue coveralls. My phone rang while I did this, but I ignored it and it stopped when the answering machine kicked in. No one left a message.

I ran upstairs, got dressed and shoved clothes in my workout bag. My phone rang again while I did this, but I continued to ignore it.

Then I ran out to my Range Rover, tossed my bag in and took off.

❦

I had a feeling Luke would come looking for me so I went to a different gym and paid for a day pass.

While working out I tried to give him the benefit of the doubt.

However, there was no denying that we'd had several hot and heavy discussions about a variety of things, and not once did he mention he had a "thing" with Jules, no matter how short.

Furthermore, not only was Roxie Luke's first guess about who I thought he had feelings for, Roxie also thought that, and I wanted to know why.

After my workout, I showered, dressed, went and sat in the Range Rover and opened my phone.

I had seven missed calls. Two were from Luke, three from Ally, one from Shirleen and the last one from Jules.

So, of course, I called Daisy.

"Sugar, everyone is lookin' for you. Where are you?" she asked when she answered her phone.

"In my car, listen Daisy—"

She interrupted me. "Ally is freakin' out. She let the cat out of the bag but, girl, it sounds a lot worse than what it was. Jules is upset. She wants you to understand what happened—"

I interrupted right back. "I want to know about Roxie."

"Roxie is freakin' out too! She likes you with Luke, we all do. This could get weird, like it was weird for a while when Vance and Luke both were—"

I didn't want to hear about Vance and Luke and Jules, I wanted to know about Roxie. "No, I want to know why Roxie thought it was her that I thought Luke had a thing for."

"Pardon?" Daisy asked.

"Last night, when Luke and I were arguing about it, his first guess as to who Ren meant was Roxie. Ally told me Roxie thought I thought it was her. Why would both of them think that?"

Silence.

"Daisy, please, tell me," I begged.

"Sugar, I know you're lookin' for a way to protect your heart. But you're lookin' in the wrong direction. I have to tell you, the best way to protect your heart is to trust it to a man who'll take care of it for you."

Right. Like such a man existed.

I did not *think* so.

"Last night and this morning, Luke and I talked a lot," I told Daisy. "He said a lot of shit to me, all of it I wanted to believe. The problem is, he declared he was through talking this morning and it seems there's a lot he left out. I can't trust my heart to a man who'd keep something from me. Especially if it's about people in his life, which will mean, if I stay with him, they'll be people in my life. That means in the Rock Chick Hot Bunch tribe I'll be the chump, and I don't want to be the chump. Can you understand that?"

Daisy said softly, "I can understand that."

"Please then, tell me."

She sighed. "First off, you have to know these girls are not your usual girls. The Rock Chicks are special and the Hot Bunch know that."

I kept silent and waited.

"Okay then," she went on. "Luke threw down with Roxie when he was playin' her bodyguard. It wasn't a big deal. He just told her he was interested if it didn't work out with her and Hank."

The news hit me like a blow.

Strike one.

"Then he kind of fell for Jules when they were trainin' and workin' together. That went a little further, because Luke went for it after everyone thought Vance broke up with her and then went out of town so he wasn't keepin' his eye on things. Nothin' came of it, mainly because Jules had already given her heart to Vance, but somethin' special grew out of that for Jules and Luke. Ava listen to me, it's somethin' sweet and special and totally innocent that grew out of it. Vance and Luke are friends and—"

Strike two.

"Any more I should know about?" I asked, interrupting her. "Jet, Indy, anyone?"

"Sugar," Daisy said softly, and she sounded disappointed. "Don't be like that."

"So let's play what if. What if Vance *had* broken up with Jules? Where would Luke be now?"

"What if is a stupid game. He didn't break up with her, end of story."

I knew where Luke would be now. I knew by his relentless, tough guy, macho man pursuit of me. He "fell for Jules" as Daisy put it. If Vance had broken up with her, right now Jules would be in Luke's loft and he'd be contemplating when he would let his and Jules's daughter date if she looked like Jules. Likely it'd be at age forty if she looked like Jules.

Then it hit me. Jules was pregnant. Hell, if she was with Luke she would be pregnant with *his* baby.

"Oh my God," I whispered, almost certain I was going to puke.

"That doesn't sound good," Daisy mumbled.

"I have to go," I said again.

"Come over to my house, we'll talk," Daisy replied on a rush. "I'll get the girls over—"

"Later, Daisy."

Yeah, much later... as in never. To cut off Luke, I had to cut off the Rock Chicks completely. And I liked the Rock Chicks a lot.

And that was strike three.

"Wait!" I heard Daisy cry before I disconnected.

I tossed my cell into the passenger seat, put my hands on the steering wheel and rested my head on them.

You think she should talk to him now? Hear his side of the story? Listen to him explain about how he tried it on with half the Rock Chicks? How he broke it off with Sandra Whoever-She-Was without batting an eye? How he didn't mention any of this shit during his "straight talk"? Bad Ava taunted Good Ava.

Good Ava didn't answer. She was too busy quietly crying.

I turned off my phone and went to a travel agent. I booked a last minute trip to an all-inclusive in St. Croix, leaving the next morning at oh-dark-thirty.

I went to a card shop, bought a card, paper and a pen and wrote Sissy a long note, explaining everything. Then I went to an Internet Café, e-mailed my clients and told them I had a family emergency that would mean I'd be out of town for two weeks, and I looked up the address for Nightingale Investigations on the web. I posted the card to Sissy, care of Nightingale Investigations. Then I went to the mall and bought a bunch of new stuff for my trip, including luggage because mine was at Luke's.

Then I went home, scanned the street for Luke's Porsche or any black Ford SUVs. Finding none there, I parked in my garage. I lugged my bags inside and took them upstairs. I was going to spend the night in a hotel close to the airport.

I dumped my shopping bags on the bed and rolled the suitcase beside it. Then I walked downstairs and arranged my purse and all the paperwork I'd need for my trip, including my tickets, on the dining room table. After that, I went to the kitchen to get a drink, a heavy one. I was going to call a taxi to take me to the hotel so I could get as drunk as I liked.

And I was going to get *way* drunk.

I was mixing it, my back to the kitchen door, when two arms closed around my waist.

Shit.

I hated it when Luke moved so quietly.

"Let me go," I whispered, and even to my ears my voice sounded broken.

"Not until I teach you a lesson."

My body went solid.

It did this not because it was Luke who was speaking.

It did this because it was Noah Dexter who was speaking.

Fuckity, fuck, fuck, *fuck*.

I fought him.

I lost and got hurt doing it. So hurt, I lost consciousness for long enough for him to carry me downstairs to my creepy basement.

The fight had been ugly. I kicked, screamed, bit, punched, tugged and tumbled.

He mostly punched, and he was better at it.

Before getting knocked out I felt wetness on my face that I was certain was blood coming from a tear in my lip or from my nose, or both.

By the time I came to, I had something over my mouth, strong and sticky, and I knew it was tape. I licked it and pushed at it with my tongue but it didn't move. He had me in the old coal room, the smallest, darkest, most cramped, most creepy part of the basement, and he was taping my hands well over my head to a steel support pole.

I made a noise that was supposed to communicate "No!", but it didn't come out as much due to the tape.

I felt sick, my head was groggy, I felt dull pain in too many parts of my body and I was scared out of my ever lovin' mind.

I got myself together enough to try to pull my body away from him taping my hands, but the tape held strong and tore at my skin. Before I could get anywhere, he moved around and pressed into me, moving from my hands and starting to tape my arms to the beam. I kept pushing against him and trying to kick at him but he just pressed deeper until my breastbone connected with the beam so hard I cried out under the tape.

"Sent some PI's after me, didn't you? You stupid fuck," he hissed in my ear, his body still pressing into the back of mine, hands still wrapping the duct tape around and around my arms. "You should have left it alone. That fuckin' redskin sniffin' me out. Someone finds you down here before you die of thirst, you call them the fuck off. You hear me, Ava?"

I swallowed and it tasted like blood. Then I nodded.

"Christ, I had to leave a mark I'd been workin' for months because of this fuckin' shit."

I closed my eyes and stopped pushing against him when he started to tape my chest to the beam. I tested the tape at my hands but it held fast.

"And you're fuckin' Stark. I cannot believe you're fuckin' Luke fuckin' Stark, but I saw it with my own eyes."

My body went still.

He felt it. He stopped wrapping tape around me and laughed.

"Yeah, I watched you, Ava. I watched you and I jacked off while I did it."

Oh... my... *God*.

Even though I really, *really* didn't want him to, he explained, "I been followin' you, but you're never fuckin' alone. I knew you'd see Stella so I went there, hopin' to nab you in the bathroom or somethin'. I watched Stark fight Zano for you, followed you and Stark home and broke into a place across the street. Lucky for me you guys left the lights on. I watched the whole thing. I wish I'd had a camera."

I was breathing heavily through my nose. I couldn't believe this was happening and I didn't want to believe what he said.

"You were hot," he whispered, pressing into my back in an entirely different way. His hand slid across my side to my breast, cupping it. "He did you against the wall. I thought you were a good girl. I knew you'd let me fuck you against the wall, I would have stayed around longer."

Then for some reason his hand went still, his body went tight and his head came up.

He hissed in my ear, "I have a gun, you make a fuckin' noise, I blow your brains out then I'll shoot whoever's up there, too."

That was when I heard footfalls upstairs.

"Ava," Luke's voice called from upstairs. I closed my eyes and visions of a bloody, bullet-ridden Luke filled my head. I opened my eyes again immediately to clear the visions.

"Let's make this interesting," Noah muttered and then he moved away to drop the tape, but he came right back and he pressed his body into mine.

I heard Luke's footsteps going up the stairs to the top floor just as I felt Noah's hand on my belt buckle. My body jerked but Noah hissed, "Not a sound or you're both dead," and I stopped my struggle before it started.

I could still hear Luke moving around the house and I stayed silent, even as Noah's hands undid my pants and one slid inside while the other one went up my shirt to cup my breast again. I could feel his fingers (not hitting the target, by the way, he never did) pressing against me, his other fingers doing a nipple roll as I listened to Luke moving around the house.

Finally, after it threatened all day, I threw up but choked it back down before it made it to my mouth.

Throughout it all, silently I was crying.

I tried to ignore what was happening to me physically by chanting in my head, *don't come down here, don't come down here, don't come down here.*

Luke didn't come down. Noah and I heard the front door slam and I knew Luke was gone.

I felt both terrified and relieved by this.

"Fuck, now I have a hard-on," Noah said in my ear, pressing his groin against my ass, rubbing against me and his hands kept at me. "You always did have a sweet ass," he mumbled in my ear. "You do it doggie-style with Stark as well as against the wall?"

I had. That was one of the three positions of a few days ago.

I did not share. Not only because I couldn't, as he had taped my mouth closed, but also because it was none of his business and he was dry humping me against a steel pole that he had taped me to, the screaming, unbelievably horrible, awful, maniac *jerk!*

I heard him groan into my neck (luckily, as was usual with Noah, this didn't take very long) and he sagged against me when he was done.

I hate you, I thought, and this time I meant it with all my heart.

His hand swept across my ass.

"Sweet," he muttered.

Then he finished taping me to the pole. When he was done, my hands, wrists, arms, chest, waist, knees and ankles were all taped to the beam and I couldn't move, not even an inch.

He got in my face. "Next time, Ava, if you don't call off the Indian, I won't be so nice."

I made an angry noise in my throat, but it was too late. He was gone.

Before he left, he closed the door to the coal room and I heard him fix the lock. The door had a padlock on the outside, don't ask me why. I'd inherited it from the former owners and never removed it, but I also never locked it.

Now it was locking me in. Even if I was to get loose, I'd be locked in my creepy basement in a room completely devoid of light. But I was taped from hands to ankles to a steel pole and I didn't know if I could get free. I had blood in my mouth, the taste of vomit in my throat and had just been violated in a very-not-nice way. Even though I knew it could have been worse, that didn't help much in the current situation.

Keep your head together, darling, Luke will come back looking for you, Good Ava whispered in my ear.

You're strong, you've been strong through a lot. Stay strong, girl. This, too, shall pass, Bad Ava whispered in my other ear.

I'm scared, I told them.

So are we, Good Ava admitted.

But we'll make it, Bad Ava said. *We always do.*

⚞⚟

For a very long time, I alternately hung there and fought against the tape. Every once in a while I'd make progress, a little more movement, but it was exhausting and I wasn't getting very far. So I'd stop and rest and work on trying to get the tape off my mouth by rubbing it against my shoulder.

This worked. I was able to pull off the tape, and it hurt, mainly because it also pulled against what I knew now was a tear on my lip. I also managed to get my ankles far looser, but couldn't get my feet free.

Eventually, having exhausted myself, I fell asleep tied to the beam.

I woke up when I heard a noise.

"Basement!" I meant to scream but it came out as a croak.

I tried again.

"Basement, basement, *basement!* I'm in the basement!"

This came out a lot louder.

I heard fast footfalls on the stairs.

"Coal room, at the back, the room with the lock on the door!" I shouted. "There's pull lights in each room. There's a padlock. The key's…"

I stopped shouting because I didn't know where the key was or even if I had the key.

Then I heard a gunshot.

The door came open and I winced as the light from a flashlight hit my face.

"Jesus fucking Christ," Lee muttered.

"Thank you, God," I said.

He moved forward, his hand going to the back of his jeans.

"Hang on, honey," Lee murmured. "I'll have you free in a second."

"Hanging on is my only option at this point," I whispered my joke, and it didn't sound very funny, which must have been why Lee didn't laugh.

He put the flashlight in his armpit and he cut through the tape with a pocketknife, ripping it free. A couple of times I made pain sounds in the back of my throat when he ripped tape off my skin, but I did my best to swallow them down. When I was mostly loose, I drooped into him even though I tried not to, but my entire body was numb. He took my weight and kept working at the tape until I was free. When he was done, he straightened. He pulled me fully into his arms, his going tight around me as pins and needles shot through my whole body.

To my horror, I started crying.

He stroked my hair with one hand and held me tighter with his other arm.

"S... s... sorry. I'm a wuss," I told him.

"You're fine."

"I'll have it together in a second," I said.

"Ava, you're fine."

I nodded.

I started deep breathing and he kept stroking my hair. After a while I got the tears in check, wiped my face against his shirt and took one, last, deep breath.

"I gotta call Luke," he said when I exhaled.

I nodded again.

"You know who did this to you?" Lee asked.

I answered immediately, "Noah."

I knew my answer surprised him by the way his body went still.

Then he pulled back, and even in the dark (he was holding his flashlight behind my back), I could tell he was looking at me.

His hand came to my neck and his thumb stroked my jaw.

In an ultra-soft voice, he asked, "You wanna tell me why your jeans are undone?"

I shook my head, his hand flexed against my neck, and I said with a hitch in my voice, "He kind of... *touched* me."

The air in the room went static in a flash, and just as quickly I felt it move with the fury rolling off Lee in waves, pounding against the walls and slamming back into the both of us.

"Let's get you out of here," he replied, his voice tight.

He started to move to pick me up, but I pulled away. "I'm okay now, I can walk."

He nodded, guiding the way with the flashlight, holding my hand. He took me upstairs, to the bathroom and led me in.

Before he closed the door behind him, he said, "You need anything, call me. I'll be right outside."

I nodded again. He closed the door.

I stood at the sink, hands at the basin, avoiding looking in the mirror and listened very carefully. Therefore, I heard him make the call.

"Vance, you with Luke?" Pause. "Okay, I found Ava. She was taped to a support in her basement. Dexter did it. I want you here. Mace, Eddie and Hank, everyone you can get. She's in bad shape, been beaten up but it's worse." He paused again. "Yeah, that's it. She was dressed but her pants were undone. She says he touched her." I closed my eyes tight at hearing these words coming from Lee. Somehow, hearing them made the whole thing seem more real. "I want the boys around when Luke finds out. I'll give you five then I'm callin' Luke." Pause. "Yeah, out."

At that, I walked to the door and pulled it open. Lee was leaning against the wall in the hall. His head came up when the door opened.

"It wasn't as bad as you think," I told him.

"Ava, honey, get yourself cleaned up."

I went into the hall and stood in front of him. "He didn't rape me or anything."

"Don't talk now. We'll talk later. You want me to help you clean up?"

I was getting panicked. "Lee, don't tell Luke he touched me. It wasn't that bad."

His hands came out and his fingers went into my waistband. Wordlessly, he pulled me to him and then did up the button on my pants that I'd forgotten about. After that, he cinched the belt.

This was so sweet, so gentle, I had to swallow down tears again.

I put my hand on his chest and leaned into him. "Lee, you tell Luke, he's gonna go gonzo."

Lee nodded. "He's gonna go gonzo."

"Please, he just, put his hand… and then put his other hand…" I stopped. "And then he took care of himself just using me to rub against."

God, this was embarrassing.

As I was talking I'd been avoiding his eyes. When I was done, I looked at Lee.

Oops.

I was thinking that Lee didn't think that was any better than being raped. I was thinking that because the fury waves were pounding again and his face, which had been gentle, had turned hard as stone.

"You're not gonna go gonzo, are you?" I whispered.

"I'm keepin' a very fuckin' loose hold on going gonzo, Ava."

I swallowed again, this time at the anger vibrating in his tone. "I don't want you boys to get into any trouble for me," I told him.

"Only person's got trouble right now is Noah Dexter, or whatever that fuckin' guy's name is."

"Lee."

His hand came up, his fingers wrapped around my head and the third hot guy in a day (or a little more than one, I didn't know what time it was, I just knew it was dark outside) leaned forward and put his forehead against mine.

Lee's forehead lean was a lot different than Luke's or Ren's.

Lee's was scary.

"You ask him to touch you like that?"

I shook my head, mainly because I couldn't find my voice.

"So he did it against your will."

I nodded my head.

"A man doesn't put his hands on a woman like that against her will. A man doesn't put his hands on a woman *at all* against her will, but *especially* not like that. A man does that, that man earns retribution. Automatic. A man does that to a woman I know, the woman of a friend of mine, a friend I trust and respect, that retribution turns ugly."

Yikes multiplied by about two thousand.

"What are you gonna do?" I whispered.

"I'm gonna do whatever I have to do to protect Luke while he does whatever the fuck he wants to do."

"What if I don't want him to do it?"

His face lost some of its scary-stony quality and went slightly gentle. "Sorry, honey. You're gonna have to let us work this out. It's a guy thing."

After he finished speaking, to my shock he kissed my forehead, let me go and then flipped open his phone, hit a couple of buttons and put it to his ear.

"Get cleaned up," he murmured to me. Then his head came up, but his eyes didn't leave mine when he said, "Luke. I found her."

Chapter 22
Precious Cargo

Since he lived so close, Tex was the first to arrive.

Lee sent him to help me clean up while Lee did whatever it was that Lee was doing. My guess, searching my house for rope to fashion a noose.

Tex sat me on the toilet seat and cleaned up the blood, put some Neosporin on my cut lip, took me downstairs and got me an ice pack for my swollen eye. He was mostly silent during his ministrations, but his mouth was tight and his eyes were shining with what could only be described as controlled hellfire.

For your information, I didn't look too bad, except for the blood down my shirt and rimming my nostrils, my torn lip, and my eye, which was already bruising. In the grand scheme of things I decided to think of it as "not too bad".

Even so, after looking at myself, I transferred my sextuple revenge from Dom to Noah, the double-extra, loser, rat-bastard.

By the time we got downstairs, Lee had all the lights blazing. I suspected he did this for me since I'd been locked in a pitch black room for however many hours. All I could think was that he was definitely on the very short Good Guy List.

Matt was the second to arrive. He took one look at me and his face got red.

Lee said one word to him.

"Focus."

Matt nodded his head once and then he focused. I could actually see him focus.

Hank and Roxie arrived next. Tears filled Roxie's eyes when she saw me and she came right up to me and grabbed my hand, holding on tight.

"Thought she might need someone who'd been there," Hank muttered to Lee.

Okay, so Hank just earned a place on my Good Guy List, too, and as I was being so magnanimous, Matt's angry red face earned him a place as well.

Tex was already on it.

"How are you doing?" Roxie asked me, leading me to my couch.

"I'm fine. Everyone's overreacting. This isn't a big deal. I knew Noah was a jerk. He just proved it irrefutably," I told her as we sat down.

She looked at Hank, but Hank, Lee, Matt and Tex were all looking at me.

"Seriously you guys, this isn't a big deal. It isn't as if this is a big surprise. He had already screwed me over once," I announced.

The door opened. I held my breath thinking it would be Luke but it was Vance.

Then I sucked in breath again when Vance got a look at me and his body went visibly tight.

I feared for my lamps because Vance looked like he definitely wanted to throw one of them, or possibly all of them.

Instead he looked at Lee and said something bizarre, "I call a shot and I don't even care if he's conscious when I get my turn."

At this, it was Roxie's turn to go tight.

"Everyone's got a fuckin' shot on this one," Tex said, sounding pissed-off.

"Shit," Hank muttered under his breath.

"What are they talking about?" I whispered to Roxie as I set my ice bag aside.

"I'll tell you later," she answered quietly. "Do you want me to get you a drink? Herbal tea or something?"

"I'd love a Fat Tire," I told her. "I'll get it." I got up and asked loudly, "Anyone want a beer?"

Roxie, Tex and the Hot Bunch were all looking at each other, but I ignored them and headed toward the kitchen. I could swear I saw Lee's eyes crinkle in a sexy smile that didn't quite involve his mouth when I passed him. I didn't know what that was about, but I wasn't in the mood to ask.

"Just me then," I said as I hit the kitchen.

When my head was in the fridge, I heard Roxie say, "Maybe she's in denial."

"I'm not in denial," I called into the other room.

"Damn," Roxie whispered loudly.

I got myself a beer and walked back into the living room taking a long pull. This somewhat hurt my lip (okay, so it hurt my lip a lot), but I powered through it.

When I hit the living room again, Lee came up to me and wrapped his arm around my shoulders curling me into his body.

It was then I saw that I got blood on his shirt where I had wiped my face.

"I got blood on your shirt," I told him.

"Forget it," he returned. "Look at me, Ava."

My gaze lifted from his shoulder to his eyes. Close up I could see he had nice eyes, warm, chocolate brown.

"You okay?" he asked.

"I'm fine."

"You should go upstairs, lie down, talk to Roxie," he suggested.

"I'm fine."

Lee looked at Hank. "Maybe we should call Victim's Assistance."

"I'm *fine*," I repeated, a lot louder and a lot snottier this time.

Lee looked back at me. "Okay, honey. You're fine," he said this in the way all men speak when they're dealing with a stubborn, unreasonable woman. I just stopped myself from rolling my eyes.

Instead I offered, "I'll clean your shirt. I'm good with stains. I can Shout it out like a pro. If I didn't go into graphic design, I was going to go into dry cleaning."

The eye wrinkle came back. It was a lot better close up. In fact, it was positively magnetic.

So that was why I was standing wrapped in Lee's arm and staring at him like a lovesick puppy when the door opened and Luke walked in.

Everyone, including me, looked at Luke.

Luke looked unhappy. Not, "oh, they are out of my favorite donuts at LaMar's" unhappy but *a lot* worse.

"Hey," I said.

Luke's eyes never left me, even when he walked forward and even when Lee's arm dropped from around me. We lost eye contact only when Luke pulled me into his arms and I had nowhere to put my face but against his chest, but I chose the side of my face that wasn't bruised and battered. He held me close, but he didn't hold me tight. He held me like you hold a newborn baby, gentle and with care.

Wow.

I forgot I was mad at him and on my way to St. Croix and I melted into him.

"I'm fine," I repeated quietly.

"Babe," was all he said.

"Let's give them a minute," I heard Hank tell the crowd.

Lee got close and I lifted my head up and looked at him. The eye crinkle was gone, his face was totally serious, and I knew what he was communicating.

I shook my head, but he nodded his. I knew this meant if I didn't tell Luke, he would.

"I want it to come from me," I told Lee.

That was when Luke's arms got tight. Lee just nodded again, looked at Luke, then he was gone.

I tilted my head back to look at Luke. If it was possible he appeared even less happy. Then his hand came to cup the bruised side of my face.

"Jesus, Ava," he muttered.

"Really, I'm fine. It's not as bad as it looks."

He bent his neck to rest his forehead against mine. "You wanna share what that was about with Lee?" he asked quietly.

"Not really," I told him, and his body went still. "But I'm going to anyway," I whispered.

I watched, fascinated, as he slowly closed his eyes, took in breath through his nostrils and then opened his eyes on his exhale while his body relaxed again. This moved me at the same time it shook me. This small thing said a lot. It said a lot about Luke, a lot about how he felt about me and a lot about *how much*.

Even with all the drama I felt my stomach go melty and I really wanted to kiss him.

Instead I broke out of his arms, put down my beer and came back to him.

Then I put my hands on either side of his neck and looked in his eyes. "First, you have to promise me you won't throw any lamps."

"Ava."

"Promise."

His arms went around me. "Promise," he said.

"And...um." My eyes slid away and his arms got a little tighter so they slid back. "You have to promise you won't *hurt* anyone, as in, maybe kill them or something."

This time, his body went solid as a rock.

"Luke—"

"He touched you," Luke interrupted me, and his voice was flat, dead and the way he spoke freaked me out.

"Luke," I repeated.

"That's why everyone's here before me. Why I saw Eddie's truck pullin' up when I was walkin' up to the house. Lee was preparing because he knew——"

"Luke," I said again.

"*Fuck*," Luke hissed, the dead, flat voice long gone, anger taking its place. My hands went tight on his neck when I felt the air in the room go scary dangerous as I realized Luke was preparing to go gonzo.

Time to tame the wild beast.

"Look at me, Luke. Please look at me."

He looked at me, but only for a beat. Then he crushed me to him, his arms pressing the air out of my body as he buried his face in my neck.

"Fuck," he repeated against the skin of my neck. "Did he...?"

"No," I whispered. "It wasn't as bad as that."

I put my arms around him and held on tight.

Then I said, "I don't want you to do anything stupid. I don't want you to get into trouble for me. Just call Vance off Noah. My face will heal and we'll go back to fighting all the time. It'll be like it didn't happen."

His head came up. He pressed his temple against mine for a second then his mouth moved to mine and he kissed me gently on the lips. He lifted his head to look at me and I saw his eyes were not gonzo, they were tender. One arm stayed around me while his other hand came up to my neck and his thumb stroked my jaw.

"Tell me what happened," he said using The Voice. This time The Voice was tinged with a sweetness that, tied up with all the other emotions I was feeling, simply undid me.

Still I fought it. "We'll talk about it later. Maybe tomorrow," I stalled.

"I need you to tell me now."

"It wasn't as bad as you probably think."

His face dipped closer to mine. "My beautiful Ava," he whispered and my stomach got tight. "Please, tell me now."

I couldn't help it. He called me his beautiful Ava and he said "please".

I told him.

Almost everything.

I left out the part about it happening while he was in the house. I figured that could wait for later (read: never).

As I told him, he showed no reaction. He kept me close, his thumb stroking my jaw, his eyes never leaving mine.

When I was done talking, he kept looking at me without saying a word.

"See," I said. "It wasn't that bad."

"I'm gonna kill him," Luke responded in a matter-of-fact voice that said he was, indeed, going to kill Noah.

It was my turn to go rock-solid. "Luke!"

"He's dead."

I grabbed fistfuls of Luke's tee at his sides. "Please don't. Please, Luke. It happened to me, not you. I don't want you to do anything gonzo."

His thumb quit stroking and his fingers tightened at my neck. "Yeah, Ava. It happened to you and you're handlin' it great, babe. You're doin' great," he said. He bent down and brushed his mouth against mine.

I closed my eyes and relaxed into him.

His head came up and I opened my eyes again.

"But that's right now, beautiful. Later tonight, tomorrow, a week from now, it's gonna hit you. It's gonna haunt you and I won't be able to stop it. It's done. And you're mine. You're mine to watch over, you're mine to take care of, you're mine to protect. I didn't protect you. I gotta live with that and it'll make it a whole fuckuva lot easier to live with knowin' he paid a price. Someone hurt you, someone *touched* you," he said this between his teeth, losing hold on his control for a moment. Then I watched him gain it back again before he went on. "And that someone is not gonna get the chance to hurt you, or any woman, again."

"I'm asking you, Luke, please leave it alone."

"I'm telling you, beautiful, I can't. It just isn't in me."

I burrowed deeper into him and shared what was really on my mind. "What if *you* get hurt? He said he had a gun."

"Only one's gonna hurt is Dexter." I opened my mouth to interrupt, but he kept talking. "Ava, beautiful, I won't get hurt. You've got nothin' to worry about." His mouth came to mine. "Nothin' to worry about," he repeated.

My arms went around him and he kissed me. It was light, gentle and only hurt a little bit. When his mouth disengaged, his forehead came to rest on mine again, our noses side-by-side.

"You wanna sleep here tonight or at the loft?" he asked.

"The loft," I answered.

"Then let's get you home."

He moved away from me, but put his arm around my shoulders and started moving to the door. I halted and looked up at him.

"Shouldn't we call the police?" I asked.

"No police. This is gonna be off the radar."

A chill went up my spine.

Then I remembered something. "But Hank and Eddie are police."

"And?"

"Aren't they going to have an issue with this being 'off the radar'?"

"Lotsa shit is off the radar that Hank and Eddie know about. They don't like it, but I suspect they don't lose any sleep over it."

All of a sudden I was tired and I didn't want to talk about this anymore. I wanted to sleep, and yes, I was happy to admit, I wanted to sleep pressed up tight against Luke's strong, warm, hard body, and I would have put that in writing if he'd asked me.

"Let me get my purse," I said.

His arm dropped and I got my purse. When I was close enough again, his arm came back around my shoulders and we walked into the front yard where everyone was standing.

"We're going to the loft," Luke told Lee.

Lee nodded.

Luke looked at Tex. "You'll lock down the house?"

Tex nodded.

Luke dug in his pocket and tossed Tex my keys. Then his eyes went back to Lee.

"Meeting first thing," Luke said.

Lee nodded again.

I glanced at Eddie, who was looking to the heavens.

Then I glanced at Hank, who was looking at me.

"Roxie will be over tomorrow," Hank told me.

"Thank you," I said, and looked at Roxie. "Thank you," I repeated.

She smiled at me, came up and kissed my cheek. "Sleep well, honey. I'll see you tomorrow," she whispered.

Luke pointed me to the Porsche, but I pulled away and walked to Lee.

I didn't say thank you to Lee. I just wrapped my arms around him, got up on my toes and kissed his cheek. I looked him in the eye a beat, hoping he understood without me having to say it (and I was pretty certain he did). I broke free

Kristen Ashley

and did the same to Tex. I didn't break free from Tex as easily, mainly because he engulfed me in a bear hug before letting me go.

"Thanks everyone," I said quietly to the crowd, feeling like a big dork, but knowing at least a gesture should be made before Luke's arm came back around my shoulders. He took me to the Porsche and we were gone.

⋙⋘

Luke was right. It hit me, and it hit me a lot sooner than I would have expected.

It hit me the minute he flipped the light switch in his loft.

Light filled the space and I felt panic seize me. I ran to the switch and turned it off. Then I flattened myself against the wall, protecting the switch with my body.

"Babe." Luke was close, his voice gentle.

"He's watching," I whispered, terrified.

I'd forgotten to tell Luke one little, but important, thing.

Luke's fingers slid under my hair to curl around the back of my neck. "Ava, come away from the wall. Let's get you changed and in bed."

"We have to go to a hotel."

"Ava."

"He's watching."

"He's not watching," Luke said softly.

His hand dropped away from my neck, came around my waist and he gently tried to pull me away from the wall. I resisted, he felt it and instantly stopped trying.

"I forgot to tell you something," I shared.

I put my forehead against the wall and Luke's body came close to my back. His arm went tight to hold me against him and his face came to the side of mine.

"Tell me," he urged.

"He followed us last night," I whispered. "He broke in somewhere, across the street, next door, I don't know. You don't have any curtains, no blinds. We left the lights on when we did it. He watched us have sex. I know because he knew we did it against the wall. He—"

Luke interrupted me, "We're going to a hotel."

Thank you, *God*.

⋙⋘

Luke checked us into the kickass, cool-as-shit Hotel Monaco in Downtown Denver. I'd never stayed there, but any hotel that had "The John Lennon Suite" *and* "The Grace Slick Suite" *and* "The Miles Davis Suite" had to be kickass, cool-as-shit, and it was.

Then we went to bed.

We were lying side by side in each other's arms. Luke was quiet, likely deciding how to dispose of Noah's body once he killed him.

"Luke?" I called.

One of his hands slid up my back under my tee. He'd located the newly-washed Triumph tee for me and I was wearing it. This I found incredibly sweet, but I was trying not to dwell on it.

"Yeah, babe," he answered.

I tilted my head back to look at his blurry, shadowy face. "Will you make love to me?" I asked in a small voice.

Don't ask me why I asked this. I just knew, somewhere deep, I needed it.

"Ava, I'm thinkin' that's not a good thing," he replied softly. "Right now, sleep is a good thing."

I found his answer both disappointing and (probably hysterically) very alarming.

"Okay." My voice was even smaller.

There was a beat of silence before Luke muttered, "Shit." He rolled into me and his hand came up to the healthy side of my face. "This doesn't bode well for my future," he told me.

"What?"

"My inability to say no to you," he said before touching his mouth to mine and his hand slid slowly down my neck, my side, my hip and then over my bottom.

"You say no to me all the time," I told him, now feeling happy in that somewhere deep down inside. I was happy that he was touching me, holding me, kissing me, taking care of me, and he didn't find me dirty and repulsive.

"When have I said no to you?" Luke asked my neck where his lips had moved.

"You don't say no, as such. You just haul me around until I'm where you want, doing what you want."

I felt his mouth move and knew he was smiling against my neck. His hand cupped my ass and he pulled me against him, but he didn't respond.

I didn't mind. I wrapped my arms around him and held on tight.

Then he started to make love to me and it was exactly that. Slow and sweet and absolutely perfect. I forgot about everything. Being taped in my basement in the pitch dark and Noah touching me while Luke was in the house.

It was perfect until Luke's hand moved down my belly and between my legs. His fingers hit the target, but instead of feeling the usual jolt of pure goodness, my body froze. I wrapped my hand around his wrist and pulled it away.

"No," I whispered. My body came unfrozen and all of a sudden I was shaking, and not the good kind of shaking. "I'm sorry. I was wrong. I can't."

I tried to move away, feeling like an idiot, but Luke's hand pulled free of mine. He rolled off me and held me close.

"Ava, hold on to me."

His voice was rough, but he didn't sound angry that I stopped the action when it was really getting good.

"I can't," I told him. "I need—"

"Quiet, beautiful. Just hold on."

I did as I was told. I felt him hard against my belly and felt like a huge dork because I was the one who started it.

"I'm sorry," I whispered, and I was. I was so sorry that my voice broke in the middle of saying it.

"Quiet," he replied.

"I got you all worked up and—"

"Babe, I'll survive."

"Luke."

"Ava, I'm good. Just be quiet."

I went quiet.

We lay there for a while, silent, holding on. The shakes left me and I eventually felt nothing in the world, nothing but our bed at Hotel Monaco, Luke and me in it.

Out of nowhere, something hit me. A flashback.

Not of Noah beating me up and touching me where I didn't want him to, but a flashback of Luke. It was a flashback of when Luke took me for a ride on his new motorcycle when he was seventeen and I was thirteen.

His Mom wasn't happy about the motorcycle, but she kept this to herself (outside of telling my Mom). His Dad hated it and he didn't keep it to himself. As usual he tore into Luke about it.

I loved the motorcycle and after I heard Luke have a rip roarin' with his Dad and Luke slammed out of the house heading to the garage, I ran over and caught him. In my thirteen-year-old-girl usual blathering, dorky way, I told Luke I loved his motorcycle and I told him exactly how much.

When I was done, Luke smiled at me, the dark look fading from his face. I'd always loved it when I used to do that for him. It didn't happen a lot, but it happened. Then he told me to hop on, and I was so excited I did without even thinking twice.

We rode for at least an hour and I thought I'd never forget that ride.

When we got home, they were waiting for us in Luke's driveway. Mr. Stark and my Mom. Luke's Dad yelled at him for taking a thirteen year old out on a motorcycle without asking. My Mom yelled at him because she was a bitch.

Calm as could be, something that always pissed Luke's Dad off (I knew, not because I saw it, but because I heard Mrs. Stark tell my Mom about it), Luke just said to his Dad, "I would never let anything happen to Ava." Then he turned to me, touched my nose and continued, using The Voice, "Precious cargo."

Why hadn't I remembered that? How could I ever forget that?

Finally, realization dawned.

I belonged to Luke. I was Luke's woman.

Hell, I had probably been born to be Luke's woman, if you believed that kind of shit.

I wasn't going to St. Croix and I didn't care about Jules and Roxie and Luke trying it on with them. Just like Daisy said, I was using that as an excuse to guard my heart.

Crapity, crap, crap, *crap*.

Not only that, Luke didn't go gonzo about Noah, probably because I asked him not to. He took me to a hotel when I freaked out at his loft. He made sure I had the Triumph tee. Lastly, he didn't have a hissy fit when I stopped the festivities right when they were getting to the point of no return, and held me, just like I needed.

So not only did I belong to Luke, he was most definitely a Good Guy.

The warm melty feeling in my stomach could no longer be denied.

Shit.

This time my hand slid down his belly and my fingers wrapped around him.

He sucked in breath then said, "Ava."

"Quiet, Luke," I replied.

I rolled into him until he was on his back, climbed on top, guided him inside me and settled.

God, he felt nice.

I was chest to chest with him, my face pressed to his neck. "I could sleep like this," I whispered.

"I know," he replied, and there was humor in his voice. My head came up so I could smile at him in the dark.

His hands slid up my back, one stopped midway to wrap around and the other one kept going and went into my hair.

"You mind movin'?" he asked.

"I guess I could do that," I answered, and I started moving, slowly, savoring it, letting it build. I would kiss him, he would kiss me, our hands would roam, but it was as if we had all the time in the world. Luke let me control it completely, didn't even try to take over. When I was close, I slid my hand down his arm and took his in mine then guided it between our bodies, straight to the target.

"Ava." His voice was back to sounding rough, and my name in that voice made my stomach turn (more) melty, mixed with a shiver going through my body. His fingers pressed and rolled, which made the melty stomach and shivery body intensify significantly.

"Yes," I breathed.

I kept moving, he kept pressing and rolling. We kept kissing in between panting and eventually it hit me, and when it did it was slow, long and *nice*. Seconds after mine was over, his hands went to my hips, holding me down on him tight, and it hit him.

He kept me where I was by wrapping his arms around me.

I pressed my face in his neck. "Thank you," I whispered.

"Babe, I'd do just about anything for you, but you gotta know, that was no sacrifice."

Wow.

He would do just about anything for me?

Ho-ly *crap*.

After he said that, I couldn't help myself. I nuzzled into him.

Then, because he said that, I took a huge risk and told him, "I've decided you're a good guy."

He pulled my hair away from my neck and replied, "About fuckin' time."

⌖

I woke up and it was just dawn. The sunlight was still weak and I woke because I felt I was alone in bed.

I sat up and looked around the room to find Luke sitting in an armchair, wearing his black cargos, shirtless (as usual), leaned forward with elbows on his knees, head in his hands.

I could tell this was an unhappy position of masculine reflection.

For a second I got scared. Then I got out of bed, found the Triumph tee and tugged it on. He watched me move toward him. When I got close, he pulled me into his lap and sat back in the chair. I felt a moment of relief that his unhappy masculine reflection didn't include something that would mean he would never pull me into his lap again, so I let my body relax and settled into him.

"Do you want to share what's on your mind?" I asked.

"Don't you have to brush your teeth?" he responded.

I smiled at him before I wrapped an arm around his abs, stuffing my face in his neck.

"I'd rather know what's on your mind," I returned quietly.

One of his arms was curled around my back, hand resting on my hip. The fingers of his other hand slid back and forth from knee to tee on my thigh. My only thought was that I could wake up like this every morning of my life.

Then Luke spoke.

"What's on my mind is that I'm responsible for what happened to you."

All morning dewy softness flew out the window, my head jerked up and I stared at him.

"*What?*" I asked, somewhat loudly.

"I'm responsible," he repeated.

I narrowed my eyes. Not because I was angry, but because I didn't have my contacts in or glasses on and I was trying to focus so I could read his face (this didn't work).

"How on earth are you responsible?" I asked.

"I went after him, he retaliated. That's how I'm responsible."

Oh, for goodness sakes.

"Luke, that's just crazy."

"It isn't, Ava. I should have seen it coming and prepared, especially when the info started to come in on him."

Uh-oh.

This didn't sound good.

"What info?"

Luke didn't hesitate before sharing, "His name isn't Noah Dexter. He's got a record, he's wanted in two states and he's been connin' women, like he conned you, for a long time."

I supposed I shouldn't have been surprised by that, but I was surprised by it.

"I still don't see how that makes you responsible," I said.

"You didn't tell me about the jewelry," was Luke's strange reply.

"What about it?"

"It was worth over sixty-five K."

I sucked in breath at another demonstration of his freaky ability to know *everything.*

"How did you find that out?" I asked.

"Your aunt's will. The jewelry was worth over sixty-five K when appraised for the will, seven years ago."

"I'm not sure I'm following."

"Dexter didn't steal five grand, he stole over seventy grand. That's a big difference. You were a larger mark than I first thought. This guy isn't a small time con man. Far as we could tell, he was running two cons simultaneously. The one with you and some other woman, much older, disabled, in her early seventies. He got her jewelry, stole her car and wiped out her retirement account. Between the two of you, he pulled in over three hundred large."

"Holy shit," I breathed, incapable of wrapping my mind around this news. I was, however, able to septuple my vow of revenge against Noah.

A disabled lady in her seventies? What a *jerk!*

"I underestimated him," Luke went on, interrupting my mental tirade. "He gets caught, his picture hits the news, women come forward who didn't report him and he's fucked even more than he *was* fucked. He's not gonna let that happen, and he would be desperate enough to do about anything to make certain it doesn't. Including fuckin' with my woman, somethin' not a lot of people in Denver would have the balls to do."

Okay, so, it was safe to say this was not good news. I felt like an even bigger idiot now than I felt when Noah took off with my money.

Time to focus, and *not* on me being an idiot.

"Luke, you aren't responsible," I stated. "I'm responsible. I let him in my life in the first place."

"Lotta women do."

"That doesn't make it any better."

"Probably not, but it's the truth."

There you go.

Time for a different tack.

"Okay then, you want to know how I felt when you first said you were going to go after him?"

Luke just looked at me.

"I felt happy," I shared. "My stomach got melty. I was glad someone wanted to take care of me."

Silence.

I persevered, even though doing so scared the shit out of me. We were in vulnerable territory here. Way vulnerable.

"Last night, you were preparing to go gonzo. You didn't because I needed you. Last night you also said you can't say no to me. If I pushed it, that I didn't want you to go after him, *really* pushed it, would you have?"

More silence.

Shit.

It was going to have to be all or nothing.

I put my hands to his neck and moved so I was facing him.

Do it, say it, the time is right, Good Ava urged.

Don't! The time will NEVER be right! Bad Ava yelled.

For once I listened to Good Ava, took a breath and bared it all.

Quietly, I said, "Yesterday, when I was in my freak out about Jules, Daisy said to me that I was trying to find ways to protect my heart but I was doing it wrong. She told me the best way to protect my heart was to trust it to someone who will protect it for me."

More silence, but his body went completely still.

"That's you. It's always been you," I whispered, my heart racing. I was scared as hell, but I forged ahead. "Please don't take responsibility for Noah being an asshole. I couldn't bear it if you did that."

I'd barely stopped talking when, without a word, Luke got up, taking me with him. He carried me to the bed and put me in it, coming down on top of me.

"You belong to me," he stated, his voice soft, his tone firm, his hands starting to roam.

I was pretty fucking happy he seemed to be delighted (in a Luke way, of course) with the news that I'd trusted him with my heart.

Still, I wasn't ready to go there just yet.

"Take it back that you feel responsible," I said instead.

"Tell me you belong to me," he demanded.

"Take it back first," I countered.

The roaming hands were getting serious so mine started to roam too, just because I didn't want to be left out.

He kissed me gently then against my mouth he said, "I'll wait. You can say it when I'm inside you."

"Seriously, you can be so annoying," I told him.

"Babe," he replied as he smiled against my mouth.

For your information, a lot later, when he was deep inside me, I gave him what he wanted.

I mean, this *was* Luke. I *was* his woman.

And I *did* belong to him.

For as long as I could remember.

Chapter 23

Gonzo

Luke and I walked into the Nightingale Investigations offices and everyone was in the reception area waiting for us.

When I said everyone, I meant *everyone*.

Lee and Indy, Jet and Eddie, Hank and Roxie, Vance and Jules, Sissy, Ally, Daisy with a tall, dark-haired, handsome man I did not know standing at her side, Shirleen, May, Tod and Stevie, Mace, Matt, Hector, Darius, Tex, Duke, and some big black dude I'd never seen before in my life.

"Holy shit," I whispered.

Luke's mouth got tight.

Everyone stared at me and I knew why. I didn't look good. I got a good look at myself in the hotel mirror that morning. My lip was torn and my eye was bruised and blackened and, that didn't count what they couldn't see, and that was the headache to end all headaches. Not to mention these people talked. No way to keep a secret in this group. News spread like wildfire.

Shirleen was the first to break out of the group stare. She walked up to me and pulled me into tight hug.

"Child," she said low, a tremor running through her voice, a tremor that communicated itself to my body.

"I'm fine," I told her, putting my arms around her and giving her a reassuring squeeze.

She just held on tight.

After a few beats she leaned back and looked at my face close up. As I watched, sweet, soft, gentle Shirleen morphed into hard, angry, pissed-off Shirleen.

"No one messes with *my* girl," she declared quietly, eyes still scanning my face. She stepped back, let me go and looked towards the male contingent of our audience. Then she repeated, "No one messes with *my* girl." This time she said it louder, angrier. It sounded like an order and the tension in the room, already high, climbed higher. Nobody seemed prepared to do a thing about it. In fact, they all seemed to be feeding off it.

Not good.

Before I could intervene, Shirleen looked at Darius. "You got me, son?" she asked.

"I got you, Aunt Shirleen," Darius replied, and my surprised gaze swung between Shirleen and Darius. I didn't know they were related.

Shirleen, not quite done, looked at Lee. "Do *you* got me?" she repeated.

"Shirleen, it'll be taken care of," Lee responded calmly, but his voice held a lethal edge.

"It better be," she said, her voice low again, this time with scary meaning. "It better fuckin' be."

Eek!

Time to move on.

I looked at Indy, hoping to change the subject. "Who's taking care of Fortnum's?"

"Fortnum's is closed for a staff meeting," Duke answered my question in his gravelly voice, his tone doing nothing to dissipate the scary atmosphere and therefore he foiled my attempt to change the subject.

"But, you can't——" I started.

"We can, we have, we're not fuckin' goin' back until this shit is *sorted*," Tex threw down.

I felt weird. Moved, but scared, and kept my eyes on Indy.

"You can't do that," I said.

Indy just shook her head. "Jane, who's one of my staff, Kitty Sue, who's Lee's Mom, and Jet's Mom, Nancy, are at the store explaining things to the customers. They'll open in the afternoon when the crowds are smaller and they can handle them. Until then… Well, Ava, you know that no one messes with a Rock Chick, not ever, but especially not——"

"Indy," Lee said low, interrupting her. I could tell she had been working herself up to rant mode. At Lee's voice, she pulled in her bottom lip, bit it and kept quiet, but I knew it cost her.

"I'm fine," I repeated, not just to Indy, but to the entire assemblage.

Everyone just kept staring.

Yikes.

"What I want to know," Shirleen started, when no one seemed to be prepared to move, "is why you all are standin' around like you don't got shit to do? You got shit to do. Serious shit. It's time to fuckin' get crackin'."

The staring stopped. Folks started to move and I let my body relax.

"Give me five," Luke said to Lee, then took my hand and walked me to the door to the inner sanctum. He opened the door, guided me through and down the hall, directly to the kitchenette he'd taken me to (or more accurately, carried me) that first time I was at the offices.

We went inside and he closed the door. He turned to me and his hand came to my jaw.

"You okay?" he asked. I nodded and he went on, "I had no fuckin' idea we would walk into that, babe, if I knew—"

I realized he was pissed at the same time I realized that he would have protected me from what just happened if he could have. And lastly, because of that, I realized Luke wasn't just a Good Guy, he might be The Best Guy *Ever*.

For this reason, I moved into him and put my arms around his waist. "It's cool Luke, they just care. It feels nice."

That was a partial lie. It felt scary and slightly humiliating that all those people knew that Noah had his hand down my pants. Instead, I was trying to focus on them rallying around me, which did, indeed, feel nice. More to the point, I wanted Luke to focus on it because he didn't look happy, and an unhappy Luke could be a frightening thing.

Luke's thumb stroked my jaw and I watched as his anger ebbed away. "All right beautiful. If you're cool, I'm cool."

I smiled at him.

Crisis averted.

Then he continued, "Before I meet with the boys, we gotta talk about somethin'."

Uh-oh.

Crisis maybe *not* averted.

"Luke, I'm not sure I can handle talking about something."

He bent down to kiss my nose and said gently, "I know, Ava babe. I wouldn't bring this up, not now, but it's important."

Crapity, crap, crap, *crap*.

"Okay," I agreed but I didn't mean it.

"Yesterday—" he began.

Nope.

I wasn't going to talk about that. I'd already talked about it as much as I was going to talk about it.

"I don't want to talk about yesterday," I interrupted.

His other arm moved around me and his hand at my jaw slid into my hair to cup the back of my head. He brought me close so my body was pressed against his.

"We gotta talk about it."

"We'll talk about it later." As in much later, a thousand years from now preferably.

"Babe, I kept what happened with Jules and me—"

I went stiff. "Jules and you *and* Roxie and you," I corrected him.

His face went hard before he muttered, "Those fuckin' women."

"Someone had to tell me," I shot back.

"*I* wanted to tell you," he replied.

"Yeah? When?" I was beginning to get heated.

"When the time was right. Only so much someone can take, you'd had enough."

"You said you were through talking."

"Yeah, for then. Not for eternity."

"You didn't say that."

"I didn't say we were never talkin' again either."

This was true.

Shit!

His face got softer and I knew that he knew he had me.

Shit again!

"Luke—"

"I don't want to fight about this," he stated.

I glared because I was perfectly happy fighting about it.

He ignored my glare. "The point is how you responded."

"I didn't respond."

"Yeah, that's the point. You shut down, shut me out and then you made plans to take off."

"What?" I asked.

Surely he couldn't know I was headed to St. Croix. No one knew, not even Sissy, until her card came in the mail, of course.

He let me go, walked to a locker, opened it and pulled out some papers which, I noticed at a glance, were my tickets to St. Croix.

Ho-ly crap!

He knew I was headed to St. Croix.

"Where did you—?"

"I went to your house. Found these on the dining room table, new luggage and a bunch of shopping in your bedroom," he replied before I could finish my question. He threw the tickets back in the locker and shut the door.

Hell and damnation.

I was beginning to realize it was not such a good thing my boyfriend was a private investigator. Although I had left that stuff out for anyone to see, still.

I was so exasperated at Luke knowing *everything*, I rolled my eyes to the ceiling and then said something stupid. There was no excuse for it. I should have protected the information with everything I had, taken it to my grave, kept it buried and never let it out, even under torture.

In my defense, I wasn't myself. Too much had happened to me with Dom, with Ren, with Noah, even with fucking Riley, and most especially, with Luke.

That was why I didn't stop myself before saying, "I can't *believe* while I was downstairs with Noah and he was demonstrating why he's the ultimate *jerk*, you were searching my house."

The air in the room instantly went thick with tension. My eyes flew from the ceiling to lock on Luke's and I realized my mortal mistake when I saw his face had gone stony. Scary stony. Fury-unleashed stony.

Gonzo stony.

"What did you just say?" he asked through his teeth.

"Nothing," I replied quickly.

"You didn't say nothin', you said somethin'."

"No, I meant—"

He advanced. I retreated.

My back hit the door and he came up close. "He was in your house while I was in your house?"

Like I did the night before, hoping it would work again, I put my hands to his neck to try to get through to him, calm him.

"Luke, please, listen to me—"

"He touched you then, didn't he?"

My eyes grew wide that he guessed this (how could he guess this?), and unfortunately, my eyes told the truth for me.

It was then Luke went gonzo. No neck touch, soft voice and pleading were going to help. No way.

355

He turned from me, and with a vicious blow and a ferocious growl, he punched the wall, his hand going clean through, drywall dust poofing out. I stared in horror as he pulled his hand out of the wall and then punched it again, leaving another hole.

He wasn't quite through. After wall punch two, he turned, walked to a locker and punched *that*. His fist against the steel made a huge noise and my horrified stare turned part terrified, part amazed when the steel buckled and the sides of the door bowed out. He hit it again, then again, and I charged him.

"Luke!" I shouted, throwing my arms around him to stop him from hurting himself. If he kept doing that he was going to crush his hand. "Stop it! Please, stop!"

His arm sliced around my waist, lifting me clean off my feet, up through the air. He took three long strides and I landed on my ass on the counter of the kitchenette. He closed in, coming between my legs, his hands, one of them bloody, moving to either side of my face. He held on and stared at me, his face hard and angry, and my heart was beating like a jackhammer.

It was then the door opened. I looked over his shoulder and Lee, Vance and Mace were there making the room seem even smaller.

"What the fuck is goin' on?" Lee asked.

Luke turned halfway to them. His eyes to the floor, he didn't look at them. I noticed a muscle in his jaw was jumping and I took this as a good sign that he was trying to regain control. He took a hand away from my face, sliced it in a sweep, palm down and low, indicating nonverbally (and likely incorrectly) that he had himself in check.

"Tell me this shit didn't just get worse," Lee said.

"This shit just got worse," Luke answered, his voice an angry growl. "Give us a minute."

I closed my eyes and when I opened them again, Lee, Vance and Mace had backed out and Lee was closing the door.

"Luke, listen to me," I begged.

He twisted back to face me and I caught my breath because his gonzo actions hadn't even touched his level of fury. He was still pushing the very top edge of the red zone.

"Talk to me," he clipped, and it wasn't a request.

"Maybe—"

"Ava, do not keep any more of this shit from me. Tell me what the fuck happened, right *fucking* now."

My body went stiff. "Luke, you seem to keep forgetting, it happened *to me*. It didn't happen to you, it happened *to me* and I should—"

He framed my face with his hands again and got close. "It happened to you, babe, but at the same time, it happened to *us*."

I pushed at his shoulders and yelled, "How dare you!"

He didn't move. Instead he kept talking.

"Last night, I put my hand between your legs and you froze. If you weren't you, if you didn't have the strength to sort your fuckin' head out and work through it, that could have had a whole different ending. It says somethin' about you that you could work through it. Hell, it demonstrates one of the reasons I want to be the one, the *only* one, who puts my hand between your legs. You were most other women we wouldn't have had last night. Most women would shut down and last night could have taken weeks, months, maybe never have happened at all. I was prepared to work through it with you. Lucky for me, you aren't most other women. That still doesn't take away the fact that it could have been a long road for both of us." He got even closer. "Sex is sex, babe, with *anyone* else. With you, it isn't. It's a fuckuva lot more. You know it. I know it. And he could have taken that away from us. After all these years we found it and he could have taken it away. Not just from you, but from me too. Do you understand?"

Tears filled my eyes, and before I could deep breathe they spilled down my cheeks.

I understood. I really understood. Furthermore, I understood I wouldn't be dancing at my wedding because Luke declared he wasn't going to dance with me, and I would be bearing him three sons (or daughters, whatever).

And I wanted that, with everything that was me, but more, Luke wanted it just as much as me.

Noah had put all that in jeopardy.

It was then my tilty-world righted, and for the first time in a long time, maybe the first time in my life, I felt my feet planted firmly on the ground.

I didn't answer but I didn't have to.

Luke watched me cry for a few beats and then said softly, "He's gonna pay for those, too."

"What?" I asked in a shaky voice, trying hard to pull myself together.

"Your tears."

At his words, I put my hands to his face and it was me who rested my forehead against his at the same time a sob tore from my throat.

So much for pulling myself together.

We stayed where we were, both holding on to each other while the tears slid down my cheeks. Finally, I sucked in breath and managed, with a tremendous effort of will, to pull myself together.

When I did, Luke's thumbs swiped at my cheeks and he whispered, "Tell me."

I closed my eyes slowly, and just as slowly I opened them.

Then, I told him. "He was taping me to the post. I already had tape over my mouth. He heard you come in and told me he had a gun. He told me if I made a sound, he'd blow my head off and then yours. I heard you call for me. I made a move to try and get away and he warned me again. We listened to you move around upstairs. He said he wanted to make it interesting and he touched me. You left, he'd got excited and he finished himself off. Then he finished taping me, told me to get you to make Vance back off and he left."

It was his turn to close his eyes.

"I could have stopped it," he murmured.

I shook my head and my hands tightened. "He would have killed us both."

His eyes opened. "He's a con man, not a killer."

"You don't know that."

"I know it."

"You can't know it."

"I know it."

"Luke—"

"I know it because I'm not a con man but I am a killer."

My breath froze in my lungs, but I still managed to breathe, "What?"

"That's part of who I was. It isn't who I am now, but it isn't something you forget how to do."

Panic filled me and oxygen came back into my lungs with a burning whoosh.

"Stop talking," I begged on a whisper.

"I've said it before, babe, but maybe you didn't clue in."

"Stop talking."

"You gotta know who you've let in your bed."

"Stop."

"You wanna end it now, you say the word and I'll walk away. I'm still goin' after him, I'm still gonna make him pay. But I'll be out of your life."

"Stop talking!" Now my hands were gripping his head, lungs burning so hot I was finding it hard to breathe.

"Say the word now. You don't, I'm never letting you go."

"Please, Luke, stop talking."

"You gotta make the decision now, Ava."

"Shut up," I whispered.

"You can't deny this and you can't deal with this later, it has to be now. I'm not gettin' used to sharin' my life with you and havin' you take off on me. You don't say the word now and you can't deal with it later and you think to leave, I'm warnin' you, I'll come after you."

"*Shut up!*" This time, I shouted it.

"You make the decision, either I walk out and leave you in here or we walk out together. We walk out together, that's it. Things get tough, we fight, it doesn't matter. We deal. You don't buy tickets to St. Croix, you don't give me the silent treatment. *We deal.* We walk out of here together and you use this, or anything else you can conjure up, to shut me out, I'm tellin' you babe, it's not gonna be good. In our scenario, we aren't switchin' roles so I'm forced to live your Mom's life while you take off and live your Dad's."

Oh… my… *God.*

He did *not* just say that.

"You didn't just say that," I whispered, letting go of his head, pulling mine from his hands and leaning back.

"I said it. You know the worst in me, and I know it's bad, but I'm not hidin' anything. I'm givin' you the chance to decide. You tell me to walk, I won't like it, but I'll do it."

Okay, that was it. I'd had enough.

"You are *such* a jerk!" I snapped and gave him a shove that was so hard, he rocked back at the shoulder.

I was too angry to realize I'd finally scored a physical push. Instead, I kept ranting.

"You know, Lucas Stark, the reason I got contacts and lost weight was because you hugged me at your Dad's funeral and later I overheard Marilyn and Sofia making fun of me, and *you*, because we looked stupid together. You, hot, handsome Luke hugging me, Fatty Fatty Four-Eyes. They said the sight of us made them throw up a little. They said you had to be gay to hug me. I vowed, *vowed*," I shouted the last word at the top of my lungs, caught in a dramatic tizzy I could not control (and didn't even try), "that you wouldn't lay eyes on me again until I could be held by you, and if anyone saw us no one would throw up a little or think we didn't look right together."

I was on a roll. So on a roll, I didn't notice the air in the room change again. Nor did I notice the look and feel of Luke change. I just kept right on yelling.

"And last night when you thought I was sorting through stuff in my head, I wasn't. I was remembering that motorcycle ride you gave me, after which you got in serious shit with your Dad and my Mom and you called me precious cargo. So I wasn't sorting through stuff in my head. *You* pulled me through last night and you didn't even know it, you big idiot."

I shoved him again, this time his shoulder didn't go back. I didn't notice that either. I just kept on raging.

"You told me that it felt good when we were growing up to know I thought you could move mountains because you needed that. Well, *you* knew what *I* grew up with! I couldn't have gotten through it without knowing *you* were across the street, and you were the only person in my life who gave a shit. Other than Sissy, you were the *only person in my life who gave a shit!*"

"Ava—"

"I'm talking now," I interrupted him, using a line he'd used on me.

I ignored the side of his mouth going up in one of his sexy half-grins and kept on going.

"So I don't care who you were for eight years, it doesn't change who you are to me. So don't give me any ultimatums and don't threaten me. I am who I am, a big dork who makes mistakes and deals the best way I can. I'm going to keep making mistakes and being a big dork because that's who I am. You can't deal with it, then you best walk out that door because that's the way it is."

I stopped talking and realized, first, that I was breathing heavily, and second, that I had been shouting the whole time and it was likely everyone could hear.

Shit.

Oh well, fuck it. Now was not the time to be embarrassed for being me.

Hell, there was never a time to be embarrassed for being me.

"You through?" Luke asked, cutting through my world-rocking epiphany of coming to terms with being a dork.

I thought about it.

"Yeah," I replied.

"Your mother and sisters come to town often?"

I blinked in confusion, not only at his change in subject, but at his calm, rational tone. Gonzo Luke was a memory.

"Not really," I told him.

"But they come to town?"

"Sometimes."

"Do I have to be nice to them?"

I took in a breath.

It had happened. I'd lost control, opened up and let Luke see my soft spot. I'd told him everything, held nothing back.

And he was smiling at me.

I felt something shift, then settle. The soft spot was still there, still vulnerable, but now that I showed it to him, I closed the door on it, locked it and handed Luke the key.

I felt goose bumps rise on my skin, but I ignored them and answered his question in a quiet voice. "Probably."

"That's gonna be hard, babe."

"You're a tough guy, macho man, you can hack it."

His arms came around me and he slid me forward on the counter so my special girl parts were pressed against his hard boy parts. My arms lifted and closed around his neck.

"Fair warning. They say shit to you I don't like, especially those fuckin' sisters of yours, I may not be responsible for what comes out of my mouth," Luke told me.

"I'm sensing that Marilyn and Sofia have earned a new title. That's twice you've called them 'those fuckin' sisters of yours'."

He ignored my comment and the fact that I impersonated his deep voice and kept to his theme. "I'm not shittin' you, Ava. I'm not gonna stand around and listen to those bitches cuttin' you down."

Apparently, Luke took me giving him my key pretty fucking seriously.

Daisy was right. The best way to guard your heart was to trust a good man to take care of it for you. Lucky for me, considering there weren't many around, I found myself a good man.

Caught up in this new knowledge, I whispered, "Okay." Then leaned forward, and even with a cut lip, I kissed him hard.

His mouth opened over mine, his tongue slid inside and even with a cut lip he kissed me back, making the hard kiss so hot I melted into him.

Oo, Good Ava breathed. *I feel so much better now.*

Weirdly enough, Bad Ava added, *I do, too.*

You do? Good Ava asked.

Yeah, Bad Ava answered. *Go figure.*

Well, finally, Good Ava commented.

Still lots of fun to have, even if we are Luke's woman, Bad Ava noted.

I'm not thinking that's a good thing, Good Ava leaned in and said in my ear.

Bad Ava giggled and she sounded happy.

⇁⇝

After our mini-post-drama make out session, Luke took me out of the kitchenette, and in the hallway, the black guy I'd never met was talking to another guy I'd never seen before and Shirleen.

"Shee-it," the black guy said when he saw us. "You white girls got attitude. Far as I can see, these boys need to get their heads examined. I'd put up with that shit for about a fuckin' second."

Any normal person would politely pretend that they hadn't heard a thing. I was learning quickly that I was not surrounded by normal people anymore.

Since normal for me was a Dad who would up and leave, a fading beauty queen of a mother who was so engrossed in her own life she forgot her daughters had one, too, and might need her help, and my two "fuckin' sisters" who were mean as snakes, I figured not normal was not so bad.

Shirleen had different thoughts and turned on the black dude. "Like black women don't have more attitude then ten of these white women," she declared, as if that was a good thing.

"Black women don't give you shit by yellin' at your ass for-fuckin'-ever. They get fed up, they quit bitchin' and burn down your house or stick you with a knife. Makes it easier. Either way, you know it's time to get your shit together and you just gotta call your insurance man."

"And you are?" I asked, before Shirleen could retort like she looked like she was preparing to do, big time.

"I'm Smithie," he answered. "You dance?"

I blinked at him, stunned by his bizarre question. "Do I dance?"

"Smithie." For some reason Luke's voice was a low, warning rumble and Smithie's eyes turned to him.

"What? You too? What's fuckin' wrong with strippin'? Daisy stripped and everyone likes Daisy. Lottie strips, everyone likes Lottie."

I was stuck on the "stripping" explanation to "do you dance?"

Then it dawned on me that Smithie must be the owner of the strip club where Jet worked as a cocktail waitress during her drama, and where her sister Lottie was currently a stripper (and the best one in the Rocky Mountain region, if rumor could be believed).

"Now that Daisy's with Marcus, she strip anymore?" Shirleen asked.

"No," Smithie answered.

"Lottie got a man?" Shirleen carried on.

"No," Smithie snapped, cottoning on to Shirleen's point.

"Luke look like the type of boy who'd let men watch his woman take her clothes off while she's dancin' around on a stage with baby oil slathered all over her body?" Shirleen pushed.

"All right, all right, fuck," Smithie muttered. "Can't a man recruit? Nothin' wrong with asking."

I looked at Luke. "I think I need cookies."

He gave me a half-grin and touched my nose.

What he did not do, I noticed, was charge out and buy me cookies.

I demoted him from The Best Man Ever to just The Best Man I'd Ever Met. Superman would have charged out. Hell, he'd have flown to get Lois Lane cookies. I was pretty sure of it.

Luke's eyes moved to the other man who hadn't said anything. The other man was huge, as in enormous. Every inch of him, as far as I could tell, was muscle.

"Jack, you in on the meeting?" Luke asked him.

I sucked in breath.

Jack.

Jack was the guy in the surveillance room that saw me start to put my hand down my own pants.

Shit!

I stared at Jack. I thought Jack would ogle me, give me a look. Something, anything, to communicate, like a lecherous, icky *man,* that he knew what he knew.

Jack didn't even glance in my direction. He kept his eyes on Luke.

"Brody and me are takin' shifts in surveillance," Jack told Luke. "Other than me, Lee's pullin' everyone off assignments until Dexter is found. Even Monty's goin' into the field."

Wow.

I didn't know who Monty was, but the way Jack said it I got the feeling this was a big thing.

"Well!" Shirleen snapped. "What you all standin' around for? Shit. That dickhead's gonna be drinkin' piña fuckin' coladas in Mexico before you all pull your fingers out of your asses."

I sucked in breath yet again, and at the rate I was going I was going to pass out. Still, I wasn't certain Luke would take to anyone, even a scary Shirleen, telling him he had his finger up his ass.

I turned to him. "Luke——" I started cautiously to try and tame the wild beast before he went gonzo again.

Luke's hard eyes moved from Shirleen to me. He wasn't happy with her, but he also wasn't going to go gonzo.

I let out a breath then started a different (read: safer) subject. "I'm not sure I want Lee to——"

"Decision's made, babe," Luke cut me off to say. "Lee doesn't often change his mind. The sooner this is over, the sooner we can all focus on other shit."

"Yeah, like the next one of you white bitches who tears into one of these boys lives. Who's up next, is it that Hawaiian guy?" Smithie asked.

"Far as I can tell, it's Ally. She's due," Shirleen countered. "That cop boy-friend of hers got himself into the FBI. He's off to DC. No way in *hell* Ally Nightingale is gonna leave Denver. Soon, she'll be a free agent."

"My money's on Hector," Jack threw in. "He's a wild man. Some woman's gotta tame him before he gets himself killed."

"I'll take that action," Shirleen said.

"Oh my God. This is cool," I breathed, excited to be in on the ground floor, *finally*, of one of these bets, especially when it wasn't one that involved me.

Luke's hand came to the back of my neck. "Babe."

I turned to face him, lost in the excitement. "Who do you think it's gonna be?"

"I don't wish this shit on *anyone*," was Luke's answer.

As much as it killed the mood, I had to admit, Luke had a point.

"Lord!" Shirleen shouted, reaching the end of her tether. "Do *I* have to go out and whack this guy personally?"

Yikes.

Luke sliced a killing glance at Shirleen before he pulled me into him with pressure at my neck and kissed me softly.

"I want you to stay in the offices, and I don't want you to do anything stupid," he warned when he was done.

The knee weakening I experienced with his kiss vanished and I glared at him. He gave me a half-grin, totally unaffected by the glare.

Then he was gone.

Jack peeled off and disappeared behind a door, but Smithie and Shirleen remained.

I looked at them.

"Well?" Shirleen asked, as if she was expecting something.

And I knew what she was expecting. I also knew what I had to do.

I may have realized, finally, that I was Luke's woman, that I belonged to him and that he could be trusted with my heart, my body, my troubles and all my vulnerabilities.

But I still was a Rock Chick.

"I need to talk to the girls," I told Shirleen.

"Oh shit," Smithie muttered. "Here we go."

"Oowee, that's what I'm talkin' about," Shirleen cried in glee.

Uh-oh, Good Ava murmured.

Yippee! Bad Ava hooted.

Chapter 24
Vibrator Ceremony

Shirleen walked Smithie and I into what she called the "Down Room".

It was a big room. It had a couch, a TV, a treadmill, a weight bench and a bunch of weights. It also was filled with Rock Chicks, Tod, Stevie, Tex and Duke.

When we walked in, everyone turned to stare.

"Hey," I greeted.

Sissy came forward and gave me a big hug. I hugged her back. She pulled away and looked up at me. I braced in preparation for her to say something that would make me cry.

"I'm thinking you aren't fuck buddies with Luke anymore," she said on a grin.

Clearly my shouted diatribe in the kitchenette announcing my elevated relationship status with Luke superseded all my other dramas, including being duct taped to a steel support and then fondled by my con man ex-boyfriend.

I looked to the ceiling.

"I'm thinkin' her vibrators are gonna get lonely," Daisy noted.

I closed my eyes.

"I'm thinking we should have a vibrator ceremony. Maybe we can all stand around in the dead of night, carrying candles and chanting while she buries them in her backyard," Ally added.

I made a low, frustrated sound in the back of my throat.

"I'm thinkin' you bitches best stop talkin' about vibrators. We got a pack of wild men in the next room plannin' a human hunt and you women are talkin' about sex toys," Smithie threw in, sounding exasperated.

I looked at Smithie and said with feeling, "Thank you."

"Who brought him?" Tod whispered loudly to Indy.

"I did. I figured we needed all the help we could get," Jet replied.

"He's kind of a killjoy," Tod went on. "I like the idea of a Vibrator Ceremony. After we're done burying them, we could make canapés and drink champagne. It's a lot more fun to talk about that than hunting down humans."

Tod was not wrong.

"Oh for fuck's sake!" Duke exploded.

"All right!" I shouted before I lost any more control. "Listen up."

All eyes turned back to me.

I took a deep breath.

Then I realized I didn't have anything to say.

So, as any good Rock Chick would, I winged it.

"Let's break this down. First, some guy hit Bobby in the head with a baseball bat. Seems everyone has forgotten that, but I haven't. I don't even *know* Bobby and I know something's gotta give with the guy who hit Bobby. You with me?"

There were a couple of nods but mostly the Rock Chicks looked confused.

"Um, he's kinda in jail," Roxie reminded me. "Remember, Hector and Darius got him? Hank told me Bobby ID'd the guy from mug shots and after that he confessed."

Oh. Yeah. I forgot the first part. The second part was good news.

I decided to forge ahead.

"Okay, that's sorted," I announced. "Then, second, last night was not good. For some reason it seems it was worse for Luke than it was for me."

"That's because you're a steel magnolia, sugar," Daisy chimed in.

She got more nods than I did.

"What the hell does that mean?" Tex asked.

"You seen the movie *Steel Magnolias*?" Daisy asked Tex.

"Fuck no," Tex stated the obvious.

"Watch it, then you'll understand," Daisy went on.

"Will someone please tell me why we're talkin' about a fuckin' Julia Roberts movie?" Duke put in.

"It wasn't a Julia Roberts movie, it was a Dolly Parton movie," Daisy snapped back.

"It was really a Sally Field movie," Jet said quietly.

"Oh pu-lease. Everyone knows Shirley MacLaine stole the whole damn show," Tod threw out.

"Someone kill me," Smithie begged.

"People!" I yelled.

Everyone quieted and turned back to me.

When I had their attention, I continued.

"All right, so second point, part A. Luke's off-the-scales pissed and Lee's none too happy either, which means Noah, my ex, is fucked. I don't mind that, I just don't want anyone I care about doing something stupid and fucking up their life in order to make Noah pay. Which takes me to part B. I'm pissed, too. I mean, the guy beat me up, taped me to a post and put his hand down my pants, but it's worse! At the same time he was stealing my auntie's jewelry and all my money, he was conning a seventy-year-old disabled lady out of her retirement fund and he stole her car!"

There were gasps all around.

Finally. Now I was getting somewhere.

"Oh my God," Sissy breathed.

"No shit?" Ally asked.

"No shit," I told her. "That means we have to find him first and make him pay by turning him over to the proper authorities."

"I know some proper authorities," Roxie said.

"Me too," Jet put in.

"Practically my whole family is proper authorities," Indy added.

"Right, they come in later. First we have to catch him," I went on and looked at Duke, Tex and Smithie. "Everyone with me?"

The girls, Tod and Stevie nodded.

Tex, Duke and Smithie did not.

Shit.

"Are you guys here as members of the Rock Chick gang or are you here as informants for the Hot Bunch?" I asked them.

"Shit, woman," Tex said, but I noted he didn't answer my question.

"I'm being serious," I told him, sounding just as serious as I was being, which was ultra-serious. "If you're here as informants, take off now. If you're not, you can stay. Either way, I don't want you talking me out of this. My crush on Lucas Stark began when I was eight years old. Now, twenty years later, he's mine. He just caved in a locker with his fist, for goodness sakes. God knows what he's going to do to Noah when he catches him. I'm not spending the next twenty to life visiting him in a penitentiary. Got me?"

Tex, Duke and Smithie just stared at me.

"Got me?" I snapped.

Tex looked at Duke "She's got spunk," he said.

"Where I come from, we call it sass," Duke replied.

"Where I come from, we call it attitude," Smithie put in.

"Oh, for the love of God, whatever you call it, are you in or out?" Jules clipped.

Smithie looked at me. "I don't know about your firsts and seconds or A's and B's. All I know is Jet told me a friend of hers got violated. I ain't down with that shit. I don't care *who* nails this motherfucker, I just wanna be in on nailin' him. So yeah, I'm fuckin' in."

"In," Duke growled.

"Fuck yeah, I'm in," Tex boomed.

I nodded to them. Once. "All righty then, here's my plan."

And I told them my plan. It was kind of a shit plan, but luckily Indy, Ally and Jules had ideas to share and they were better than mine. In the end, I felt all right because instead of a half-assed plan, we had a pretty decent one.

When we were done, Tod raised his hand and I nodded to him.

"Can I just ask, after we find this guy, can we talk about the Vibrator Ceremony? I'm thinking of making us all kind of choir-like robes to wear, but with sequins and some satin sashes as belts. Maybe in chartreuse."

It was then I was wishing someone would shoot *me*.

⌲⌯

The gang handed out assignments. Everyone prepared to move out and I approached Jules.

"Hey," I said.

"You hanging in there?" she asked, looking at me closely.

I nodded. "Listen, I… um…" I started, but May came up to our group and I stopped.

"It's okay. You can talk in front of May," Jules told me.

"About *anything?*" I asked.

"Hon, if you mean about you freakin' out yesterday about Luke makin' out with Jules on her couch while Vance was watchin' on the monitors in the surveillance room, then yeah, you can talk about anything," May put in.

My bugged out eyes swung to Jules. "Vance was watching?" I breathed.

"Yeah, I didn't know that. Neither did Luke. Vance installed cameras in my house during my troubles and he was on duty in the surveillance room the night Luke and I... um..." Jules stopped then started again. "Ava, you have to know, it didn't go very far."

"Vance was watching?" I breathed again. I didn't know Vance very well (read: hardly at all), but I figured Vance was a lot like Luke. "Did he throw any lamps?" I asked.

I saw Jules relax before she grinned. "No, but he wasn't too happy."

"I'll bet," I said, thinking she got off easy.

"Did Luke throw a lamp?" May asked.

"Yeah, after he caught me with Ren," I told her.

May looked at Jules. "Who acts like that?"

I thought this was a good question, but I didn't share. Instead I said, "Jules, listen, I don't want you in on this operation."

Both Jules and May looked at me. May's eyes narrowed. Jules looked surprised.

"Why? She's The Law. Right now, way I see it, she's the best thing you got goin' for you," May said.

I looked at Jules. "I can't explain it now, but I think Jules understands."

I saw the light dawn on Jules. It didn't dawn on May. Therefore I reckoned May wasn't in on the pregnancy news.

"You can't cut her out of the action just because she made out with your boyfriend," May protested.

In any normal situation, a girl would be obligated to cut out another girl because she made out with her boyfriend.

This, however, wasn't a normal situation.

Still.

I ignored May. It was up to Jules if she wanted to share that I was protecting her because she was pregnant. Instead, I looked for a compromise.

"Can you be the information person? Operate a Command Central? People can check in with you. You can keep tabs on things, where people are, what they've learned. I don't know, that kind of shit?" I asked.

Jules smiled. "I can do that."

"Hang on a second, Jules can drop a guy twice her size. I don't—" May cut in.

"I'll explain it later," Jules interrupted her.

"But—" May went on.

"May, I'll explain it later," Jules repeated.

May looked from Jules, to me, back to Jules.

"You're keepin' somethin' from me," she accused.

"I'll explain later," Jules said again.

"Hon, you better explain later," May snapped, really not happy to be out of the loop, but she said no more and moved away.

Jules and I watched May retreat, then Jules turned to me. "It isn't that I don't want her to know. I just want to be further along before I tell her. I don't want her to get all excited and then... it's just that, I have a history of... if I lose it, I just want Vance and me..." Jules stopped and looked away.

I grabbed her hand and gave it a squeeze.

She looked back at me and said quietly, "Thank you for keeping it a secret. There aren't many of those in this tribe."

I'd noticed that.

Instead of answering, I pulled on her hand to bring her closer and I hugged her. I hugged her because I was happy for her and Vance. I hugged her because she obviously didn't think I was a screaming dork for my freak out the day before. Lastly, I hugged her because she was proof that Luke had good taste in women and he had settled on me, which said a lot about both of us.

"Is there gonna be lots of huggin' and carryin' on or we gonna get this shit done?" Tex boomed from somewhere close.

I sighed. So did Jules.

We broke our hug and I looked at Tex.

"Let's get this shit done," I declared.

⊰❈⊱

Indy, Ally, Tod and Stevie went to go talk to Brody, a friend of theirs and an employee of Lee's. Apparently he was a computer genius and Lee's hacker. They were going to pump him for any information he had on the Noah Investigation.

Jet, Roxie, Daisy and Smithie went to get provisions, including stun guns, Tasers, pepper spray and handcuffs.

May and Jules went to Jules's house where we were all going to meet later.

Shirleen, Tex, Duke, Sissy and I went to my house so I could get my Range Rover.

We trooped in my front door, Duke first. He stopped dead, barely clearing the doorway from the entrance hall to the living room.

Shirleen slammed into his back, I slammed into Shirleen's back, Sissy slammed into me and Tex boomed, "What the fuck?" from the rear.

"What the fuck is right," Duke growled, staring into my living room.

I looked around everyone in front of me and saw through the doorway that Uncle Vito was sitting in my armchair.

Shit.

What was Uncle Vito doing there? I did *not* need this.

Time to run interference.

"Hey Uncle Vito," I called, pushing my way through, even though Shirleen tried, and failed, to hold me back.

Duke was more successful. His arm wrapped around my upper chest and he hauled me back against his body.

That was when things got worse.

See, first, I forgot for a second (don't ask me how), about my face. Second, I didn't know that Ren was standing by the fireplace, nor did I know that Dom was lounging full out on my couch.

The Zano Family took one look at me and the air in the room went electric.

"Get her outta here," Duke rumbled, feeling the air and pushing me backwards.

Uncle Vito slowly stood and Dom came out of his lounge as Shirleen yanked me back. Unfortunately, Sissy was pushing forward. There was general confusion as we were bumped and shoved, but the confusion got sorted out quickly when Ren and Dom entered the equation.

Ren caught my arm and pulled me out of the fray and fully into the living room. Dom caught Sissy and pulled her in.

I was more worried about Dom getting to Sissy. I was even more worried when the electricity ratcheted up to radioactivity when Dom got a look at the fading purple marks under Sissy's eyes.

"Dominic," Uncle Vito said in a low, warning tone as Dom prepared to go berserk.

"Look at me," I heard Ren order.

Oops.

I forgot Ren had hold of me. I looked at him. I just had a chance to notice we had nearly identical cut lips (for some reason his looked sexier, which I found pretty fucking unfair) when the radioactivity in the room became highly unstable.

"I'm gonna fuckin' kill him," Ren whispered.

"Lorenzo." Now Uncle Vito was saying Ren's name in a low, warning tone.

"We been at this half an hour and already things are out-of-control," Duke grumbled.

I ignored Duke and focused on Ren. "It's okay, Ren. Everything's fine."

Ren's hands came to either side of my neck and his thumb gently pressed into the underside of my chin. His eyes were on the tear on my lip and his face was tight.

"I'm gonna fuckin' kill him," he repeated.

"Really, it's okay," I said. "Luke's looking for Noah. We're looking for Noah—"

Oops again.

Clearly I'd made an incorrect assumption because Ren's head gave a jerk. His eyes came to mine and they narrowed. I'd surprised him.

"Stark didn't do that to you?" Ren asked.

It was my turn to have my head jerk.

"Of course not," I snapped, sounding exasperated.

"*Dexter* did that to you?" Ren's voice was trembling with fury.

"What in *the* fuck?" Dom asked from somewhere else, but I knew he was talking about me.

I didn't know what was worse than unstable radioactivity. Perhaps it was the sun exploding, which had to be the power of what it felt like the room was preparing to do.

"You wanna step back?" All of a sudden Tex was at our side and he wasn't asking a question. Ren's body didn't move but his head turned. He didn't step back and his hands didn't move from me.

"No," was all he said, but you could tell he meant it.

"Fair warnin'. You step back or I'll fuckin' make you step back," Tex boomed.

"Please, don't—" I started.

"Lorenzo, son, step back," Uncle Vito demanded from behind Ren.

Ren and Tex continued their staring contest.

"Lorenzo, I want to hear what Ava has to say. I'm askin' you, step back," Uncle Vito pressed.

Ren's eyes came back to mine, then they dropped to my mouth again. One of his hands moved so his thumb could gently touch the cut on my lip.

His gaze shifted to mine. His eyes were troubled, anger warring with something else, something softer, and quietly he said, "Honey."

This cut through me because I realized, right then, Ren didn't just want to fuck me. Ren liked me. Ren didn't just like me. He *liked* me.

"Ren," I said softly, and I sounded sad. Sad enough for him to understand without me saying it that he didn't have a chance in the world.

He closed his eyes. This cut through me, too. Deeper this time, because he was a good guy and he deserved to be happy. He had just picked the wrong girl. Not that I could make him happy. I was kind of crazy, I had a bad temper and I fibbed a lot. Luckily, Luke "enjoyed" that kind of thing. Regardless, I lifted my hand to his cheek.

"Oh fuck," Shirleen said from somewhere behind me.

That was when the room exploded.

Mainly because, with his usual perfect timing, Luke walked in.

Worse!

Behind him came Lee and Vance.

And no one looked happy.

In a flash, Tex stepped back. Lee and Vance took positions, the heat of the exploding air pressed in, and Luke came at us, eyes on Ren. Ren went still, preparing for attack.

Worse than parking-lot-fistfights-mayhem was about to ensue. I knew it, I felt it and I had to stop it.

I pulled away from Ren and got between him and Luke.

"Luke—" I put my hands up.

Luke collided with them and halted. His eyes flashed to me and they were scorching.

"Get outta my way, babe."

I scrambled for something, anything, to make Luke to calm down.

"He just found out about Noah," I said.

Luke went solid and his brows snapped together. "You told him he touched you?"

Oh fuck.

Fuckity, fuck, fuck, *fuck*.

"*Touched* her?" Ren said low from behind my back.

Oh *fuck*.

Fuckity, fuck, fuck, FUCK.

Luke's eyes moved to Ren for a beat then they came back to me. He searched my face, then his gaze dropped to my hands on his chest and then, for some reason, I felt his body relax.

I had a moment of relief before it was swept away. Because, for some ungodly reason, Luke shared, totally open and brutally honest.

Luke looked at Ren as his arm slid around my waist, pulling me to his side. "Yeah, he touched her. He beat the shit out of her. Duct taped her to a steel support in her basement. Put his fuckin' hand down her pants and dry humped her. Then he left her in the dark for hours before we found her."

Ee-yikes.

"You have *got* to be shittin' me," Dom snarled, and I peeked around Luke to look at Dom. His arm was around Sissy's neck and his face was red. Sissy's face was pale, as, I suspected, so was mine.

Apparently Dom had forgotten that, days earlier, he'd stun-gunned me and tried it on with me in the back of his BMW.

However, even I had to admit that wasn't as bad as what Noah did.

I shifted fully to Luke's side and his arm curled around my neck. I chanced a glance at Ren and saw he was studying his shoes, one of his hands at the back of his neck, the other one at his waist. This was a different position of masculine reflection, and I figured Noah's luck, already short, had run out.

But it was Uncle Vito who spoke next, and his voice was Scary with a capital "S".

"No one fucks with family."

Okay, so it was actually *now* when Noah's luck ran out.

"I'm not family," I protested.

Ren's head came up. His hand at his neck dropped and his eyes locked on mine.

"You're family." His voice was terse.

"I'm not," I repeated.

"You're family," Dom snapped.

"No, really—" I started.

"Ava, Sissy is family, and since you're Sissy's family, like it or not, in a roundabout way, that makes you a Zano. And no one fucks with a Zano," Uncle Vito declared.

Hell and damnation.

"You get him, I want him," Luke said, and I looked up at him.

It was then I realized why he shared. It was then I knew he trusted that I could hack it if he shared. It was then I knew that he knew Ren didn't just want to fuck me, but he had feelings for me, deep ones. It was then I realized Luke knew how *all* the Zanos felt about me. And finally, it was then I realized Luke was using the Zanos to get what he wanted. Payback on Noah.

It was actually really clever in a manipulative and annoying way.

"Hang on a second——" I started.

"Done," Uncle Vito agreed.

My heart stopped beating and I looked from Uncle Vito to Luke and back again.

"Wait——" I started again.

Luke talked over me. "Ava's activated the Rock Chicks," Luke surprised me by informing my now not-so-secret plan to the Zanos (how did he know *everything?*). Ren, Dom and Uncle Vito looked at me, and Luke went on, "I know enough to know I'm not gonna be able to control her, or any of 'em. I want him found before they find him."

Uncle Vito looked to Lee. "Your brother and Chavez involved in this?"

"Not officially," Lee answered.

Uncle Vito smiled a scary smile. My heart clenched an unhappy clench. Shit!

"Everyone, can we just——" I started, yes *again*, then Luke interrupted me.

He turned to Tex and Duke. "You keep her protected. Something happens to her, I hold you responsible."

"What the fuck you think we're doin' alignin' ourselves with the girls rather than the hunt?" Tex boomed, clearly affronted.

Luke ignored him and looked at Dom. "Your shit sorted?"

"Not exactly, but this takes precedence," Dom answered.

"Damn straight," Duke agreed.

"Once this is over, we need a family meeting," Uncle Vito cut in and his eyes moved between Sissy and me. "That's why we came here. Dominic wants to talk to Sissy. Lorenzo doesn't agree, and I've allowed him in on the meet.

Ava, you want in and Sissy wants you there, you can be there, too. I'm presiding."

I looked at Sissy. If anything she looked even paler. We both knew that Uncle Vito presiding meant Sissy was screwed.

"I want Ava there," Sissy said.

"Ava's there, I'm there," Luke announced.

Oh crap.

"You're not family." Ren had clearly had enough.

"Ava's not anywhere near you unless I'm with her," Luke replied.

This made Ren smile.

Oh *fuck.*

"Boys—" I started, yes, again, to be interrupted, yes, *again.*

This time, it was Uncle Vito.

"All right, I'm done with this," he declared and his eyes came back to me. "I want you with Lorenzo. Not only do you look good together, you two are a couple, that means you'll be in the family officially and I don't lose my Thanksgiving euchre partner. Anyway, you'd make a good mama, give Lorenzo lotsa babies. You got the hips for it."

Luke went still beside me at the very mention of Ren and my "lotsa babies" and the thought of Ren anywhere near my hips, but I was too busy rolling my eyes to the ceiling to deal with Luke's reaction.

Seriously, how much could a girl take?

Uncle Vito went on, "You got something serious going with Stark, say it now or we gotta have a different kind of family meeting."

My eyes went away from the ceiling and moved to Uncle Vito. Then they went to Ren and I felt my face go soft.

"Luke and I have something serious," I said quietly.

"Fine. That's done," Uncle Vito replied, and even though he didn't look happy, I could tell he was going to let it go.

Ren wasn't so prepared to let it go. "You fuck her over, you got trouble," he said to Luke.

Luke didn't respond.

"Yeah, we're not goin' through this Noah shit again," Dom threw down.

"Oh for goodness sake," I snapped when Luke, who had again relaxed beside me, got tense and his gaze cut to Dom.

"Shut up, Dom," Ren said before Luke could respond.

"I'm just sayin'—" Dom said to Ren.

"Yeah, right. You were just sayin'. Let's talk about when you pulled me back from goin' after Dexter after he fucked Ava over. I nailed him then, this shit wouldn't have happened and Ava wouldn't have got hurt," Ren shot back.

Ho-ly *crap*.

Ren wanted to go after Noah when he fucked me over? That was huge.

Luke, already tense, went solid and my body copied his reaction.

"Well, I didn't think—" Dom started.

"You never think," Uncle Vito threw in. "You hadn't talked Lorenzo outta that shit months ago, he'd be the one with his arm around Ava's neck right now and Angela would be callin' Father Paolo about Catholic classes," Uncle Vito looked at me. "You're in the family officially, you gotta turn Catholic. Just warnin' you in case it don't work out with you and Stark."

I could feel Luke preparing to go gonzo when I heard Shirleen say, "I would think this was fuckin' hilarious, standin' around chatting about fuckin' Catholic classes, but there's a shithead out there and we're givin' him plenty of time to get away after he put his hand down my girl's pants!"

When she stopped talking, she was shouting. One thing you could count on, that was Shirleen bringing the matter to hand.

"Luke," Lee said, and he and Vance moved toward us.

Thankfully, I figured this meant the latest drama was at an end.

"Right," Luke muttered, and tore his angry gaze away from Uncle Vito and looked at me. "I came by to tell you not to do anything stupid because I know you're gonna do somethin' stupid."

"I am *so* sure," I snapped, unable to stop myself.

He curled me so I was facing his body. "Whatever the day brings, babe, at the end of it, we're together. Got me?"

That took the wind out of my sails, mainly because I liked what he said.

"Well then, okay." I still sounded kinda bitchy, but my heart wasn't in it.

"I don't like what you're doin', but enough time has been wasted so there isn't any left to argue about it," Luke told me.

I nodded.

"You wanna stay at the hotel again?" he asked.

I shook my head. "I think we should stay here. I don't want to be scared of my own house."

It was his turn to nod. His face started to get soft and his eyes warm and I was relieved he understood. Then he bent his head and touched his mouth to mine.

"Stay close to Tex, Duke or Jules," he said, face still close.

"Jules isn't, um… working in the field during this operation," I mentioned, my eyes slid to Vance. I bit the uninjured part of my lip and looked back at Luke. "You… erm… know why. Jules and I decided she's in charge of Command Central."

The angry went out of Luke's face and body.

"Ava babe," was all he said, but he said it in The Voice and my knees wobbled.

"Luke," Lee pressed, still standing close and breaking the moment.

Luke didn't look at Lee as he said to me, "Gotta go."

I nodded again.

"Stay safe," he finished.

Then he touched his mouth to mine and was gone.

Vance stopped at me before he took off. I held my breath as, blank-faced but eyes intense, he reached out, took a lock of my hair and tugged it.

Then he was gone, too.

I let out my breath.

Dom led Sissy to my side, his eyes on my closed front door.

"You give Stark that hickey?" Dom asked me.

Oh shit, not the hickey again.

I turned to glare at him, but he just grinned at me.

"Nice," he said, nodding slowly.

That was when Sissy pulled out from his arm and punched him in the stomach.

"Now that's what *I* call nice," Tex boomed.

I burst out laughing.

"The family meeting is gonna be interesting," Duke noted, a huge smile on his face as he looked at a doubled over Dom. Sissy stood beside him, hands on hips, wearing the Sissy Glare.

Ren ignored this, He approached, pulled me into his arms and held on tight.

"Been wanting to do this since you walked in," he said quietly in my ear.

I sighed, deep and huge, mainly because I just realized that Ren gave good hugs.

After a while, I told his neck in a soft voice. "You know, you shouldn't be hugging me."

"I know, and I don't give a fuck," Ren replied.

Oh well, Luke was gone, just this once. My arms went around him and I squeezed.

"You're a good guy," I whispered.

"Yeah. Too good. I wanted to give you time after Dexter. You needed it. I shouldn't have given it. I should have moved in."

He was right. He should have moved in. However, if he had I wouldn't have had my chance with Luke. There was no way to tell if Ren and I would have been better or worse so there was no reason to dwell.

"Could I talk you into handing Noah over to the police if you catch him?" I queried.

Ren's head came up. He looked me in the eyes then he shook his head.

"You're going to hand him over to Luke?" I asked.

Still silent, Ren nodded.

"Men," I sighed.

Ren's hand came up and he touched the cut on my lip. His eyes got scary angry for a brief flash before he hid it.

"Be safe, Ava," he said gently, and finished, "Be happy." Then he pulled away and nodded to Dom. "Let's go."

"Sissy—" Dom started.

"Save it for the family meeting," Sissy snapped.

"Sis, baby," Dom tried again.

"Save it!" Sissy repeated, this time on a hiss.

"Save it, Dominic. Yeesh, you give me heartburn," Uncle Vito broke in, patting his heart with his hand. "Been givin' me heartburn for years. Lorenzo, when you're head of this family, beware, it comes with heartburn. Now, let's go."

Eek.

Ren's future included Head of the Zano Family. Thoughts of me in pressed slacks and flouncy blouses doing lunch with the ladies in between Botox injections paraded through my head. I had to admit, I was pretty glad I had dodged *that* bullet.

"Don't even think about it," Ren muttered, close and bent low to my ear. "I become head of the family, first order of business is have Dom whacked so no heartburn. Second, buy a house on St. John where we would live for half the year, drinking rum for breakfast and fucking under the stars."

His head came up. I blinked at him. He smiled at me and it was an ultra-sexy smile.

My heart started racing.

Uncle Vito led the way and then *they* were gone.

"Now, can we get to the business of findin' this jerk-off?" Tex asked impatiently, looking like he was about ready to come out of his skin.

"You okay?" Sissy asked, voice filled with concern.

No, I wasn't okay. All of a sudden, my mind was filled with having sex with Ren under a warm, balmy, tropical, starry night and they were happy thoughts.

If Luke knew, he'd have a shit fit.

"Yeah," I lied, taking in her pale face. "You okay?"

"Yeah," she lied back.

We looked at each other a beat then, even though there was nothing funny and definitely nothing happy about our situation, just because we'd survived yet again, we grinned.

Chapter 25
Barlow Bitches from Hell

"Shee-it, Kumar, you had the left bower? Why didn't you take the second trick with that motherfucker?" Tex boomed across my dining room table at poor Mr. Kumar who was *not* getting the hang of euchre.

Uncle Vito, who was sitting across from me, chuckled and winked. We had won five games in a row as partners.

"I don't understand this bower business," Mr. Kumar complained. "How can a jack be higher than an ace? How can only one card of a different suit be the same as another suit? Then jacks are just jacks when they are another color? Then it all changes on the next deal of the cards? This game is too confusing."

Shirleen walked into the dining room from my kitchen carrying a fresh iced tea. "Of course it's confusing. First off, you're only playing with half a deck. Any card game that you play with half a deck has to be half-assed."

Uncle Vito and Tex cut their eyes to Shirleen.

Uh-oh.

"Euchre is the *only* card game worth a shit. It ain't half-assed," Tex declared.

"Give me poker any time," Shirleen retorted.

"I know poker," Mr. Kumar put in hopefully.

"Poker is a common game," Uncle Vito threw down.

Shirleen's eyes narrowed.

Hell and damnation.

"I'm going to bed," I announced, getting up from the table.

"You can't go to bed, it's best out of eleven," Tex protested.

I stared at Tex. "In the beginning, it was best out of three, then it was five, then it was seven, then nine, now eleven?"

"We have to win *one*," Tex told me.

I looked at the ceiling.

"Girl, get outta my way. I'm gonna kick the shit outta this euchre business. Kumar, you be Vito's partner. Tex and I are gonna whup some euchre ass." Shirleen shoved me out of the way and pulled Mr. Kumar out of his chair.

I took my opportunity and headed toward the stairs. "Don't be too loud. I can't sleep with noise," I said over my shoulder.

"Only sound you'll be hearin' is Vito goin' *down*," Shirleen informed my back.

I just stopped myself from laughing before I walked up the stairs.

No way Uncle Vito was going down in euchre. Tex might be from Indiana, in his words "the spiritual home of euchre", but nobody beat Uncle Vito.

Nobody.

Even if he was saddled with Mr. Kumar as his partner.

I got ready for bed.

Well, today wasn't as fun as I thought it would be, Bad Ava groused.

Are we giving up? Good Ava asked hopefully.

"No," I told the mirror as I slathered on moisturizer.

Oh poo, Good Ava snapped.

Yippee! Bad Ava yelled.

Needless to say, the Rock Chicks operation was a bust.

Lee had gotten to Brody first, therefore when the Rock Chicks interrogated him, Brody hadn't talked under threat of certain torture from Lee (read: losing his "bodacious" job).

So we started by going to Noah's old apartment, but he was long gone. We spread out, "canvassing the neighborhood" (as Indy called it), knocked on some doors, but only one person was home and they didn't know anything.

Jules at the Command Central made some calls and found out who the landlord of the property was. She called him and asked about Noah, but there was no forwarding address.

We trekked back to my place. I dug out my address book and called all of Noah's friends (there were two), but neither of them had the same phone numbers.

Then we swung by several of the places Noah used to hang out, but no one had seen him in months and no one knew where he was now.

Out of options, Indy, Roxie, Jet and Jules promised to "pump" their men for information and I went home with Tex as bodyguard and Shirleen for company. Uncle Vito came over to see how I was doing, and not long after he arrived Mr. Kumar showed up for the same reason.

Euchre ensued. The rest was history.

I put on a kelly green camisole and a pair of chocolate brown, drawstring pajama shorts with big green polka dots and got under my covers.

I picked up the phone and called Luke.

"Yeah?" he answered.

"Hey," I said.

"I hear the Rock Chicks called off the bad guy search for the night."

"We're not giving up," I told him.

"Run out of leads?"

We had. Or, more to the point, we never had any leads and we just ran out of ideas.

Still, he didn't have to sound so happy about it.

"We'll get more leads tomorrow."

I heard his soft laugh.

Jerk.

"Since you aren't here, I'm taking it you haven't found him yet, either," I noted.

"I'll get him."

The way he said that gave me a shiver up my spine.

New subject.

"Are you hunting all night or are you coming to my place?"

"I'll be there."

"When?"

"Soon."

"When's soon?"

"Soon is soon."

"Luke."

"Babe."

Silence.

Stalemate.

I broke the silence. "All righty then, just wake me up when you get home."

"Why?"

"I want to know you're safe."

"You want me to fuck you."

For goodness sake.

So he was right. He didn't have to point it out.

"Who's full of himself tonight?" I asked.

"Someone's gonna be full of me tonight." He used The Voice and its edge was smooth as velvet.

That got a belly melt.

"I'm tired," I told him, ignoring the belly melt and The Voice. "I'm going to sleep."

"Sweet dreams."

I could hear the smile in his voice before I heard the disconnect.

Then I heard Tex boom, "Shee-it, Shirleen."

I turned off the light and settled under the covers with a smile on my face.

Funnily enough, I didn't feel scared at all of my house.

***

I felt my body roll and it wasn't me rolling it.

Then I felt hands roaming.

"Hey," I said sleepily as Luke's 'tache hit my neck, his lips coming with it.

"Babe, you want me to fuck you when I get home, it's a good idea not to go to bed with so many clothes on," Luke told my neck.

"It's just a camisole and shorts."

His hands went into the camisole. Up, and then it was gone.

"It's just shorts," I corrected.

I felt him smile against my mouth before he kissed me.

"Was anyone here when you got here?" I asked when our lips disengaged.

"Tex, watchin' a movie. Shirleen was crashed on the couch. They both left when I got in."

I felt warmth spread through me and it didn't all have to do with Luke's hands and mouth.

"They're good people." I was talking to his throat at the same time I was discovering the fact that he was naked. I took advantage and ran the tips of my fingers over his tight ass.

"The best," Luke replied, then his hand came under my chin, tilted my head up and he kissed me again.

After he kissed me, I wasn't in the mood to talk anymore.

So we didn't.

***

My body was rolled, my torso pulled up and I opened my eyes as Luke shifted me into his lap.

He was fully dressed, and either it was a gray day (not many of those in Denver) or it was early dawn. I guessed (correctly) it was early dawn.

"What's going on?" My voice was scratchy with sleep.

"I want a kiss before I go," Luke replied.

I squinted at him. "Where are you going?"

"Shit to do."

I came fully awake. I did not *think* so.

Time to try a new tactic in order to save Luke from doing something that could land him in prison.

I cuddled into him and slid my arms around his waist.

"Stay here with me." I was working the sleepy voice, hoping it would have an effect.

His hand went up my back and into my hair, twisting it gently in his fist.

I thought I was getting somewhere, but he said, "Sorry, babe."

Shit.

"I'll make you breakfast," I tried again.

He shook his head.

"I do a great frittata with bacon and cheese."

He gave me a sexy half-grin, but kept shaking his head.

"Pancakes?"

More shaking of his head.

"Waffles?" I kept going.

Now it was his body shaking, with laughter.

Crap.

Crapity, crap, crap, *crap.*

Time to pull out all the stops.

I pressed close and put my lips to his neck and ran them up the side until my mouth was at his ear.

"I'll do my punishment," I whispered and his body went still.

Now I knew I was getting somewhere.

I pulled his tee out of his cargos, slid my hands inside and up the muscles on his back. My mouth moved around, lips on his jaw until they were against his. Our eyes caught. We were ultra-close and I saw his were ink.

Yep, definitely getting somewhere.

"You can watch," I said low, my heart beating fast, half hoping he would say no, half excited about the possibility that he would say yes.

"Fuck," he muttered, and I was pretty certain I had him.

That was why I smiled.

He saw the smile. His eyes went molten and he repositioned me so I was straddling him.

I sucked in breath, thinking he was taking me up on my offer and not wanting me to touch myself while straddling his lap. At the same time I was pretty fucking turned on about the idea of touching myself while straddling his lap.

One of his hands cupped my ass, the other one stayed in my hair and tilted my head down to his.

"Babe," he said.

"Yeah?" I breathed.

"You scared?" he asked softly.

I licked my lips and nodded.

"But you'd do it anyway?"

I nodded again.

"Would you do it even if you weren't tryin' to manipulate me into not doin' somethin' you don't want me to do?"

He knew my game.

I wasn't surprised. First, he knew everything. Second, I was being pretty obvious.

I thought about it a beat. Then, a bit more hesitantly, I nodded again.

His eyes dropped to my mouth and he muttered, "My beautiful Ava."

I tremor shot through my body at his words and he kissed me, hard, long, wet and very, *very* nice.

When he stopped kissing me, I was deep in a Luke Lip Fog and his hand slid from my ass up my spine.

"Tonight," he whispered. "I want you right here, but with my cock inside you, while you make yourself come. Right now, beautiful, as much as it kills me, I'm gonna find Dexter."

That cut through The Fog.

"Luke."

"I know you think you're protectin' me, but I told you, this is somethin' I gotta do."

"Luke."

He ignored me and carried on, "My woman is sittin' in my lap with a torn lip and a black eye. This is not just about revenge. It's about sendin' a message."

My body started getting tight.

"Luke."

His arms moved to wrap around me. "Beautiful, I want everything you offered this morning, but I can't enjoy it until I know you'll be safe. What I do puts you out there. Anyone who thinks to fuck with you has got to understand there'll be consequences. What I'm doin' will make you safe."

"You can't guarantee that."

"I can sure as fuck try."

My body finished getting tight and I glared at him.

"This is who I am," he told me.

"I don't like it," I retorted.

He half-grinned again. "Yeah, you do."

How unbelievably arrogant.

"No, I don't," I snapped.

The grin went full-fledged. "Babe."

I tried to pull away. His arms went tight.

"Let me go," I bit out.

"Not gonna happen."

I went back to glaring and Luke burst out laughing. "One thing's certain, life with you is never gonna be boring," he informed me.

He said that like he wasn't sure it was a good thing, but he was looking forward to it anyway.

If I wasn't naked, I would have put my hands on my hips. Instead, I tried to pull away again.

His hand went back into my hair. He tilted my head down and he kissed me. I fought it for a few beats, lost the fight and kissed him back.

When he stopped kissing me, he was back to grinning. "Try not to do anything today that'll get you in trouble."

"*You* try not to do anything that will get you incarcerated," I shot back.

He laughed again (the nerve!), touched his lips to mine, shifted me aside then he was gone.

I know you don't like it but I think he's sweet for wanting to protect us, Good Ava shared.

It isn't sweet, it's HOT, Bad Ava chimed in.

Yeesh, Bad Ava thought everything was hot.

I crawled under the covers and fell back to sleep.

⚡

The phone ringing woke me up.

I rolled and nabbed it off the nightstand.

"Yo," I muttered.

"Babe."

Obviously, it was Luke.

I got up on an elbow. "Please tell me you aren't calling from a police station."

He laughed like what I said was extremely funny (which I thought it was *not*) then said again, "Babe."

"What?"

"Ma called. She showed up at the loft again, wants to take us to breakfast. I told her I couldn't go, but she could take you. She's heading to your place now."

I shot into a sitting position.

"Excuse me?" I asked.

"She'll be there soon."

"I can't go to breakfast with Mrs. Stark. The girls and I have plans."

"You gotta go. She's lookin' forward to it."

Shit!

I knew what he was doing. He was stopping me from searching for Noah like I had tried to do with him earlier that morning.

And he was better at it.

"I cannot believe you," I snapped.

"Ava babe, you were sleeping. If you were all fired up to find Dexter you would be hunting. It's just breakfast. You and the girls can go after Dexter when you're done with Ma."

"Call her back, tell her I have plans."

"Can't. She would be disappointed. I don't like to disappoint her and I get the impression she wants time just with you."

Mrs. Stark wanted time just with me? This was not good. In fact, this freaked me way the hell out.

"Call her back," I repeated, then I heard a knock on my door. "Shit!" I cried. "She's already here."

"I'll make it up to you," he told me as I jumped out of bed and started searching for my clothes.

"Impossible."

"Nothing's impossible."

"No, Luke, mark my words. *This* is impossible. I'm seriously pissed at you."

"Ava."

I pulled on my panties the phone in the crook of my neck. "You're lucky I'm even speaking to you right now. Get ready. Once we're off the phone this episode bought you at least forty-eight hours of the Ava Barlow Silent Treatment."

"Jesus, you're cute when you're pissed," he said, and he sounded like he meant it.

Argh!

Without another word I yanked the phone from my ear, pressed the off button and threw it on the bed. Then I pulled on my camisole and pajama shorts, rammed my glasses on my nose and ran downstairs.

I threw open the door and stared. Mom, Marilyn and Sofia were standing on my doorstep.

What... the... *fuck?*

"Oh my God!" Mom shrieked. "What happened to your face?"

Shit.

"Mom—" I started.

"Did Lucas Stark do that to you?" Marilyn asked, staring at me as she opened my screen door.

"Of course not," I replied, pissed that she would think that, and having a sinking feeling that she invoked Luke's name.

They knew.

"How did your face get like that?" Sofia asked, pushing in behind Marilyn, all of them shoving forward, all of them carrying suitcases.

Okay, it was so official, it could be written on a tablet of stone.

My life *sucked*.

"What are you guys doing here?" I asked, trailing them into the living room.

"Ava, don't change the subject. How did your face get like that?" Mom snapped.

We were standing in my living room. They had dropped their bags and they were all staring at me. All of them looked glamorous, dressed to the nines with glossy two hundred dollar hair styles, designer clothes, handbags that cost the moon and stars and faces made up as if they had just bought a session at the MAC counter.

Hell and damnation.

"I have a situation," I said, sounding like it was nothing. "I'm sorting it out."

Me, Luke and half of Denver.

"Now," I continued, sticking to my earlier theme. "What are you doing here?"

"Josie Stark called, said she had breakfast with you and Luke and that you two were seeing each other," Mom told me, sounding put out. "She said it looked serious."

Ee-yikes.

Mrs. Stark thought it was serious. It was, of course, serious. However, a week ago, it wasn't supposed to be.

"She was pleased as punch," Mom went on, now sounding extremely put out, which, for my Mom, was a very bad thing. "What I want to know is why am I hearing this from Josie Stark? Why didn't my own daughter tell me this news?"

"Mom—"

"Are you dating Luke?" Marilyn asked before I could formulate an answer to Mom.

"Marilyn—" I started again.

"I cannot believe *you're* dating Luke," Sofia put in and she sounded incredulous.

Bitch.

I felt my temper rise at the same time I felt like a knife had been plunged into my gut. My eyes moved to Sofia, and as usual, I tried to hide the hurt. Though it wouldn't matter if she saw the hurt, she didn't care and never would.

"Ava. Answer me," Mom demanded before I could say anything to Sofia.

My eyes moved back to Mom. "Why are you here? Why didn't you just phone?"

"We had to see it with our own eyes," Marilyn informed me, sounding like me being with Luke was akin to finding a vision of the Virgin Mary in your morning coffee.

I was saved from having to answer by the phone ringing at the same time we heard a, "Yoo hoo," called from the front door.

Luke's Mom had arrived. Saved by Super Mom Stark.

I fought the urge to grab Mrs. Stark and run screaming from the house. Instead, I walked to the phone and tagged it.

"Yo," I said into the phone, turning and giving a lame wave to Mrs. Stark, who was staring at my family in genteel shock. Then her eyes hit me. She saw my face, the genteel went out of the shock and she stared at me with unhidden concern.

"Yo, girl. We're pickin' you up in twenty minutes," Shirleen said in my ear. "Ally got Brody shitfaced last night and got some info outta him. We got a battle plan."

"Um, I have a situation here," I mumbled, walking into the dining room with the phone as I watched Mrs. Stark greeting my Mom and sisters with warm Mrs. Stark hugs that, if you asked my opinion, they did not deserve. Unfortunately, Mrs. Stark didn't discriminate, not even against Super Bitches.

Shirleen's voice was sharp. "What kind of situation?"

"My Mom and sisters showed up unexpectedly and Luke arranged for me to go to breakfast with his Mom. They're all here and I don't think I can get away."

Silence.

"Shirleen?"

"Shit, that boy is good," she told me, sounding impressed.

He was, and it pissed me off.

"Yeah, and it bought him forty-eight hours of Ava Barlow Silent Treatment," I informed her.

"Not sure that's good retaliation. Luke don't talk much," Shirleen noted.

He might not talk much to other people, but the shit he said to me rocked my world.

"I have to go," I told her.

"No problem. We'll move on the leads we got and we'll keep in touch."

"I'm missing all the fun," I complained, sounding like Bad Ava.

"You find a way to ditch 'em, let me know. I'll come get you."

"Thanks, Shirleen."

"No reason to thank me. I haven't had this much fun in months. Later."

Disconnect.

I turned toward the living room.

"We're all going to breakfast," Marilyn announced, a bitchy smile on her face.

Marilyn had two smiles, fake-sugar-sweet and bitchy. She mostly used bitchy with me. It was clear she was looking forward to this and I didn't take that as a good sign.

"Yeah, that way you can tell all of us what's going on with you and Luke," Sofia chimed in.

I looked for an excuse and my eyes caught their suitcases. "Why don't you check into a hotel first? Then we'll make it brunch," I suggested, thinking that would buy me time to come up with an excuse to ditch them.

"We're staying with you," Mom said, foiling my plan.

I stared.

"Yeah, we have it all figured out," Sofia told me. "Mom can sleep on your futon and Marilyn and I'll sleep in your bed. You can sleep on the couch."

Of course, I'd get the couch in my own damned house.

I didn't have the time, or the energy, to fight the fight. I needed reinforcements. Macho man with a great mustache and tight ass reinforcements.

"I need to take a shower," I said.

"We'll wait," Mom replied.

I looked at Mrs. Stark. She was smiling at me and I could swear she was trying to communicate that it was all going to be okay.

She was *so* wrong.

I ran upstairs, straight to my bedroom. I closed the door, nabbed the phone and called Luke.

"Yeah?" he answered.

"Luke—" I began.

"I thought you weren't speakin' to me," he sounded like he was smiling.

"My Mom and sisters are here."

Silence for a beat then, smile gone from his voice, he asked, "Come again?"

"Your Mom told my Mom that we were together and it looked serious. My Mom gathered the Barlow Bitches from Hell and they all came, in their words, to 'see for themselves'."

"Why the fuck would they do that?"

"I don't know!" I cried, but quietly so my family wouldn't hear. "They're the Barlow Bitches from Hell. Why do they do anything?"

"You sound agitated," Luke pointed out the obvious.

"*Did you hear me?*" I squealed then sucked in a controlling breath before I went on more quietly. "My *Mom* and *sisters* are *here* to *see for themselves* that we're *serious.*"

"Babe, calm down."

"Calm is not an option. I need cookies. I need tequila. I need cookies drenched in tequila. I can barely cope with my family when my life isn't complicated to the point of insanity. But, may I remind you, my life is complicated to the point of insanity!"

My voice was again rising.

He was quiet for a moment then he said, using The Voice, "Ava, you can handle it."

I took a deep breath and replied, hating that I had to admit it, but bottom line, I had to admit it. "I want to say I can, Luke, but I can't. They're going to chew me up and spit me out. They always do."

"Is Ma there?"

"Yes."

"She'll look after you."

"Luke, even Super Mom Stark is no match for the Barlow Super Bitches. You know that."

Another moment of silence then, "I'll be there in fifteen."

I went still and stared at the wall. "What did you just say?"

"Hang on, I'll be there in fifteen."

I kept staring at the wall, completely unable to comprehend the fact that Luke was going to drop the hunt for Noah and come to my rescue.

"Seriously?" I asked.

"A coupla hours ago I told you no one fucks with you. I meant *no one* fucks with you."

Oh… my… God.

"Luke—"

"See you in fifteen."

Disconnect.

I love him, Good Ava told me.

We are SO going to touch ourselves tonight while he's inside us, Bad Ava promised.

There was no time to contemplate payback for Luke's latest demonstration of why he was *The* Best Guy *Ever*. I ran to the bathroom, brushed my teeth, washed my face, put in my contacts, took a quick shower, pulled a comb through my wet hair and slathered peony-scented lotion on my body.

I was rushing back to my room when I heard the front door open and Sofia, Marilyn and Mom all cried at the same exact time with the same exact sickly, sweet girlie voices. "Luke!"

Yuck!

I yanked on jeans, a tight, black tee that said "Harley Davidson Motorcycles' on the front in brown with a sage green horseshoe around the words and sparkly green sequins on the letters. I added a kickass black belt and black flip-flops. Because I was unable to do anything but, I added a massive dose of silver at ears, neck, throat and fingers.

Then I ran downstairs.

The women were sitting drinking coffee and gazing at a still-standing Luke, all but Mrs. Stark, like he was a god fallen to earth. Marilyn and Sofia's looks had the added dimension of openly showing they wanted to rip his clothes off.

I will repeat: my life sucked!

I walked into the room and Luke's eyes cut to me.

"Hey," I greeted.

His eyes dropped to my chest as I approached him. When I was within reaching distance, his arm slid around my waist and he curled me into his side.

"Harleys are sweet, babe, but we're a Triumph family."

Ho-ly *crap*.

Did he just say that?

I looked at him. His eyes were warm and affectionate.

Yep, he just said that.

He kissed my neck, lifted his head, stared in my eyes and murmured, "You smell like flowers."

"Peonies," I told him.

He gave me a half-grin. "Nice," he murmured, using The Voice with the Velvet Edge.

My knees wobbled.

"Oh my God," Marilyn breathed, which was quite a task considering her mouth was hanging open.

"This is lovely," Mrs. Stark cut in, jumping from the couch, looking nearly giddy with happiness. "Now we can all go to breakfast."

"Why does Luke have a gash on his face?" Sofia asked. "Is it the same reason Ava has a black eye?"

"We'll talk about it at breakfast," Mrs. Stark said firmly, happy giddiness fading fast.

"Ma, I can't go to breakfast," Luke told her and my heart clenched.

Shit.

So much for Luke coming to my rescue.

"Oh no! Why not?" Mom asked.

"I thought, you coming by—" Sofia started, but Luke interrupted her. He did this by pinning her with a look that would make Satan himself shiver in the fiery depths of hell.

"I came by for Ava because she's too sweet to tell you what I'm gonna tell you."

Uh-oh.

I had the feeling Luke was in the mood to be brutally honest.

"Luke—" I started, but he kept talking.

"You'll have breakfast and then Ava's got some shit she's gotta do. So I'll answer your questions right now. Yeah, Ava and I are together, it's serious, it's headin' somewhere important, and anything else is none of your business. You don't like that, too bad. You get breakfast with her then she's gotta take off. During breakfast, you'll be nice to her. I hear anything different, you answer to me. Is that clear?"

Yep, Luke was in the mood to be brutally honest.

"How did this happen? When did it happen? How *could* it happen?" Marilyn asked. She was, in the face of the impossible fact of a Luke and Ava (and apparently Triumph motorcycles) togetherness, incapable of being clear she understood Luke's threat.

"It happened because she's Ava," Luke answered like that was all the reason needed, and my knees wobbled again at the same time my throat got tight.

"That would be why I'd think it *couldn't* happen," Sofia said under her breath, but loud enough for everyone to hear.

My body got stiff, but Luke's body got preparing-for-gonzo tense. It was then I realized my "fuckin' sisters" weren't just bitches. They weren't very smart either.

"Sofia," Mom muttered before Luke could retort.

"Sofia," Mrs. Stark cut in at the same time as my Mom and she sounded pissy, something I'd never heard from her before. "What on earth is the matter with you?"

I looked at Mrs. Stark and blinked. She looked unhappy. Not just unhappy but nearly Lucas Stark Gonzo Unhappy.

Wow, definitely pissy and then some.

"Goodness me, we all know they've had something special for years. You act like you didn't grow up and see it like everyone on the block did. Mrs. Weinberg said years ago they would make a sweet couple, and when I told Maggie Regan a few days ago, she said she knew it would happen all along. It's not just me who thinks this is hardly surprising. I just wish it hadn't taken so long."

Mrs. Stark took a deep breath then her eyes moved to her son and she continued.

"As for you, we are not a Triumph *or* Harley Davidson family. I keep telling you, Lucas, motorcycles are dangerous. You're going to give me a stroke, riding around on those things. Now that you've got Ava, you need to think before you race around in your Porsche and on those bikes."

"He's got a Porsche?" Marilyn breathed.

"You've got bikes? Plural?" I asked, staring up at Luke.

"What's with the suitcases?" Luke asked, ignoring Marilyn and my questions, his eyes on the bags, his mind on a topic he obviously thought was slightly more pressing than the varied options for transport that he owned.

"We're staying here," Mom informed Luke.

Luke's mouth went tight.

"Ava's sleeping on the couch," Marilyn shared.

At that, Luke's entire face went tight and he looked at Mom. "Two choices, either I put you women in a hotel or Ava and me go to a hotel."

Mom stared at Luke. "But—"

Luke cut in, "I don't have a lot of time. The one thing I know is, Ava isn't sleepin' on the fuckin' couch. You have to choose. Now."

"Lucas, language," Mrs. Stark put in, and I was pretty certain an hysterical giggle was going to burst forth at Mrs. Stark chiding her son for his language.

"Choose," Luke clipped, and at his tone my giggle died an early death.

"I'm not sure," Mom said, and I could tell she desperately wanted to take Luke up on the offer of a free ride, but thought it might appear rude and greedy in front of Mrs. Stark.

Luke could tell, too.

"You stay here. Ava and me will go to a hotel." He looked down at me. "I get things taken care of, I'll take everyone to dinner tonight. I don't and you don't, I'll arrange for your family to have a nice dinner and you do what you gotta do."

"But we came here to see you and Ava," Mom protested.

"Ava has shit to do," Luke replied.

"We came all this way," Marilyn added.

"Yeah, and you didn't tell Ava you were comin', and I'll repeat. She has shit to do."

"But—" Marilyn kept going.

"Take a close look at your sister then take a look at me. Does it look like we got time to drop everything because you hit town with no notice?"

Ho-ly *crap*, but Luke didn't take any shit. I was impressed more than I was normally impressed.

"What's going on?" Mom asked, eyes narrowing on Luke.

Luke looked at the ceiling. I tore my gaze away from him and looked at Mom.

"I told you," I answered. "I have a little bit of trouble. Luke is helping me and we both are trying to sort it out."

"What kind of trouble?" Mom pushed.

"How many kinds of trouble get you a cut lip and a black eye?" Luke asked, aiming his angry stare at Mom. "There's only one kind of trouble. The bad kind," he finished.

"I'm her mother!" Mom, it was clear, had just lost patience. "Why don't I know what's going on? Not only is her face all banged up, but she's dating *you*, of all people. I mean, that George boy I can see Ava with, but *you?*"

Luke looked at me, not knowing George, and I felt the knife that was plunged in my belly twisting. George was serious history. Pre-weight loss, pre-Rick-Dave-and-Noah, a sweet guy, but a geek and so not in Luke's league it was sad.

The fact that Mom still thought I was out of Luke's league hurt like hell. I'd worked hard to be a Barlow Bombshell, but that was totally lost on her. For the past week, four seriously hot guys had been after me like I was the best thing since sliced bread, but in my head that evaporated. Mom thought me doing the impossible—landing Luke—was bigger news than me being "all banged up", and that was killer.

"George?" Luke asked me.

"Her first boyfriend," Marilyn answered helpfully.

"He wasn't my first boyfriend," I mumbled, even though he kind of was.

"You and George were cute together. He was all snugly soft. Perfect for you," Sofia threw in.

"Snugly soft is right," Marilyn said.

"The soft is right. Dough boy," Sofia giggled

"This is unbelievable," Luke growled low, watching the Barlow Super Bitch Byplay with an angry gaze. I could tell his control was slipping and I couldn't do a thing about it.

"Didn't he pop your cherry?" Marilyn put in and my stomach plummeted as my lungs seized.

Luke went totally still.

Here we go. They had warmed up and were ready to throw down.

"Marilyn!" Mom snapped, not protecting me, more embarrassed that Luke and Mrs. Stark could hear.

"Well, he did," Sofia told Mom.

"That's no reason to share," Mom continued.

"I knew the minute it happened," Marilyn stated, so into the Barlow Super Bitch Fest she ignored Mom, Luke's scary anger filling the room, Mrs. Stark's horrified, furious gaze and me. "He always followed her around like a little puppy. After he nailed her it got worse."

"She probably popped his cherry, too," Sofia told Marilyn and they were now holding a conversation like no one else was in the room.

"Can you imagine?" Marilyn bugged her eyes out at Sofia at the very thought of Dough Boy George and Fatty Fatty Four-Eyes fumbling around popping each other's cherries.

I was back to wanting to run screaming from the house, except I couldn't seem to get my limbs to move.

"Quiet," Luke said, softly but lethally, and all eyes turned to him.

"Lucas——" Mrs. Stark began, but Luke kept talking.

"Your sister is standin' in front of you with a busted lip and a black eye, her man at her side, and you bitches are talkin' about... whatever the fuck it is you're talkin' about," Luke said, his voice vibrating with anger.

"Did you just call us bitches?" Marilyn asked, her eyes wide and her voice filled with offended surprise.

"You act like a bitch, I'll call you a bitch, and you're actin' like a fuckin' bitch," Luke answered.

"Oh my God," Sofia breathed.

"He's kind of a straight-talker," I put in quietly.

"You were men, I would teach you some manners. Though growin' up you never had any, so I don't imagine you'll start now," Luke carried on. "Difference is, back then I wasn't in the position to say what I'm gonna say now. Back... the fuck... down. Ava tells me any more of that shit you just treated us to goes down, you're both out on your asses and you aren't comin' back. Your sister is a memory for you and you two cease to exist for her. Is that understood?"

Marilyn and Sofia stared at him.

"*Is that understood?*" Luke barked.

They jumped at his tone then nodded, as anyone would.

Ho-ly *shit*.

Luke looked at my Mom. "It's up to Ava what she wants to tell you about her troubles. She doesn't feel like sharin', that's her choice. You'll deal with it. I hear you don't, it's not gonna make me happy."

"But——" Mom cut in. She looked confused, shell-shocked and as if she didn't know how to feel.

Luke leaned forward a bit at the waist, and thankfully Mom went quiet.

"Take your daughter to breakfast," Luke ordered in a low warning tone that said he was, quite simply, done. Then he looked at me. "Breakfast doesn't go your way, beautiful, you call me. I'll send someone to get you."

"Okay," I whispered, but I had a feeling breakfast was going to go my way.

His arm got tight and his voice got quiet as he ordered, "Walk me to my car."

Without looking back, we walked to the Porsche. He turned and leaned against it, pulling me between his legs and into his arms.

"Your fuckin' sisters," he swore, his eyes on my house, and I could tell he was still angry.

Kristen Ashley

I leaned into him, putting my hands on his chest. He took in a breath and looked down at me.

"You're like a flower that grew through a crack in the sidewalk," he told me.

I didn't say a word. I couldn't. I'd forgotten how to speak.

"I want you checkin' in," he demanded.

"Okay," I said, finding my voice.

"We would stay at the loft tonight, but—"

"I know," I cut him off.

"After this shit is over, I'll have blinds put in."

"Okay," I repeated.

"You gonna be able to get through breakfast?"

I nodded and told him. "I think I owe you again."

"Yeah. You're rackin' up quite a debt," he bent his head and touched my lips, then his body relaxed and his face went soft. "I like it," he muttered.

For some crazy reason, tears started to fill my eyes and Luke saw them.

"Babe."

I put my hands to either side of his neck. "Thank you."

His arms went tight and his forehead came to mine. "You just paid off this particular debt."

At that announcement, I melted into him.

"You still owe me," he went on.

I smiled because I didn't mind, not one bit. "I think I like it that you protect me," I confided. Don't ask me why, I just did.

It was a good thing to do.

"Ava," he whispered, his face soft, his eyes ultra-warm, his arms getting even tighter.

"No one's done that, not like that. Not even Dad."

"Beautiful—"

"Thank you, Luke."

"You already said that."

"I wanted you to know I meant it."

One of his arms stayed wrapped around my waist, the other hand slid into my hair and his mouth came to mine.

"You're clear," he said against my lips.

"Clear?"

"You just cleared all your debt."

Oh... my... *God*.

"Really?" I asked.

He nodded.

He *was* The Best Guy *Ever*.

"You're still makin' yourself come while I'm inside you tonight."

Oh yeah, I was definitely going to be doing that, *and* I was looking forward to it.

I licked my lips, which meant I licked his lips, and his eyes went ink.

"Fuck, you're somethin' else," he muttered, and I could tell he meant this in a good way—a *very* good way—and happy vibes shot through me.

"You don't think I'm weak and spineless for not standing up to my sisters?"

"Been wanting to say a few things to them for years, so no. I'm fuckin' glad you gave me the opportunity."

I love you, I thought, but did not say.

Something shifted on his face as I thought this, but whatever it was, I couldn't read it. Whatever it was, it was profound, it was raw and it was beautiful.

I could swear he guessed my thoughts and he liked them.

My knees gave out and he took my weight without a word said between us.

After a few beats, my voice sounding husky, I said, "You better go."

"Yeah. Be safe, be smart and don't let them give you any shit."

"Okay," I said again. "Don't do anything I wouldn't do," I told him.

"Babe." He gave me a half-grin, thankfully breaking the moment, right before he touched his lips to mine. I pressed in, my arms sliding around his neck, and his lip touch turned into a full-on make out session.

He let me go, set me on my jelly legs, rounded the car, got in and he was gone.

I walked back into my house and when I got into the living room I knew everyone had been watching.

Mrs. Stark was smiling at me, huge and happy.

Surprisingly, my Mom was, too.

Marilyn and Sofia looked jealous as all hell.

That made *me* smile.

"All righty then," I declared. "Breakfast."

Chapter 26
Manipulate a Macho Man Underwear

Breakfast went my way because Marilyn and Sofia were mostly silent, probably half afraid to say anything, half pouting. Mom was silent, too, at first, but she didn't seem to be pouting, she seemed to be thinking. For the most part, Mrs. Stark and I gabbed and giggled, then Mom joined in and surprisingly I had a great time.

While we were on our last cup of coffee I excused myself and called Shirleen to come and get me. I went back to the table and we left the restaurant (again, Le Peep in Cherry Creek and granola pancakes, without the bacon this time). I gave out hugs to Marilyn and Sofia (you could tell their hearts weren't in it, but then again, neither was mine) and Mrs. Stark (her heart was definitely in it). Marilyn and Sofia wandered away as I gave my house key to Mom.

"I'm worried about you," she told me.

This statement startled me and my eyes caught hers. She looked genuinely concerned and this rocked me, mainly because I'd never seen that look on Mom's face before.

"I'm fine," I told her.

She shook her head then put her arms around me. I went stiff because her hug seemed genuine, too.

"Ava, I want you to know, I didn't mention George because... well, because of the reasons Marilyn and Sofia thought I did," she whispered in my ear. "I mentioned him because he was steady, he cared about you and he would never leave you."

Erm... *what?* My Mom cared? About *me?*

Ho-ly *shit.*

Maybe I *was* in an alternate universe.

I felt my throat get tight. "Mom——"

Kristen Ashley

Her arms tensed and she pulled me deeper into her. She held me for a bit then let me go, but placed her hands on my upper arms and looked me directly in the eyes. Hers were wet. Because of that, mine got wet, too.

Hell and damnation.

"From what I saw today, Luke's the same way. More," she said quietly, and her hands squeezed my arms. "It's obvious he's cut up about whatever's going on with you. I'm glad. Not that he's cut up, but because you need a man who cares that much. I'm happy for you, sweetie."

Oh... my... *God*.

I couldn't help myself. I pulled her in my arms and held on tight while I deep breathed. She did the same thing.

We let go and she touched my face, then said, "I hope Luke gets this sorted so we can have a nice family dinner tonight. I'll talk with Marilyn and Sofia. It'll be okay."

"Thanks, Mom," I replied, and maybe for the first time in my life, I meant it.

She kissed my cheek and then walked to Mrs. Stark, who was looking away but wiping her face, and I knew she had heard. I stood and watched as they went to their cars. Mom and Mrs. Stark stood beside Mrs. Stark's Audi and it looked like they were settling in for a chat.

I left them to it and went to the local Starbuck's, where I had arranged for Shirleen to come and get me, and I got myself a skinny vanilla latte. I decided I would think about this latest life revelation later when I had Sissy and cookies drenched in tequila.

Or, better yet, Luke, a warm bed and a dark room.

That thought made me smile as I walked out of Starbuck's.

Shirleen's Navigator was at the curb. Tex was in the passenger seat and he jumped out when he saw me.

"Hey Tex, did you win any euchre...?" I stopped talking when he snatched my cup right out of my hand and threw it in a trash bin.

"This family don't *do* Starbuck's," he boomed then turned and shouted at Shirleen. "The girl needs coffee! Fortnum's! Now!"

Eek!

The Rock Chicks all met at Fortnum's except Indy and Ally, who were off to some prison to interview one of Noah's friends who'd managed to acquire a five year state accommodated stay.

Ally hadn't gotten "some" info out of Brody. He sang like a canary under the influence of Red Bull and vodka (ee-yikes!).

Unfortunately, Lee and the Hot Bunch knew that Brody wasn't exactly discreet so they hadn't shared much. What they did share was that they'd tracked down both of Noah's buddies. One was in prison, the other one Brody didn't have information on.

Ally also learned that Noah had a gazillion aliases, but the name he was born with was Walter Ellis. He was wanted in Nevada and California and he'd been on the con practically since babydom. For a percentage of the con, Noah's informant (now wiling away his days fashioning license plates and likely shivs) would troll legal records, pointing Noah in the direction of malpractice payoffs and highish stakes inheritances. Nothing too big so as to fly under radar, but nothing too small that wouldn't be worth the effort.

Lastly, Brody shared the name of the lady who Noah had conned while he was conning me. Her name was Winnie Conrad, she was seventy-two and had a spine operation go bad when she was sixty-six which took away the use of her legs. After a years-long battle, she got a payoff for the botched operation which enabled her to buy a decent, handicapped accessible house in a decent neighborhood, as well as augmenting her meager retirement money which allowed her to live, and pay taxes and utilities, in a nicer neighborhood. Noah got his hands on what was left of the payoff, which set her back to scraping by, but somehow she had managed to keep her place.

Jules had done some research from Command Central and discovered Mrs. Conrad's address in Aurora.

Shirleen informed me that the Rock Chicks worked hard on my behalf, pumping their men for information. This didn't work, but apparently they had fun trying. Also, they'd all had fun sharing their escapades over coffee while I was at breakfast. I didn't find any of that hard to believe, but I was pretty pissed I'd missed out on the gossip.

Tex made me a skinny vanilla latte to replace the one he threw out and we hit the road. Jet, Roxie, Smithie, Duke, Tod and Stevie took off to Noah's old neighborhood to knock on some doors. Tex, Daisy, Shirleen, Sissy and I took off to pay a visit to Winnie.

We pulled up to Winnie's and saw she was sitting in a wheelchair on her porch enjoying the sunny, warm day. She was a round black lady, hair recently set, dressed in her Sunday best. She had likely just got home from church. She was drinking an iced tea.

We trundled up and she stared, but then again anyone would stare. Sissy and I had black eyes (Sissy's was fading, but mine still looked angry). Shirleen's afro seemed to have grown two inches in the last week. Daisy's hair rivaled Shirleen's in size and volume, she had five-inch, shiny white, platform go-aheads on her feet and her body was encased in skintight denim with enough rhinestones to supply Celine Dion's wardrobe technician for emergency mending on a concert tour. And finally there was Tex, who looked like a recently reformed serial killer (and that was being nice).

We were undoubtedly not the popular choice for Sunday visitors.

"It's all right, Mrs. Conrad. We may look crazy but we ain't gonna hurt you," Shirleen assured her as we hit the porch.

Winnie didn't look like she believed Shirleen.

"How do you know my name?" she asked.

"We're lookin' for Walter Ellis, AKA Noah Dexter, but I think you knew him as Jeremiah Levine," Shirleen answered.

Winnie sucked in breath. Her kindly face got hard then she muttered, "Jeremiah?"

"Yeah. You know who we're talkin' about?" Tex asked.

Winnie looked at Tex then her eyes scanned all of us. "What now with Jeremiah? I had some boys come talk to me earlier this week about him. I don't know anything and I don't want to know anything. Good riddance to bad rubbish, I say. I haven't seen him in months and I like it that way."

I couldn't blame her.

Shirleen grabbed me and pulled me forward. "See this girl here?"

Winnie nodded, her eyes wide as she looked at me.

"Well, while Jeremiah was rippin' you off, he was also rippin' off my girl Ava. Stole her money and her dead auntie's jewelry. A little while ago she got herself a man who found out this little piece of ugly history. He's the kinda man who doesn't like that shit much and went lookin' for payback. Jeremiah felt the heat, got angry, and a coupla days ago, took it out on Ava. You get what I'm sayin' to you?" Shirleen asked.

The wary hardness went out of Winnie's face. It went soft as she gazed at me.

"Oh honey," she whispered.

"I'm fine," I told her, smiling just to prove my point.

"You don't look fine to me," Winnie said, and I could see the concern in her eyes.

"No, really," I promised quietly.

I got closer and knelt down by her chair.

She looked down at me. "Was it your man who came by earlier this week?"

"Probably," I said.

"Which one was he, the Native American or the one with the mustache?" she asked.

"The mustache," I answered.

She smiled and reached out a hand to me. I took it and she squeezed.

"He's cute. Drives a Porsche, looks good in it, too," she told me then went on. "He's got a great mustache. Most men would look all kinds of fool with that mustache, but he works it real fine. *Real* fine. Seems a good sort. A whole lot better than Jeremiah."

She had that right. *All* of it.

"Right now, he's also kind of angry," I fibbed. It wasn't exactly a lie, more a significant understatement. "After Noah... or, sorry, Jeremiah beat me up a couple of days ago, Luke's payback turned to retribution. I'm trying to find Jeremiah before Luke does and turn him in to the police so Luke won't do anything gonzo and get himself into trouble."

She shook her head and squeezed my hand again. "Seems to me Jeremiah could use someone metin' out gonzo retribution, but I'd hate to see your man get himself into trouble. I'd like to help, but like I said, I haven't seen Jeremiah in months."

"You have an address? Phone number? Did you meet any of his friends? Did he say anything to you that might help us find him?" Daisy asked.

Winnie let go of my hand and looked at Daisy. I stood up and stepped away.

"Like I told those boys that came lookin' for him, I don't know anything. My family tried to find him after he..." Winnie stopped talking and looked away and I could tell she was embarrassed.

I kind of understood how she felt, but I was a white woman with a somewhat hefty inheritance that Noah luckily couldn't figure out how to steal. She was an elderly, disabled black lady living in Aurora, Colorado, *not* a penthouse on Central Park in NYC. You could tell she wasn't exactly rolling in it. What Noah got from her probably cut deep into whatever end-of-life living-in-a-wheelchair safety net she had.

This pissed me off so much, for a moment I considered calling off the Noah chase and letting Luke do whatever Luke was going to do. Then I realized it could mean I wouldn't get to process all my life's complications in a warm bed with Luke lying next to me, so instead I vowed octuple revenge against Noah, rat-bastard.

"This is beginning to tick me off," I announced, crossing my arms on my chest. "We're not getting anywhere. We keep running into dead ends, but they're dead ends that the Hot Bunch moved through days ago. We're never going to catch up. Luke's gonna find Noah and I'm not altogether certain Eddie and Hank are going to keep this whole thing off the radar when Noah turns up with a cap busted in his ass."

"Sugar, Luke ain't gonna be aimin' at Noah's ass," Daisy told me.

"Listen to you, 'a cap busted in his ass'. You're cute," Shirleen said. "I can see why Luke likes you. Outside of the fact you got a great ass, that is. Luke strikes me as an ass man."

She was wrong. Luke didn't discriminate. He was a whole package man.

"I have an idea," Sissy threw in, and everyone looked at her. "You, Indy and Jules lure your boys home somehow. I don't know, pretend you've got flu or food poisoning or something. We'll assign each one of you a buddy. The minute they get close to you in bed, you give the high sign. We'll jump out of a closet, stun gun them and cuff them to the bed. Then we can keep searching, and maybe talk Eddie and Hank into helping us on account of they're cops and will want to do this lawful like."

This was a terrible plan, but I did allow myself a moment to think of Luke cuffed to a bed. It was an intriguing thought.

"I ain't cuffin' Luke to no bed," Tex boomed, tearing me away from my intriguing thoughts. "Fuck, I'm not cuffin' Lee or Vance to a bed, either. Those boys would lose their badass motherfucker minds. I got a girlfriend and fifteen cats. I get tortured and killed, who's gonna take care of Nancy and my kitties?"

I stared at Tex. Tex didn't strike me as the type of guy who had "kitties", much less actually used the word.

"I'm checkin' in to Command Central, see if Jules's got anythin' new," Shirleen announced, walking off the porch and around the house all the while flipping open her cell.

I turned to Winnie and crouched beside her again. "You doing okay? After…erm, Noah—"

Winnie shook her head but said, "Got a large, big-hearted family. They're takin' good care of me."

I smiled at her again, reached out and gave her another hand squeeze. Then I pulled a pen and a stray receipt out of my purse and wrote my name, home and cell numbers on it and handed it to her.

"Your family just got larger. You need anything, even if it's just company, call me."

She took the piece of paper and looked at it then she looked at me. "He got your auntie's jewelry?"

I nodded. "The jewelry didn't mean much, wasn't my style, but Auntie Ella meant the world to me and it was hers and she wanted me to have it. I try not to think about it but it sucks that it's gone."

"Maybe you should let your man do what he's gotta do," she suggested.

I stared at her thinking maybe she didn't just get back from church. The Bible said an eye for an eye, but it also went on about forgiveness being divine. Nothing like mixed messages. Still, even though Luke looked the part of a kick-ass angel of vengeance, I couldn't be totally sure he was God's chosen tool to send Noah straight to hell.

"The thought had crossed my mind," I admitted. Winnie grinned and I went on, "Problem is, Luke moved in across the street when I was eight, which is about the time I fell in love with him. He was always hot, even when he was twelve, but I was fat, had glasses and mousy hair. Didn't matter, he liked me all the same even back then. It took us a while to hook up and I'm not anxious to get unhooked."

It was her turn to nod. "I can see your point."

I got closer. "I'm a little worried Noah, or Jeremiah, or whoever he is, is getting kind of desperate. Who knows what he'll do, but if he finds out we've all looked you up—"

"I'll give my grandchildren a call," she interrupted me. "They'll keep an eye on me."

"Could you check in with me just to set my mind at ease?" I asked.

Her grin went ultra-warm. "Be happy to."

I gave her another hand squeeze just as we heard the deep bass thrumming from a moving vehicle on the street. A shiny, dark blue, older model Lexus with gold trim pulled up in front of the house, seriously loud rap assaulting the quiet neighborhood. The rap cut off and four young black women of varying shapes and sizes, but all dressed and made up as if they were just about to stroll into a club, rolled out of the Lexus.

"Uh-oh," Daisy muttered as she stared at the girls heading up the walk.

I stood up as Sissy asked, "Uh-oh, what?"

The leader of the pack was short, round and had her black hair in big fat ringlets that were bouncing around her head and face. She wore fire engine red lipstick and it looked good on her.

Daisy was moving behind Tex and I didn't get a good feeling about it. Daisy was not the kind of woman who hid without good reason, and I didn't relish finding out what her good reason might be.

"What's going on?" I whispered toward Daisy.

"You! Bitch! I see you!" The ringlet girl was clickety-clacking on her high-heeled, bronze, peek-a-boo toe pumps and she was pointing at Daisy.

What now?

"Think you can stun gun me *twice* then walk away?" Miss Ringlet demanded.

Stun gun? Twice?

Uh-oh was wrong.

Eek! was more like it.

I looked at Daisy and Daisy was done trying to hide behind Tex. She came out in full view and she'd morphed straight to Attitude.

"I didn't stun gun you!" she shouted back. "Indy did, but only after you charged her, and that time I wasn't even there. Then Jet did it, but only after you called Ally a bee-atch and punched me, so I had to take you down."

Eekity, eek, eek, *eek*.

"Olivia Conrad," Winnie waded in. "What you thinkin' waltzin' up to my porch, all attitude? These are my friends."

"Ain't no friends of yours, Big Momma," Olivia answered, having arrived on the porch looking ready for action.

"What's going on?" I asked, and Olivia's eyes swung to me and they got big.

"Shit, girl, what happened to yo' face?" she asked, forgetting her tirade when confronted with the busted up vision of me.

"Noah Dexter beat me up," I told her.

"Noah who?"

"You know him as Jeremiah Levine," I explained.

At my words, Olivia, already ready to blow, pushed the lever up to engage the rocket launchers.

"*That no-good motherfucker beat you up?*" she screeched, and I was pretty certain my eardrums were close to bleeding.

"Duct taped her to a steel post in her basement," Daisy shared, then went ultra-generous with information. "Once he'd taped her, he stuck his hand down her pants, dry humped her and then left her in a basement coal room for hours before one of our boys found her."

Shit.

Olivia's eyes bugged out and all her girls sucked in breath.

"*What?*" she shrieked, and the windows on Winnie's house shook.

"You didn't tell me that last part," Winnie Conrad said from beside me, her voice sounding not sweet old lady who goes to church on Sunday *at all*.

"Well——" I began, turning to Winnie, but I was interrupted.

Olivia turned to Daisy. "What's this got to do with you, bitch?"

"Olivia, girl, watch your mouth," Winnie put in, but Daisy ignored Winnie.

"She's a Rock Chick and I'm a Rock Chick. Rock Chicks look out for each other. We're after Jeremiah, Noah, whoever the hell. And don't call me bitch, comprende?" Daisy answered, her own rocket launchers fired up and blazing, ready to roar.

"I hear what you're sayin', lookin' out for your girl but no one disrespects me," Olivia shot back.

"You punched me in the face. What'd you expect me to do?" Daisy fired her bullet.

"I wasn't aimin' at you. It was a mistake. You got in the way when I was aimin' at your *other* girl. What'd *you* expect *me* to do?" Olivia retaliated.

"I expect you to get over it. It all started when Indy stun-gunned you during a bar brawl and she was protectin' her man by stun gunnin' *your* man and you got all attitude," Daisy carried on.

"What? She got a right to protect her man and I got no right to protect mine?" Olivia asked what I thought was a valid question.

"Your man had skipped bond. Indy's man's a bounty hunter. Sounds to me like your man ain't worth your troubles. Not that I judge what he's gotta do to make a livin'. I just judge the motherfuckers stupid enough to get caught," Daisy retorted.

Hmm, I didn't think that was the right thing to say.

"Tell me you did *not* just say that," Olivia demanded, her head bobbing, her ringlets bouncing.

Yep, I was right, that wasn't the right thing to say.

"Sugar, I said it," Daisy replied.

Everyone tensed.

Time to de-escalate the hostilities.

I went for the sympathy tactic.

"Listen," I put in. "I think Mrs. Conrad and I have been through enough without a catfight between my girls and her girls on her porch. Everyone, please, help us out and stand down."

"We don't got time for this silly-ass girlie shit anyway," Tex boomed. "We got a dickhead on the loose."

The Rock Chick Posse and the Pissed-Off Black Women Posse turned to glare at Tex.

Shit.

Foiled again by Tex being a lunatic.

"Don't look at me!" Tex shouted, if it could be believed, sounding even louder. "Jee-zus, huggin' and cryin' and badass motherfucker showdowns in livin' rooms and takin' a break from the action to have Sunday breakfast with your man's mother, what the fuck? We gonna take a side trip to the mall next or do we want to find this fuckin' guy?"

"Actually, I could use a side trip to the mall," Sissy put in. "I didn't bring enough clothes with me from Wyoming and I don't want to go back to my house. It depresses me."

"What's wrong with your house?" one of Olivia's girls asked.

"Drive by, AK-47 through the living room. It's a mess. All my pottery, dust."

I stared as all of Olivia's girls nodded, accepting this as if Sissy had said her house had been accidentally flooded by the normal, everyday but annoying occurrence of blocked pipes.

"I could go to the mall, too," Daisy added. "Marcus is takin' me out to dinner tonight and I don't have a thing to wear."

A thought hit me and I said, "I need thirty minutes in the lingerie section. Luke and I have special plans tonight."

Tex looked to the heavens. "Lord, forgive me for what I'm about to do."

"What are you about to do?" Sissy asked.

"Wring all you all's necks," Tex boomed back.

"We take Tod and Stevie to the mall with us, we'd be in and out in thirty minutes. Those boys don't fuck around at the mall. They got, like, a different kind of gay-dar," Daisy told Tex. "It's the kind that they can hone in on the best outfit, pair of shoes, or whatever you need, find your size without even askin' and feed you the shit in your dressing room without you havin' to leave it. They don't spare your feelin's either. If it don't look good, they just snatch it from you and find you somethin' else. They could do it in the Olympics, they're so good."

Tex scowled at Daisy, completely unimpressed.

"We have no leads. It wouldn't hurt, a quick stop to the mall," Sissy pointed out and I couldn't stop my smile. Sissy going head-to-head with Tex meant the old Sissy I knew was back. Three weeks ago, Sissy probably wouldn't have had the gumption to say "boo" to Tex.

"What're you grinnin' about?" Tex demanded, his scowl now directed at me. "A second ago, you were thinking of cuffin' Luke to the bed to get ahead of him in this hunt."

"Luke?" Olivia cut in, staring at me. "Big Momma told me Luke Stark paid her a visit this week. We talkin' 'bout Stark here?"

"Yeah," I told her.

Her eyes got big again. "You seein' Stark?"

My smile grew wide. "Yeah."

"Shee-it, girl. I seen him around. I seen him lots. That boy is *fine*. That boy's ass, hon-*nee*, that ass could win awards. You sure bounced back from Jeremiah all right. Good for you," Olivia smiled back.

"Are we goin' to the mall or what?" Daisy asked.

"I could go to the mall," Olivia said.

The Rock Chick party stared at her.

"I could join the hunt for Jeremiah, too. Wouldn't mind takin' that boy down," Olivia went on and then turned to her girls. "He's the one stole from Big Momma."

"Rat-bastard," one of her girls muttered.

"That's what I'm saying," I muttered back and got a bunch of big, white grins.

Shirleen, who'd missed all the action, and not only didn't look like she cared but didn't bother to ask, hoofed up to us.

"We got a situation," she announced and everyone's eyes swung to her. "Smithie's cornered in someone's yard by a couple of German Shepherds. Any of you good with dogs?"

Crap!

This just keeps getting better all the time, Bad Ava took that opportunity to chime in.

Oo, puppies! I love puppies! Good Ava exclaimed.

"I'm good with dogs," Sissy said.

"Right, let's go," Shirleen didn't waste any time. She waved at Winnie and took off toward her Navigator. Everyone followed suit, except I leaned over and gave Winnie a kiss on the cheek, and Olivia gave her a big hug finished with a kiss on the top of her head.

"Be safe," Winnie called after us as we walked through her yard.

"We goin' to find Jeremiah after this dog business?" Olivia asked, following us.

"Yeah, after the mall," I told her.

Daisy pulled up short and gave Olivia a look. "We good?"

Olivia shrugged. "I'm over it. The man took Big Momma's money, she almost lost her house. Fuck that. This hunt takes priority."

"I hear you," Daisy replied.

I could swear I heard Tex growling to the heavens.

"Can I ride with you?" Sissy asked Olivia. "I'm thinking, once I divorce my stupid, cheating husband, I'm going to get a Lexus. I've never been in one, but they're sweet. I'd like to experience the ride."

"Get yo' skinny white ass in there," Olivia answered, which Sissy took as a yes.

Olivia, her posse and Sissy all scrunched into the Lexus, the rest of us shoved into the Navigator. Shirleen pulled out and Olivia tailed us.

"Let me get this straight," Tex boomed from the passenger seat. "Now Dexter has got Lee and his boys, Ava and the girls, the Zano family and four crazy black women after him. Indy and Ally are at a prison on a fool's errand, 'cause that boy ain't gonna talk. Smithie's pinned in a yard by dogs, and after we do a dog rescue, we're goin' to a lingerie department?"

"That's right," Daisy replied.

He blew out a huge sigh. "Shee-it," he muttered (but it still came out as a boom).

⌘

Shirleen hadn't gotten the story exactly right.

Smithie wasn't cornered by two German Shepherds. Smithie was *treed* by two German Shepherds.

By the time we got there, Smithie was perched on a stout limb twelve feet up and the two dogs were at the trunk, snarling and barking so viciously, white slobber was lapping at their doggie lips.

Sissy valiantly tried cooing at them. One of the dogs broke off, still snarling, and chased her to where we all were standing behind a ten-foot chain link fence at the side of the house. She rushed through the gate and Jet threw it closed behind her.

Luckily, the dog preferred Smithie-meat, likely noticing that Sissy didn't have as much juice on her bones, and ran back to the tree.

"Motherfuckers!" Smithie yelled at us. "Do somethin'! I been up here an hour."

"That isn't true. He's only been up there half an hour. Forty-five minutes, tops," Stevie corrected.

"Anyone tried to stun gun the dogs?" Daisy asked.

"You wanna walk up to one of those dogs and stun gun it? I don't *think* so," Tod put in.

"We should have brought Tasers," Roxie said.

"Indy and Ally have the Tasers," Jet reminded her.

"Maybe we should call the fire department," I suggested.

"You wanna explain to the fire department why a black man with no connection to the owners of this house is in their yard?" Duke asked.

"Why *is* he in the yard?" I asked Duke.

"Search me. I was down the block, not gettin' shit about Dexter, by the way, when I got the call from Roxie," Duke answered.

"I think he said he heard something and thought the owners were back here. He came around to talk to them and got caught by the dogs. Though I can't really be sure since he was yelling the story and cursing a lot while he told it, so I didn't follow," Roxie put in.

"Why don't we go buy a few steaks and bring them back? Lure the dogs away," a voice said from behind us, and my body got tense when I recognized it.

I turned stiffly to look, hoping that I was hearing things, and not the usual Good Ava and Bad Ava nonsense, not even caring that it would mean I had finally lost what was left of my mind, and everyone turned with me.

Mrs. Stark and my Mom were standing behind our tribe. It had been Mrs. Stark with the steak idea.

For the second time that day, I had to ask, what... the... *fuck?*

"*What are you doing here?*" I screeched. Yes, I screeched, totally unable to control the shrill in my tone. I'd lost it. I was done. This was too much. I could take no more.

"Who are they?" one of Olivia's girls (earlier she had been quickly introduced as Rhonda) asked.

"Hello. I'm Josie Stark, Luke's Mom. And this is Christine Barlow, Ava's Mom. Pleased to meet you," Super Mom Stark came forward and started shaking hands and bestowing warm smiles on everyone as if she was at a church mixer.

Everyone shook her hand, but they all continued to stare at her.

"You're Luke's Mom?" Shirleen asked, staring wide-eyed with wonder at Mrs. Stark.

I wasn't surprised at her reaction. Luke seemed more the type to explode fully formed out of a pit of blistering lava, not spring from the loins of a woman with a conservative hairstyle, low-heeled, faultlessly-shined, bone-colored pumps and sporting a short-handled, matching-bone-colored purse two steps up from a granny bag.

"Sure am," Mrs. Stark stated proudly.

"I love this!" Daisy squealed and then giggled her tinkly-bell giggle. Jet, Roxie and Shirleen were grinning at each other huge, and I feared they were about to join in on the giggles.

"Um…" I cut in before hilarity could ensue. "Again, can I ask, what are you doing here?"

Mom and Mrs. Stark were warily looking Tex top-to-toe, obviously not certain what to make of him.

Mom tore her eyes away from Tex first. "Well, Josie and I were talking. We're both worried about you. So we sent Marilyn and Sofia to the mall and we decided to follow you. Make sure you were okay."

"What?" I asked, even though I heard her answer. I just didn't want to believe it.

"I know it's none of my business," Mrs. Stark, obviously not hearing me or deciding not to answer, turned to Olivia. "But you're a pretty girl. I like your lipstick. It's the perfect color for you. You have a lovely grandma. A girl like you, well, she shouldn't be out with a boy who has bounty hunters after him. I don't know you, but I'm a mother and I'm pretty good at sizing people up, and one look at you, I know you could do better."

Mom looked at me. "We listened at the side of Mrs. Conrad's house. You were wrapped up in things, didn't see us." Her eyes got soft. "Ava, sweetie, I had no idea. Your troubles."

Fuck.

Fuckity, fuck, fuck, *fuck*.

"I'm fine, Mom, honest. I'm over it," I assured her and turned my attention back to Super Mom Stark. I wasn't certain Olivia Conrad was the kind of girl who liked anyone getting into her business, especially middle-class, white Super Moms. I thought that might be more pressing at this juncture than Mom finding out I was conned, beaten up and violated by a total jerk. I would deal with Mom later. "Mrs. Stark——" I started.

"That Louis, he was no good," Rhonda told Olivia, I thought unwisely. "I was always sayin' you should cut him loose."

"Mm-hmm," Olivia's other two girls, Tamika and Camille, murmured their affirmation in unison.

"Well, I loved him," Olivia defended herself.

"You loved his big dick," Camille put it then she looked sheepishly at Super Mom Stark. "Sorry, but it's true."

Kristen Ashley

"Sex is not love," Mrs. Stark declared sagely.

"If it's good nookie then it's close enough," Shirleen muttered under her breath.

I stared at them, stunned speechless at the fact that Mrs. Stark seemed to be intent on holding an impromptu woman's talk show on a stranger's lawn. The dogs were barking, Smithie was up a tree and Tex looked like the kind of guy *no one* wanted loitering around the neighborhood. I was pretty certain it was dumb luck that the police hadn't already descended on our party. I was also pretty certain that dumb luck wasn't going to hold out.

Before I could intervene, Duke did.

"Time for the honesty," he growled, looking, scarily enough, at me.

"I'll say, brother," Tex boomed, crossing his arms on his chest and also glaring at me.

Before I could run away or will my body to spontaneously combust, Duke walked up and stared at me, straight in the eye.

"I know you're tryin' to protect Luke and I'm okay with that 'cause you care about him and he's a good man. He deserves to have a good woman carin' about him. I'm not okay with standin' out in the bright sunshine with the neighbors watchin' and a black man in a tree. I'm not sure I want to explain to Luke Stark why his mother's been fingerprinted. I'm equally unsure of my desire to explain to him why I let his woman get fingerprinted. What I am sure of is that *you* don't want to explain it to him either."

"Duke—" I began but he kept talking.

"I don't disagree with what he's doin'. Someone put their hands on my wife Dolores, hell would get paid and I'd be the one huntin' down the jackass who'd be payin' it. You got a whole bunch a people caught in the middle here and your shit is so far south we're hangin' onto a pole by our fingernails. Pretty soon we're gonna have some angry badasses descending if this shit doesn't get sorted and fast. Girl, I'm tellin' it to you straight, give up the ghost. You got no idea what you're doin'. Sort this shit out and sort it out now."

My eyes bugged out. "What am I supposed to do?"

"You know what you gotta do," Duke's gravelly voice rumbled low.

I did know what I had to do. And I knew I had to do it fast. Mainly because I didn't feel like getting fingerprinted. Also, the fingerprinting ink would likely stain Mrs. Stark's bone-colored handbag.

Hell and damnation.

With a heavy sigh, I pulled my phone from my purse and flipped it open. I scrolled down my phonebook, found the name I needed, pressed the green button and put it to my ear. It rang twice as I walked several feet away.

"Yeah?" Luke answered.

"Luke?"

"Beautiful, I wanna say I have time to talk but I'm doin' somethin' important."

I wanted to know what important something he was doing, but Smithie was up a tree. I didn't have time to ask.

"I'm sorry. I wouldn't call, but I've got a situation."

Silence for a beat then, "Talk to me."

"Well…" I started then stopped, mainly because I didn't know where to begin.

"Ava," Luke sounded impatient.

"See, the thing is…" I started then stopped again and before Luke could say anything I rushed on, deciding to let it all hang out. "We went to visit Winnie Conrad. She's a nice lady, but she didn't have much for us. The thing is, her granddaughter, Olivia, showed up while we were talking with Winnie and apparently somewhere along the line, both Indy and Jet had stun-gunned Olivia and Daisy got in a catfight with her. She wasn't so happy seeing Daisy at her grandma's place and there was kind of a mini-incident. Then she found out who I was, what happened to me and that we were after Noah so she decided to join the hunt, after we go to the mall and get Smithie out of the tree that is."

I heard noise as his hand covered the mouthpiece of the phone. Then I heard words and they were indistinguishable, but even though I couldn't make out what he was saying, I could tell whatever it was, it wasn't happy.

Then he came back to me. "Let's talk about why Smithie's in a tree."

"That's why I'm calling. Two German Shepherds have treed him in a stranger's backyard. He was canvassing Noah's old neighborhood. I'm not clear about how that happened, but the dogs aren't happy and we can't get him down."

"Call the fire department."

"He's in a stranger's yard and we don't have a good story about why."

"Call the fire department."

"Luke, he's in a stranger's backyard. He's a black man in a stranger's backyard. And there are, like, twelve of the now-extended Rock Chick gang hanging

421

out beside the house. We don't have time for me to describe Daisy's outfit and you've seen Tex. I'm not sure the fire department is going to let us slide."

"Ava, call the fire department. I'll call Eddie. Smithie won't have any trouble."

"I'm not quite done with my story."

Silence.

Or, more accurately, scary silence.

I continued, "See, my Mom and I had a nice chat after breakfast, but I'll tell you about that later. Anyway, your Mom and my Mom got worried about my troubles and they decided to follow us. They're here, too. Your Mom thinks we should get steaks for the dogs, but she's also counseling Olivia on her man troubles."

More silence.

I persevered.

"So, not only do we need to get Smithie out of the tree without anyone getting arrested, someone needs to do something about the Moms because so far Olivia has been cool about the counseling. I think she's coming to terms with her man troubles, but, you know, we don't know her very well. Your Mom has the best of intentions, but from what I've seen, Olivia can throw some attitude. I don't know, she might turn at any moment. Not to mention Tex is totally pissed because we have to swing by the mall—"

"Ava. Quiet."

He said it in the tone where I knew he meant it, and if he had been close I knew I wouldn't have had the words but a hard shut-Ava-up-kiss.

Then he said, voice still low and angry, "Give the phone to Ma."

"Okay," I agreed readily and didn't delay, but turned to the huddle. "Mrs. Stark, Luke wants to talk to you."

She smiled happily, looking like she didn't have a care in the world, and walked up to me. She took my phone, put it to her ear, listened for about five seconds, smiled and said, "Of course. Be safe."

She handed the phone back to me. Her eyes giddy happy, she ignored my open-mouthed stare and she walked back to the huddle.

Then she said something truly frightening.

"Christine, we have to go. Luke says we need to make a reservation at a steakhouse. I'm thinking Buckhorn Exchange or Morton's. If we get in at Morton's, we can dress up."

Slowly, with creeping dread, I put the phone to my ear. "Why is your Mom making reservations for dinner?"

He ignored my question. "Lee's calling Eddie right now. Eddie will deal with Smithie. You go to the mall. I'll pick you up at your place at seven."

My body got tight and I repeated, "Why is your Mom making reservations for dinner?"

"You can call off the Rock Chicks and tell Winnie's granddaughter to stand down. We got Dexter in the holding room."

My tight body went stone-still and my lungs evacuated all oxygen.

"Luke," I whispered.

"After the mall, if you want, you can have Tex or Duke bring you here if you got something to say, or do, to Dexter."

"Luke—"

"You got two hours. You're not here, we're finishing with him."

"Luke—"

"Two hours, babe."

"Luke!" I cried, fear taking hold of me as oxygen burned a wake into my lungs.

He didn't hear me, he had disconnected.

The tribe gathered around as I numbly flipped the phone shut. Sissy knew me better than anyone. She read my body language, got close and took my hand.

"The hunt's off. The Hot Bunch got him," I whispered and everyone looked at each other.

"Well, that was no fun," Olivia remarked. "Just a brother in a tree. I hope the mall works out. I need me a good top if I'm gonna find a decent man. This season, there ain't no good tops. I need cleavage. Cleavage was last season. I can't find cleavage anywhere."

"Sugar, you okay?" Daisy asked, eyes sharp on me.

No, I was not okay. I needed a new plan and I needed it fast.

I closed my eyes, took in a deep breath and then, as usual, I winged it.

I opened my eyes and looked at Duke.

"Eddie's going to take care of Smithie," I said and Duke nodded. Then I looked at Jet. "Can you call Indy and Ally, tell them it's over?" Jet nodded too. Then I looked at Tod and Stevie. "I need an outfit for Morton's and really good underwear. The outfit has to be the fuck-me outfit to end all fuck-me outfits.

Kristen Ashley

The underwear has to be good-enough-to-manipulate-a-macho-man under-wear. The kind he can't say no to. Can you do that?"

"You betcha, girlie," Tod told me on a huge smile.

My eyes went to Roxie. "I need the works and I need it fast. Once Tod and Stevie get the clothes and shoes, can you do the works?"

She knew exactly what I was asking and answered, "Of course."

I turned to Olivia. "Go to your grandma, I'm going to be calling her in half an hour. If she agrees to my plan, you both have to be ready to roll."

"This mean I'm not goin' to the mall?" Olivia asked.

"I'll take you to the mall tomorrow," I told her.

"Works for me," she replied.

Finally I looked at Tex. "Luke says you'll take me to the offices after I'm ready. Will you do that?"

Tex's gaze cut to Duke, then back to me. "No problem, darlin'."

My eyes moved to Shirleen and I said simply, "I need you."

Without hesitation Shirleen returned, "Whatever it is, I'm there."

Sissy squeezed my hand. "You want me to come with you, too?"

I turned to her. "No, I need you to babysit Marilyn and Sofia, and I want you to come to dinner with us tonight. Can you do that?"

"Absolutely," she answered.

That was when we heard sirens.

"What the fuck!" Smithie shouted. "Where did you all go? Is anyone fuck-in' there? I'm in a fuckin' tree. Jesus fuckin' Christ."

Tex got close and his huge hand settled on top of my head. "Let's go," he said, the boom muted but still there.

I nodded.

I looked back at the Rock Chicks as Tex, Shirleen and I headed to the Navigator. There were smiles, waves and chin lifts.

I waved back but didn't smile.

I was too busy freaking out about what I was going to do next.

Chapter 27
Octuple Revenge

Tex drove his bronze El Camino into the parking garage under the Nightingale Investigations offices and I saw Olivia wheeling Winnie's wheelchair around the side of her Lexus.

Tex parked and barely had the car shut off when he shot out, hauling ass over to Olivia. I followed as fast as I could, which wasn't very fast in four and a half inch, spiked heels.

"Shee-it, girl, you're about five foot two and wearin' pumps. You shouldn't be doin' transfers. It ain't safe. Get outta my way, I got it," he boomed to Olivia and I watched with surprise as he pushed her aside while he explained to Winnie, "Don't worry. Jet taught me how to do this. Nancy, my girlfriend, Jet's Mom, was still recoverin' from a stroke when we got together. She'd get tired, she'd need her chair."

Olivia and I stood back as Tex expertly transferred Winnie from car to chair.

"You're good at that," Winnie noted when she settled in.

"Nancy don't need her chair now," Tex shared. "But it ain't somethin' you forget how to do."

See, told you Tex was a good guy.

Winnie gave him a grin and patted his hand then looked at me. "You ready?"

No. No, I was not ready. But I had to be ready. Luke had given me one option and I was going to take it.

Luckily, Daisy was right about Tod and Stevie knowing how to shop. Not only was I wearing the Fuck-Me Outfit of All Time, I had on Manipulate A Macho Man Underwear that would make John Rambo forget that Vietnam even existed.

Not to mention Indy and Ally showed up at Roxie's. Indy gave good hair and Jet was a dab hand at makeup—experience gleaned from her days working at a strip club. Daisy stepped in and did a cover up job of my black eye that was so good, if someone took a before and after photo, it would win awards.

Therefore I was vamped out like nobody's business.

Indy had curled my hair in tight banana curls then she ran her slimed-up-with-hair-gunk-fingers through it, shaking it all around so my head was a mass of sexy, wild, soft curls.

Jet had done my makeup sultry, giving me dark, smoky eyes, barely there blusher and lots of lip gloss.

Tod and Stevie's Fuck-Me dress was a deep, forest green. It was strapless and fit like a glove from cleavage to hips. It stopped just above the knee and on one side had a deep slit nearly up to my hip. The shoes were killer, totally sex on heels. They were black with pointed toes, high, pencil-slim, spike heels and a thin, complicated ankle strap that took me (and Roxie) ten minutes to figure out how to fasten.

But it was the underwear that made the outfit, and you couldn't even see it. You just felt sexy wearing it. Way sexy. Off the charts sexy.

The undies were two-piece in a deep green, one shade down from forest. A strapless bustier and skintight satin panties. The bustier was covered in black lace and the panties were also heavy on lace in all the right places. The backs of the panties were cut high (not thong high, but close) so they showed lots of ass. The back of the bustier was dipped low so it showed lots of skin.

The underwear wasn't the most comfortable thing I'd ever worn, but what the hell. No pain, no gain.

"Yeah. I'm ready," I answered Winnie.

"She ain't ready," Olivia muttered.

I decided to ignore Olivia. I had to focus and I didn't need negative thinking.

We took the elevator up and went to the offices. Shirleen was sitting behind the reception desk talking on the phone.

When we walked in, her tawny eyes came to me, bugged straight out of her head and she said, "Dorothea, I gotta go. My girl's here and shit... I don't even know what to say. Words won't describe it. I'll get my phone, take a picture. You have *got* to see this."

Shirleen hung up and dove under the desk, coming up with her bag at the same time digging out her phone.

"Shirleen, I don't have time for pictures," I told her.

"Girl, you want a photo record of this. Trust me," she returned, pulling out her phone, dropping her bag on her desk and bleeping buttons, tongue sticking out the side of her mouth. "Now how does this thing work?"

"Give it to me," Olivia ordered, sashaying toward Shirleen. "I got the same phone. I take pictures all the time."

I looked at Tex, beginning to feel desperate. By my calculations I had, like, a minute before Luke and the boys "finished" with Noah.

"Will you go get Luke?" I asked Tex.

"Oh, Luke knows you're here," Shirleen informed me, and the way she said it gave me goose bumps, and not the good kind.

As if he knew (which he probably did) that it was his cue, the door to the inner sanctum opened and Luke was there. A man I hadn't yet met was with him, slightly older than any of the Hot Bunch. Blond military haircut, piercing blue eyes and the standard issue, Nightingale Hottie tight-muscled, zero-body-fat body.

I didn't have time to check out the latest member of the Hot Bunch. I only had eyes for Luke.

He was feeling the same way. He did a full body sweep, rocked back on his heels and crossed his arms on his chest. Then he did a slight shake of his head like he couldn't quite believe me, but one side of his mouth curled up in a half-grin as if he thought I was amusing.

Really not the reaction I was hoping for.

"Hey," I greeted.

"Shit, Luke, you don't put a ring on her finger, I will," the blond guy said.

Now *that* was the reaction I was hoping for.

"You got a wife and five kids," Luke told him, but didn't take his eyes off me.

"Oh yeah, for a second I forgot," the blond guy replied.

It was then I realized I wasn't breathing so I forced the air out of my lungs.

"Babe," Luke said, still not moving from his position just inside the room. "You wanna tell me why Mrs. Conrad and her granddaughter are here?"

I stopped breathing again.

Shit!

Get yourself together, girl! Bad Ava shouted.

You made this plan, you have to carry it through. Be strong! Good Ava encouraged.

I started breathing again, mainly because I had no choice.

"I figured it's not fair I get to have my word with Noah since he did the dirty on both Mrs. Conrad and me. I asked her if she wanted to say a few things and she did. So I invited her to the party. You don't mind do you?"

The blond guy burst out laughing.

Luke did not.

"Yeah, I mind." Luke, as normal, was brutally honest.

"Well, that's not good," I forged ahead. "Mrs. Conrad and Olivia came all the way downtown from Aurora. It's tough for Mrs. Conrad to get around. It would suck if she made this trip for nothing."

Luke tore his eyes from me, looked at Winnie, and without remorse he said, "This is a closed party."

"Luke!" I cried. He was ruining my plan!

"Got it!" Shirleen yelled and everyone looked at her. She had her cell phone pointed facing our direction and a little picture of me was on it. "That's a good one too. That's so good, I may make it my wallpaper."

"Shirleen, we're in the middle of something here," I told her.

"Oh yeah, sorry," she mumbled.

She bent her head and started beeping more buttons on her cell phone, likely sending my photo to half of Denver.

I looked back at Luke. "Can we talk privately?" I asked.

"Nothin' you can't say in front of Monty," Luke replied.

My eyes moved to the blond guy. "So, you're Monty."

"That's me," he said.

"I'm Ava," I introduced myself, though he probably knew who I was. Still, I didn't want to seem rude.

"I know that, darlin'. I manage the surveillance room. We monitor Luke's loft and we monitor Fortnum's. Seen a lot of you."

My mouth dropped open. Monty smiled. I felt the heat hit my face. Monty's smile got bigger.

"You monitor Fortnum's, too?" I whispered.

"Yeah," Monty answered. "You can thank me later."

I blinked before I asked, very, *very* stupidly, "For what?"

"For not showin' Luke the video of you crawlin' on all fours down the side book aisle."

It was then Luke laughed.

Okay, abort plan, time for a new plan.

I turned to Shirleen. "I'm done here. We can leave. I need cookies. STAT."

"Girl, I did not traipse around town, droppin' off Tex, goin' to your house to get your perfume—" Shirleen started.

"My house is two blocks from Tex's," I cut in.

"So? Then you had me callin' everyone and their brother," Shirleen shot back.

"You just called Olivia!" My voice was rising.

"Well, I didn't do all that for you to give up at the first hurdle. Shit, girl," Shirleen finished.

Argh!

I turned back to Luke. "Can we *please* speak privately?" I tried again.

He pressed his lips together. Not with anger, more like he was trying to stop them from twitching. Then he said, "You got five minutes."

He motioned toward the door. I walked through it and stopped. He passed me and I followed him to a door down the hall I'd never been through before. We went in and I saw it was an office. Big desk, chairs in front, couch on the back wall. The same décor as the reception area. I stopped inside, close to the desk, and turned to Luke, who'd closed the door behind us.

"You can't stop yourself, can you?" he asked before I could say anything.

"What?"

"Cleared your debt this morning, less than eight hours later, they're pilin' up again."

My eyes got wide. "What do I owe you for now?"

"Arrangin' for Smithie to be taken out of a tree."

Oh. That.

"That's just one little thing," I told him. "And you did that for Smithie more than for me."

"Smithie was in the tree because of you."

That was kind of true.

Hell and damnation.

"What else do I owe you for?"

"The debt you bought for struttin' in here dressed like a man eater."

"I'm not dressed as a man eater."

His eyebrows went up.

Okay, so I was dressed as a man eater.

"Why do I owe you for that?" I asked.

He shook his head. "Ava babe, I know the game you're playin' and you're gonna pay for playin' it."

I crossed my arms on my chest. "And what game is that?"

"The same game you played this mornin'. You don't want me to do somethin' I want to do and you're usin' your sweet body to get it. As much as I like the view, babe, the intent behind it pisses me off."

His words angered me so much I looked around for something to throw at him.

Before I could find anything, Luke demanded, "Ava, look at me."

My eyes went to him, but I didn't look at him. I *glared* at him.

He ignored my glare and went on, "We aren't playin' your game. You get your word with Dexter, then—"

I interrupted him. "For your information, this dress is *not* for you. It's for Noah."

That got a reaction.

At first I saw I surprised him, which surprised me because I didn't think Luke *could* be surprised. Then the surprise faded fast and I saw he was ticked off. I knew this because his eyes narrowed, his brows drew together and the air in the room started closing in because his ticked off energy was electrifying it.

"Come again?" he said low, but I was too angry myself to be scared of him.

"See," I started to explain. "I had vowed revenge against Dom. Every time Dom would do something jerky, I'd double it, triple it, whatever. I kept a running tally. Then once Noah hurt me, I transferred my revenge to him because he deserved it more. Then I started adding on whenever I'd find out he did something bad. I got up to octuple revenge."

I twisted, dropped my purse on the desk, came back around, lifted up my hands and held my left pointer finger with my right hand and started counting down my plan.

"One, I walk in there looking *fine*. Not looking beat up and broken, but looking *good*. That way, he sees what he gave up. He could have had me, but he used me and threw me away. He might be too coldblooded to care, but it'll make *me* feel better."

I added my middle finger to my hand.

"Two, I'm in there with you and he knows we're together. You're better than him, hotter than him, richer than him, everything more than him. I want to rub his face in it."

I added my ring finger.

"Three, I'll say what I have to say. I don't know what that is yet, but I'm winging this as I go along. I'll figure it out."

I kept adding fingers.

"Four, he has to see Winnie. He may be a snake, but he can't be so low that he won't flinch when he's confronted with yet another one of his victims, especially when she's in a better place with good people around her no matter what he did to her. Five, Winnie gets to have her say. Six is whatever you're going to do to him. I don't have a seventh and eighth part of my revenge yet, but I figure I might kick him. With these pointy shoes, that'll hurt like—"

I stopped talking because one second Luke was three feet away, the next second he was using his hard body to back me up until my thighs hit the desk and he was pressed in, full frontal.

"What are you doing?" I cried, grabbing his upper arms in order not to stumble on my teetering heels.

His hands were on me, his head bent and his lips went to my neck.

"I'm gonna fuck you, right here on Lee's desk." His voice was low again, but not with anger this time. With something entirely different, and a shiver slid across my skin. "The eighth part of your revenge is you walkin' in there with your face soft, satisfied and sexy as hell like it is after I make you come."

Ho-ly *shit*.

My special girl parts went into full spasm.

He was pulling up the skirt of my dress at the same time, stepping all over my plan.

"Luke! You're going to mess up my makeup."

My skirt was bunched around my hips and Luke's hands were at my ass.

"I don't care." His mouth glided up my neck to my jaw.

"Someone can walk in," I kept at it.

His fingers were moving across lace and satin. His head came up, he leaned back, looked at my hips and his body went still.

"Jesus," he muttered as he slid the skirt up higher so he could get a better look. Then his eyes lifted to mine and they were ink. "Those for Dexter, too?"

431

"No!" I snapped, slapping at his hands. "You're ruining my surprise, for *you*, which was supposed to be for later on tonight."

At that he grinned. Not a sexy half-grin. An even sexier, full-on, white smile.

"Stop smiling at me," I bit out, shoving my skirt back down. "I'm losing my revenge mojo here. I was all psyched up and you got all testosterone on me. Or more testosterone than normal".

"Ava."

I got my skirt in place and raised my eyes to his. His were still ink, but they were amused ink and I knew his intent.

"Don't you kiss me, you'll mess up my lip gloss," I ordered. "Jet spent ten whole minutes on my lips and I don't want her time wasted."

His arms came around me and his face got close. "You're cute when you're bossy."

I rolled my eyes to the ceiling.

"Look at me, babe."

I looked at him.

"The eighth part of your revenge can be him rottin' in prison for the next decade."

I sucked in breath and stared at him.

After a few beats, I whispered, "You're not going to kill him?"

He shook his head.

I kept staring at him then something hit me. "Were you ever going to kill him?"

His arms got tighter. "If I'd have seen him after I found out he touched you, or when I found out he did it while I was in your house, maybe. Since then, no."

Oh... my... *God.*

"Why on earth didn't you tell me?"

"Because you were in less danger traipsin' around with the Rock Chicks. Didn't hurt that it served the added purpose of keepin' your mind off inventing ways to push me away."

I should have known Luke wasn't going to kill Noah. He was a good guy. Hell, he was *The* Best Guy *Ever.*

Still, I was annoyed.

"I was worried to death you'd do something gonzo."

His forehead came to mine. "Yeah, that's what kept your mind off inventing ways to push me away."

I could just not believe him.

"You're incredibly annoying," I snapped, pulling my forehead away and putting my hands on his chest and pushing (which didn't work, per usual).

He ignored my comment and started his own topic. "I'm gonna kiss you now."

"You are not," I said, but his lips were coming toward mine and I couldn't tear my eyes from them. "Luke, my lip gloss!" I protested right before his mouth hit mine.

In the end I had to repair my lip gloss and Luke had to wipe Jet's application off his mouth with the back of his wrist.

Not to mention his kiss was so thorough, Luke was going to get part of his revenge, because even after shaky-handed lip gloss application, I was going to walk in to see Noah in the waning throes of a serious Luke Lip Fog.

❦

"Who's that?" I asked, staring at a guy I'd never seen in my life. He was sitting on the side of the bed in the small, sparsely furnished (read: bed only), secure room at the back of the offices, a room they called the Holding Room.

Hector and Vance were in with him. He had a fat lip, a swollen nose and was holding his torso straight like bending would cause pain but otherwise he looked healthy as an ox.

And he was not Noah.

Luke had walked in the room in front of me. Tex wheeled Winnie in the room behind me. Monty was standing outside.

I stopped at Luke's side, Tex and Winnie stopped at mine.

"Fuck," the man said, his eyes on Winnie.

"What do you mean, who's that?" Hector asked me.

"I mean, who's this guy?" I turned to Luke. "I've never seen this guy in my life."

"But, that's Jeremiah," Winnie told me.

I turned to stare at her, thinking she might be confused, but you could tell by the blistering look she was aiming at the guy she was far from confused.

Wow.

433

"Okay," I said to Winnie. "But it isn't Noah."

"You're shittin' me," Luke said from beside me, and I turned back to him.

"No," I replied, and I watched his mouth get tight. I looked back at the guy.

He had Noah's loose description. He was stocky, his hair color was not quite brown, not quite blond and he had blue eyes. But Noah was slightly slimmer and definitely cuter.

"I can't believe this. I got all psyched up to confront Noah and I get this guy?" I cried in exasperation.

I mean, really, what the hell?

Luke turned to Tex. "Get me Brody."

"I don't know where he—" Tex started.

Luke moved. It was a barely-there movement, but it made a chilly statement.

"Calm down, badass. I'll find Brody," Tex muttered and took off.

"Been waitin' all day for this to come out," Jeremiah said, grinning through his fat lip. "The Nightingale Boys fuck up. It's beautiful. Walt's gonna piss his pants laughing."

Uh-oh.

All of a sudden I realized the seriousness of the matter. I felt the danger in the air and I felt a freak out start to happen.

"Maybe you shouldn't talk," I advised him and I thought I was being nice. A lot nicer than he deserved considering he was Jeremiah.

Jeremiah's eyes slid to me and they were so cold, my freak out magnified to creepy proportions.

"Walt and I drew straws for you," he told me, voice and smile oily slick. "Once we got a look at you, we both wanted a shot. I got the short straw, which meant I got Aunt Jemima here, and Walt got a good taste of you. He said you tasted sweet as cherry pie."

Mrs. Conrad had gasped at the Aunt Jemima comment. I felt, rather than saw, Luke go still. I was frozen to the spot from the minute he began talking.

"Ava, get Mrs. Conrad out of here," Luke ordered, voice controlled but it held an angry edge.

I still couldn't move, but I could talk and I was pissed way the hell off. Pissed enough to disregard Luke's order.

"You aren't very smart, are you?" I asked Jeremiah.

"Smart enough to get her money, her car—not that she could use it—and a whole shitload of gold from you."

"But not smart enough not to get caught, and not smart enough to know you just fucked yourself by not keeping your mouth shut," I returned.

"Cherry Pie, been dyin' for a good eye full of you and you gotta know, it was worth it," Jeremiah retorted, his eyes sliding the length of me, and I added a long hot shower to my evening schedule.

"Ava, get out of here." Luke's voice had turned deadly.

"You keep digging deeper," I ignored Luke and said to Jeremiah.

"They can't do dick," Jeremiah taunted.

It was my turn to smile. He was *so* wrong.

"You don't know who you're dealing with, do you?" I asked him.

"Ava—" Luke began.

"Yeah," Jeremiah broke in, standing and everyone in the room tensed. "Supposedly shit-hot PIs, but not shit-hot enough to know they got the wrong guy."

"Yes, I will give you that," I allowed. "They should've known no way I'd give a piece of my 'cherry pie' to a guy like you. It was lucky when you two were deciding who would screw me over that Noah got the long straw. At least he was cute. You wouldn't have got a first date."

The smile fled from his face.

I went on, "Anyway, fortune favors the bold and if these boys are nothing else, they're bold. They may have been looking for Noah, but they found you, which works just as well because Mrs. Conrad might have a few words to say to you."

"I don't give a shit what Aunt Jemima has to say," Jeremiah snarled.

You would think I couldn't move faster than three shit-hot PIs, especially wearing four and a half inch spiked heels. But I could.

I was on Jeremiah in a flash, hands on his shoulders, and lucky for me, a slit in my skirt deep enough for my knee to connect pretty fucking hard with his gonads.

He dropped to his knees, hands to his crotch, a long groan escaping his mouth.

A steel-band-like arm wrapped around my waist and I was pulled back several feet, my body pressed tight against Luke's.

I ignored Luke and his arm and hissed to Jeremiah, "Be nice."

"Fuck you," Jeremiah moaned, and it didn't sound all that convincing, probably since he had temporarily lost *that* particular ability.

I looked at Winnie.

"Mrs. Conrad?" I called, sounding sweet as sugar. "Do you have anything to say?"

Winnie's eyes were on Jeremiah, but she answered me, "I think you covered it."

There you go.

Time to move on.

I turned in Luke's arm and lifted my eyes to his. "I'm guessing you're not coming to dinner with the Moms."

Luke just stared at me like I'd broken into a tap dance while singing "Mr. Bojangles".

"All righty then," I declared. "Don't worry about getting blood on your clothes. I'm really good at stain removal."

I leaned into him, hand at his chest, and gave him a quick lip touch. Then I pulled out of his arm, but lifted my hand to wipe the lip gloss off his mouth with my thumb.

"Don't be too late," I whispered and I watched one side of his mouth go up in a half-grin.

Then, all business, I turned to Mrs. Conrad and grabbed her wheelchair.

"Welp, better go. We don't want to be around when Luke's meting out gonzo retribution. It might get messy and this is a new dress. Do you want to go to dinner with my family and Luke's Mom? My treat," I asked conversationally as I wheeled Mrs. Conrad out of the room.

"That would be lovely. Would be a shame, we both got all dressed up but had nowhere to go," Mrs. Conrad replied, cool as could be, as if we were wheeling through a park, not exiting what amounted to a cell.

"We're having steaks," I told her. "You like steak?"

"Girl, I love steak. Who doesn't like steak?"

"I like steak," I agreed.

We passed a smiling Monty. We stopped outside the room and I turned to look in. Hector was already moving toward Jeremiah. Vance was watching me and he was wearing a very attractive shit-eating grin. My eyes slid to Luke. His were on me and my heart stuttered when I watched, fascinated, as he winked.

Then I shut the door.

"I'm Ava Barlow. I'm staying with Lucas Stark. Can I have my room key, please?" I asked the reception clerk at Hotel Monaco.

He tapped on his computer, something came up and he read it, smiled at me and gave me my keycard telling me the room number. I took it with a return smile and headed to the elevators.

Dinner had been a blast. Marilyn and Sofia had opted out, still pouting. Olivia, Shirleen and Winnie had opted in, and Sissy met us there with the Moms. We ate, moved the festivities to the Cruise Room, meeting Indy and Jules. We drank martinis (of course, Jules didn't drink martinis, seeing as she was preggers), enough to get loose, not enough to get drunk and Shirleen dropped me off at the hotel.

I exited the elevators, found the room and let myself in with the card.

The room was dimly lit with one lamp. Luke was in bed, on his back, hands behind his head, chest bare, covers to his waist, looking Zen.

"Hey," I greeted, throwing my purse in a chair.

"Come here," he replied softly and my knees got week.

I told my knees to behave and asked, "How's Jeremiah?"

"Incarcerated," he informed me. "Hank got an anonymous tip, sent a car out. Uniforms picked him up, took him to the hospital to stitch him up and now he's behind bars. Winnie needs to go in tomorrow to press charges." His voice dropped low and he continued, "Now, come here."

I took in a deep breath, let it out and walked to the bed.

When I made it to the side, Luke's hands came from behind his head. He did an ab curl, caught my waist and pulled me down on top of him.

When we had settled, his fingers sifted into the hair at the side of my head and slid back, taking the weight with it and holding it behind my head.

"I like your hair like this," he murmured.

"Indy did it," I shared.

His eyes came to mine. "We got plans tonight, you and me."

"I already had dinner with the Moms."

He gave me a half-grin. "I wasn't talking about those plans."

I knew he wasn't.

Shit!

"Babe, move your foot, your shoe is about to pierce the skin on my shin."

Shit again!

I moved my foot and muttered, "Sorry."

"Take 'em off," he ordered.

"I can't, the straps are too complicated. I have to wear them to bed, then I have to wear them until they fall apart. I'll never—"

He flipped me on my back then his hand slid down my side, my leg, to my ankle. Within thirty seconds he had both shoes off.

"How did you do that?" I asked, eyes wide, thinking the wonders of Luke would never cease.

He didn't answer. His fingers found the zip at the side of my dress and tugged it down.

"Luke, I want to hear about Jeremiah," I told him.

Zipper down, he slid the dress up, up and then it was off. He tossed it aside, lifted up on his elbow and his head bent to look at me. One of his hands came back to my body, gliding across the bustier at my midriff.

"Jesus," he muttered, eyes ink, face soft.

Okay, suffice it to say, he liked the underwear.

"Luke!" I cried. "Focus!"

His gaze moved to my face. He looked part amused, part impatient and part sexy as hell.

"We got him to talk," he told me.

This didn't surprise me.

"Do I have to get my stain removal gloves out?" I asked.

He shook his head. "Not a big fan of mess, babe."

Thank God for that.

He kept talking, "Jeremiah, real name Kurt Reid. He's been partners with Walt Ellis for five years. Worked Nevada with him, then Colorado. Their shit is linked. So much, Brody got the intel mixed up. Brody's also got a meeting tomorrow with Lee, eight o'clock."

I had a brief moment to feel sorry for the unknown Brody before Luke went on.

"Sometimes they would do the con together, sometimes they hit different marks. With you and Winnie, they hit different marks. He knew all about you. Ellis, or Dexter, knew all about Winnie. They also have a safe house in Durango. Reid says Ellis is there. Hector and Vance are on the road tonight checking it out."

"So it's close to over."

"Babe, for you, it *is* over."

I was cool with that. I probably had only one knee to the 'nads in me for this lifetime and I'd given it to Kurt Reid.

I was cool with that, too. Kurt Reid was a jerk.

"Okay," I said to Luke.

He smiled at me. My stomach got melty.

Then he moved. My panties were gone in the blink of an eye. He rolled, taking me with him, and before I knew it he was seated on the side of the bed with me straddling his lap.

Ho-ly *shit*.

"Luke, we need to talk about a few things," I tried to stall.

His head bent and his lips traced the lace above my breast.

"No talking," he said there, not feeling in the mood for me to stall, and truth be told, I was even beginning to lose the mood.

I stuck with it. "We have to talk. There's lots to talk about."

His head dropped back and his hands went to my hips. He lifted me up, shifted my hips forward and when he set me down again, he was inside me.

Wow.

Nice.

"What did you want to talk about?" he asked as his hand slid down my arm, fingers curling around my wrist. He brought my hand between us and pressed it in so my fingers hit the target.

Ultra-nice.

"Ava."

"What?"

"You wanted to talk."

I did? Shit, I did.

His fingers moved my fingers until my fingers took over. Then his hand moved to my ass. The other one slid up my back and his neck bent, lips hitting the skin above the lace again while his 'tache tickled it.

"Um—" I mumbled then moved, sliding slightly up and down, as my fingers rolled.

This was *hot*.

Ava, focus, Good Ava admonished.

Yeah, focus. Focus on how hot this is. Yum-mee, Bad Ava cooed.

Yikes!

I had recruited the Rock Chicks for this operation and they had worked so hard on it I had to see it through. If I didn't, they might throw me out of the club.

So I persisted, "I just wanted to tell you I like my house. I like my Range Rover. And I don't think you should go to Vito's family meeting."

His head dropped back again and he looked at me. His hand at my spine slid around and cupped my breast, thumb sliding across my nipple over the lace, and that felt so good I made a little sound in my throat.

Between his thumb, my fingers and his hard boy part, I was quickly losing the will to manipulate macho man Luke into doing what I wanted.

He started talking, "We'll stay at your house while the blinds are being put up. Once the blinds are up, we'll try the loft for a while. We'll see how it goes and we'll decide. Work for you?"

I moved up and down, not slightly this time, but more.

Then I ground into him and breathed, "Okay."

"The Range Rover's gotta go, babe. It's not safe." His voice was growing rough.

"I like my car." My voice was still breathy.

"We'll get you another car. I'm thinkin' Mustang."

I liked Mustangs. Mustangs were super-fly.

"Okay," I repeated.

My fingers pressed in. It felt good and I licked my lips as he watched.

"Christ." This time, his voice was definitely rough.

"The family meeting—" I went on.

"You aren't near Zano unless I'm with you." The roughness had a new dimension now.

"Why?"

"He wants this." His thumb did another nipple swipe while his hips bucked and I bit my lip as heat shot through me. "And I'm not givin' him the chance to go for it."

My other hand curled around his neck and I looked at him.

"But," I whispered and then slid my fingers to where we connected. "*I only want this.*" I dropped my forehead to his. "You don't have to trust Ren, Luke, but you can trust me."

At my words and my touch, his eyes went molten. His hand slid into my hair, twisted and he kissed me, hard, hot and deep.

When his lips disengaged, he murmured, "You got it, beautiful."

Yay! My mind screamed.

There it was. Proof positive. Luke *was The* Best Guy *Ever.*

"Thank you," I said softly.

Then I went back to focusing on my target, and while I did this Luke watched. It wasn't embarrassing. It was sexy and it was hot. After a while, it was so sexy and hot I arched back, ready to let it happen, but he pulled me forward again.

"I want you looking at me," he demanded, voice now hoarse.

I tried to look at him, but my eyes were half-mast. I was deep in a hot sex fog and couldn't focus.

"Jesus," he muttered. "I'm gonna come just watching you."

I smiled and leaned forward, thinking to kiss him, but instead I gasped his name just as I climaxed, hard, my mouth against his.

I wasn't even close to finishing before he flipped me to my back. My arms wrapped around him as he lifted my hips and slammed into me, over and over again, prolonging my orgasm, and once the first one was done, another one rolled in right after it. Luckily, the second one coincided with Luke's.

It was heaven.

In the end, my manipulate-a-macho-man plan only half worked.

I won on the Family Meeting, lost on the Range Rover and tied on the living arrangements.

I could live with that.

Chapter 28
Two Kinds of Women

In the middle of the night I woke up, limbs tangled with Luke's in Nighttime Alpha Position.

I pressed into him. He fell to his back, I rolled over him and he came with me.

I settled on his other side, assuming Nighttime Beta Position, hooking my thigh around his hip.

His arms came around me. "Babe," he muttered, voice sexy-husky-drowsy.

"No pain tonight?" I whispered.

His arms got tight. "Not anymore."

I cuddled closer to his warm, hard body then fell back to sleep.

⌇⧟⌇

Wake up call number one:

Luke, sliding the covers down my back while saying softly, "Ava babe."

"Sleepy," I replied as I snagged his pillow and hugged it to my body.

I heard a chuckle. My torso was pulled up, I kept hold of the pillow at my chest as I was twisted, and the pillow and I hit something solid. I burrowed my face into Luke's neck as I wrapped my arms around him (and the pillow) and I mumbled, "Kiss me quick so I can go back to sleep."

I didn't really want him to kiss me quickly, but I did want to go back to sleep.

The pillow was tugged. It slid out from between us, my breasts hit bare chest and my eyes opened.

"I don't want to just kiss you, beautiful. I wanna fuck you," Luke said.

I lifted my head to see Luke, fresh from the shower, towel wrapped around his hips, cheeks cleanly shaven and droplets of moisture still on his shoulders. As if possessed by Bad Ava (and I probably was), I leaned forward and licked a drop off his collarbone.

Then Luke demonstrated the undeniable fact that days of hunting inter-mixed with fighting with me, lots of sex, parking lot fisticuffs and not much sleep had absolutely no effect on him whatsoever. It was so energetic we ended up on the floor, having rolled there after a short wrestling match over who would get to put their mouth (me) or their fingers *and* mouth (Luke) where (I lost).

After, he moved us to the bed, me on top, one of his arms locked around me, the other hand drawing patterns on the small of my back. He had a knee lifted and I was part straddling, part wrapped around his thigh, my nose pressed into the space between his ear and jaw.

Then Sissy's idea from yesterday popped into my head.

"Luke?"

"Yeah."

"Do you keep handcuffs on you all the time?"

"No."

"Most of the time?"

"Depends. Why?"

"Just wondering."

The arm locked tighter and the hand stopped drawing and cupped my ass.

"Why?" he pressed.

I lifted up on my elbow and looked at him, feeling weirdly shy even though I was sprawled on top of him naked after having energetic, part wrestling sex. "How would you feel about being, um… cuffed to the bed and, erm… letting me have my way with you?"

He half-grinned and I thought he liked the idea, and it made my very sensitive, post-orgasm, special girl parts tingle.

"I like to be the one in control, babe."

My eyes narrowed. I dropped down and started to roll, but he foiled my escape plan and came with me. This meant both his arms went around me, holding me to him, and his thigh was pressed deep between my legs.

His hand fisted in my hair and tugged it back gently so I would look at him.

His face was not amused, it was soft. "I might not like that particular idea, Ava, but I do like that you're up for adventure."

"I've just decided it's missionary position until the end of time," I retorted.

That's when he face got amused. "Bullshit," he murmured.

He was right, it was bullshit.

Still.

"Are we gonna fight over how we have sex?" he asked.

"Maybe," I replied, sounding bitchy.

"So now that we don't have anything to fight about, you're inventing things?"

"I'm not inventing things! You're not being fair. How come you get to cuff me to the bed and I don't get to do the same to you?"

"Because I'm stronger than you."

This was true. This also didn't make me happy so I scowled at him.

He got close, or, I should say, closer. "Make you a deal. Tonight, I'll bring the cuffs. Whoever manages to get the other cuffed to the bed gets to play."

That was hardly a good deal for me.

"You just pointed out the obvious. You're stronger than me."

"Babe, you're not using your imagination."

I have a good imagination, Bad Ava reminded me, her voice dripping with anticipation.

Me too, Good Ava surprised me, her voice sounding dreamy.

I smiled slowly.

Then I said, "Deal."

He touched his lips to mine, eyes open, and murmured, "Never thought life could be this sweet."

My stomach got melty. "Really?" I whispered.

He rested his forehead against mine. "There are two kinds of women. The ones you go to bed with and the ones you wanna wake up with. Lots of the first, not many of the last. If a man's lucky, he'll find the last."

He touched his mouth to mine again and I took that as a definite sign I was the last.

Oh... my... *God.*

My whole body went melty.

"You got somethin' you wanna say?" he asked softly.

He knew. He knew I loved him. And he wanted me to tell him.

Eek!

I shook my head.

"I'll wait," he said.

Then he kissed my nose and rolled off the bed. He dressed while I watched, came back to me, sat on the bed, pulled me into his arms and kissed me long and deep.

Then he was gone.

I cuddled into the pillows, smiled to myself and went back to sleep.

~⌖~

Wake up call number two:

My phone in my purse, all the way across the room, started ringing.

I pulled myself out of bed, ran across the room, nabbed my purse and yanked the phone out, flipping it open and putting it to my ear.

"Yo," I greeted.

"Hi there, sweetie. Your sisters and I are going to breakfast. Do you want us to come get you?"

It was Mom.

I was definitely digging the New Mom. However, I'd rather have a tooth extracted without Novocain than go to breakfast with my sisters.

Still, they were family.

"Okay," I agreed. "But I need a change of clothes, can you bring some?"

"Sure thing. I'll have Sofia go up and—"

"No!" I interrupted sharply. God only knew what horrors Sofia would drag out of my closet as payback for yesterday. "You pick," I told her. "Jeans, t-shirt, belt, flip-flops and bring some of my silver jewelry."

"Which pieces of jewelry?"

"Any of them."

"Can do. We'll be there in about twenty minutes."

I told her my room number and we disconnected. Then I scrolled down to Luke and pressed the green button.

"Yeah?"

"It's me," I said.

"Babe, your name comes up on the display," he informed me, a smile in his voice.

"Then why do you answer 'yeah' if you know it's me?"

"That's how I answer the phone."

"Well, you could say something else like 'hello' or 'Ava' or even 'babe'."

"You want me callin' you 'babe' now?"

"It's better than 'yeah'."

"Let's see if I got this right. Now we're arguing about how I answer the phone?"

Okay, he had a point.

"Sorry," I mumbled.

"Dexter was wrong. You don't taste like cherry pie. You taste a fuckuva lot sweeter. If you didn't, babe, you'd be a pain in the ass."

"Did you just call me a pain in the ass?" I asked.

He sighed.

Time to move on.

"Where are we staying tonight?" I changed the subject.

"Your family gonna be in town?"

"I don't know."

"The hotel if they are, your place if they're not."

I looked at the bed. It had a padded headboard, no slats for cuffs.

"If we stay here or at my place, we can't play our, um… game."

"We'll play another night."

He didn't sound too broken up about it.

"Lotsa games to play, babe," he went on softly. "I'll get creative."

I felt my knees wobble. If he hadn't already *been* creative, I was looking forward to creative.

"Okay. Did Vance and Hector get Noah?"

"No."

My stomach clenched. What did he mean "no"?

"No?" I asked.

"They didn't go to Durango. Got a tip. He's in town, they're trackin' him and they're close. I'm just about to go out to assist. I want you to stay at the hotel. This shouldn't take long."

"But I'm going to breakfast with my family."

Silence for a beat then he told me, "I'll get a man on you. Don't leave the room until he knocks on the door. You've met everyone now. It'll be one of ours."

"Okay."

"Don't do anything stupid."

"Luke!" I snapped.

"Promise me."

"Why do you keep saying that?"

"Last time you called me, beautiful, Smithie was up a tree."

Shit!

I hated it when he was right. And he was right all the fucking time except for with Kurt Reid, but that wasn't his fault.

I gave in, "All right, I won't do anything stupid."

"Christ, you're cute." The smile was back in his voice.

"Am I cute or a pain in the ass?" I asked, the bitch in my voice.

"Both. And you can be a bitch, too, and for some fuckin' insane reason, I like it all."

What did you say to that?

I didn't have a chance to say anything. He disconnected.

I took a shower, and when I got out my phone was ringing again. I padded to it wrapped in one of the hotel's robes. It said, "unknown number', but I flipped it open anyway.

"Yo."

"We goin' to the mall or what?"

It was Olivia. How she got my number I didn't know, but it was a moot point now.

"We're going to the mall. I have to have breakfast with my Mom and sisters first."

"I could do breakfast," she invited herself, which I was realizing was kind of her way.

Olivia would definitely make breakfast with my sisters a better experience. Hell, Genghis Khan would make breakfast with my sisters a better experience.

"Meet us at Hotel Monaco as soon as you can get here," I told her.

"I'll be there in fifteen minutes," she replied.

"Gotcha."

She disconnected, but I had another call coming in before I got the phone flipped shut, so I took it.

"Yo."

"Where are you?"

It was Riley, and I remembered I was supposed to meet him at the gym that morning. "Shit, Riley. I'm sorry. I forgot. My life's a total—"

He cut me off, "That guy still in the picture?"

I sighed.

Then I said quietly, "That guy's name is Luke, and yeah, he's still in the picture. He's probably gonna be in the picture for a while."

Silence then, "Ava, I'm guessing that you guessed where I'm at with this. Can't say I'm thrilled that this Luke character shows up and your life becomes a disaster."

"Luke didn't do it. He's fixing it."

"Fixing, not fixed, means he's taking his fucking time."

"Riley, that isn't fair. You don't know what's going on. It's not good and he's barely getting any sleep, he's working so hard to fix it."

More silence then, "You sure about this guy, Ava?"

I went back to speaking quietly. "Yeah, Riley. I'm sure." Then for some bizarre reason I shared, "I'm in love with him."

It was his turn to sigh. "You comin' into the gym today?"

I closed my eyes because what he said meant we were going to be okay and that was a relief.

I opened my eyes again "I have to go to breakfast with my family. Do you want to come?"

Now why did I ask that? He was hot. He wasn't just the personal trainer at the gym, he part owned it. Marilyn and Sofia would be all over him

Luke told me not to do anything stupid, and there I was, doing stupid shit. I couldn't even control it.

"Since you're not here, got nothin' on. I'll be there," Riley responded.

Crap.

Crapity, crap, crap, *crap*.

"Um… I should warn you my sisters are kind of… how do I put it?" I used Luke's words. "Man eaters."

"You'll protect me," he teased, and I drew in breath. The old Riley was back.

I told him where to meet us and flipped the phone shut just as a knock came at the door.

I looked out the peephole and saw my mother standing there so I opened the door and she shoved in. She was alone. I glanced out in the hall, but no Marilyn and Sofia, so I shut the door behind her.

"This hotel is something else!" she cried, looking around. "Luke must be doing well. Really, *really* well. A Porsche and putting you up here?"

She wasn't wrong. Hotel Monaco was super-fly.

"Where are Marilyn and Sofia?" I asked.

She turned and stared at me, ignoring my question due to the fact that something just dawned on her. "Why *are* you here? Doesn't Luke have a house where you can stay?"

"He's having some work done on his loft," I semi-fibbed. "He was staying with me until you guys came."

"Loft?"

"Yeah, in LoDo."

"Luke has a LoDo loft?" she breathed, eyes faraway happy.

Okay, so yes, it was true, a LoDo loft was quite something but really, enough was enough.

"Mother. Hello? Where are Marilyn and Sofia?"

She blinked and came back into the room. "They're downstairs having coffee." She dumped a bag on the chair and continued, "There's your clothes. Take your time, we'll enjoy coffee and let you get ready. Just meet us downstairs when you're done."

She came forward, kissed my cheek and left. The door hadn't completely shut on Mom when my phone rang again.

I flipped it open. "Yo."

"Hey chickie. I heard the revenge gig was a bust."

It was Ally.

"Um—"

"I know all about it. Brody fucked up. Lee came home last night not a happy camper. He's not hip on looking like an asshole. Not to mention he trades a lot on his reputation as a badass motherfucker who's got it goin' on. Brody fucking up means all the boys took a direct hit to their reps and Lee is dis-fucking-pleased, let me tell you. He told Indy, she told me and we're doin' our best to keep it amongst the Rock Chicks."

"That sounds like a good idea," I agreed.

"How did Luke take it?" she asked.

"He wasn't happy, but I was kind of more involved in the conversation with the guy they did get. He was the one who conned Winnie, and you would *not* believe, but he called her Aunt Jemima right when she was in the room."

Silence then, "Please tell me you're lying."

"No. I wish I was."

"Holy crap! What a dick! What did Luke do when he said that?"

"Nothing, he didn't get a chance. I got there first and kneed him in the 'nads."

I heard a hoot and then, "Righteous!"

I smiled. "We're going to breakfast, want to come?"

"Who's we?" she asked.

"Me, my Mom, my sisters, Olivia, Riley and whoever Luke sends to be my bodyguard."

"Didn't you say your sisters are bitches?" she asked.

"Yes. Please say you can come. I need Bitch Buffers."

"You got it. I'm at Fortnum's. Duke, Jane, Tex and Jet are here so they can hold down the fort. Daisy's here, too. I'm sure she'll come with."

"Thanks. We're meeting in the lobby of Hotel Monaco whenever you can get here."

"Be there soon as we can."

We disconnected and I flipped my phone shut. I opened the zipper on my bag and saw that Mom didn't do too badly, though she didn't exactly follow directions. There were jeans and a goodly amount of my silver to choose from, but instead of any old tee, she picked an army green, boat-necked, long-sleeved tee with tiny orange and hot pink flowers flowing from the hem at one side to come up in a swirl on the midriff. She'd decided against flip-flops and added a pair of dark brown suede shoes with a peek-a-boo notch in the toe, a high, thin, wedge heel and a thin strap around the ankle. As a finishing touch, Mom threw in a matching brown suede belt with a heavy oval silver buckle.

Okay, so she wasn't exactly an Entirely New Mom, but she was a Somewhat New-ish Mom. She *had* put in the jeans. I wasn't going to quibble.

I got dressed, put on my silver, strapped on the shoes and went to the bathroom to do something with my hair. Mom had stocked me with comb, hair products, travel-sized face stuff, loose powder, mascara, blusher, deodorant and perfume, most of which was probably hers because mine was scattered to the four corners (read: at Luke's and at Roxie's).

I did my best with what I had, considering the cut lip and black eye were still there (but finally fading) and was walking into the bedroom when my phone rang.

I flipped it open. "Yo."

"What's this about breakfast?"

It was Shirleen.

"Hey Shirleen. Did Ally call you?"

"Fuck no. Luke told me before he took off. I'm in the lobby and I'm hungry. Matt's comin' up to your room. Get your ass in gear."

I couldn't help it, I started smiling. "All right, keep your pants on. We'll be down in a second."

"Be snappy."

Disconnect.

There was a knock on the door before I completely flipped the phone shut. I shoved it in the back pocket of my jeans as I walked to the door. It started ringing again, but I ignored it while I opened the door. I had a smile of greeting for Matt on my face.

The problem was, it wasn't Matt knocking on the door.

It was Noah.

Fuckity, fuck, fuck, *fuck!*

Chapter 29
Convoy, Chaos and Cookies

"My life sucks," I told Noah.

He pulled a gun out of the pocket of his jacket and pointed it at me.

I stared at it. "You have got to be kidding me," I said.

"Not even fuckin' close," Noah replied

My cell in my back pocket quit ringing just as the phone in the room started ringing. I didn't have a chance to do anything about it as Noah grabbed my arm and pulled me out of the room. The door closed behind me, shutting out the sound of the ringing phone.

"What are you doing?" I asked.

"I don't know," Noah answered.

He didn't know?

"What do you mean, you don't know?" I snapped.

"I mean I don't know, shut up. We're takin' a ride."

We were walking toward the elevators, Noah's hand on my arm pushing me in front of him. One elevator dinged and opened. Matt walked out and halted when he saw us. His body went tense and within a second Quick Draw Matt had a gun. I didn't even see where he got it. He just had it trained on Noah.

Eek!

"Let her go," Matt demanded, and any normal person would obey him, mainly because he sounded scary, not to mention he had a gun. This surprised me because I didn't think he had it in him to sound that scary. Sure, he was a hottie with a great body, but he didn't seem as badass as the rest of the boys. At his tone I realized I was wrong about that. Way wrong.

Noah had his gun pointed at my back. When he saw Matt's gun, he moved it to my temple.

Uh-oh.

"Back off," Noah demanded.

Matt's eyes were at my temple. His mouth went tight, he took two steps back and we took two steps forward.

"Call the elevator," Noah ordered, and I suspected he was talking to me, mainly because he still had my arm in his hand and he shook me. I tagged the elevator and it opened immediately.

Matt didn't take his eyes off us and I didn't take my eyes off him as Noah backed us into the elevator, all the while turned to face the doors.

Matt stood outside the doors, eyes on me and they were active which I took as a good sign mainly because, at that point, I was holding on to anything I could get.

The doors closed.

Shit!

Noah took the gun from my head and put it to my back again.

"Noah, this is a bad idea." I told him.

"I think you know by now, Ava, that my name is Walt," he replied.

"Okay then, Walt, this is a bad idea," I repeated.

"Got no leverage. They messed up Kurt. They messed him up bad. Motherfuckers. They aren't gonna mess me up. Fuck that. You're the only leverage I got. They won't come near me if I got you."

I wasn't certain that was true. "Noah, I mean Walt, I'll talk to Luke. Just let me—"

"Time to talk to Stark was after I taped you to a post."

"I tried. Luke didn't feel like giving up. He's not big on that kind of thing. Maybe I can be more convincing this time."

"You had your chance."

Shit a-fucking-gain.

The doors opened and we stepped out. Noah stopped, jerking me to a halt, and he went still.

I was looking at the floor. My eyes came up and I saw Ren, Sissy, Dom and Uncle Vito standing there, looking like they were waiting for the elevator.

What the fuck?

"Hey guys," I said, trying to sound casual.

They all had their eyes on Noah.

"Are we having the family meeting?" I asked, still trying to sound casual.

"We were," Dom replied. His eyes hadn't left Noah.

"I'm kind of busy right now," I told Dom.

At that, Ren's body moved, but he halted when Noah put the gun to my temple.

"Move back," Noah ordered.

None of them moved. They changed, but they didn't move. Sissy's face went pale. Ren, Dom and Uncle Vito went solid.

"Move back!" Noah shouted, getting nervous, and people turned to stare. I heard a few audible gasps and a small scream when eyes hit us.

I didn't think Noah getting nervous was a good sign so I said softly, "You guys, please move back."

"This ain't a good idea, son," Uncle Vito advised Noah.

"Move back," Noah repeated.

"She's a Zano," Uncle Vito went on.

"She's not a Zano," Noah flashed back.

"She's a Zano," Ren said firmly.

For goodness sake, were we going to go through this again? *Now?*

"It'd really help me out, say, not to get my brains splattered across the Hotel Monaco lobby, if you guys would *step back!*" I shouted the last part.

"What's the breakfast hold up?" Shirleen was trundling up. She skidded to a halt. My eyes went to her and hers were wide. "Shit! Is that Noah?" she asked me.

"My name is Walt," Noah corrected.

"Whatever. You crazy, boy?" Shirleen asked, her gaze moving to Noah.

"Everyone, get out of our way!" Noah demanded, now not only nervous but losing patience, and I guessed this was a *very* bad sign.

"Yeah, you're crazy. Do you know you got a gun to the head of Luke Stark's woman?" Shirleen informed him and then continued to share. "He ain't gonna like that much."

"Shirleen—" I started.

"Ava...?"

That was my Mom.

Hell.

And.

Damnation!

Mom peeked around Shirleen.

"*Ava!*" she shrieked when she saw me.

"Mom, calm down," I said.

"What's happening...? Holy crap," Marilyn had arrived, Sofia at her side. Did I already mention my... life... *sucked?*

"Everyone, get fucking back!" Noah yelled.

"That's my sister," Sofia told Noah.

"I don't care, get fucking back," Noah clipped.

"*You have a gun pointed at my sister's head!*" Sofia screamed.

"Take that gun away from her head, right now, you jerk!" Marilyn shouted.

"Guys, you aren't helping," I told them.

"This is outrageous. We're in the lobby of a nice hotel. This kind of thing doesn't happen in the lobby of a nice hotel," my mother snapped. "Not to *my* daughter anyway. Put the gun down."

"Ava, get rid of these people," Noah said in my ear.

"Folks, can we all just—" I began.

"Has anyone called Luke?" Mom asked, she was digging through her bag. "I'm calling Luke. Who has his number?"

I'll ask again. Why me? Why me? *Why me?*

"Please, everyone can you just—" I began again.

"Holy shit." That was Riley, who had come around Sofia's right side and jerked to a stop at the sight of Noah and me. "*What the fuck are you doing?*" Riley exploded, staring at Noah and looking not like a mild mannered personal trainer, but just like a badass motherfucker.

Even in my current circumstances, I was impressed.

"Do I know you?" Noah asked.

"Yeah, you know me. I'm Ava's personal trainer. I was at her birthday party last year."

"Oh yeah. You ever finally get the nerve up to fuck her?" Noah asked, sounding nasty.

There were gasps all around, but I heard a couple of growls. One I suspected came from Ren, the other one I knew came from Riley.

I was beginning to wish he'd just shoot me.

Then we heard, "What the fuck!"

It was Ally. She'd rounded the other side of Ren, and Daisy rounded her side.

Everyone stopped and stared at the new arrivals.

Ally looked normal. Jeans, kickass belt, cowboy boots and vintage AC/DC tee.

She wasn't the reason everyone stared. Everyone stared because Daisy did not look normal. Daisy had the bottom of her platinum blonde hair in pigtails, the top teased out to maximum volume and she was wearing a baby pink velour Juicy Couture tracksuit that was skintight. If that wasn't reason enough to stare, she had the top zipped down to expose so much cleavage, the actual presence of the top was unnecessary except for the fact that it covered her nipples, thus stopping her from being arrested for indecent exposure.

"Well, I'll be goddamned," Daisy said, staring at Noah and me.

"What's the hold up?" We heard from the back. "The longer we take on breakfast, the longer it'll take to get to the mall—"

The person stopped speaking because she'd pushed her way to the front and we saw it was Olivia.

"Muthafucka," she breathed when her eyes hit me.

"All right people!" I shouted. "Everyone move back. *Back!*" I screeched.

Everyone moved back except Ren and Dom, because somehow they disappeared, vanished, no longer in sight.

Crap!

Noah moved us forward. My posse stayed close but moved back. We did this all the way across the lobby, everyone else in the hotel watching our progression in stunned silence as I heard the noise of faraway sirens.

When we hit the doors, Noah took the gun from my head, grabbed my hand and pulled us through. He ran down the sidewalk, taking me with him. I stumbled, nearly falling on my high-heeled wedges and I cursed my mother for her meddling into my wardrobe choices. Though flip-flops wouldn't likely have been any better. I'd learned that lesson the hard way.

He didn't break stride and kept dragging me. I righted myself just as we ran into traffic, straight to a car that was stopped at a light.

Noah pulled open the door, shoved the gun in the driver's face and clipped, "Out."

"But… this is my car," the driver said, eyes wide, obviously not thinking clearly, because all of a sudden on a sunny Denver day he found himself staring at a gun.

Noah moved the gun to the side, pulling the trigger and drilling a round into the pavement.

I jumped, the driver jumped and then Noah pointed the gun at the driver again.

"Out!" Noah shouted.

The driver got out.

Noah shoved me in first. I scrambled over to the passenger side and Noah got in behind me. Before I had myself settled, we took off on a squeal of tires, running the red light and making cars swerve and honk.

"Noah!" I yelled. "I mean, Walt! You're gonna kill us."

"Shut *up!*" Noah shouted.

I put my seatbelt on, which wasn't easy. Noah was driving erratically, jerking the wheel back and forth, passing cars, speeding up then stopping fast and running red lights willy-nilly.

Once I got my belt on, I turned to the front.

You would think I'd be scared. I wasn't scared. I was pissed way the hell off.

I'd had *enough.*

"This just cuts it," I grumbled. "I cannot believe you kidnapped me. First, you charm your way into my pants. Then you steal my money and Aunt Ella's jewelry, leave me high and dry and make me swear off men. Then!" My voice was beginning to rise. "I find myself a good guy, *the* best guy *ever*, and he wants to protect me and he goes after you. Instead of taking it like a man, you take it out *on me.*"

"Ava, shut up."

"I will not shut up. You're a jerk. You dry humped me. What was *that* all about?"

"You have a sweet ass," he said, as if that explained it.

"So? It isn't *your* sweet ass anymore. It's Luke's," I snapped. "Did you tell your partner I tasted like cherry pie?"

"You do," he replied on a reminiscent grin.

I growled then bit off, "Men!"

The phone at my ass started ringing, I leaned forward and pulled it out.

"Don't answer that," Noah ordered.

"Fuck you," I shot back, saw the display said, "Luke calling" and flipped it open. "Yo."

"Babe," Luke replied.

"I've been kidnapped again," I informed him.

"I know. I'm following."

I turned my head to look around my seat and saw Luke's Porsche behind us. He was at the wheel talking to me on the phone. Next to him was Ren's Jag, Ren driving, Dom sitting beside him. I kept looking and saw Ally's Mustang behind Ren, Daisy sitting beside Ally, more people in the back. I couldn't really see, but I suspected they were my sisters. Olivia's Lexus was beside Ally, Shirleen sitting next to her, what I reckoned was my Mom in the back. I couldn't be certain, but I thought I saw Riley's Pathfinder trailing the pack. They were all speeding and weaving, following Noah and me down Speer Boulevard in a highish speed chase.

Fuck.

Fuckity, fuck, fuck, *fuck*.

"You got a convoy," Luke told me.

I turned forward. "I can see that."

"Get him to slow down," Luke demanded.

"He isn't exactly listening to me."

"Ava, get off the phone," Noah cut in.

I looked at Noah. "Be quiet, I'm talking to Luke."

That was when we heard sirens. Not far away sirens. These were close.

"Fuck!" Noah snapped. "Get off the fuckin' phone."

"Kiss my ass!" I yelled.

"Beautiful, not sure it's a good idea to get him riled," Luke said in my ear.

"I don't care if he's riled," I told Luke.

"I care if it means he's gonna put a bullet in you," Luke returned.

He had a point.

"He's concentrating on driving," I assured Luke.

"Ava, I'm not gonna say it again, get off the *fucking* phone," Noah shouted.

"Glad to see I'm not the only man in your life who has to repeat himself," Luke remarked.

"I don't think you're funny," I told Luke, even though I kind of did.

I heard his chuckle in my ear as Noah snapped, "I wasn't being funny."

"I'm not talking to you," I told Noah.

A black Explorer pulled out from a road to our right. We shot by him and I saw Lee driving, Matt in the passenger seat. I didn't have a chance to wrap my head around where they had come from. Instead I looked behind us and saw that Luke and Ren also shot by Lee. The Explorer angled in to cut off Ally and Olivia, aided by a couple of squad cars.

"What's happening?" I asked Luke, turning forward again.

"You buckled in?" Luke asked me.

"Yeah. What's happening?"

"Get him to slow down. If he doesn't slow down, get him to buckle up," Luke replied.

"Luke, what's happening?" I demanded.

"Brace, babe, this ends here."

Disconnect.

Oh shit.

Shittity, shit, shit, *shit!*

I flipped the phone closed. "Noah, slow down."

"You should have told him to back off," Noah returned.

"Noah, seriously, they have something planned. Slow down."

He turned to me, lifted the gun to point at me and said, "Ava, for the past week, you've been nothing but a pain in my ass."

I'd heard that before, kind of.

"Well, good," I flashed back. "You deserve it."

He kept glancing back and forth to the road and me, gun raised and pointed at me. What with him driving like a freak, his inattention to the road did not make my situation any better.

"Noah, pay attention to the road."

"Call him back and tell him to stand down," Noah ordered.

"This is Lucas Stark we're talking about. He doesn't stand down," I explained.

"This is great, just great," Noah grouched like it was all my fault.

"You could have taken off, gone to Argentina or something. You didn't have to beat me up and tape me to a post. That was like waving a red flag at a bull. Then you kidnap me? How stupid are you?" I snapped.

"Shut up."

"I'm just saying."

"Shut... *up.*"

"Noah, slow down or buckle up," I told him, trying to be nice.

He was still driving like a maniac, swinging his eyes to the road and to me. "Buckling up means takin' the gun off you, and how am I gonna shoot you if I put the gun down?"

I had no answer to that and I was done. If he shot me then, hopefully, I'd survive. Jules got shot in the belly and chest and now she was happy and preggers. However, if Noah shot me, Luke would rip his head off. No hope for future happiness and babies in his life because he'd be dead.

So I shrugged. "Suit yourself. Don't say I didn't warn you."

"You weren't this fuckin' irritating when I was bangin' you," he informed me.

"I liked you then. I thought you were a good guy. Now I know you're slime," I retorted.

He didn't reply. I crossed my arms on my chest and then, up ahead, I saw another black Explorer pull out in front of us. It didn't turn. It pulled into the intersection and stopped dead.

Ho-ly *shit!*

"*Noah!*" I screamed because he wasn't watching, he had his eyes on me.

I saw two squad cars pull out and angle in at the front and back of the Explorer. They stopped, too, blocking the intersection entirely.

"Look!" I managed to get out. Noah looked, made a choking sound in his throat, took the gun off me and slammed on the brakes at the last minute.

But we were going way too fast.

We rammed into the back of the Explorer and the front of a squad car, and the air was filled with the eerie, frightening sound of crunching steel and breaking glass.

We barreled right through.

I didn't see much after that because I'd been thrown forward. The air bag popped out and I hit it, or it hit me, whatever. We kept going, slower this time, and only stopped when we crashed into something else with a loud bang and more crunching steel.

I sat there dazed for a second before I began fighting the air bag. I managed to lean away from it, turned to look at Noah and immediately bile filled my throat.

He was out of his seat, head and shoulders through the shattered windshield, waist and hips resting on the steering wheel and air bag. He wasn't moving but he was groaning, his eyes open, and blood was everywhere.

My door was pulled open, the air bag went "poof", it deflated and I turned to see Luke.

"I think he's hurt," I whispered.

Luke didn't respond and he didn't look at Noah. He unbuckled me and his hands started roaming, moving along my limbs, his indigo eyes scanning my body, his face hard.

"She's good," he clipped. To whom I didn't know. He shoved his arms in, one under my knees, one at my back and lifted me clear of the car. That was when I saw Matt.

I blinked as I looked around after Luke got me out of the car, not hesitating as he carried me away. I heard sirens, I saw Hector and Vance on Noah's side of the car and heard Lee say from somewhere, "Do your best to stabilize him, but get him loose."

Daisy, Ally, Mom, Marilyn, Sofia, Olivia and Shirleen were all rushing forward. Riley was running up after them.

"Back to your cars. Get outta here. *Go!*" Luke roared, and the women started walking slowly backwards then turned and hoofed it to their cars. Riley stopped, eyes on me. He must have been assured at what he saw because he turned and hoofed it, too.

Suddenly I was jostled. One second I was in Luke's arms, the next I was in Ren's.

"Take care of her," Luke ordered.

Without hesitation, Ren moved, taking me to his Jag.

"I think I should—" I started but Ren interrupted me.

"Quiet, honey," he said softly. "Can you stand?"

I nodded. He put me on my feet and opened the passenger side door. I got in and he shut the door. Dom slid in the back. Ren rounded the front and angled behind the wheel. He just started the car when it happened.

Boom!

I jumped and let out a little scream as the car Noah and I had been in exploded.

In a flash, Ren's hand tagged the back of my neck and he pulled me down toward his lap, his torso landing on top of me. I heard, rather than saw, pieces of car landing everywhere with sickening thuds, some of it hitting Ren's Jag, making it bounce.

"Oh my God," I whispered to Ren's hard thigh.

After the thuds stopped, Ren came up, I came up and my hand went directly to the door handle as my eyes scanned the landscape. I stopped my attempt to exit the car and find Luke when what I saw penetrated my stunned brain.

There were pieces of burning car everywhere. There were also members of the Hot Bunch and uniformed officers all recovering from whatever safety positions they'd assumed.

From what I could see, all were fine, no one injured. Hector and Vance had been shielded behind the wrecked Explorer, an unconscious Noah lying on the ground at their feet. Matt was coming out of a crouch behind a squad car. Lee, apparently protected by an invisible Badass Shield, was simply standing in the middle of the mayhem, staring at the burning remains of the car.

Luke, much like Lee, was standing smack in the chaos, pieces of car on fire all around him, and his eyes were on me.

I gave him what I hoped was a jaunty wink and a stupid half-wave.

He shook his head and half-grinned.

I dropped my hand and turned to Ren.

Then I said, "I need cookies."

⌁

"Miss Barlow, I'm gonna have to repeat, next time you get kidnapped or your house gets broken into or you get beaten up and violated, it's a real good idea to call the police," Detective Jimmy Marker told me, sounding slightly aggrieved.

I pulled out the Oreo I was dunking into milk Tex had given me, popped it's soggy goodness into my mouth and munched.

"Okay," I said, mouth full, hoping that I would not be experiencing any of those things anytime soon (read: ever again).

I was in Fortnum's and so was most everyone else.

Duke, Tex and Indy were manning the espresso counter.

Shirleen was standing guard beside the couch I was sitting on.

Uncle Vito was sitting across from me.

Sissy was on one side of me, Mom on the other. Sissy, by the way, had missed the car chase, staying behind with Uncle Vito at the hotel.

Marilyn and Sofia were at a table across the room. Sofia had been crying, like, a lot. Apparently, her little sister having a near-death experience bounced the bitch right out of her (good to know, not that I'd ever do *that* again). Marilyn was having trouble taking her eyes off me as if, at any second, another bad guy was going to come in and spirit me away.

Riley was sitting at the table with them, elbows on knees, jaw in his hands, eyes on me.

Daisy was sitting on the arm of the couch, Ally sitting on the other one.

Roxie and Jet were sitting on the book counter, Hank standing next to Roxie, Eddie standing next to Jet.

Jules was sitting in the armchair next to Uncle Vito.

Olivia was standing at the espresso counter, enjoying a cappuccino and an Archway peanut butter cookie.

Ren and Dom were standing just inside the door, talking in low voices, Santo and Lucky a few feet away.

Ren had ordered Santo and Lucky to bring me cookies and they obviously obeyed orders well. There were Oreos, Chips Ahoy, four different types of Milanos and a plethora of other Pepperidge Farms choices, Nutter Butters, Pecan Sandies and a variety of Archway and Entenmanns on the coffee table in front of me.

Tod and Stevie would have been there, but they were flight attendants and they were both flying. However, Indy was watching their chow dog, Chowleena, and Chowleena was sitting on the couch between me and Sissy, panting. So I figured Tod and Stevie were there in spirit.

Detective Marker rose from the armchair at the side of the couch.

"I got what I need," he announced.

I nodded as Indy came forward and handed me a fresh skinny vanilla latte. I set down my milk and took the latte. Then I sipped.

Heaven.

"Who's up next?" Detective Marker asked Indy, sounding resigned, but apparently deciding it was best to prepare for the next disaster.

"I'm thinkin' Mace," Indy replied.

"I got my money on Ally," Shirleen put in.

Ally twisted to Shirleen. "Me?" Then swiftly (and weirdly), her eyes sliced to Ren before they went back to Shirleen when she kept talking.

"That blond boy's headed to DC. You think you'll escape this shit? You're a Nightingale," Shirleen replied.

"Darius needs a woman," Daisy threw in.

"Huh," Shirleen grunted. "Darius would put up with this shit for about a second."

The doors flew open, the bell over them clattered and Smithie came in.

"What'd I miss?" he yelled to no one in particular.

"Ava, held at gunpoint. Kidnapping. Car chase. Car crash. Car explosion. It's over," Jet explained. "I missed it, too. I was working," she sounded disappointed.

"Thank Christ for that," Eddie muttered.

"Amen," Hank added under his breath.

"Shee-it," Smithie said.

I reached for a cookie, found the variety too complex, and bit my lip in indecision.

"Ava, give it up with the cookies," Riley told me.

My eyes moved to him, "But—"

He shook his head. I glared but sat back.

"What'll it be?" Tex boomed at Smithie.

"Latte with some of that butterscotch syrup," Smithie replied, walking in.

Detective Marker moved to leave when the doors flew open again, the bell over them clattered, and three big guys I'd never seen before rushed into the store, guns raised and pointed at Dom.

The room went still.

Ho-ly *shit*.

What now?

"Nobody move. Vincetti, you're comin' with us," one of them ordered.

No. This was not going to happen. I could take no more. I was going to put an end to this, right... fucking... now.

I stood. "Not so fast," I snapped.

"Ava—" Ren started, eyes on me.

I stomped up to the men with guns. They stared at me as I did so, obviously taken aback by my bold behavior. I didn't care. I walked right up to one and yanked the gun out of his hand.

"What the fuck?" he clipped, staring at me with his gun.

I twisted, tossed the gun five feet to Eddie who, at the last minute, came out of his frozen stupor (a stupor caused undoubtedly by my crazy-as-shit actions) and caught it.

"Do you know there are three policemen in this room?" I asked.

The men looked around.

"No shit?" one mumbled.

"No shit," I replied. "What's your deal with Dom?" I demanded.

"He stole money from us," one of the men said.

"So?" I asked.

"A lot of money," another one said.

"So?" I repeated.

"We want it back," the one I took the gun from said.

I turned to Uncle Vito. "Can you give them back their money?"

"I already told 'em I'd pay 'em," Uncle Vito replied.

I turned back to the men. "Okay then, what's the problem?"

"The man we work for don't like it when people steal from him," the first man said.

"Charge interest. Make it worth his while. This isn't rocket science boys. Yeesh," I returned.

"That sounds like kind of a good idea," the second man said.

"Twenty-five percent," the first man told Uncle Vito.

"Ten percent," Ren returned.

"Twenty," the first man haggled.

"Ten," Ren repeated.

"Fifteen," the first man tried again.

"Ten. You take it or you got war with the Zanos," Ren told him.

The three men shifted, not liking this idea, but still not wanting to give up. I sighed, heavy and huge. Men!

"For goodness sake!" I snapped.

"We just want Vincetti," the third man said.

"Dom's a Zano," Ren replied.

"We don't want family trouble. Just cut him loose," the second man threw in.

Ren shook his head. They all looked at each other.

"All right, ten. Fuck," the first man relented.

"Tell The Man he'll have it in the hour," Uncle Vito cut in.

Finally!

"While we're here, we should get a coffee. I hear it's good here," the second man told the first man.

The third man's eyes were on Eddie. "You think I could have my gun back?"

Eddie's answer was to shove it in the back of his jeans, then he pulled his badge out of his back pocket and clipped it on his belt.

"Shit," the third man mumbled.

"What'll it be?" Tex boomed.

The newest bad guys moved toward the espresso counter and some of the tension went out of the room. Not all of it, seeing as Detective Marker sat back down, obviously deciding not to leave. Hank, Eddie and Duke took different, slightly more aggressive/defensive positions within the coffee area.

The door opened, the bell rang again and I turned around to see Luke, Vance, Matt, Lee and Hector striding in.

Luke's eyes scanned me then they scanned the room then they stopped on the cookies. After he got a good look at the cookies, his eyes cut back to me.

"Babe," he said on a half-grin.

"If there's any time that's Cookie Time, *this* is Cookie Time," I stated the obvious.

"Why are Sid's boys here?" Lee asked, standing by Luke.

"Who's Sid?" I asked in return.

Lee's head inclined toward the new bad guys.

"Oh, they were after Dom," I replied.

"I know that. Why are they in my fiancée's bookstore ordering coffee?" Lee went on.

Ee-yikes.

He sounded pretty unhappy.

"The situation is cool," Dom put in. Lee's eyes moved to him and they were even less happy.

Luke's arm slid around my shoulders and he pulled me into his side. Without delay, I relaxed and put a hand to his abs, hooking my other thumb in the middle back belt loop of his cargoes.

"Ava settled it," Ren informed Lee. Then, done with this topic, his gaze came to me. "You're okay?"

I nodded. "Thanks for the cookies."

He smiled and said quietly, "Anytime."

Luke got tense beside me at the very mention of Ren ever buying me cookies again in this lifetime. Ren's eyes moved to Luke and I got tense.

They had a Badass Faceoff for several beats then Ren jerked his chin and Luke did the same. Ren's eyes came back to me. He gave me another smile, this one softer, less cocky and very sweet.

"Take care of yourself, honey," he said.

Then *he*, weirdly, gave *Ally* a swift, unhappy look before he was gone.

"That's our cue," Uncle Vito stood.

"But we haven't sorted things out with Sissy," Dom protested.

"We'll do it tomorrow." Uncle Vito walked around the coffee table and bent to give Sissy a kiss on the cheek.

"Hang on, my shit's sorted now. I want to talk to Sissy," Dom pushed.

"Piss off, Dom," Sissy said, standing and walking Uncle Vito to the door.

"Sis, baby," Dom cajoled, giving her one of his killer smiles.

Sissy shot him a look, clearly immune to Dominic Vincetti's killer smile. This made *me* smile.

"Tomorrow, after Ava's recovered from the drama," Uncle Vito ordered.

"Uncle Vito," Dom said.

"Tomorrow," Vito snapped.

Dom turned to Sissy, the killer smile gone. His face, I was shocked to see, looked serious. "I fucked up. I admit it, all right? I fucked up. It won't happen again."

Sissy kept on giving him the Sissy Glare.

Dom turned to me. "I fucked up, with my wife and with you. It was a shit thing to do."

"You got that right," I told him.

He turned back to Sissy and promised, "I can make it good between us again."

She continued with the Sissy Glare, and against my will, I began to feel sorry for him. He had a huge audience, but he seemed not to care. Any man would be humiliated, except maybe a man who genuinely wanted his wife back.

Wow.

I couldn't process this and didn't try. Instead I looked at Sissy to ascertain if she needed bestest best friend assistance and I saw she wasn't backing down.

"Just think about that," Dom urged quietly, and it sounded like he sincerely wanted her to think about it and he wasn't lying through his men-are-jerks teeth.

And somehow, I suspected he wasn't.

Then he and Uncle Vito were gone.

I watched as Sissy deflated right in front of me. All the bravado leaked right out of her.

"You okay?" I asked.

She shook her head.

"I think we've moved on to Tequila Time," I said.

She nodded her head.

"My place!" Shirleen yelled. "I got tequila. I got rum. I got vodka and I got mixers. I even got popcorn. Someone should bring some tortilla chips and guacamole because I haven't had breakfast and I'm definitely peckish."

"I'll bring cashews," Indy said.

"I'll bring the chips and it'll only take a minute for me to mix up the guac," Jet put in.

"I'll bring turkey, swiss and rye. We'll make sandwiches," Roxie offered.

"Fucking hell," Hank muttered

More offers were called as Luke curled me into his body. I looked up at him and his face was soft.

"You goin' to the party?" he asked.

"How's Noah?" I queried instead of answering.

He hesitated, pulled his lip between his teeth then let it go and shook his head.

I did not take this as a good sign.

I sucked in air then breathed, "Is he dead?"

Luke shook his head again. "Broken neck. Bone pierced the spinal column. He'll be paralyzed from the neck down for life."

I shut my eyes tight. I really hated Noah. He conned me, stole from me, beat me up and worse. Still, even after all that, being paralyzed was a high price to pay. This hit me hard, and even though he was a jerk, I felt bad for him. Bad enough for my throat to get tight.

"Look at me, babe."

I opened my eyes, caught his and told him, "I don't feel like partying."

His other arm went around me and got tight. "I didn't think so."

"That sucks for Noah," I whispered.

"It sucks for Noah," Luke agreed.

"Why do I care?" I asked.

"Because you're a good person," he answered.

"Do you care?"

As usual, brutally honest, he replied, "Nope."

I rested my forehead on his shoulder. His fingers slid up and curled around my neck.

"It's over," I murmured.

"Yeah," he said.

My arms went around his waist and I pressed in close. His fingers started kneading the muscles at my neck.

"What do you want to do, beautiful?" he asked.

I thought about it. An idea came to me and I tilted my head back to look at him.

"Do you have a bike?" I asked.

He watched my face. "Got three."

Of course, he had three.

"Can we ride?" I requested.

Luke grinned. "Absolutely."

Chapter 30

Bliss

The elevator doors opened and I flew through them.

"Late!" I shouted, running to the dining room table. "I'm late!" I repeated unnecessarily.

I threw the shopping bags I was carrying on the table and scanned the loft.

Luke was sitting in the recliner. He was tipped back, footrest up, hands behind his head, watching the Rockies on the flat screen (even though if you stopped to listen you could hear the damn game through the windows, we were that close to Coors Stadium). The new blinds were mostly closed all around so as not to let the glare of the sun hit the TV.

Mace and Matt were sitting on the couch with their feet up on the coffee table and hands curled around bottles of beer. Big Bobby, now fully recovered and back at work, had one of the new dining room table chairs (black lacquer, gray suede upholstered seat and back, sweeping lines, kick fucking ass) turned backwards and he was straddling it. Hank was sitting on the kitchen counter and he was holding a beer by its neck. Eddie's head was in the fridge.

All the men had turned, eyes on me, as I ran across the loft to the dresser.

"Olivia came by, we got to talking and got behind on the decorating. Then Olivia, as she always does, invited herself to the party. *Then* Tod and Stevie decided everyone needed new outfits so, even though we had *no* time *at all*, we took a trip to the mall." I stopped at the dresser, babbling on like they were actually listening to me (which they probably were not) and I looked over my shoulder at Luke. "I think I spent too much money."

I heard a phone ringing and Hank moved to answer it as Luke's eyes cut to the dining room table. He took in the bags then his eyes moved back to me.

"An outfit takes six bags?" he asked.

"I also bought shoes," I told him as I heard another cell phone ring.

"An outfit and shoes take six bags?" Luke slightly amended his question.

I turned back to the dresser and started digging through it, half in a panic. "I might have bought some other stuff."

"I'll be there in fifteen." I heard Hank say to his phone.

"I'll pick it up on my way home." I heard Eddie say to his.

I found what I was looking for and snatched them out of the drawer with too much hurried energy. I managed to keep hold of the bra but my lavender satin panties with black lace flew through the air, landing on the floor five feet behind the couch.

All the men's eyes went to the panties. My eyes went to the panties.

I thought perhaps that was the perfect time for me to learn how to become invisible just as I heard Luke chuckle.

"Time to go." Big Bobby jumped up from his chair, swung it around and carried it back to the table.

I saw Mace and Matt make a move to get up as I ran to the undies and snatched them off the floor, balling them up in my fist and hiding them and the bra with my arms.

"No, it's okay. I'll get ready in the bathroom," I told them, pretty sure I was blushing, considering my face was on fire. "Finish the game."

"Gotta go anyway," Eddie put in. "Jet needs me to pick up some ice and drop it by Fortnum's."

"Apparently Roxie's new dress has a back zip that she can't reach," Hank sounded partly amused, partly like he wasn't intent on getting home to zip *up* the dress, but rather the other way around. Little did he know that I knew her dress didn't even have a zip so someone was about to get lucky.

On that thought, I smiled to myself. I ran to the bags, grabbed the ones I needed and ran to the bathroom.

"See you all there," I called over my shoulder and slammed the door to the bathroom.

I pulled off my clothes and jumped in the shower.

⊰⊱

The six weeks since my troubles finished hadn't exactly been uneventful.

First up, we had the family meeting. Uncle Vito surprisingly stayed quiet while Dom tried to talk Sissy into giving him another chance. Ren and I kept quiet, too, even though I really, *really* didn't want to and I could see Ren felt the same way. In the end, we didn't have to say anything. Sissy told Dom to go jump in a lake and walked out of the room. I looked at the Zanos then gave out hugs (yes, even one to Dom, mainly because he looked like his world just came to an end) and followed her.

It wasn't over. Not by half.

For the next month, Dom pursued Sissy like a man possessed. It appeared that not only did the shot she took to the face wake up the protective, hot-blooded, Italian husband, but Sissy's bitchy attitude was turning him on. Big time.

He ended up kidnapping her.

Which meant I ended up calling in Luke and the boys (again).

Luke and Vance found them in a condo in Vail, but he came back sans Sissy.

"Why did you leave her there?" I demanded when he arrived at my place in the dead of night, woke me up and told me he found Sissy but didn't have her.

"Babe," he said, sitting on the bed and taking off his boots.

I waited for him to say more. He didn't.

"Luke!" I snapped.

He twisted, angled onto the bed, landed full on top of me and my breath went out in a whoosh.

"They worked it out," he told me after I'd sucked oxygen back into my lungs.

I narrowed my eyes at him. "She thinks he's scum."

"They worked it out," he repeated.

"I don't believe that."

"Trust me, they worked it out."

"How do you know? Did Sissy say that? Sometimes Dom can be—"

"Babe, trust me. I wouldn't leave her there if I didn't think it was a good thing."

That shut me up because Luke really wouldn't do that.

"Oh, all right," I finally grumbled.

"Now." His eyes were ink. "Let's talk about what you owe me for finding her."

I didn't quibble. I'd learned that quick payback for the many times I fell in debt with Luke was definitely the way to go.

Anyway, every single time I was pretty certain I got more out of it than Luke did.

Second up, just as he promised, we had stayed at my place until the blinds were put in at the loft then we moved to his. We still weren't sure which way to go. I liked my back porch and funky office. Luke liked the loft's security and central location. In the end, Luke told me to do what I had to do to make the loft mine, thus the dining room table (so Tex, Mr. Kumar, Uncle Vito and I could play euchre which we did, quite a bit) and a variety of girlie things for the kitchen (but not too girlie; I bought all the KitchenAid appliances in black, the rest in black or red). Luke had my furniture moved into storage and had an agency rent out my place. The plan was we'd keep both properties. If we decided to move to my place later, we'd still have it to move to.

It was a decent compromise.

Even though I didn't share it with Luke, I didn't really care where we lived, just as long as we ended the day, and started a new one, in the same bed.

Last, the New Mom—and apparently the New Marilyn and Sofia—were driving me up the flipping wall. They had let me into the Barlow Bombshell Club, which meant daily phone calls, lots of unsolicited advice on everything under the sun and constant getting into my (and Luke's) business. At first, I thought it was kind of cool. Then I found it kind of annoying.

When I complained about it to Luke while lying full out on the couch, Luke on his back, being Zen, me pressed into his side, not reading the book I had propped on his chest, Luke said, "Gotta choose, babe. They are who they are. Either you're in the club or you're out."

I sighed. He was right yet again. In the club it was.

I got out of the shower, did the whole celebration preparation on body (the peony-scented lotion, Luke's favorite), hair (loose and wild, Luke's favorite) and makeup (party time drama, no other choice; it was party time) and turned to my shopping bags.

I'd brought in the shoes, but grabbed the wrong bag of clothes. My party dress was still on the dining room table.

To save time which was slipping away fast, I tugged off my robe, put on the undies and strapped on the shoes (Tod found them at Nordstrom's; metallic purple, high, spike-heeled, strappy sandals) and ran out to get the dress.

I stopped in mid-run. Luke was standing in the kitchen, head back, muscular throat on display, finishing a beer.

He had on a charcoal gray suit, a shirt the same color, throat exposed at the collar. I hadn't seen him in a suit since his father's funeral.

Luke looks good, Good Ava breathed, hand at her neck.

No, Luke looks GOOD, Bad Ava was fanning her face

They were not wrong. Luke didn't look good. Luke looked *good*.

"You look good," I told him.

His head came down, his gaze came to me and he went still.

"Jesus," he muttered, eyes doing a body sweep.

I came unstuck from my Luke Looking Good Fog and ran to the dining room table.

"I grabbed the wrong bag." I started sorting through bags then asked Luke, "Can you grab my perfume?"

He didn't grab my perfume. Instead, I felt his heat at my back. He leaned forward and I had no choice but to lean with him. He did an arm swipe, the bags went flying and I felt his hand pressing in the middle of my back.

"Luke," I said, my eyes on the bags on the floor, my voice stunned.

He pushed me down toward the table as the thumb of his other hand hooked into my panties, yanking them down to just below my hips.

Oh wow.

My special girlie parts quivered.

"Luke!" I gasped.

He didn't answer. He kept me pressed to the table even though I tried to come up. His hand was moving at my bottom, I heard his belt clink, his zipper, then without warning, he slid inside me.

I stopped trying to rise, and my arms, of their own volition, slid straight out in front of me, palms flat against the table, my bottom pushing into Luke's hips.

"Luke." It came out a lot different this time. His hand left my back and both went to my hips, holding me still as he moved.

My breath started coming heavy.

Like everything with Luke, this was *hot*.

I moved with him, made happy noises low in my throat, then he slid out, swept my panties down to my ankles, twisted me around and lifted me onto the table. He pulled the panties, which were tangled at my shoes, free, tossed them aside and moved between my legs, lifted my hips and slid inside me again, bending his torso over mine.

I lifted my head. One of his hands stayed at my hip while he slammed into me, the fingers of his other hand slid into my hair, and he kissed me, long, deep, wet and lots of tongue.

"We're going to be late," I panted when his mouth disengaged.

"Don't fuckin' care," he said back, his voice rough.

My hands came up. One curled around his neck, the other went to his jaw, my thumb trailing his 'tache while my hooded eyes stayed locked on his mouth.

"God, you're beautiful," he murmured as my thumb moved to trace his bottom lip.

"I could live my life, you inside me," I whispered back.

He stopped stroking and ground in deep. Shivers slid through me and I licked my lips. His eyes went molten and he kissed me again.

Mouth against mine, he admitted, "Got no control when it comes to you."

"Is that a bad thing?" I was getting close, my voice hitched in the middle of the sentence and I was losing focus.

He didn't answer my question. Instead, eyes on mine, he muttered, "Give it to me, babe."

"What?" I asked, but I didn't wait for his answer. It hit me. It was magnificent. I felt it rush through me as I said his name softly and smiled.

"That's just the way I like it," Luke whispered against my smiling mouth while I came.

Then his lips pressed hard against mine, he drove into me one last time and he groaned into my mouth.

⚜

"I knew that was the dress for you girlie," Tod told me. "Your man is over there looking at you like he's spent the last year at a males-only monastery in the depths of a mountain range, inaccessible by cars and a treacherous, death-defying two week walk from civilization."

I looked at Luke and Tod was right. Luke was looking at me. However, Tod was wrong. Luke wasn't looking like he wanted me. He was looking like he had already had me and he liked what I gave him.

My knees wobbled.

"We did it on the dining room table before we got here," I told Tod.

"Mm-hmm. Like I said, the dress," Tod replied.

My dress was pretty, though it was not me, but Stevie convinced me I could make it work. It was girlie, floaty and lavender. It had twisted material to make straps. It showed lots of chest, but not lots of cleavage. The bodice was cut on a slant, a wispy tear of material falling from it. It fit close and fell on a floaty slant at the hem, exposing one knee and a lot of leg on one side. The back was low, just above my bra strap. It was demure on the face of it, but the way it clung and moved was seductive as all hell.

"I hadn't even gotten my dress on yet. I was still in my undies," I shared.

Tod turned to me, mouth open, then he looked back at Luke. "Swear to God, these boys should be locked up. It isn't safe, men with that much testosterone coursing through their blood free to roam."

Daisy came storming up to us. She was wearing an ice blue, body-hugging, strapless dress, the bodice held up by what could only be a miracle.

"Where are they?" she snapped.

"How should I know?" Tod asked.

"Did you call Indy?" Daisy shot back.

"No, I don't want to disturb her," Tod told her.

"Why not?" Daisy's voice was rising. "The hors d'oeuvres are getting cold and I talked Tex into wearing a suit and I think he's beginning to get cranky."

Our eyes swung to Tex and it did appear he was getting cranky. We knew this because cranky energy was emanating from him and he was fiddling with the tie knotted at his throat.

"I didn't call her because this *is* a wedding, Daisy. I didn't want to interrupt," Tod explained.

"I cannot *believe* we weren't invited," Daisy groused.

"Daisy, girlie, we are invited. We're here aren't we? They just wanted the ceremony small," Tod returned.

"I know, but still," Daisy gave in, but still sounded put out.

Tod put his arm around her shoulders. "You did a good job with decorations and I like the waiters you chose. You've got an eye for fine male ass."

I looked around Fortnum's, which had been closed for a private party.

It had been transformed and somehow (you had to give Daisy credit, as Head Party Planner she'd done a bang-up job), it was tasteful and elegant. The normal coffee house furniture had been carted away and replaced by chairs covered in white linen as well as white wicker tables. Festive white balloons and clear Christmas lights were everywhere, even lining the ceiling. The place was awash with white peonies in big glass vases. Handsome waiters carrying trays filled with glasses of champagne or hot hors d'oeuvres were wandering around and light, classical music was playing.

We had done the decorating ourselves, and as a wedding gift, paid for the party, although everyone bought real gifts, just because.

Shirleen and Daisy sprung for the waiters and the furniture rental. Tod, Stevie, Smithie, Tex and Duke got together and paid for the catering. Roxie, Jet, Ally and I bought all the flowers and decorations. Lee and Indy, of course, insisted on springing for the booze.

Luke materialized at my side, his lips coming to my neck, giving me an immediate and involuntary shiver just as Roxie, wearing a pale pink boat-necked front slim skirt brushing the knees, back completely bare, rushed up and whispered with excitement, "They're here."

"They're here!" Shirleen, in turquoise from head to foot (even her wild afro had turquoise glitter sprayed in it) cried from across the room, nearly bouncing up and down with excitement.

I turned to Luke and looked up at him. "They're here," I breathed.

His eyes scanned my face for a beat then he put his forehead to mine and, close up, I watched his eyes smile.

By the way, it was fascinating to watch, let me tell you.

Jet moved around one side of the room, Ally the other. They were carrying baskets of big, white tissue disks of confetti. Everyone took a massive handful then, en masse, we all closed in on the door, forming a semi-circle. There was Tod and Stevie, Daisy and her husband Marcus, Smithie and one of his women LaTeesha, Olivia with Winnie sitting by her side, Tex and Nancy, Jet and Eddie, Hank and Roxie, Big Bobby and his girlfriend Carol, Matt and his girlfriend Daphne, Shirleen and Darius, Hector and some blonde I hadn't yet met, Mace (alone), Monty and his wife Gillian, three guys named Zip, Heavy and Frank that I met when I arrived at the party, Duke and Dolores, Ally (alone, too; just as Shirleen predicted, she'd broken up with her boyfriend when he had gone to FBI training), and Luke and me.

The doors opened and Jules's Uncle Nick walked in beside an older Native American lady. They smiled. Jet stuck her basket out, they grabbed a handful of confetti and assumed their positions in the circle.

All eyes moved back to the door.

May walked in, looking lovely in baby blue, complete with huge hat. She was carrying a small bouquet made entirely of peonies so deep pink they looked like velvet. She grinned, grabbed some confetti and took her place in the circle.

Two young boys walked in. I had met them a few times before, one short, skinny and white, one tall, filling out well and black. They went by their street names, Sniff and Roam. They looked uncomfortable in their suits (but handsome), but even more uncomfortable under the scrutiny of the crowd. Their eyes found Luke and they walked straight to him, ignoring the confetti basket, and shoved through to stand behind Luke and me.

Indy and Lee walked in, Indy looking amazing in a mint green dress that was even more girlie than mine. Lee had a pink rose pinned to his lapel, and, it must be said, he looked hot in a suit, too. They grabbed their confetti and just managed to get into position when the couple of honor walked in.

Everyone sucked in breath.

Jules's gleaming jet-black hair was down, slightly curled in massive waves falling around her shoulders. She wore an ivory silk sleeveless dress, empire-waist, cross-over bodice with hint-of-cleavage vee. It fit snug all the way down to her knees so you could clearly see the slight bump at her belly. She had on a pair of baby blue high-heeled sandals, a wide leather strap across her French manicured toes, a soft, satin ribbon coming up from the sides of the shoe, wrapping around and tied in a bow at her ankles. She was carrying an enormous bouquet of white peonies and roses and she was, quite simply, glowing. She had a diamond at her neck and some kind of chunky, cool as shit silver bracelet on her wrist, a gorgeous promise ring on her right hand, not to mention the huge rock on her left ring finger, nestled now with a wedding band.

Vance was at her side, white rose at his lapel, dark suit, dark shirt, and dark tie, his black hair pulled back in a ponytail. I didn't know what the masculine form of glowing was, but whatever it was, Vance looked it.

"Congratulations!" Daisy shouted, breaking the silence. She jumped forward and threw her confetti.

We all followed suit shouting, and confetti flew so thick in the air it seemed to be snowing. It drifted around slowly, floating softly as it fell around the newlyweds.

I saw the tears glimmering in Jules's eyes as she looked around at her friends then she turned, Vance's arms closed around her and she shoved her face in his neck.

That was when I felt my throat close.

"Shit," Indy, standing close to me, muttered.

Lee mumbled, "Honey," and slid his arms around her.

She pressed a red trying-not-to-cry face into his chest and wrapped her arms around his neck.

That was when I felt my throat begin to burn and I took a step back, for some reason needing to escape.

So I looked to escape as fast as my purple shoes would take me.

I whirled and ran, dodging well-wishers and waiters, and made it halfway down the middle aisle of books before an arm caught me at the waist and I was turned to face Luke.

My head tilted back and my gaze met his. His face was soft, his eyes were searching. My eyes were filled with tears.

"Babe," he murmured. "Talk to me."

I shook my head and took a step back. Both his arms went around me and he pulled me close. Therefore, no retreat.

Eek!

"No running," he said, voice soft but firm. "Talk."

"I don't think…" I started, then stopped.

Get it out, get it out, get it OUT, girl, Good Ava demanded.

Yeah, for goodness sake, let's get this over with. I need more champagne, Bad Ava sounded bored.

"Ava," Luke said low when I didn't start talking.

I cleared my throat, took a deep breath, straightened in his arms and said, straight out before I could stop myself, "I don't think I've ever been this happy."

His head jerked back and I knew that was not what he was expecting to hear.

Then his face changed. He looked at me in a way he had never looked at me before, and whatever was in his face made my lungs seize.

His arms moved. One went low, very low, past my waist, his hand going lower, pressing into my behind so my hips were fit snug into his. The other arm slid up my back so it was wrapped just under my shoulder blades and I felt his fingers against the side of my breast.

"I'm scared," I told him in a small voice, and I felt a shiver slide through my body. I also felt suddenly cold, so I pressed in close and put my hands on his shoulders. I closed my eyes tight then opened them and whispered, "Luke, I'm scared to death. I've never been so scared in all my life."

"Tell me, and I swear to God, I'll make it so you won't be scared ever again," he promised.

I blinked at him. "Tell you what?"

"You know what."

"I don't know what." After I said it, I knew what and my body went tense.

"Babe, I've been waitin' since that day your family breezed into town."

That was when I knew that he knew all along. How he knew, I did not know. But then again, he knew everything.

"Do I have to say it?" I asked quietly.

He gave me a half-grin and an arm squeeze. "Yeah, you have to say it."

I sighed.

He did another arm squeeze.

My hands slid up from his shoulders to his jaw and I looked him in the eyes.

Oh well, I had been waiting since I was eight. I had created extravagant daydreams about it. I had dreamed of it at night. I had written about how I would do it in my diary. I had hoped for a chance to do this for over twenty years. I had even prayed for it.

There was no reason to wait any longer. If I waited any longer I'd be a serious wuss.

And there was one thing I knew about myself after the last couple of months: I was no wuss.

"Lucas Stark," I whispered, "I love you."

I hadn't let my mind move forward past the actual saying of the words to process what I thought his response to my telling him I loved him would be.

However, even in my wildest imaginings it wasn't what I got.

His arms did another squeeze, this one so tight it crushed me to him. He kissed me. The kiss was so hot, so hard, so deep, it bruised my lips (truth be told, I didn't really mind).

Then he let me go and I was in such a Luke Lip Fog that I went back on a foot, my hand curling around his upper arm to steady myself, but I didn't have to do that. Mainly because, all of a sudden, I was no longer on my feet. Instead, I was thrown over Luke's shoulder, his arm wrapped around the backs of my thighs. He turned and started walking back toward the party.

Oh... my... *God.*

He was not carrying me to the party! Was he?

"Luke!" I hissed. "Put me down."

He kept walking.

"Luke! Everyone is going to—"

Too late. We hit the open area. People were chatting, laughing, glasses were clinking.

As Luke walked through, the chatting, laughing and clinking glasses stopped and I looked around from my position hanging over Luke's back, my hands at this waist, my head lifted up and I saw everyone stare.

"You the man!" Sniff shouted at us, and there were a few low laughs.

I decided, in that moment, I was going to *kill* Luke.

"We'll be back," I heard Luke say to someone, then he walked through the door and I saw he was talking to Vance and Jules who were both watching us go. Vance wearing his shit-eating grin, Jules's eyes wide.

I gave them a lame wave.

Jules burst out laughing.

Luke kept on walking.

⚜

I sucked back the last of my champagne, slammed the glass on the table, turned my head and shouted, "Waiter! Fill 'er up!"

Luke, who was lounging next to me in one of the lovely little linen-covered chairs, had his arm draped on the back of mine. His hand curled around my neck, he twisted me toward his body and his mouth came to my ear.

"How drunk are you?" he whispered.

I jerked my head back, gave him a glare and crossed my arms on my chest. Luke chuckled.

With his he-man, tough guy, macho man antics, he had bought himself an undefined period of the Ava Barlow Silent Treatment.

Okay, so he had whisked me back to the loft in his Porsche, dragged me in, made love to me slowly and told me he loved me right before I had my *second* Luke-induced orgasm of the night, and that was all good. Very good. Super good. *Ultra*-good.

Then he had taken us back to the party, and I knew that everyone *totally* knew I had just been laid, and good. That meant I was embarrassed for the second time that night by Luke.

The waiter came up with another glass of champagne.

"Thank you," I said with feeling, smiling sweetly at him.

"Sugar, don't you think you need to eat somethin', considerin' you're drinkin' enough for all of us?" Daisy asked, sitting across from me.

"I'm not hungry," I answered.

"She's pissed-off." Shirleen, sitting beside me, smiled.

"Damn straight," I returned.

"Girl, I don't know what you're pissed about. A fine man carted me off to give me the business, and good, if your face and hair was anything to go by, I'd be doin' fuckin' cartwheels," Shirleen replied.

Luke's thumb started stroking my neck. I turned and glared at him again. He burst out laughing.

He was *so* annoying!

I turned back to Shirleen. "You say that now. It happened to you, you might not say it. You might do what I'm doing. I think a sentence of at least a week of Ava Barlow Silent Treatment is too nice. Maybe I'll make it two."

"Silent Treatment!" Daisy cried then giggled her tinkly-bell giggle. "Girl, you wanna get back at him, you cut off his water, comprende?"

Intrigued, I leaned toward Daisy. "Cut off his water?"

"No nookie. None, nada. No fingers, no mouths, no tongues, no kisses, no *nothin'*. Complete cut off. Works for me every time," Daisy replied.

I sat back nodding somewhat drunkenly. "Daisy, you are the *shit*. I like that idea."

Luke's hand curled around my neck again. He twisted me toward his body and his mouth came back to my ear. "You try to cut off access to that sweet body of yours, beautiful, you'll find yourself cuffed naked to my bed for a week," he hesitated, "maybe two."

Ee-yikes!

He lifted his head. Our eyes caught, we got into an Ava Barlow and Lucas Stark Glare to the Death Contest and, per usual, I lost.

I jerked away from him and gave him another good glower, but turned back to the table and shared, "I don't think cutting off his water is gonna work."

Shirleen threw her head back and laughed.

I, personally, didn't think anything was funny.

Roxie and Hank came up and Roxie collapsed in a chair while Hank grabbed a couple of glasses of champagne.

Roxie looked up at Hank. "You're next for Lee's job."

"What you mean, girl?" Shirleen asked.

"Lee was Vance's best man, Hank's Lee's best man. Indy and Lee are getting married in a few weeks," Roxie explained.

Shirleen blew out a sigh. "Gonna be an expensive year for the friend of a Rock Chick. You all see Jet's finger?"

Everyone turned to look at Jet's finger. On it was a princess cut diamond with an unmistakable meaning.

"Oh my God!" I mini-screamed.

"She didn't say anything to me." Daisy's voice was stunned and she sounded upset.

"Eddie asked her a couple of days ago," Roxie explained. "I only know because I dragged her into the bathroom and made her spill. She didn't want to take any of the limelight from Jules."

Daisy rolled her eyes. "That's Jet's way. She's not big on attention."

I felt a light touch on my shoulder. It wasn't a Luke Touch so I looked up to see Jules standing there. Her eyes were on Luke.

"Can I steal her?"

Luke lifted his chin. I got up, Jules took my hand and we walked away. She stopped and pulled me girlie close.

"You okay?" she asked.

God, she was *so* nice. Here it was, her wedding day, and she was worried about me and my latest drama.

"Let's not talk about me. Are *you* okay?" I returned.

Her face got soft. Her eyes moved around the room until they fell on Vance and her hands went to her belly. I saw the solitaire there. The band of her engagement ring was slim, the setting was plain, the diamond was magnificent. On her right hand was the super-fly silver band I knew (because she told me) was the promise ring Vance had given her last Christmas.

"Bliss," she said.

I looked from her belly to her eyes. "What?" I asked.

"Bliss. For the first time in my life, I feel bliss." She got close. "Do you feel it? With Luke?"

That was when I got close.

"I told him I loved him tonight," I shared.

She nodded and her lips tipped up in a smile. "The fireman's hold out the door, right?"

"Yeah. Why do these guys act like that?" I asked.

She shrugged. "Who knows?" Her eyes went back to Vance. "Thank God they do, though."

I grabbed her hand. "I'm so glad you're happy."

Her tippy lips turned to a full-fledged smile just as Indy came near.

"Are you guys talking about the fireman's hold?" she asked softly.

"That was hot," Ally said, coming up beside me.

"I'll say. Luke's making the rest of the Hot Bunch look like amateurs." Roxie joined our group.

"They're gonna have to step it up," Ally said, and then we all giggled at the thought of the Hot Bunch "stepping it up". If these boys stepped anything up, civilization would go back in time about fifty thousand years.

Jet shoved in and her arm came around my waist.

"You okay, you know, after the fireman's hold?" she asked.

"Are *you* okay, after you got engaged a couple of days ago?" Jules cut in.

Everyone looked at Jet and her cheeks got pink. "I didn't want to steal your thunder," Jet said to Jules.

Jules grabbed her cheeks in each hand, pulled her forward and gave her a big old kiss, right on her forehead.

This started a bunch of sloppy girlie kissing, hugging and carrying on. Daisy, Shirleen, May and Nancy joined in and it got sloppier and louder.

Finally Tex boomed, "Will someone change this crappy music? We need some goddamned rock 'n' roll!"

The Rock Chicks all turned to stare at Tex. He tugged his tie off, threw it in a plate filled with half eaten hors d'oeuvres and aimed a scowl at us.

This made the girl huddle burst into laughter.

Then someone put on some rock 'n' roll.

My hand was tagged, pulled and I moved in its direction, following Luke. Once he got me away from the gaggle of Rock Chicks, he turned me into his arms.

"Done bein' mad at me?" he asked.

I glared, giving him his answer. He ignored the glare, bent his head and nuzzled my neck.

"You may be mad at me, but you still love me," he said close to my ear, and he sounded pleased with himself.

He was right, as usual.

I didn't share this.

His head came up and he rested his forehead against mine as his hand came to my jaw, his thumb stroking my cheek.

"Babe, I'm not gonna let the woman I love telling me, finally, that she loves me slide by without a celebration."

"You didn't have to carry me out through a crowd of our friends, acting like a caveman."

He smiled at my broken silence.

"It's who I am," he said, quietly, honestly and without a hint of remorse.

"It's annoying," I told him, but I had to admit, just to myself, I didn't really mean it.

"Yeah." He said this like being annoying was an acceptable personality trait. Then, deciding to move on to a different subject, he asked, "Is Jules happy?"

I melted a little. I couldn't help it. It was a nice party, these were great people and Jules and Vance were folks who deserved happiness.

"She said this is bliss."

His head slanted, his fingers splayed against my jaw, his thumb slid along my lower lip then his mouth came to mine.

With his lips against my lips, I watched close up as his eyes went ink.

Then he said, "She's right."

The Rock Chick ride continues
with **Rock Chick Reckoning**
the story of Mace and Stella

Made in the USA
San Bernardino, CA
25 April 2014